NO RESERVATIONS

E. V. TOUCHTON

THE GENTRY LIFE LLC

First Edition

Copyright © 2019 by E. V. Touchton/Megan Touchton-Bartlett

ISBN: 979-8-9893909-2-2 (Hardback)
ISBN: 979-8-9893909-0-8 (Paperback)
ISBN : 979-8-9893909-1-5 (E-Book)

Library of Congress Control Number: 2023923024

First Publication 2023

Edited by Molly Touchton

Cover Design and Cover Illustration by Purvi Jhavar Sharma

Cover Formatting David McMahon

Interior Artwork by Steven Paulo Davis

AUTHOR'S NOTE

A little heads up:

In this book, several characters speak fluent Munster Irish, and another is a born and bred southern Louisianan—a Cajun man, through and through.

The why and the how I made the verifiably insane decision to have several major characters fluent in a language I don't speak, while phonetically writing another with an accent/dialect I don't have...

Is a spoiler filled explanation for another day.

For now, I will say this—I did do my language research due diligence—it's in the spoiler-free, post-story "chapter", Caveat-ing Language.

For now, I hope you have as good of a time reading this book as much as I did writing it—because I had an absolute blast.

As Remy would say, "Have your enjoys".

CONTENTS

DEDICATION

This book is dedicated to my mother, Tammy.

Okay Mommy, you were right and I admit it. Spending one of my senior year electives on an official typing class was a very, *very* good idea. There. I said it.

Also.

If you were still hanging out on the corporeal side of Life, I know you'd be running one helluva publicity campaign, including negotiations with newly cultivated connections in film adaptation circles, clearing the way for all sorts of cinematic fun--you *never* did anything by half.

Also-also.

I miss you like hell, and love you even more.

THE
GENTRY'S
TABLE

PROLOGUE

JULY 31

"To the gentry's table
To the table's garden's door
Drop me at the roots
Return to master once more."

The voice echoed in Brad's mind as he stepped onto the Victorian mansion's manicured lawn.

Brad had been on some crazy trips, but this time... He didn't remember the dealer's face. Not even the needle's prick--his favorite part--and how did he end up downtown? And since when did he start dreaming up dumb-ass poems about tables having gardens and doors?

The voice sounded again, louder, *"The table's garden's door."* The urgency of the command made Brad's heart race, his mouth dry.

He took a few more steps. A garden peeked through moon-flower-laced latticework. He climbed over the fence of morning glories, onto the porch.

He reached out, touched moonflower vines, traced them down to the gate. *The table's garden's door.* He grabbed the handle, but it didn't budge. Brad's eyes drifted to the sign left of the mock gate. The Gentry's Table.

The *Table's* garden's door. Oh.

His muddled brain then heard something new...soft bells, but not bells. Voices. But different from the command between his ears...

Welcome! Welcome!

This wasn't the first time a heroin ride had included voices--or blackout travels to mystery destinations--but tiny, flying women with butterfly wings--that was new. Their voices were gentle, musical--and shouldn't have been able to compete with his Master's command.

But hear them he could.

The Master's voice became more garbled as glowing ladies stroked his face, beckoning him to follow. He looked toward the garden, but in his mind, he heard:

Oh no, child. Much nicer inside.

"But the garden. I need the garden."

Oh yes! We have a Garden! And it has a Lounge! Come see it! Come inside! You'll be safe!

Safe? It had a beautiful sound, though Brad hardly remembered what it meant. *Safe.*

He followed the--*fairies?*--to ornately carved mahogany doors. Through the doors, and into a large dining area.

The flying women chimed at the edge of his hearing, *Come to the Lounge!*

Brad gave way to their encouragement. He took cautious steps through his awareness' swimming haze...winding past tables and chairs. To a narrow hallway, its cozy lighting a soothing contrast to the dining room's airy exposure.

To an old-fashioned gate leading to the Garden Lounge.

His feet faltered as he descended brick steps. Greenhouse style walls made the edges of the room almost invisible, and climber-lined lattice-work over slanted glass roof provided dappled shade. The combined effect made Brad feel like he was stepping into a storybook fairy garden. A comfortable daze enveloped him as he entered.

Stumbling, he caught himself on cheerful wicker furniture with daisies woven through the gaps...then sunk his face into an arrangement of mimosa blossoms and dried eucalyptus, inhaling deeply.

You need to come further.

He resisted, but fluttering voices reassured him.

Don't worry--Leanne will know what to give you. She always knows.

The Master's command churned incoherently in Brad's awareness as warm, friendly lights drew him inside. Past blushing rose loveseats with sumptuous pillows...past dining chairs pulled to dark cherry hardwood tables...

Just a little further.

The voices encouraged him as his feet rebelled, pulled to obey his Master's order. The voice in his head had sped up, but Brad couldn't understand a word of it.

Stay! Stay and eat! You're safe here!

Brad sighed with relief as he dropped into a high back grandfather chair. Lines of tension eased from his forehead as he rested his head against cool, black leather. His left hand relaxed its grip on the contents of his jeans pocket.

"Hi there!"

Brad heard the greeting, but his mind was too clouded and his body too relaxed to respond with anything other than his eyes. He looked up. Red hair. Hot. No wings, though.

"Good afternoon," she said, gently, as though working hard to affect a non-intimidating air.

Brad wanted to say something clever. What came out: "No one at the desk. I seen the door and just gone through it. That okay?" His voice was lackluster--but at least he didn't sound high.

"Absolutely." The woman looked at him a moment longer. Maybe he was doing okay. Pretty smile as she said, "I'll get you a water and be right back." He watched her as she walked away.

Some time passed. The command kept echoing in his head, but he was too relaxed to care. He thought about the redhead...

"I never forget a face."

Oh shit. She was back. Brad tried to smile, but he couldn't move.

She kept talking. "So I know you've never been here." Brad looked at the plate in her hand. "I'm Leanne Gentry, and this is my Garden Lounge. As its chef, I'm delighted to offer you this complimentary *amuse bouche.* It's a Black and Blue Stinger." Leanne set the star shaped plate down. A puff pastry, filled with blueberries, blackberries, and some flecks of red.

Despite the drugs in his system, Brad felt hungry. He took a bite. Tears welled at his eyes as berries burst in his mouth, their sweet juices taking him back to his granddaddy's garden, the wild berries they'd picked. The memory of it was happy, and his mouth felt it. Happiness spread to his body and mind. He took a second bite. And a third. Thank God she gave him something sweet. Something spicy in there, too. Made the berries sweeter.

Thirsty. He lifted the glass of water. A whiff of fresh lime reached his nose as his lips brushed the thick wedge lodged on the rim. The water was cool, clean, and...

As the purifying energy entered his system, Brad gagged--his need to absorb it at war with the voice in his head, the burning on his back.

He gulped, gagged and gulped again. The Master's voice ricocheted inside his skull, screaming about the fucking doors and the punishment he could expect for disobedience. Brad took a third sip, and felt a surge of pride as he successfully fought it down.

He was sick. He couldn't stop. He was sick. He needed to eat. He took another bite, defiant and determined. Despite the nausea and the screams, he ate...and ate...tiny bite by tiny bite. He felt like he was fighting for his life, for his soul. The next sip of water burned as a righteous fire, cooling his body and burning away impurities.

Burning impurities. Burn them away--destroy everything. All of him. Gone.

He wasn't making sense. Nothing made sense.

He almost felt clean--at least on the inside. Like he'd showered, but still wore filthy clothes.

Another sip, and the screaming increased, causing his hand to shake, spilling... The shock of it froze his entire reality--his only awareness, slow seeping from the front of his clothes to his back.

Brad's own cries escaped when the lime infused water reached the patterns on his back. His skin burned, burned and the Master's voice came back.

"The Door, you worthless bastard. Take it to the Door."

Tears fell from Brad's eyes as he whispered, "Stop...it burns...it hurts..."

"You will burn until you obey."

A chorus of soft voices competed. *Let us help!*

No...no...no...Brad's left hand struggled around in his jeans pocket. He yanked something from inside. A wet, twisted root, its two tendrils snipped and tied together.

"You will burn until you obey. Take it to the door!"

Brad clenched and unclenched the object, then dropped it to the floor as he scratched at his shirt, his chest. The pain drowned all the voices, consumed his senses--he needed to escape...

He rushed to the glass walls, his hands and forehead pressed against the cool, smooth surface.

Let me leave!

We can help!

Let me leave!

So consumed with pain and panic, Brad was barely aware as the Lounge released him by dissolving the glass wall. He fell onto soft, thick grass. He stumbled a few feet, then collapsed under a magnificent oak tree, his hands grabbing onto exposed roots, life lines on an open ocean.

We're so sorry. We tried. So sorry.

The words repeated, but fell on deaf ears. Brad's eyes opened and closed as he passively experienced a parade of hallucinations. Flying fairies, pealing bells, their ever-changing knells causing the roots of the oak to gild into glowing metal patterns--forming an opening in the wide trunk. An enormous cat walked to him, and if a cat could look alarmed, frightened, and overwhelmed by pity, all at once, this one did.

"I regret I cannot help you."

The talking cat then walked to and through the metal pattern on the oak's trunk and vanished.

Brad almost laughed--how was he to know the door was in a fucking tree?

Moments or days or hours passed...he opened his eyes to more bells.

A tall man stepped from the tree-door. He had dark, curly hair, shiny armor, and a drawn sword. The knight lifted his sword to the darkened sky, its blade reflecting moonlight. The blade grew brighter, then faded, then shrank into something small enough to be pocketed. Armor morphed into dark jeans and a black polo shirt. The knight-man strode to the building.

Brad's eyes closed again. He was so tired. Of pain. Of fear. Of life. He was fading...

***

A slap landed hard on his cheek. He gasped, opened his eyes. His Master.

"Where is it?"

He tried to speak as the Master yanked him to his feet. "Where is the poppet?"

Before Brad could answer, the Master's hand clamped his mouth shut. A trail of lights had ignited at the Victorian's top floor, lighting a path to the glassed-in room.

Help? He'd accept it this time...

Two women walked into the garden. One in a long, blue dress, the other in a sexy green nightie. Blue Dress spoke. "What did you hear?"

Sexy Nightie answered. Shit, that was the waitress from earlier.... "I don't know that I *heard* anything. Just...something in the Garden. Something *feels* wrong."

The Master spun Brad around. Face to face, he growled, "Without making a sound, point to my poppet. *Now.*"

Brad's hand trembled as he raised his arm to the Lounge. Just beyond glimmering glass, a faint, glow throbbed on the floor. Wrathful comprehension erupted on the Master's face--the ground trembled.

Blue Dress spoke again. "Oh gods. Leanne, now I feel it too." She pulled out her phone.

Brad looked at Leanne. So close...He tried to scream for help, but choked. He could hear his Master growl at her, "You cannot Hear us. You cannot See us. We are Unknowable to you." Brad shuddered as a cold sheet fell upon them, an impenetrable veil against her sight.

But Sexy Nightie swung around, shouting in some foreign language as she settled her shotgun on men she couldn't see...and shouldn't have sensed.

Hope stirred in Brad's chest. God, maybe she *could* help...

"Who's there?"

"You cannot Hear us. You cannot See us. We are Unknowable to you."

Leanne took a step closer, the shotgun mere inches from Brad's nose. Then her head tilted, and with a sudden movement, she raised the gun away from Brad, and switched its sight to the Master's face. Again addressing blank space, her voice barked the order, "Answer me!"

Unable to resist her thrall, Brad tried to answer. He did. But the Master's hand was clamped across his mouth.

"You cannot Hear us. You cannot See us. We are Unknowable to you."

Her eyes never moved, but at the veiled speech, Leanne slowly lowered the shotgun. "Yeah, you better hope I don't find your cowardly ass."

Oh God, no...terror surged through Brad as he felt the Master react to her taunt. He tried to scream, but the hands were squeezing, clenching, crushing his throat...everything went away but for indistinct shouts and red flares zooming around him.

2 HOURS EARLIER

CHAPTER 1 - JUST TAKE THE HELP

"That's it. I've had it. I'm *done*." Leanne Gentry slammed the door.

She stormed into the main dining area of The Gentry's Table, the restaurant she and her sister ran from their Victorian home. "Never again." She threw her purse onto a freshly made table and flopped into one of the grandfather chairs facing an enormous fireplace.

From the sanctuary of the back office, Anya Gentry had detected the wave of frustration well before she heard Leanne's voice, but still startled when her older sister slammed the door. That was pretty impressive--Anya hadn't realized those doors *could* slam.

She shook her head as she walked through the main kitchen, pausing only to take the wine bottle offered by their friend and head chef, Remy. She smiled as the tall Cajun smoothed out his food stained, Archbishop Rummel '05 t-shirt, bowed, and pushed the door open.

With a raised eyebrow at the mess on the table, Anya poured a generous glass of their favorite red blend. Leanne's arm shot out from the side of the chair, hand open for the full glass of wine.

Making a show of checking her watch, Anya sat down and said, "10 pm. And here I thought spending several hours on a dinner date was a good sign."

Leanne groaned. "No matter what I said, Dan's response was, 'great idea', 'love that', 'sure, we can order that, it's my favorite'--and apparently thinking I wouldn't notice when he broke out in hives because he's allergic to the goddamn mushrooms!!!" She took a sip of her wine. A very long sip. Anya refilled the glass. "So off to the emergency room we go." She leaned forward, and gesturing with her free hand, continued, "It's not that I'm happy he got sick--I'm glad he's fine. But *seriously*! If you don't have the balls to say 'Hey, I'm allergic to that, it'll make me violently ill, how about some fucking mozzarella sticks?', you should expect to get sick, and often." She slumped back, sloshing a bit of wine on the already stained shirt. Anya could guess what caused the first discoloration--and shuddered. "I mean," Leanne continued, "If he can't even be straight about *food*--"

Another slosh, another splotch on the blouse. "Watch yourself, dear. That's alcohol abuse." Anya could hide the grin from her voice, if not her eyes.

Leanne shot her a grim look, then dissolved into rueful, despairing laughter. She put down her glass, folded her arms on the table, and buried her face in them.

"And it's awful, to feel so annoyed with him. He's just--"

"A fellow you'd unintentionally walk all over," Anya finished for her. She liked Daniel very much, but the *Ledger-Enquirer* reporter was accommodating, infatuated--and out of his depth. With her sister, he was like a moped trying to keep up with a Harley-Davidson.

"Or *poison*." Leanne's voice was muffled by the drape of hair covering her head and arms. She lifted her head, and with a piteous expression, asked, "How is it, I'm so bad at this? I can fix everyone else up. Protection, love, money, sex life--I can help with all of that. Cook 'em a dish of this or that. Bam. Done. Even that kid today. He was a total wreck. Needed a *fuck-ton* of protection, and some purification, because if he wasn't high as hell, then I'm a freakin'--"

Anya cut her off. "Well, there's the difference. When casting for others, it's easier to be objective about magickal cures. It's your job, and you're phenomenal at it. It's why people come to the Garden Lounge. The problem is--"

"I shouldn't have to use--."

"Please." Anya interrupted, no-nonsense. She enjoyed the rare opportunity of telling her sister to shut up. "You know damn well how effective it is. It's half of how we make our living." She paused, considering her next words. It wasn't that Leanne lacked experience with men as friends, or as a lover here and there--but dating? Between their nomadic childhood and passion for education, dating had always been a luxury for which Leanne barely had time, let alone patience.

When their shared dream of sinking roots came to fruition, they replaced travel and culinary programs with the freedom to stay home--to create for themselves the kind of life their dear parents would never need or understand. Anya looked thoughtfully at her sister. Ready to settle down--and completely at sea on how to go about it. Or so she thought. Anya took a breath and continued.

"What *you* don't like is admitting you need help." She met Leanne's stare. "So take tonight off. Remy and I can handle clean up just fine on our own. Get to work. For yourself, this time."

"Wait. *You* were in the kitchen tonight?"

"Our roundsman quit. I've got it covered." Anya was adamant when Leanne rolled her eyes. "No, I mean it. Floating from station to station, filling in where people need, it's pretty much what I do when I'm in the kitchen anyway. Tonight, it'll just be more official." She sighed. "Go on, you know what you want. Just put a spell together and do it."

Leanne nodded. "Yeah, I guess. Hey." Self-pity gave way to curiosity as her brain jumped subjects. "That kid. How was he, after I left?"

Anya shrugged. "I checked on him like you asked. But he was gone."

"That's weird. I was sure he was going to sleep it off."

"Well, his food was gone, at least." No need to mention the spilled water and broken glass. Leanne worried enough as is.

Leanne's brow creased in concern. "Well, that's good. Maybe he's all right, then."

Anya hoped her sister was right. Leanne took justifiable pride in her work with the Lounge...but the sad truth was they couldn't save everyone, so before Leanne had a chance to dwell...

"So. Spellwork. The perfect match for you."

"Yeah. Okay. Guess it wouldn't hurt."

Sure, they'd go with that. Out loud, Anya said, "That's the spirit." She patted her sister's arm *without* the stain on it. Sisterly love only went so far. She delivered a parting shot as she returned to her duties, "And for the Goddess' sake, shower and put on some clean clothes." She shut her eyes a moment before turning away. "Trash the shirt."

＊＊＊

A few blocks down from The Gentry's' Table, a crowd mingled cheerfully outside the Cannon Brew Pub. Standing a few inches taller than the rest, a Columbus Police detective stood still, scanning outdoor tables for his partner. The summer evening felt good--a light breeze rustled the heavy air down Broadway, carrying street noise and live music on it. The smell of cigarette smoke mixed with fried food, beer, and the silty scent of the Chattahoochee River.

"Hey, McOrnery!! Over here, man!"

Detective Fergus McAnrai resisted the temptation to roll his eyes. His smile was a mix of admonishment and amusement as he sat down. "No need for name calling and false accusations."

"Fine, Mc*Ahhn*-ree, fine." Detective Shane Harris pronounced it properly--mc-CONN-ree. "You ain't a stubborn sumbitch at all. Don't know where I got that."

Shane's warm, chocolate eyes creased with mischief as he rubbed his hand over light brown hair. In his easy Georgia drawl, he asked, "So, you change your mind about coming out tonight?"

With a short laugh, McAnrai said, "Nope." Stretching long legs under the table, he automatically turned his attention outward, watched several uniforms patrolling the weekly block party. As much as he missed his hometown, he loved Columbus' summer concert series. Families settled in with camp chairs, Solo cups, and children armed with footballs and frisbees. Huge oaks lined the wide median and draped protective arms over impromptu games while parents enjoyed performances by local cover bands.

Tonight was an extra performance, a fundraiser for something. McAnrai nodded his head to "Witchy Woman" before turning back to his friend. In an effort to switch topics, he looked down at the menu and said, "God, what I would give for a real cheesesteak."

Shane cut off the lame diversion by saying, "Boy, you need a life beyond work. Come out tonight. My cousin Meredith's band is playing at The Loft."

Ignoring him, McAnrai continued, "Don't get me wrong--Cannon makes a good steak sandwich, but--as for anywhere else? Bah." One too many times he'd been served a couple of open hamburger buns topped with chunks of sirloin, covered with a slice of melted cheese. He grimaced. Philadelphia-born, the newly pinned homicide detective had never gotten used to the South's all too common, and tragically literal, interpretation of Philly cheesesteaks. Or to being called 'boy' for that matter. By someone his own age.

Shane responded with a stare.

Sighing, McAnrai said, "No thanks, I'm done for today." He took another swallow of his well earned, just-got-off-duty beer. At Shane's expression, he added, "Look, I told you--I like Meredith just fine. Enough *not* to make her my next ex-girlfriend." And enough not to fight over religion. Most of the locals he'd met raised their eyes at his Catholicism...gods, if they only knew...

"That's what I like about you, Mac, that Irish optimism."

McAnrai opened his mouth to speak, but at that moment, a young girl ran up to their table. She rushed past Shane to grab McAnrai's arm, her voice low. "You're a policeman, right?" Her face was flushed, her eyes wide and urgent.

McAnrai and Shane both put their beers down in sync, and replied, "Yes."

Her eyes never left McAnrai's. "There's some yelling. A lady yelling like a, a," she paused, searching for words. "Like a screaming leprechaun. At the Gentry's Table. And--and there's fireworks."

McAnrai looked at Shane. Answering his look, McAnrai said, "Fireworks and a screaming leprechaun at the Gentry's Table." His words held a touch of snark--manufactured as the girl's story sounded, McAnrai felt a pull to her words. At Shane's shrug of agreement, he turned back to her and said, "Sure, we can get there easy."

As they put money on the table and rose to leave, McAnrai's mind rapidly tracked over what he knew of the place. Great bar--he was friendly with its bartender. On more than one occasion, he'd enjoyed a few drinks with him and the Cajun guy running the kitchen. Good guys.

The Table itself was run by a couple sisters. He'd met one of them. The PR one--and her name was...Anya? Nice girl, cool head. Hard to imagine her screaming for any reason. Any happy reason, that is. His nerves prickled, and his feet picked up their pace.

Just three blocks away, past the River Center parking garage, McAnrai and Shane arrived at the grand Victorian that was home to the Gentry's Table and its bar, the Magick Brugh. Red sparks flying from the treeline welcomed them to the party.

They stepped quickly but carefully through neat rows of vegetables and herbs. A woman's voice yelled, "Who's there?" It was loud, commanding, and not directed at the approaching officers.

A cold gust of wind blew from the back of the property, pushed past McAnrai and Shane, sending a shudder through their shoulders, and almost knocking them off balance. A shadowy figure holding something long and reflective came running from behind the house, as though chasing the creepy wind.

Shane muttered, "What the--?"

Drawing their sidearms from their holsters as they ran up the front porch stairs, through broken latticework, and into the garden behind it, McAnrai called out, "Police! Freeze!"

The vague outline froze. Thin moonlight reflected off the barrel of a sawed off shotgun.

Stepping closer, they saw the shotgun was being held by a...

Soooooo...the 'screaming leprechaun' was a woman. Long waves of hair floated in a mass around her face, with flashing eyes and a churning temper the men could feel hitting them in waves. McAnrai's eyes tracked wisps of sparkly red light floating around her--those must be the last of the reported fireworks. But they didn't seem to be coming from anything in particular. Other than her.

From *her*. He blinked. What the hell...?

When she saw them, the red flares disappeared. Adjusting the stance of her bare feet to include the two armed trespassers, she demanded, "And who are you?"

"Like I said, *police*. Drop the gun." McAnrai's voice was far lower, but it possessed an authority that got her attention. Under the steady gaze of his brown-black eyes, she relaxed her grip on the firearm--but didn't drop it.

Just then, the lights from the house turned on behind the woman, outlining her as an hourglass silhouette with a crown of untamed, crimson red hair. McAnrai circled around, moving so the light came from his side. Once there, his eyes adjusted to see her free hand smooth the emerald-green satin nightgown. He caught his breath. Nightgown implied far more material than she was wearing. It wasn't quite a negligee, but the spaghetti straps of the simple slip struggled to cover the full curves of her--

"Badges." It was not a request. The plainclothes officers held up their credentials. Her eyes narrowed.

McAnrai cleared his throat and raised his eyebrows. She lifted her chin, and with slow deliberation, placed her shotgun on the lawn. As she rose, her appraising eyes never left McAnrai.

Shane's muttered, "Feels like a standoff" drew a frown from McAnrai. Back to the woman, McAnrai hid his eye roll at Shane's continued, if subdued commentary. "My boy. Getting taken down by a half-naked leprechaun."

A refined voice came from inside. "Leanne, I think we can relax." Anya smiled. "I can speak for Officer McAnrai's profession, and I'm ready to let him vouch for his friend, there."

McAnrai turned and saw Anya Gentry descend the steps. She wore a pale blue linen dress, and a rope of pearls was clasped around her neck. Her auburn hair, every bit as long as the leprechaun's, was pulled back and her understated makeup was perfect--she could not have presented a more stark contrast to the wild woman on the lawn. Even the small, pearl handled pistol she held at her side had a delicacy that prevented any undermining of this woman's restraint and decorum.

With each of her approaching steps, the policemen could feel the electricity in the air dial down. When she stood in front of them, the atmosphere had cooled to a serene pool. Well, a serene pool with a wicked generator in the middle. McAnrai could still feel energy radiating from the other woman. It was almost audible to him. McAnrai shook his head slightly, tried to focus.

Anya pocketed her pistol and reached out to shake hands. "Impressive response time since I didn't get a chance to call 911. I assume you heard the disturbance?"

McAnrai nodded. "Heard about it anyway. Everything okay?"

"Oh, I do think so. Now, anyway." Her smile was affectionate, if a little sarcastic, when she nodded to the wild woman on the lawn and said, "I see you've met my reclusive sister, Leanne," she gestured to the curvy redhead, who, to McAnrai's surprise, didn't seem at all embarrassed by her attire, or lack thereof. If her faint accent had left him guessing, this was confirmation--*not* a southern belle. "You'll have to excuse her--"

"They don't have to excuse anything," Leanne interrupted. "What *would* be helpful, though, is checking to see where our trespasser went. I couldn't see him, but I sure as hell felt someone lurking about."

Though still noticeable, her brogue had faded along with her wrath. McAnrai fought a grin. It was both funny and inexplicable--that in all the times he'd eaten at the Table (or had a pint at the Brugh), how in all hell had he missed *her*? And he was a noticing kind of guy--so unless she was trying to stay hidden...?

To be fair, if she was the type to ward off criminals wearing nothing but a negligee, a shotgun, and a snarl, it made sense for her sister to run the public side of the business.

"I don't know, Leanne," Anya gave her sister a long look. "Maybe it was all in our heads?"

"Hardly. That was a helluva creep fest back there, and--" Leanne stopped herself short, met Anya's gaze, and tilted her head to the side. "On the other hand, I have been running on very little sleep. That may have been my own making."

The officers stared at the sisters' exchange. Clearing his throat, McAnrai said, "First things first. I'm McAnrai, and this is Harris." And if Leanne is imagining things, then so was he. He looked to his partner. Shane seemed to be brushing off the same thought but was just as unwilling to admit a strong breeze gave him the willies.

Out loud, McAnrai said, "Well, whatever it was, safe to say it's gone now."

Anya agreed, "Oh yes. I think so." She stepped over to Shane, slipped her arm in his, and led him to the house. "I don't suppose we need to make a formal statement of this, do we?"

Shane accompanied Anya inside, leaving McAnrai alone with Leanne. He drew a sharp breath as Leanne adopted a playful formality by lowering herself into a mock curtsy. "Well, kind sir, I'd very much like my gun back." The intense force that had been so violently palpable was gone--replaced by warmth. Her twinkling eyes assured him the storm had indeed passed, and in its place was a good-natured woman, calling a truce. To his own amazement, McAnrai picked up the shotgun himself and handed it to her, trying not to stare as he did so--it had been a while. A *long* while.

"Why, thank you so much." Leanne straightened up and rested her hand on his arm. Discarding her impish tone, she nodded toward the door. "You look like you could use some dinner." She tilted her head and stared him up and down--he had the strangest feeling he was being studied, even searched, by those large, sea green eyes. She bit her lip, then grinned, pleased with herself. He met the long stare.

With a dazzling smile, she asked, "How about a cheesesteak?" His eyebrows shot up in surprise and inquiry, but she had already started up the stairs. Looking over her shoulder, she winked and said, "We even fly rolls down from Philly."

McAnrai watched as Leanne walked through the door. Holy shit, those legs...

Hunger hit him, and hard. He followed.

He'd never been a praying man, but gods, he thought fervently, *please* let her be single.

CHAPTER 2 - A MATCH MADE IN FAERY

They stepped through the private garden entrance Anya had opened. McAnrai could hear voices from the public dining room--he turned to join them, but Leanne stayed his arm.

"C'mon, Detective." She turned her back to him and walked down a short hall. Looking over her shoulder, she added, "Not a homicide, and you're off duty."

Another smile. This one was less sparkle, more invitation.

Grinning to himself but frowning out loud, he walked after her, and asked. "What makes you think I'm off duty?" His eyes were playing tricks on him--the door rippled like water before it opened. He pinched the bridge of his nose--it had been a longer day than he thought.

They entered a softly lit kitchen. It was very clean and cozy without being crowded. Leanne opened the refrigerator and started pulling out supplies. As she reached into the deep recesses, McAnrai looked away with the short, knowing laugh of someone solving a riddle. She was doing this on purpose. He smiled to himself, and asked, "No, really. How did you know I was off duty?"

Ignoring his question a second time, Leanne swirled her hair to a loose knot on the back of her neck. It started to unravel, but stayed behind her shoulders. She turned to the stove.

McAnrai's gaze held more than one level of curiosity. How did she know he was off duty? That he worked homicide? His brow furrowed as his expression darkened.

How could he get a straight answer from her? *Any* answer? And what would happen if he grabbed a handful of her hair and crushed her mouth with his? While he desperately hoped he knew the answer to the last question, the first three rankled.

His eyes followed her natural, flowing movements...she was only making a sandwich. Hoping it presented as annoyance, McAnrai scrubbed his hand over his face. Jesus, he had to get his shit together.

"There's a beer fridge built into the island if you're interested. I'll have a lager." The suggestion just high-handedness enough to needle him.

His eyes narrowed. "Oh, I'm interested." But instead of moving, he added, "In a few things." As much as he was enjoying the performance, McAnrai was annoyed. Other than sizzling meat, the room had been silent while she cooked and he stewed. For a man accustomed to being answered when he queried, gracefully dodging--no, blatantly *ignoring*--his question was an easy way to piss him off. And this slippery seductress bit was *not* lessening his frustration. At. Fucking. All.

Jaw set, arms crossed, feet planted in a firm stance, he stared at her back and waited. He was done asking questions. It was time for answers.

As if she heard him utter his ultimatum aloud, Leanne looked up from the creamy meat and cheese mixture she had just poured into the open roll. With a satisfied smile, she sighed and placed the pan in the sink. Clearing her expression, she turned around, and gave her full attention to the handsome detective. Broad shoulders, strong, yet lean build. Fantastic mouth. The stern expression enhanced it. She couldn't wait to see how it smiled.

Leaning back and meeting his stare, she crossed her arms in a gentle mimicry of his body language. "You're coming *from* work because you have the harried look of a man who'd already had a long day. This ruckus went down at shift change, and while there's a slight scent of beer, you're sober. I got "detective" by your easy authority and..." she paused to flash a cheeky grin, "I'm gonna add 'homicide', because I am *just* that fucking smart."

She tilted her head and raised her eyebrows as she removed the apron. After gently ruffling her hair back to normal, she carried the plate across the kitchen and asked, "There, is that good enough for now?"

He suppressed a grin, but when she stopped just inches in front of him and reached around his torso to set the plate behind him, he said, "For now." His emphasis was clear. There would be more answers. She should make no mistake about that. He spared a quick glance at the cheesesteak as it went by--the scent of the shredded, cheese-soaked beef mingled with the sauteed onions. Damn.

It was the merest of expressions, but it didn't go unnoticed. She grinned.

What would happen if he grabbed...

Leanne looked up at him. Barely a foot apart, their eyes held each other at a standoff. McAnrai's earlier assessment was correct--he *was* being examined. Searched. And she found what she was looking for.

Honorable. Obstinate. Homesick. A strong sense of compassionate decency keeping his capacity for violence in steady check. A pain-ridden heart, its injuries hidden behind a thick shell of dark humor.

He was the breed of man who held himself so rigidly in check, when the crack happened, the results were...He was close, she could tell. So, what would push him that last inch...?

McAnrai held his ground--and his breath--as Leanne stepped closer. His brain raced, desperate to keep up with the rest of him. The light, floral scent of her hair felt like rising tendrils, caressing his face, erasing his awareness of anything but her. What would happen if he grabbed a handful...

Inches apart, she said in a low, direct voice, "And you're starving because no one's served you a decent meal in years." His eyes flashed as she tilted her head to the side. He wondered if she could read his mind, his uncertainty a tense balance between hoping she can't and please God, please say she can.

Her eyes bore into his, her lips slightly parted. She leaned closer and whispered, "Bring it."

As it turned out, he was wrong about what would happen.

His guess was entirely too conservative.

***

"So, I have a confession to make." Leanne rolled onto her stomach and rested her chin on McAnrai's shoulder. It was three in the morning, and they had just started to doze when her conscience pricked at her.

"Hmmm? You're forgiven." He lifted his arm to welcome her closer. She slipped her head onto his shoulder.

"No, I'm serious. You need to listen to me." Arm around his waist and leg resting on his, she drummed fingers on his chest. He growled and rolled to face her.

"Fine. Tell me all your secrets." Despite the hour and exertion, his eyes were alert.

That sure as hell wasn't happening tonight. Smiling but nervous, she looked away. "Look, I need to tell you--I'm--well, I'm a--"

"Witch? Yeah, I caught that." He closed his eyes and settled back into the deep feather bed. "Glad that's settled."

Leanne's head snapped toward him, "Wait, what? How did you know?" But McAnrai had put his back to her and was feigning sleep. "No, seriously." she sat up and leaned around his shoulders to see his eyes shut and a wide grin on his face.

He opened one eye. "I can't answer your questions--I'm fast asleep."

She rolled her eyes--but turnabout *was* fair play. "Fine, but there's more. Please, this is serious."

At the change in her voice, he relented. "Okay." He let out a deep breath and sat up a bit, propped on a pillow. He rubbed his face with his hands and ran his fingers through his hair. "Out with it, woman. In all these hours we've known each other, what terrible thing did you sneak off and do?"

"No, it was earlier tonight, before everything. I was working u pstairs...well... I was doing spellwork." Her hands were twisting the sheet's edge. "That's where I was when I got that bad feeling about the garden--I was right in the middle of raising the energy for my purpose, got interrupted... What?"

McAnrai chuckled. "Nothing, go on," He adopted a deliberately straight face, "You were confessing your witchy ways to me. Is this where I become puritanical?"

A tentative smile touched her lips as it became clear the first points had landed safely. She continued, "No, that's not it. It's the spell, it... it was about attracting... well...you."

At that, he looked down at her and cupped her face in his hand. "C'mere." She rose a little. His expression was serious, but reassuring. "Tell me."

She sighed. "I'd hit my wall. I was fed up, tired, and--" Their eyes met.

"Lonely. Yeah, I can relate to that."

Encouraged by the kindness flowing from him, she slid back down and laid her head on his chest. "So Anya convinced me to do the work--to attract the perfect man for me. My match."

He jerked his head back and looked down at her. "So, you put a Faery-land come-hither on me?" His tone was somewhere between incredulous and amused.

"Ah, *hell* no." Sitting straight up in an immediate reprieve from feeling sheepish, she shot him an offended look. Eyebrows raised, she said, "Ya think I need to *force* a man to want me? Because--" McAnrai cut her off with a kiss.

Pausing for breath, he said, "*No*. I'm not saying that at all." He pulled her close again, kissing her. Slow, sweet and warm, it was almost successful in distracting her from further conversation, but she broke off and pulled back.

"You know what the come-hither is? The kind the Fae use?"

"Well, I can see your confusion. A nice Italian name like 'McAnrai'." He stopped and drew her to him again. "Look, what I'm hearing--you planned to make a big noise to get my attention. Then, if I liked what I saw, I'd stick around--and if *you* liked what *you* saw, you'd let me. How'm I doin' so far?" She nodded. "Well, good on ya, it worked. I'm here, and I like everything I've seen. Better than liked. In fact, I've better-than-liked it several times." He let his hand slide down her back, cupping her hip...

"Okay, okay. You made your point." She kissed his shoulder, and added with a smile, "Several times."

Tension broken, and McAnrai grinned. "Okay. *Now*, that's settled." He wriggled himself back to lying down, and let out a magnificently contented sigh as Leanne wrapped herself around his side. They both started to nod off.

"McAnrai?"

"Hmmmm?"

"What's your first name?" She lifted her head, then smiled at his annoyed expression.

"Ask me another." He pulled the sheet and blanket to cover both of them.

She considered a moment. "Why did you laugh when I told you about raising the energy?"

At this, he chuckled again, "Just the idea of you going crime-fighter in a negligee." Unable to resist the opportunity for a little payback, he added, "And I got 'witch' from the tattoo."

"My tattoo?" He felt a surge of satisfaction at the look of surprise and inquiry--now on *her* face.

"The one of the moon phases--the pentagrams as the full and dark moons kinda gave it away."

Ahhh. Hairline on the back of her neck. She nodded. "Impressive. That one's tiny."

"Well, I'll admit, I didn't get an up-close look until the fun on the stairs." He smiled at the memory. "Though, after reading the spiral on your hip--"

"Whoa, wait." Her eyes shot open. "You could read that?" She sat up, her movement so abrupt, the whole bed moved. "It's written in

Ogham." Celtic history was largely run as an oral tradition, but their Tree Alphabet, Ogham, could be used to phonetically form words, as Leanne had done with her name's translation.

"And in Irish. Secretive little *leanansidhe*, aren't you?" His eyes fluttered shut, and his breathing became a deep, steady rhythm. She sunk down again, resting her head on the crook of his shoulder. In a dreamy, wistful voice, he said, "I have my own little *leanansidhe*." Even in his sleep, he held her close, stroking her hair.

Reads Ogham *and* Irish, and understands both well enough to know her name means 'faery lover'. It dawned on Leanne that, just maybe, she was getting more than she bargained for. She considered for a moment. She couldn't believe she hadn't allowed for how literal the Goddess was--she *had said* she wanted to meet her match. Initially startled by the fast succession of revelations, watching McAnrai's chest rise and fall as he slept, listening to his strong heartbeat, Leanne felt herself drifting to a peaceful slumber.

Thinking he was out cold, she muttered, "Guy should be a detective--he'd be pretty good at it."

"I know, right?" He adjusted their positions to sink his face in her neck, kissing it one last time before they both finally fell asleep.

CHAPTER 3 – SEVERAL IMPOSSIBLE THINGS BEFORE BREAKFAST

"Okay. How about you think about that, and I'll grab us some refills?

Leanne watched McAnrai walk to the kitchen, then smiled to herself as she turned back to the garden's early morning bustle. While it would be several hours before the Magick Brugh opened officially, there was already a smattering of visitors from the Other Crowd.

Without any uninitiated humans around, faeries who either couldn't (or wouldn't) pass as humans enjoyed the early morning (or late evening) atmosphere of the Brugh's garden. The iridescent dragonfly wings of flower faeries reflected shimmery hints of sunrise as they buzzed through flowering vines and bushes, tending to them as they go. Butterfly-winged sylphs fluttered in and out of the morning glory and honeysuckle vines weaving a canopy with the exposed beams above.

Curling her legs under herself, Leanne rubbed her neck a little. A life-long morning person--she loved her sunrise routine. And today she was sharing it with--she let out a long, contented sigh.

She didn't have words for McAnrai yet--but they would come. For now, she was still reeling from the night they just spent--they both were. Reeling, but in a good way. And now...of the dozens of faeries present, not one was hiding their true forms from him. The only thing more amazing than her friends' willingness to let McAnrai see their natural state...was his complete comfort with the spectacle.

The man knew faeries. Hell, even Remy had needed an introduction, and *his* family was as neck deep in magick as the Gentrys. But not McAnrai. He was comfortable with them. With her witchcraft. With everything.

He knew faeries. And they knew him.

She thought about McAnrai's question, and smiled as she watched him return, coffees in hand. It *had* seemed strange that she and Anya had bypassed locales known for elite fine dining and cosmopolitan lifestyles to plant themselves in Columbus. A beautiful city, but not well-known on the global foodie stage. But it was that very quality, the relaxed lack of presumption, that made Muscogee County the perfect destination. Without fame and glamour breathing down its neck, Columbus, Georgia seemed built to be one thing--a home. For two life-long nomads, the gentle, predictable security of a place like this held an appeal they could not deny.

Out loud, she said, "At first, it was 'Mom's of Ireland, but Dad's Army--and they frequent Ft. Benning--let's settle wherever they'll often be' kind of thing. But," she paused.

Anticipating her words, McAnrai said, "That's not why you stay."

Leanne shook her head. "No."

He leaned over, kissing her before sitting in the next rocking chair. "My turn. Getting stationed at Benning led to indefinite house-sitting for my grandmother." He took a long sip, savored the dark roast. "Which is how this Philly-born, Irish-pagan ended up living in the Bible Belt." He leaned back in the rocking chair. "I like it here, a lot. But I'm not settled. Like, I know I shouldn't leave, I *know* I belong here, but...I never felt at home, not unt--" His voice trailed off into his coffee as he caught the compromising words.

Leanne pretended to be distracted by garden gnomes pruning dead flowers and leaves from the lilac and gardenia hedges. The last several hours had been amazing, but the sudden influx of emotion, to say nothing of their recognizing it, was overwhelming. Overwhelming in their absolute comfort and synchronicity with each other, and over-whelming in the sense of who-the-hell-can-actually-feel-that-way-after-a-few-hours. Impossible, right?

Especially for two people who had never believed in love at first sight.

So these hard-core feelings. Understanding their import--hell, their existence--that was more than enough to digest for now. The fact that Leanne's strongest Talent, her Empathy, made it so she was actually feeling McAnrai's emotions along with her own--and therefore *literally knew* how he felt. Sharing *that* could wait.

Changing the subject (somewhat), McAnrai tipped his mug at the engraved cast-iron cauldron embedded into the wall at its porch entrance, his expression quizzical.

Leanne waggled her brow and said, "That? Ah, well. The Brugh's sign, it's--a hint on how to pronounce it."

"Have a brew at the Brugh?"

She laughed, nodding. Yes, the Magick Brugh was a bar, in the strictest sense of the word, but not the kind that appealed to boisterous soldiers from Ft. Benning or co-eds from Columbus State University. Not that it didn't attract a wild patronage; it simply drew a very specific flavor of exotic. When the Gentry's Table opened, the Brugh and its garden were designed to be an easy way for Anya and Leanne to socialize with their friends from the Other Crowd.

Most humans didn't realize that at any given moment, at least half of the party-ers were from the Realm of Faery.

"Nothing like hiding in plain sight, eh?"

McAnrai's laugh was deep and rich, "Nothing at all. Nothing at all." He drew a long, relaxed breath. At her unasked question, he said, "After my mother died, I pretty much grew up in my dad's pub." With a quick glance, he added, "Your place reminds me of his."

They sat in silence for a few minutes, enjoying the coffee, and each others' company. With reluctant sigh, McAnrai looked at his watch, and groaned. "I need to leave for work."

Leanne nodded. The moment should've been awkward, but it wasn't. Just two people, gazing at each other. McAnrai cleared his throat, and said, "The hell with it. Okay, I know it's way, way too soon to say something like this, but--"

"Hardly too soon, young man--in fact, you've barely arrived in time." Both Leanne and McAnrai turned at the words, and upon seeing the newcomer, McAnrai started. Enormous even by Maine Coon standards, forty-five pounds of sleek, muscular feline stepped to the end of the bar overlooking the garden, and leapt to the floor.

"Harley!" Leanne's face broke into an apprehensive smile. "Good morning, darling. Haven't seen you in a while." She looked from Harley to McAnrai, and hesitated. The mystical menagerie in the garden was one thing, but Harley was...

Ah well. Cat's outta the bar now.

Recognizing and dismissing her concerns, Harley padded over and sat in front of them.

"It is about time you showed up." Harley's voice had the melodic lilt common to all benevolent Fae, and rolled in a smooth baritone, his accent reminiscent of the classic London Stage. Addressing Leanne, he said, "I'm sorry, my dear. But sometimes expediency for the greater good outweighs prudence. Besides," he turned to McAnrai, "Master Fergus doesn't seem too intimidated by me."

Leanne started at the flicker of annoyance she felt from the man. Before she had a chance to say anything, McAnrai said, "Funny. You don't look like my grandmother, Sir Sith."

Sir Sith. McAnrai knew he was facing a Cait-Sith--which meant he knew enough about the Faery Realm's apex feline predators to understand surviving interactions with them depended on respect.

Yet mouthing off anyway...Leanne swallowed at Harley's cocked eyebrow--this could get very unpleasant, very quickly.

But Harley chose amusement over evisceration. "See what I mean?" Maintaining eye contact with McAnrai, he continued, "You understand of course, that, in the interest of time, I needed to confirm your mettle."

Leanne was fascinated by the exchange, and even more by its implications. She prayed McAnrai appreciated them as well--that Harley's tolerance to his sass was the closest anyone, anywhere could expect to an apology. If he didn't…

She needn't have worried. McAnrai nodded, and said, "I can appreciate your position, Sir. Perhaps we can exchange preferred titles now?" Receiving a nod, he said, "My name is McAnrai."

After a long moment of consideration, the Cait-Sith nodded. "And you may address me as Harley."

CHAPTER 4 – BAD MANNERS AND GOOD FEELINGS

A small, electronic chirp interrupted the peace of Anya's morning cup of tea. She looked at her phone. One notification--a missed call from Mayor Kimberly Shetland. Her expression darkened as she listened to the message. Yes, they were catering her daughter's rehearsal dinner. Yes, her daughter had become a C-list Hollywood name whose sights were set on upgrading. And *yes*, making sure the debutante's upcoming nuptials to an ambitious B-lister would help that promotion. But not one of those was a bloody excuse to call a woman at not-even-six in the morning to request, no, *demand*, a second tasting. A *second* fucking tasting. Tonight. The dinner was three days away.

Motivated by a combination of consideration for her staff and spite for the mayor, she decided to finish her tea before spreading the news. *Slowly.* Sip by sip.

***

The kitchen crew's usual good humor wore thin as the day went on--and by the tasting, the lack of a roundsman left the entire kitchen sniping at each other, and Remy with an ironic dilemma. He drizzled a final touch over the pound cake, the rum glaze from his *grandmere* made an elegant touch to a typical Southern dessert. He arranged four--not five, since the mayor's brother had ditched at the last minute--*four* perfect slices on a platter which he then handed off. "*Fini,*" he said. The young waitress lifted the platter with a practiced flourish, and turned on her five thousand dollar smile. Remy still saw strain around her eyes. "Chin up, G. *C'est fini.*"

She dropped the smile and glared at him. Exhausted by the mayor, her spoiled daughter, the handsy assistant, *and* the damn reporter, she snapped, "If they don't tip me, I'm gonna straight up lose my shit. They've been here *three hours.*"

"Yes, *bebe,* I know." Professional smile back in place, she left, and Remy reached into his pocket. Taking fifty dollars from his wallet, he handed it to the busboy. "You see dis makes it to her table, you."

"Got it, boss man."

Remy turned around and almost ran into the young man who was *still* following him like a puppy. His sigh was impressive.

"Look, chief, I don't have time for an audition right now, *comprenez-vous?*"

The lad started up right where he'd left off. "My name is Troy Morgan, and I know what I'm doing in the kitchen, I promise you. I'm good. Just give me a chance." He followed Remy around the bar and back toward the kitchen. The head chef stepped through the door and shut it in the young man's face.

Witness to the exchange, Anya stepped forward to introduce herself as Troy stepped back and turned around. The resulting collision set her firmly on her rump.

"You must be Troy." Anya flashed a smile at him and exerted some soothing energy in his direction. Remy could make anyone crazy when he was flustered. She offered her hands, and the newcomer lifted her to standing. Anya glanced at his biceps appreciatively before clearing her throat.

"Yes, ma'am." Calmer, but still tense.

"You say you're pretty good in the kitchen?"

"Yes, ma'am, I am. I came in for a beer and overheard your barkeep talking about how your roundsman just quit. Since I'm looking for a job, it seemed like fate." His dark eyes made Anya think of a puppy. And that hair. Black and wavy. Looked soft--unlike what she could see of his body. Damn, he even made a black polo shirt sexy. She gave her head a slight shake...wait...

"You overheard *Forrest* talking?" Anya raised an eyebrow at the unlikeliness of anyone hearing their bartender saying anything beyond the usual noises of "sympathetic listener". She turned her gaze toward their brilliant, but reserved brew and bar master. "*Our* bartender?"

Troy followed her gaze there and back. He sheepishly grinned. "I overheard Mr. Hawkins talking--"

Another look...

"Yelling about the roundsman quitting, and Forrest was his sounding board."

"Well, okay then. Points for discretion." Anya smiled, slipped her arm into the crook of his elbow, and led him toward an open space at the prep bar. "I feel like I've seen you around before?"

"I've come in a few times. I like the atmosphere. Feels like home."

Anya couldn't help it--she was charmed. "We work very hard to make everyone feel at home." She put special emphasis on the word 'everyone' to see if he would bite. Her instincts suspected a faery nature, so she waited, but he didn't respond to her showing Talent like that. Usually, that broke down the wall for shyer ones, letting them know they were safe to be themselves here. No response from him.

Huh. Her mistake.

"Yes, ma'am, you do a good job with it."

Anya found herself smiling back. It was strange, she thought. Between the sisters, Anya was the one less inclined to go on instinct. But here, she had no real reason to like this man except that she just *did*. She wasn't easily enthralled, but this guy, *Jesus*. If he kept looking at her with those soft eyes, and if he'd stop calling her ma'am like she was fifty years older than him, she'd be tempted to--well--she'd be tempted.

She gave her head a little shake and smiled at Troy, who was waiting for her to say something, anything. "All right. I'm starving, and ready to be wowed. Supplies are all around you. Help yourself and knock me out."

She saw a glint of triumph in his eyes as he scanned a quick inventory of supplies. In a few minutes, he assembled several small slices of French bread with fresh goat cheese, caramelized onions, and crumbled bacon. Troy turned around and presented it to Anya. She inhaled those as politely as possible, while he made a watermelon, mint, and feta salad.

"With a little more familiarity, I'll be able to work faster and be more creative. And I'll know the menu."

Anya stared at him. She had been famished and he had just pre-pared, from what they had laying around, two of her favorites.

"Well," she said. "You've got my vote. But," she added when his face lit up, "we don't hire kitchen staff here without Remy's go-ahead and gods-bless. Come back tomorrow around lunch and take it up with him." At Troy's look, she added, "I'll tell him to expect you."

"Yes, ma'am, thank you--"

"And stop calling me ma'am. I can't be but a little bit older than you. Also, when you meet Leanne, call her anything *but* ma'am. She'll skin you alive and have Remy use what's left of you for shepherd's pie. My name's Anya, and I'll expect you to use it."

Anya extended her hand, but Troy skipped it and engulfed her in a bear hug. "Thank you so much!"

She patted his back awkwardly. She didn't much "do" the Southern "hug all y'all and ya mama" touchy-feely stuff. She reserved said touchy feely stuff for being touchy-feely. With a fella. A naked fella. *Good Lord*. "You're welcome."

"Oh!" Troy sank into a squat, eyes focused on the ground next to her feet. "Looks like you dropped--" he paused as he rose to his full height, "what looks like a charm. Maybe from when I knocked you down." He held up the tiny silver sword. "Here."

Anya caught her breath as he took her hand, caressing it as his fingers adroitly explored the contents of her bracelet. For the moment, his shy uncertainty was gone as he smoothed an empty length of chain to rest on her wrist. He slipped her a sidelong glance and asked, "You don't mind if I just fix this for you, do you?" Without waiting for an answer, his concentration returned to unlocking the latch and coaxing the charm to its intended link.

Honey, you can fix any problem you damn well want. In fact...

"Go ahead. Thank you." When he looked at her again, Anya said, "Now go on home. See you tomorrow, all right?" She smiled as he disappeared out of the kitchen.

Anya had a good feeling about him. A very good feeling.

CHAPTER 5 - THE GIFT IN THE GARDEN

Two heads of red hair bobbed from the flowering mounds of the Brugh's garden. Hummingbirds and honeybees zoomed through the air, swaying and swerving through the shower of strewn clippings.

"Well, you can't say that spell didn't work. Daaay-um." Anya laughed as Leanne grinned. "A gloriously wild night, *and* he's in the game, *and* he's got an endorsement from Harley?"

Leanne added. "Oh, and when I told him about the Lounge, ya know what he said?" She straightened up and put her hand on her hip. "That it's no wonder he kept sending people to us--that he often found himself recommending us to people with problems."

"Wow." Anya turned from the lantana and stared.

"Yeah. Which he thought was weird...but not so much now."

"And Harley likes him." Anya paused and frowned. "Even after the sass?"

Shrugging her shoulders, Leanne said, "Yeah. Something about being short on time."

"And then he just disappeared."

"Harley did. McAnrai left for work the old fashioned way." Leanne continued with her shears, albeit absently. "The weirdest part is that it felt like they knew each other. Or at least Harley knew him. I dunno."

"Careful, darling. Watch out for the wee ones." Anya pushed back a long flowering branch of orange and red lantana blossoms. She snipped a few dying branches and tossed them behind her. Faeries, bees, and birds continued to swoop in harmony with each other.

Leanne blew out a breath. "Of course. Sorry, dears." Tiny white lights flashed and then faded to invisibility. The sisters looked up as the hummingbirds also lost interest and zoomed away, while the bees traveled over to the honeysuckle.

"And his name is Fergus? Shame he hates it. Bodes well for you." Anya's smile was as sly as her words.

Leanne laughed. "Oh, I'm not touching that."

She wiped her face with the hem of her shirt, as Anya's muttered, 'I dunno--sounds like you already did'.

"What's that, sister-mine?"

"What? Nothing!"

"Riiiiight. I'm going to grab the newspaper and head in." Wiping her hands on her jeans, Leanne worked her way out of the garden. Months of effort had gone into the design. The Gentry's' gardens were lush, exotic and were often in complete defiance against the laws of Nature. Georgia's nature, anyway. How Anya got her prize peonies to grow in Georgia's top summer heat was a mystery to the locals. It also sparked no small amount of petty gossip with those who cared about such things as gardening competitions. Still, the haunting beauty of their gardens was a large part of the establishment's attraction.

Leanne walked down the Brugh's porch. She could see Remy leading the kitchen staff through the day's agenda. She sighed to herself, thankful Anya had high hopes for the fellow from last night.

She walked through the double screen doors connecting the front and side porch, down the steps. Stepping into the formal garden, she reached for the poorly aimed morning paper. She bent over to pick it up, but the sight of the body stopped her mid-reach. Frozen, Leanne didn't register the faeries freezing in the air around her before speeding in the direction of the Faery Garden, toward Anya, toward the Portal.

***

The boy from the Lounge. His body was posed on the stairs--resting against the white pillar, feet dangling into the formal flower bed below. Filthy hair hung as a stringy curtain on his face. No shoes. Leanne approached slowly, a ball of dread hardening in her stomach. She saw track marks covering the kid's ankles and feet. Ugly, infected sores criss-crossed his insteps and worked their way down between his toes.

"What is it?" Anya came running around the side of the house. "I could practically hear you--" She stopped short and turned her head, following Leanne's line of sight. "Oh my gods." Her hand covered her mouth. Anya pulled out her phone and dialed 911.

Leanne took a step closer and extended her right hand toward the body. Blowing out a deep breath, she concentrated. Usually, death itself was instant, and spirit moved on. But for those whose lives ended by violence, or whose lives had been full of pain and fear, at least some of their energy remained, confused and afraid. It was this that Leanne was trying to read--and help.

"Chaos. Pain." Leanne's brow furrowed as she drew energy to her hands. She gasped. Gods, it *hurt*. And this was just a shadow of what this boy--no. Brad; his name was Brad--had felt in his last moments. She could well imagine how intense the real pain must have been.

Leanne felt Anya's hands on her shoulders, felt her sister's strength flow into her and blend with her own, a protective force welling up against the hostility clutching to Brad's spirit.

Predatory energy swirled, coalesced. An image formed. Shades of gray, of black, of a darkness so deep the color was felt rather than seen. Experienced rather than witnessed. "It was a man." She squeezed her eyes shut against the pressure. "Such hate." The vision slipped, became malleable. He was tall, but otherwise indistinct, his features hazy.

Leanne inhaled and felt Anya brace herself. She directed her thought, her voice, the power of her Talent at this last bit of life force. *"You've thrown off this mortal coil; be free."* Leanne grounded herself in the earth, her bare feet rooted to soil, to red Georgia clay, and the bedrock beneath. *"You are free,"* she whispered fiercely and threw her arms up to the sky. Sharp rays of sunlight illuminated the energy, pearlescent flames snapped around flickering aggression, pressing inward. The malicious energy fought to maintain control, but the sisters' combined efforts were stronger. Brad's spirit broke free, bursting into thousands of silvery-black butterflies. They glided on the air a moment before evaporating into the ether.

Brad was released, sent Home. Whatever it was that had tried to trap him, that force faded from black to gray, retreated into the surfaces around the body.

"That was lovely," Anya murmured. She wiped the beginnings of tears.

Leanne nodded once, exhausted. She slipped to the ground, let her head hang between her knees, taking deep breaths.

The sound of sirens grew louder. Two police cruisers pulled to the curb.

The cavalry had arrived.

Within minutes, an unmarked, forest green SUV pulled up behind a cruiser and Leanne sighed in relief. Long-legged and solidly tall, McAnrai moved with the grace of a big cat, his strength felt more in his presence than his build. His eyes swept over the boy's body and fixed on Leanne. He went straight to her and crouched down. His eyes searched her for any sign of injury.

McAnrai stroked Leanne's cheek with the back of his fingertips and asked, "Are you all right?" His voice was low, gentle.

Leanne nodded. "I found him like this. He's been dead a while. I didn't touch him, of course."

McAnrai nodded. "That disturbance last night--"

Leanne buried her face in her hands. "Was real. McAnrai?"

"Yes?"

"He was a customer. Came in yesterday. Served him in the Lounge."

McAnrai grimaced. At least this wasn't getting complicated. With a small, reassuring smile, and a discreet squeeze of her hand, he stood and said, "I'm going to go look around. I'll be back in a minute."

McAnrai glanced again at the boy on the front porch. He shook his head and muttered to himself, "It never gets easier."

CHAPTER 6 – ROUND ROBIN REACTIONS

McAnrai strode over to where Dr. Shelby Mitchell knelt beside the body. She looked up when his shadow blocked her sunlight. "Morning, Mac. We caught a weird one today."

Doc, you have no idea. He looked from the body on the porch, then up and around the front garden and sidewalk. Frowning, his mind raced, processing how he was going to handle the ramifications of his...situation. His dark sense of humor ticked off the events of the last twelve hours. Investigated a disturbance that included a mostly naked, red headed bombshell who carried a sawed-off shotgun, and whose temper literally ignited its own fireworks when roused. Then spent several hours having the best sex of his life with said bombshell who was a witch named for the Irish faery goddess of sex--but when a guy's lucky enough to have a woman who embodies the talents of *that* namesake, he doesn't complain.

Morning was enlightening. Leanne-short-for-Leanansidhe runs a magickal restaurant with her witchy sister (named for the Irish goddess of vegetation, because of course). They do this from their home, a building which is a veritable metropolis for nature faeries. Bonus points for waking up desperately in love with Leanne. But that's okay, not to worry about any of that love at first sight bullshit--the deadly faery cat he almost offended implied that he and Leanne have known each other longer. Lots longer. So extra bonus points for past-life-reincarnation epiphanies.

And that was before he finished his fucking coffee.

Not gonna lie--things were moving a little fast for his taste...but he was strangely comfortable with it.

And then a call from dispatch. Dead body. At Leanne Gentry's house. On her front porch, to be exact.

And oh yeah--McAnrai looked again at the body--he'd seen enough death in his life to make a guess at how long this kid's been dead. And if it's been less than ten hours, McAnrai was a fucking faery himself. Yes. He, Fergus McAnrai, one of Columbus' finest, had spent the night at a damn crime scene.

But hey. Let's see what his friend the *Muscogee County Coroner* found strange.

"What's that, Shel?"

She snorted. "Where to start." She pointed at Brad's hairline. "Burnt shoelace tied into his hair." She slid a gloved hand under the shoulder, lifted slightly. "Painted pattern on the back." She set him back into place, as both she and McAnrai turned to the front of the house on their left, and then toward the sidewalk on their right. "And then there's that."

"Yeah." McAnrai rubbed his temple. "Okay, how the *hell* did a strangled body, in plain view on *Broadway*, go unnoticed until ten in the morning?" He shook his head. "Shit, the staff alone should've seen him." To say nothing of the goddamn *homicide detective* who walked by a dead body on his way to work and didn't notice. At. All.

What. The. Fuck.

Shelby pointed at marks on the boy's throat. "The killer used his hands." She tilted her head and checked herself, "I'm going with 'he' from the hand prints' size, plus their angle. Technically, it could be a crazy tall woman with large hands, and or our victim could've been sitting or kneeling." She thought a moment.

"You don't think that, though?" McAnrai brought his hand to his mouth, rested his jaw on his thumb.

"No, I do not." Her dark, elegantly sculpted eyebrows were furrowed as she shook her head. "This wasn't planned. It feels like--" her voice trailed off. "We have distinct hand prints, but you see that extra bruising? Killer honest-to-God wrung this boy's neck. And broke it." Shelby looked up at McAnrai. "That ain't easy to do."

"No, it is not." He looked away, pondering the implications. "So.. .crime of passion, lost his temper." He paused, then added, "But then went through the trouble of transporting the body here, carrying it up steps, and positioning it. He *methodically* dropped his *impulse* kill here. But why?"

The coroner stared at the body. "Especially since this boy was *meant* to be seen." In answer to McAnrai's look, "He was *placed* here with intent. As a message."

McAnrai thought he had a pretty shrewd guess as to what that message was, and clenched his jaw.

***

Leanne heard Anya call her name. She looked toward the porch and did a double take past her sister's purposeful, returning stride. When they met, she nudged Anya. "Do you see her?"

"See who?" Anya squinted in the bright sunlight, then started, "What on earth?"

Sitting in the grass at the corner of the porch, an unusually beautiful Irish wolfhound was paying very close attention to the police activity. At first, the sisters were amazed at the officers' ability to ignore such a large beast in close proximity. A uniformed woman walked by, her elbow brushing the dog's ear.

Anya said, "They're not ignoring her. They don't see her *at all*."

EMTs readied Brad for the stretcher. The hound's golden coat shimmered as she sniffed her way around Brad's body, paying special attention to an imaginary line encircling him. Police avoided walking into the enormous canine, taking awkward routes that no one acknowledged. Despite her cornsilk coat glimmering in the shade, the Cu-Sith remained invisible to everyone but Leanne and Anya.

Leanne glanced at her sister. "She must be from Faery--using glamour to stay invisible."

Anya's eyes widened with mild sarcasm. "And mortal wolfhounds don't tend to glow." Anya bit her lip. "So she's a Cu-Sith. But what interest would a Faery hound have in this boy?"

Leanne's eyebrows creased. "It wouldn't."

They exchanged a glance and said at once, "She was sent."

When she had seen enough, the hound lifted her golden muzzle in a brief salute to the sisters. They watched as the Cu-Sith trotted around the back corner of the house and disappeared with a shimmer under the shared shade of the oak, ash and hawthorn trees. To be more exact, through their Portal into the Faery Realm.

Leanne nodded. "Yeah, but who sent her?"

"That *is* the question." After a pause, Anya said, "I'll check in with my friends in Faery when I finish up out here."

Leanne opened her mouth to speak, but before she had a chance, another car peeled up to the curb. The mayor's personal assistant jumped out and hurried to them. "What the hell is going on here? I've been trying to get in touch with you for an hour!" Bailey Traywick was huffing by the time he reached them. A high school football star gone to seed, his paunch pushed at the buttons of his tailored shirt.

Leanne felt her blood pressure soar. She stepped forward and opened her mouth, but Anya laid a restraining hand on her wrist. To an onlooker, it would seem like a touch of comfort. Leanne thought she might be bruised later. With a silent *harrumph*, she moved back.

Anya smiled. "And we are sorry for that inconvenience. Unfortunately, you can see we've had quite a morning here. Leanne found a body on our front porch. We've been away from our phones."

While Bailey had the grace to redden, shame didn't stop him from pursuing his line of questioning. "Is this going to screw anything up for us? The mayor wants everything perfect for her daughter."

Anya tightened her grip on Leanne. *Definitely* a bruise.

Leanne gritted her teeth while Anya continued, her voice even. "We understand. The police should clear the scene in an hour. Even so, our preparations are already well under way." She smiled. It dazzled in the sunlight. "You can tell the mayor everything is under control."

Shoulders squared with his own importance, Bailey stepped forward, intentionally invading Anya's space, and placed a heavy hand on her shoulder. She released her sister's arm and took Bailey's offending hand in both of hers. Her fingers brushed against his pulse and her thumb stroked over his knuckles. She looked into his eyes and gradually dialed down the wattage of her smile. His breathing and pulse both slowed. She continued the gentle stroking. "Everything is under control. You have nothing to worry about, and now it's time to leave."

Bailey looked a little bemused. "Under control. Nothing to worry about. Yes, I understand. Thank you. I have to go now." He blinked a few times and left almost as quickly as he came.

"Well, that was a little much," Leanne said. "What's that about free will, again?" She rubbed her wrist and gave her sister a wry look.

Anya shrugged. "That was his own choice to leave. He needed to be able to tell Mayor Shetland that he'd brought the hammer. He did, and I reminded him to leave. Nothing more."

Leanne raised an eloquent brow. "They may not be on fire, but your pants are at least smoldering."

Anya grinned but held steadfast against her older sister's critical look. Anya continued, "Unofficial member of Columbus' royalty or not, I don't like being tread on. He was being a dick, so I reassured him, and then told him to Go Away."

Leanne didn't argue but that brow remained raised. Nephew to the mayor, Bailey's parentage was an open secret--and his sense of entitlement made the most of it. "There's that. Well, I'm glad to see him go. When he looks at me, I feel greasy the rest of the day. This wedding can't be over soon enough."

"Agreed," Anya rubbed her hands on her jeans. Looking up, she started, and asked, "How you doing?"

Now that the initial shock had worn off, Leanne's natural introversion was taking over, and her ability to be pleasant and polite was almost gone. "How are you for wrangling people without me?"

"Absolutely. Go inside. Clean up. I've got this."

Leanne left, and Anya looked around as the professional crowd began to thin. Her expression creased with worry when she noticed Remy among those left. He wasn't interfering, but his sharp eyes missed nothing. As she walked to him, she could hear his thoughts as they frantically calculated what to tell the staff--and what *not* to tell them. Anya took a deep breath, focused her mental shields--blocked out the sound of his mind replaying his own memories of violence and death.

***

Efforts for revitalization notwithstanding, downtown Columbus still had its rough moments. So to the kitchen crew, the noise from the first police car didn't attract much attention. Nor did the second. Eventually, Remy had stepped out for some air, and then...

The young Hurricane Katrina survivor couldn't resist the masochistic pull of the crime scene unfolding in front of him--he took it all in as his memories blared an ugly accompaniment.

After a few minutes, his eyes found Anya. She walked over and explained everything, right down to how she and Leanne had released the boy's spirit. "We're going to earn our keep today, love. I sent Leanne upstairs. She won't be down today or tonight."

Remy nodded toward the door Leanne had passed though. He asked, "She's okay?" His dynamic with Leanne had long since evolved to a deep, platonic, friendship--but Remy's protective instincts weren't the type to fade.

"She will be." Anya gave him a reassuring smile.

He hugged Anya and said, "*Mais oui*. We'll handle it. *De rien*."

Remy took a deep breath, then returned to the kitchen. His domain. The one place in his world where sense was made--even if it was with noisy peace and orderly chaos. He prepared himself for the task of informing his staff, and feebly hoped it wouldn't cause much more stress in the already frenzied atmosphere. His sous chef was watching him, and his heart twisted. Remy wished he could protect her from this. As a fellow New Orleans ex-patriot, he knew seeing this body would be even worse for her. A flash of alarm flickered in his eyes--he wondered if the body was still visible.

Correctly interpreting his face, Laidi Thibadeaux's voice was calm but somehow frozen. "What is it?"

Nervous, Remy rumpled his straight, sandy brown hair and looked at her. Resting his hand on her elbow, he asked, "Ya trust me, *chere*?" He kept his voice low, gentle, as if any sudden movements or noises would push her past him, into the scene out front. She met his eyes, glanced to the door and back. A mixture of comprehension and horror flickered across her face, then were replaced by the threat of anger. She snatched her arm away from him.

"I don't need you to protect me." She made a movement toward the porch.

Stock still but for the jerk of his head, to speak over his shoulder, his voice was sharp, "I didn't ask what ya *needed*. I asked if ya *trusted* me." He turned, and lowering his voice, he added, "Please, *ma mie*, I'm *askin'*, not tellin'. Please stay." A couple more seconds and the view should be cleared...

He added, "Don't tell me you wouldn't try to spare me, you. And damn-well expect me to bend."

Laidi pursed her lips, then nodded at the fairness of his words. Closing her eyes, she willed herself back to food prep.

Remy and Laidi's exchange had remained private, but not unnoticed. The staff all looked to their head chef as he told them what he could.

"So tonight's gonna run easy, just like any night. We'll keep it toget'er for Leanne, make sure we don't roust her, *non*." He paused, counting heads. Dammit, that kid had picked a shitty time to quit. He turned to the bartender. "Forrest? You still got dat boy's number? Troy?"

"Sure do."

"*Bon*. Get his ass up here. Let's see if he can deliver."

A touch of a smile brushed Forrest's face. "No need, Rem." He jutted his jaw toward the front steps. "Take a look."

Torn between relief and suspicion, Remy said, "Got handy timin', you."

Troy met the look evenly. "Anya Gentry told me to come back at lunchtime." He flashed a manila folder to the side of his face, then offered them to Remy, professional smile in place. "My references."

There was *not* time for this, Remy thought as he pinched the bridge of his nose, closed his eyes, and took a long breath. And all but one of the women in the place had already given this guy approving once overs...

On the other hand, he'd impressed Anya.

Remy waved off the file. "We're takin' you today. Impress *me* and we'll talk about sumtin' more permanent, yeah?" He spared a few quick seconds to watch as Troy took to the tables, the latter's intuition guiding him unerringly.

Remy turned his back to the rest of the kitchen, and took a shuddering breath as his thoughts darkened. At twenty-six years, he had already seen too much death in his life, courtesy of that bitch Katrina. He'd lost so much in that storm--and he was one of the lucky ones. A quick glance to Laidi--they had both been robbed of whatever childhood innocence they'd had, but Laidi had lost her world. Her neighborhood, her family--all gone. His expression softened as he looked over at her. Best sous chef he'd ever met, and her dimpled smile, and curving, petite form made her the best one he'd ever seen for looks.

Good thing *she* hadn't given the new roundsman a look-over.

CHAPTER 7 - GOTTA ASK, GOTTA TELL

D r. Shelby Mitchell sat at her desk in the Muscogee County Morgue. As buoyant as her disposition was, she relished the isolated nature of her work. Between the generic horrors of the completed autopsy, even on a good day, she needed some cushion time before she had to interact with people. But today's case...

Shelby pressed her fingers against her eyes and took a deep breath before turning her attention back to her notes. Eyes still closed, she brought her personal recorder back to her mouth. Pressing the button, she continued, "The mix of substances found on the subject's back, in his hair, in his bloodstream--yes, weird as hell describes them, and the combination of them, but *nothing* compared to the problem of the feet. Covered in--something, three different 'somethings', actually. She stopped the recorder. To no one in particular, she said, "But what the hell are they?"

She picked up a bagged piece of paper. "Oh, and the grim, little something extra I found." She pressed record, and spoke into the microphone. "A note pulled from victim's trachea, showing killer has taken a personal interest in Detective McAnrai, and the Gentrys as well."

She stopped the recorder and put it away. With a short sigh, Shelby shoved her chair back, and returned the bagged slip of paper to the box marked Evidence.

She muttered, "And to think, I left Atlanta so I could lead the quiet life down here?" She looked up as her assistant, Garrett, walked into her office.

"Oh yes, good call, there. Remind me not to ask you for input when I'm playing numbers." The precise voice and cheeky attitude of her assistant made her grin in spite of herself.

"Hey, there. Hope your day's going better than mine."

Garrett Nyles grinned back, his bright blue eyes twinkling. "Besides a friendly little tussle, I'm just ducky." In response to her questioning look, he rolled his eyes and elaborated, "His Majesty, Payne Hilton, called us *himself*." He adjusted his stance and lengthened his facial expression to fit the solemn, deep bass of the might-as-well-be-mayor. "*Something* must be done. It's a *disgrace* that a body was found on a property the public will associate with the Hilton family. My niece's wedding rehearsal, blah, blah, *blech*."

Payne Hilton. Shelby had been seated next to the man who ranked among Columbus' royalty on more than one occasion--banquets, board meetings, luncheons. Recalling what she knew about Hilton's complete lack of anything resembling a sense of humor, she chuckled at Garrett's imitation. He smiled and added, "You're welcome, by the way."

"Thank you kindly. What for?"

"Said call came while you were getting prepped for the autopsy. I told them you were mad at work on the very case at hand and couldn't possibly be torn away--but that I'd faithfully convey his concerns." He walked closer, set his reports in her inbox, and his bottom on the clear edge of her desk.

"I bet that went over well."

"Oh, darlin', *just* like a lead zeppelin," he blithely piped. "Anyway, police chief in a snit, 'mayor' in a snit, solve it yesterday or it's the gallows for us." He brushed his wispy, blonde bangs from his eyes and peeked out the door. "Looks like *your* day's about to get brighter." With a playful bow, Garrett left for his office.

"Hey Garrett?" The young man turned, eyebrows raised. Shelby reached into her right hand drawer, past her .38, to the emergency stash. "Catch!" The chocolate bar went flying.

He plucked it from the air and grinned. "Something from the surprise drawer? And *Lindt*? For *me*? Nice."

"Dealing with that jerk? You earned it, hun. Thanks for real." She flashed him a warm smile as he went back to work.

McAnrai poked his head around the door frame, "Got a minute?"

"Maybe even two." Shelby rose from her chair with a rueful smile of welcome. "I haven't finished my official report from this morning, so you're outta luck if that's why you're here."

"Actually, no, but I'd love a copy as soon as you can get it to me." He held the door, as if to close it, "Do you mind?"

"No, but--" She raised her hand toward the front of her office called out, "Careful about--" Her words were cut off by the loud noise coming from the big detective's throat.

"*JESUS H. CHRIST!*" All six feet, three inches of badass, Philadel-phian Irishman jumped an inch off the floor and a bit more back. In a voice just a touch too loud for polite, McAnrai asked, "What the *fuck* is that?"

Accustomed as she was to this reaction, Shelby shook her head. "Boy, you sound like my grandmama watching a horror movie." She smirked at his expression . "Now gather up what's left of your manliness and have a seat."

Gesturing to the elegantly mounted specimen, McAnrai laughed and turned to his friend. The friend he thought he knew well. *That's* why she kept the door flush against the wall, why she always met people in the reception-esque area just feet from her office. He had assumed it was her own need for boundaries. Apparently, it was a courtesy to the visitors.

"What. The. HELL. Shelby."

Rolling her eyes and gathering the papers from her desk, Shelby made her way to the comfortable seating. She set the papers down on the coffee table, and continued walking to McAnrai. "That's Beulah'."

"Beulah. Fucking *Beulah*? No. That's a, a goddamn tarantu--"

"Don't talk about her like that. She's a lady."

Incredulous, McAnrai stared at the ornate woodwork framing the softly lit recessed shelf--it must have been custom-made by the same artist who framed the Spelman and Emory certificates flanking it. The occupant of this luxurious nook was positioned on a pale, bark-printed, satin covered base--and by God if that mounting base didn't look like a plush pillow.

McAnrai's eyebrows neared his hairline as he turned to Shelby and retorted, "A *lady*? This thing would give Peter Parker nightmares. That leg span's at least a goddamn foot across." The velvety gray and brown arachnid was leaning on its back six legs, its front two raised high, the red markings of its mouth visible over the black and white pattern of its underside. Almost as if it, er, *she*, was looking at him skeptically as well.

Shelby tapped her French manicured nail against the glass, as if in greeting. McAnrai half expected the monstrosity to take the nearer raised leg and meet the nail tip from the other side, like some sort of twisted handshake. And if it did, he was *so* fucking outta there...

With a dry, little double smooch sound at 'Beulah', Shelby whispered, "You'll have to excuse my colleague." She shot him a playful look of reproach, "And you should know better than to overestimate a lady's figure. She's a delicately feminine eight inches from tiptoe to tiptoe." Answering his look of 'that's not any fucking better', she added, "She's pretty standard size for a huntsman." In a derisive undertone, she muttered, "Tarantula. Hah." Shelby laughed and moved farther into her office, to her mini fridge. "Drink? I've got iced tea and Coke." She gestured to the shiny leather couch across from her desk.

"Nothing stronger? I'd think you'd need some for your visitors' medicinal needs. Or do they just end up joining the horizontal ranks?" He took a deep breath, and enjoyed the sensation of his blood pressure returning to normal. "Christ, I think I understand arachnophobes, now." Hell, he may even *be* one now.

"She *is* a wonderful guard--makes me feel good and safe when I'm alone down here." Though the rest of her domain had the clinical sterility expected of a morgue, Shelby's office was her refuge. The color scheme was cozy, with dark leather bindings on the books and warm, muted colors for the walls and rugs. Dark, hardwood bookcases lined the walls, the same rich cherry woodwork that framed Beulah's outpost graced the cabinets hiding her filing system and mini-fridge. The lighting was more than enough to work, but soft enough to be a warm, comfortable contrast to the harsh glare required for her operating tables.

McAnrai gave an enthusiastic nod. "Oh, I bet." Looking--and damn-well *walking*--away from the nightmare sentinel, the transplanted northerner lifted his insulated bottle of lightly sweetened tea as he sat down. "No thanks. Brought my own."

With an admonishing frown, Shelby popped open her can and said, "Boy, I'm gonna have to teach you how to take your tea. What you're drinking?" She shuddered, "Shouldn't be allowed."

"A scolding on what shouldn't be allowed from a woman who happily shares an office with the long-lost granddaughter of Ungoliant?" Moving on, he said, "I like my tea sweet, but down here? *Coke* has less sugar in it."

"So what's your point?" She sat down next to him, file in hand. "Trade?"

McAnrai sighed and pulled out his folder. "Not much from my end. He's in the system, but nothing huge. Brad Casey. Petty theft, shoplifting...drugs more recently--possession, then use." He shuffled his papers, "Foster kid. Between being bounced around by the system, and occasionally running away, he never settled with one family."

"Therefore unlikely to be reported gone."

McAnrai nodded. "Yep." He looked at the file in her lap. "Time of death?"

"Several hours before he was found. I'd say, a little before midnight. And while I stand by his being killed somewhere else, yes, condition of the body implies he'd been on the steps about as long."

He nodded. "So, definitely before the restaurant staff got there..." He let his sentence trail off. "It's going to be fun explaining this to the boss man." Or to Shelby. He noticed her look--not that she actually suspected the Gentry's' crew either, but it was pretty odd for each of them to have casually stepped around a strangled boy.

He continued. "The only way of it, then, is that he must've been killed *well* before he was moved, set in a similar position, then placed at the Gentry's' later. I doubt the newspaper boy would've ignored him as well. And the rest of the early morning foot traffic--he was in plain view of the street." McAnrai could tell by her expression that the coroner wasn't satisfied--he didn't like the theory himself.

"There's more." Shelby opened the file and pulled out a page. "Now, I'm no botanist, but I'm a fair competitor amateur, with some excellent back up." She pointed at the top photo on the table. "These substances on his feet? I can tell they're from three different plant specimens, but damn if I know *what* plants. Nor does our boy-wonder, Garrett. Nor does my very new, very *expensive* software from Texas A&M."

McAnrai took the page's accompanying photos. He bit the inside of his cheek, considering his options. He was uncomfortably certain the solution was lying somewhere beyond the realm of easy to explain. Hey Cap, no worries. The reason everybody walked past a dead body? It was hidden by magick. Unidentifiable trace evidence? More magick. Hey Shelby, don't worry about that stuff you can't ID. They're probably just magick plants from the Faery Realm. Here's an idea, the woman who found the body? She's my new girlfriend, and you're friends with her sister, so you know they're witches--let's have them take a look around...

Yeah. That would go well.

He shuffled through the papers as he wrestled with his options, but Shelby wasn't fooled.

"You have an idea."

Oh, what the hell. It wasn't like the Gentrys were living a subtle life. Buuuuuut...there was a big, damn difference between seeing your friends as a 'one-with-the-earth' types, and learning they're both Professor McGonagall as played by Sally and Gillian Owens.

He let out a short sigh, and looked at her. "It's a little out of the box," he paused as his inner monologue burst into laughter. A little out of the box. "But before you send it out, maybe show Anya?"

Shelby considered his words. "You may have something there."

McAnrai lifted the photos of Brad's back, pointed at the marks themselves, "There's an extra level to this."

Shelby nodded. "You bet. But the base "paint" isn't human blood." Her mouth twisted in disgust. "It's canine."

The detective's eyes flashed with anger. "That motherfucker."

"Mmm-hmmm." Returning the talk to calmer ground, Shelby said, "And the why of that is probably as important as the plant-life mystery."

McAnrai watched as Shelby thought. He knew she trusted him, and the Gentrys hell, her friendship with Anya is how he had met Leanne's sister in the first place. But they both answered to people who were less inclined that way. Giving McAnrai all this was part of her job, but civilians were another matter entirely.

Finally, Shelby pushed the file across the table. "Maybe you could look through it tomorrow?" She smiled, "I know it's your day off, and all, but you're the type to go the extra mile."

McAnrai smiled back. "I'm sure I'll be able to spare some time tomorrow."

"I'll need to keep the note, though. That goes straight to Evidence."

"Well, if you really think you should." Well played. His affection for Shelby surged so, he almost forgave her for his arachno-cardio event. Wait--

He tilted his head. "Note?" McAnrai didn't like her grim expression. Not at all.

She handed him the plastic bag. "I discovered it during the autopsy--lodged in his throat."

He took the bagged note and read it.

Tell your whore she failed, Detective.

McAnrai felt every muscle in his body freeze, heard the blood roaring in his ears. Before trusting himself to speak, the detective closed his eyes and took a slow, deep breath. What had started as a bad feeling at the crime scene solidified into grim certainty. It *was* personal. When he opened his eyes, McAnrai returned the piece of paper.

And then there was the other aspect...

Shelby's expression stayed neutral as she said, "So, someone over there is yours?" Her eyebrow did creep up a bit at McAnrai's hesitation. She added, "Honey, it's either super recent, or not Anya, otherwise I'd already know."

Falling back into the soft couch, McAnrai sighed, his rage checked in favor of the relief he felt from her ripping off this band-aid.

With a long exhale, he said, "I'd say a gentleman doesn't kiss and tell, but..."

"But it looks like you done spent the night at a crime scene. Son, you best consider this a free pass on chivalry."

"Yeah." He rubbed his face. "You're right on both counts--recent and not Anya."

"Leanne?" Shelby let out a bit of a laugh. "Well, damn, then. You better fasten your seat-belt."

Suppressing a smile of agreement, McAnrai addressed the crime scene photos. "Honest to God. I didn't see him. I mean, I'll admit to being distracted by," he paused, looking for the least awkward word for a whirlwind of mind-blowing epiphanies and sexy flashbacks. And Shelby's knowing smile wasn't helping. "To being distracted. But I walked down those steps--not five feet away. It was a bit of a blur, sure, but..." his voice trailed off helplessly. He was not accustomed to his memory having holes of any kind, let alone astronomical ones.

"But how the hell did you walk past a body?"

"Exactly." His voice was soft as the enormity of this problem sank in. "You're sure of how long it had been there?"

"If it weren't for the sheer number of people who'd have to be blind not to've seen it, I would be." She smiled reassuringly, "Mac. I know how busy the foot traffic is there. At least a dozen other people, probably more, also missed it. This isn't about trusting you, even though I do."

McAnrai felt a bit better that he didn't have to beg for trust, but, "Either there is one crazy conspiracy--"

"Or something seriously strange is going on."

He thought about the note, its subtext.

As if she could read his thoughts, Shelby said, "It's not uncommon for male killers to just think all women are whores, but her 'failing'?" She looked at McAnrai, "If Leanne knew this kid, even only as a customer, this note implies the killer knew he went to the Lounge specifically," she paused at the surprised look on McAnrai's face, "Yes, I know the Lounge is where they serve the food that's 'charged'." She mimed the air quotes and smiled at his expression. "And yes, I've eaten there myself. But," she pointed again to the note, "this shows the killer knows about the Lounge, knows Leanne tried to help his victim, and..."

"Knows I spent the night. Wait..." his voice trailed as another thought hit him. "This was a passion kill, right?" He leaned back, looked at the ceiling. "Saying she failed means he knew she was trying to help--but whatever she did pissed him off wholesale. There's got to be something in that."

Shelby nodded. "Well, at least we have a handwriting sample. And only an entire city to compare to it."

They both looked at the note. Through clenched teeth, McAnrai said, "No one, and I mean *fucking no one* tells Leanne about this note. Agreed?"

Shelby's eyes expressed understanding and agreement.

At her nod, McAnrai set his hands on his knees, and rose, speaking with slow deliberation. "Okay. I should get going." He gave her a tight look, "Unless there's anything else?"

"Nope. Just let me get it typed up and it'll be on its way." She stood and joined him, set her hand on his arm. Their eyes locked in a mirthless camaraderie. McAnrai nodded his thanks, and left without another word.

CHAPTER 8 - CALL AND ANSWER

L eanne took slow steps through the front door of the house. As the immediate shock wore off, the situation's enormity settled on her. She meandered toward the entrance connecting the restaurant to her home, her sanctuary. The fans hanging from the twelve-foot ceilings turned lazily, their mahogany blades a stark contrast to the smooth cream of the ceiling. The sheer, pale blue curtains flowed with the gentle breeze rising from the floor vents pumping the room with air conditioning. Passing out of the bright natural light of the main room, she walked down the hallway, past the restrooms, and the subtly hidden Garden Lounge.

Its entrance had returned to its regular form, a beautifully detailed mural of a gate opening to an enchanted garden. Like everyone who worked here, she could enter the Lounge at any time, even when its access was disguised as it was now.

She looked away as she walked by. Leanne had made it her specialty to identify, address, and meet the magickal needs of the people granted entry by the room. She didn't want to even think about the Lounge, what it did, or how it had failed.

No, it hadn't failed, she corrected herself, *she had.* Leanne felt guilty, sick. And the beginning of angry.

She put the flat of her hand on the solid oak door at the end of the hall. The wood beneath her hand rippled as the protection wards she and Anya had in place relaxed. The door opened with a click, and she entered their private kitchen. As the door shut behind her, she felt the wards slip back into place.

Safe in her home, Leanne felt herself relax.

Cheerful daisies smiled from tall vases scattered around the room, mirroring the blooms painted on the pale cream walls. The windows welcomed the afternoon sunshine pouring in from the Garden and its Lounge.

Grabbing what she needed from the fridge, Leanne climbed the stairs to the private living space. She could feel her tension ease with each step, and when she entered the upstairs dining room, exhaustion hit her. Having lost all interest in what she was carrying, she set the bowl and the quart of cream down on the dining room table, and made an abrupt right, crossing over into the living room. Her weary gaze fell on the row of low, squashy couches lining the semicircle of the room. Grabbing a large pillow, she curled up on the closest cushion and fell asleep.

***

Harley padded up the four steps behind the couch and continued along the small walkway lining the entire length of the low seating. Like the other walls in the living room, the wall behind the couch was lined from waist height to the twelve foot ceiling with shelves brimming with books--fiction, non-fiction, and a good number of handwritten journals. The couches were flush to the wall, and a wide sill provided a walking path behind them. The Cait-Sith stepped around the old-fashioned sliding ladder the humans used to reach the highest shelves and continued over the few scattered books that had been left in easy reach of the couch. He never took his eyes off Leanne's sleeping form, though his gait slowed as he approached her. Inches from her face, his gaze intensified as he settled into a watchful crouch.

His quick, analytical mind took in every detail. Sweaty, dirty. She'd been gardening. Smears across her face where she had wiped away a few tears.

There was something else--he sniffed delicately, inhaling the faint, woody notes of a man's cologne. *McAnrai*, he thought. Strong, intelligent, the man had the capacity to balance profound love with cold-blooded ruthlessness. All traits thoroughly admired by the Cait-Sith. Harley had started to wonder if Leanne's man was ever going to show up. Considering the storm that was coming, the Faery Warrior found great solace in once again having McAnrai as an ally.

Lastly, he could feel, almost see, traces of the energy Leanne had just battled. Malignant. *Familiar*. His eyes narrowed as his certainty cemented. Would Leanne recognize it? It had been almost twenty years, and while he was beyond ancient by the reckoning of humans, she had been but a child.

Sensing his presence, Leanne's eyes fluttered open. "Oh, *Harley*." He jumped down into her lap. She wrapped her arms around him, something he always pretended to tolerate rather than enjoy. He pushed his head into the crook of her neck, purring.

"There, there, little one. I'm here now." He could feel her sobs shaking him, no small feat, considering his size. He kept talking, using his voice to calm her as she smoothed her hands over his deep, soft fur.

Harley had entered Leanne's life when she was nine years old. Michael and Niamh were good Irish Catholic parents, but it was easy to forget that "Irish" is a notable disclaimer along the lines of how one defined "strict religious upbringing." While in Ireland, visiting the different Faery mounds, and crossing through the portals into the Faery Realm for picnics and parties was as much a part of the Gentrys' lives as visiting their mortal family and friends.

On one such visit, this very confident, curious girl had wandered away from the festivities, following the sound of pained, feline cries. By the time she had reached him, Leanne was lost and more than a little scared. That fear led to her reckless decision to free him from, had she but known, a gruesome death.

Now, almost twenty years later, the life-debt Harley incurred that afternoon in the Faery hollow had evolved to a relationship closer than friendship and more mystical than family. As he waited for her to calm, he thought about what he could tell her. What would keep her safe. What was permitted. "I'm here, little one."

"*Now* you are." She let out a long breath. "Where were you, earlier?"

"I was visiting the relations."

Leanne's jaw dropped. "Okay, that I did not expect."

Harley tilted his head in acknowledgement. In all the years they had been together, he had never returned to Faery without her. In response to her shocked expression, he took a short breath and readied himself, "Well, darling, there are some things I need to tell you." He jumped onto the sill behind the couches. Leanne smiled faintly as he started to pace, readying himself for what she called his 'informative sit-downs'.

Between the nap, the catharsis of her tears, and his steadying presence, Leanne had regained enough of her composure to take a more thoughtful look at Harley. "Yes, professor, but let me clean up a bit first. Besides," she glanced over at the dining room table, and his empty dish, "I'm thirsty, and you need a refill." Leanne gave him a sidelong look as he feigned disinterest. "It smells like the bread has been delivered."

Harley didn't miss the knowing smile as she watched him dash from the sill to the table--he simply didn't care. For all the dignity, decorum, and reserve born of Sidhe lineage and several centuries, if there was one thing to make him act like a kitten on Yuletide morn, it was the promise of farm-fresh cream and a warm baguette.

***

When she returned from the kitchen, Harley was where she left him, though his excitement had him marching in place. She handed him the warm bread and filled his saucer. Regaining some sense of formality, he grabbed the loaf with his front paws, and sat at one of the dining chairs. Leanne waited while he dug in. It was so rare for him to take such unguarded enjoyment in something--she felt like a fond mother watching her child playing with a new toy. Halfway through the baguette, he slowed down enough to speak again.

"You see, darling," his refined accent rolling around the hunks of cream-soaked bread with jolly abandon, "you may feel like you made a conscious choice to work with my Lady, but--"

"*Your lady*?" With a twinge of jealousy, Leanne eyed him.

Hearing her mistake, he rolled his eyes. He took another large, drippy bite. "Not "my lady", my *Lady*. Your Lady as well, if you want to look at it that way." He chewed, swallowed, and took another bite. "When you came of age, you chose, or thought you chose, to dedicate yourself to a life working with the Celtic gods and goddesses."

He paused to see if she was following him.

"Yes," she prompted him.

"What you've never appreciated, though I've told you dozens of times, is that one does not simply decide to work with the Celtic pantheon. *They* decide if and when to work with *you*." He smeared the end of the bread into the final drop of the cream. Popping it into his mouth, he leaned back and closed his eyes, savoring the last mouthful. Fatigue and satiation from his treat were catching up to him. He slinked out of the chair and made his way back to the living room.

Curling up on the couch together, he continued. "The day you freed me--you shouldn't have been able to hear me at all. My voice was--" he yawned, "--was able to call past my enclosure by Her grace." He looked up at Leanne and could see that she was still in the dark.

"If She heard you, why didn't She free you?" Leanne stopped herself, and piled on another, more pressing question, "And who do you mean by "Lady"?"

"Leanne, she *did* free me. My Lady answered Her soldier's call by summoning one She knew would grow to be powerful, a priestess even. She recognized your strength, and knew you would be able to responsibly wield that power. Even though you were too young to appreciate it, on that day, you were one chosen by Her. On that day, I incurred a life debt to you, and started fulfilling my assignment from Her--to be your teacher and guardian for the duration of your life."

"Wait, you're a soldier? And again, for whom?" The Cait-Sith were few in numbers, with only the strongest surviving in the modern era, so she always knew Harley was powerful. She never suspected him of having a rank. To a goddess. And if she understood him, *the* Goddess. Belatedly, she added, "Priestess?"

Harley stood, stepped onto the coffee table. He drew himself to his full height, bringing his gaze above her eye level. Never one for undue humility, he exuded now a pride even she'd never seen. His eyes, ordinarily the pale green of a delicate seafoam, now glowed a brilliant emerald. The bronze flecks through his coat became more pronounced, and flickered with the illusion of a luminous coat of armor.

"Leannan Fiachra Gentry, I am *The* Cait-Sith, the Harlequin, Lieutenant for the Threefold Goddess of Life, Death, and Rebirth, Her Sovereignty The Morrigan, Warrior Queen and Divine Mother."

The armor faded. His eyes settled to their familiar hue. He ambled away from her, to his favorite section of the sofa. He snuggled himself into the deep cushions and looked at her through half lidded eyes. As he dozed off, he whispered, "You never suspected?"

CHAPTER 9 - TEQUILA HELPS THE GRIME WASH OFF

Leanne watched Harley sleep for a few moments, more than a little frustrated that he would just drop that kind of bomb and then go to sleep. Not that she was surprised. Though he loved her as he did, Harley was still Fae-- if and when they were willing to share information, a smart girl accepted the form in which it came.

Digesting what Harley *had* shared, Leanne walked past the hearth and toward the hallway leading to the bedrooms. The afternoon sun poured in streams through the French doors of the balcony gracing the front of the house. If what Harley said was true, and of course it was, why on earth would She assign Harley the job of being a guardian for a random little girl, twenty years ago?

There was no way she was ready to even attempt wrapping her mind around the Morrigan Herself viewing a nine-year-old as a recruit.

Grabbing a clean towel from her bed's storage bench, she walked into her private bath. The cool marble felt gorgeous against her hot feet. Never one for hot showers, Leanne dialed back the temperature. The cool water felt fresh and wholesome against her skin. The energetic mire washed away with the dirt and sweat as clouds of cool mist filled the room, imbued with notes of fresh lime and neroli. Inhaling, she felt it purifying her inside and out. Any second now, she thought, the energetic residue from her fight with the killer's spell would be gone. It would take more than a shower to *feel* it again, but at least she would *be* clean. Turning the knob all the way to cold, she let the icy fingers massage her scalp, leeching off the threatening headache. She let the water run for a few more minutes.

Refreshed, Leanne turned off the water and reached for the large, plush towel. She stepped out of the shower and caught the scent of vetiver incense floating in from her bedroom. Smiling, she dried off her face as she walked out into her bedroom, towel hanging down her front. The gossamer tendrils of light, musky smoke spiraled up from the censer hanging over her desk like a tiny potted plant. Looking past the spiraling scent to her bed, she saw McAnrai.

"Well, aren't you a bold one." Despite the literal thrill of seeing him, she was still getting used to the rapidly developing relationship.

"Just following orders." He was standing at the foot, dressed in faded jeans and a smile. As though reading her mind, it faded, and he added, "But I can leave?"

That adorable, merciless bastard. Broad shoulders and a powerful, if understated, build, she was certain McAnrai drew looks even when clothed. His shiny, dark brown hair was just long enough to need a comb--as it did now. Her heart beat a little faster, and she said, "Don't you dare."

McAnrai flashed a boyishly naughty, mixed cocktail of a smile. A *helluva* smile. He tossed one of the shot glasses to her.

Catching it with one hand, she laughed. "Nice try, but I've still got m'towel."

"Hey," he tossed her a slice of lime, "don't criticize the technique until you can prove it didn't work."

Leanne's other hand caught the lime wedge, and McAnrai let out a short, sharp breath as the towel dropped. He took slow steps, savoring the view as he drew closer to her. Kicking the towel out of the way, he slipped his hands around her waist and drew her close for a kiss. She dropped the glass and lime wedge on her dresser and wrapped her arms around his neck. Slow, smooth...

Glancing at the frosty bottle of tequila, the bowl of ice, and cut limes on the nightstand, she groaned. "Sweet man, I've got to get downstairs. And doesn't your job have some very clear rules about cruel and unusual punishment?" It was her duty, obligation, to get her shit together and lead her crew...

"Like I said, I've been given specific orders--something about 'keeping her happy ass upstairs'." Leanne started to protest, but he kissed her again, wrapping his arms around her back. Pressing her close, his lips played with her ear as she whispered, "Besides, some cardio should finish the job that shower started."

He met her amused gaze as he walked them to the bed. He wasn't wrong, and she knew it. After any intense spiritual experience, good or bad, exercise is the fastest way back to reality.

"Cardio, huh?" Her words smiled through their kiss.

"Vigorous cardio." McAnrai dropped his weight and lifted his woman off her feet, growling with anticipation as her arms tightened around his shoulders and her legs wrapped around his waist. His mouth explored her neck as Leanne slipped her toes just inside the belt of his jeans. He felt her feet slide down the back of his legs, pushing the last of his clothes to the floor. They sank onto the bed, his hands sliding down her back, guiding her hips onto his lap.

Leanne let herself luxuriate in the pleasure, the safety, the heat of his energy, and felt a little jolt. Something extra. Or, rather, her mind's eye could *see* it, imprisoned behind thick glass--living, exposed muscle, throbbing, bleeding, suffering. Begging for salve. There was something he didn't want her to know. Pain he didn't want to share. This was more than McAnrai trying to make her feel better. More than preventing her from fucking up everything in the kitchen by going down there in her state. *He* needed *her*. She ran her fingers through his hair, whispered, "*A chéadsearc, a chéadsearc...*"

As her weight settled on his lap, McAnrai felt some of the poisonous tension leave his own body. Violence, blood, murder--that was nothing new for him. But today was different. This wasn't just another homicide; this was a direct attack on everything he loved, held dear. Everything *his* to protect. Yeah, he'd made his peace with that part. Fast or not, she was *his,* and thank the gods, she knew it, too. He could tell she did. In exact time with the thrill that thought gave him, he heard her whisper, "*Mine.*"

"Yes I am." McAnrai's voice was guttural with need. His fingertips dug into her back. His. His. *His.* Pressing her body to his chest, he could feel Leanne's heart speed up at the sensation, experiencing pleasure, rather than discomfort at the continued force from his fingertips. Dragging to her waist, climbing up her back, into her hair, her kisses sent bolts of insane pleasure through him as his own lips traveled across her collarbone, her throat, his heartbeat chanting its mantra: His. His. *HIS.*

Leanne could feel the authority radiating from the man, his heart beating against hers, the strength in the hands digging into her back, dragging beautiful trenches to her hips, sliding up and clutching at the roots of her hair. She didn't have the words to explain her emotional exhaustion, her need to hide from everything, from everyone but him. She kissed his forehead, his eyes, his mouth, his beautiful mouth...

McAnrai needed to escape, if only for a while, escape into the bliss of their physical needs. He closed his eyes tightly, hiding his face in her neck, under the curtain of her hair, fighting to keep his emotions under control. He willed his hands to relax, ordered his fingers to spread wide, slide firmly, but gently over her skin. Back, front, arms, legs, belly, breasts...

McAnrai shuddered with pleasure as Leanne's fingernails lightly traced up his back, into his hair, her fingertips turning in, caressing his scalp. His lips moved in a slow dance across her skin while her hands slipped from the back of his head to his cheeks, gently guiding his lips back to hers. Wrapping his arms fully around her, he moaned at the sensation of her breasts pressing against his chest. At the sound, Leanne leaned further into the kiss, pushing McAnrai onto his back, the urgency of her emotions playing out against his body.

At once, they stopped, drew apart slightly, eyes met...

Her eyes..slightly unfocused, completely feral...

At that moment of connection, McAnrai's mind was finally swept clean of all thought, a primal growl erupted from his chest...In one fluid movement, he rolled onto her, into her, his lips hardly leaving her jaw.

CHAPTER 10 – GREAT STARTS AND GREAT MINDS FOR EVIL TIMES

Leanne woke to wild winds and steady rain pounding against the glass of her bedroom windows. They were well into hurricane season, though she couldn't remember Columbus being in line for any this week. Then something else occurred to her...

She smiled. Hopefully, the police had gotten all they needed from the porch before Anya had started. Leanne hadn't been the only one in need of purification, and from the sound of it, Anya was giving the property a very thorough cleansing.

So much for that sunshine the news promised. Leanne wondered just how frustrated the local weather announcer became when she and her weather-bending sister had settled here. The loud crack of thunder rattled the glass in its panes and was followed by another. And another. Damn. Anya was *serious.*

She rolled over to appreciate McAnrai's sleeping form. Flat on his back, her eyes slid over his broad chest, tanned, with an assortment of tattoos and scars--a few whose stories he'd shared, and others she knew better than to ask about. She admired his profile. High cheekbones, straight nose, strong jawline, full lips. Black lashes fluttered and eyes opened. He rolled to face her, pulled her into his arms.

"And a good morning to you, babe." The kiss was slow and relaxed, an enjoyment of the moment and of each other. "How'd you sleep?"

"Very well, thanks to you." She sighed. Almost to herself, she added, "It would've been so hard if you hadn't been here with me." She kissed him again.

"Nah, it was hard *because* I was with you. Oooof!!" He laughed as the pillow hit his face. He stretched, searching the nightstand with his hand. Lying back on the pillow, he looked at the face of his grandfather's old fashioned watch. "Shit. I should start getting ready to go." He shot her a quick sidelong glance. "No chance of breakfast, is there?"

"What, you think I run a restaurant?" She grinned, "Oh, I *guess.* We might have some food downstairs." Leanne swung her legs off the side and started to stand. "Ugh," she crawled back under the covers, "but you're cooking it."

McAnrai started to protest, but she cut him off with a laugh and a kiss. "Take it as a compliment, sweet man." She took pride in the blush that peeked through his golden complexion, and even more pleasure in watching him dress. "Besides, by the smell of it, I think Anya beat you to it."

***

Anya was curled up in the breakfast nook, sipping her tea. She watched the rain drench the gardens beyond the kitchen window. At McAnrai's footfalls, she turned. "Hope you're hungry. I might have overestimated how much to make."

McAnrai inhaled the rich aroma of blueberry pancakes, bacon, sausage and, bless the girl, was that coffee? "You're a goddess among women, Anya." He grabbed two plates and started piling them with food. "I'm starved." He poured two mugs of coffee.

With a soft laugh, she said, "Cream's over there." She walked to the sink and rinsed her mug. Glancing down at the two large manila envelopes on the counter, "I assume these are yours?"

"Yeah, I left them down here last night, thanks." He picked them up and checked the writing. *From the Desk of Dr. Shelby Mitchell* and *Attn: McOrnery.* He shook his head at the nickname he earned at the academy. For some unaccountable reason, it had followed him ever since. Sure, it was a play on how his name was pronounced, but calling him inflexible was an exaggeration. He was only stubborn when he was right.

He slipped the envelopes under his arm and arranged the rest of the food and drink. Shoving a small, rolled up pancake in his mouth, he rolled his eyes ecstatically as a ripe blueberry burst into the fluffy, vanilla-infused cake. He lifted the tray and gave a muffled "Thanks again" to Anya before returning upstairs.

***

It had been a restless night for Remy, and dawn found him wide awake and cranky as hell. Well, he thought, kicking off the covers, might as well make the most of an early start. Resigned to a long day, he rolled out of bed. After a shower and shave, he ran a comb through his light brown, shoulder-length hair. With a glance to the rain pounding mercilessly against his living room window, he grabbed his hat and swung his arms into his dark, calf-length trench coat. As he locked his door, he threw a quick glance up the steps to Laidi's apartment. She hadn't looked good when they left work yesterday, though, he reflected, that was hardly unexpected. He had almost knocked on her door last night, before thinking better of it.

It was usually an easy stroll to work from his apartment on Broadway, just two houses down and across the street. Today, the torrential rain made his morning stroll more of a jog.

When he got to the Table, he skipped up the front steps and rustled in his pocket for the keys. Once through the front door, the raging storm was muted, replaced with gentle music. He walked through the restaurant's official entrance, turned a sharp left toward the Brugh.

He paused, his senses pleasurably blurred as he felt, rather than heard, a soft melody floating around him. He smiled as he looked up at its source--the sylphs were deftly weaving through the openings of the vine-laden latticework overlooking the bar's porch. It tickled him that, of all of the strange and wonderful things he'd seen since meeting the Gentrys, the only faeries who resembled the traditional 'Tinkerbell type' were these. Tiny humanoid forms with delicate, iridescent wings fluttered about his head. Though their skin tones spanned every shade from palest pink to rich ebony, the sylphs were dressed in sweet, pale colors, and each cast a luminous glow--to watch them swim through the air, to see the cheerful, multi-colored orbs as they dashed in and out of hiding, it was mesmerizing.

For someone who had been disillusioned so young, it was pleasant to occasionally lose himself in wonder for a minute or two. He knew by the time the Table and Brugh opened, the Other Crowd would have shifted, and this storybook atmosphere would be replaced with a bright assortment of Fae who could pass as regular humans. Well, usually passed. There was that one incident with the leprechaun and the *poitín*...

He hung his hat and coat in the locker, tilting his head to the genial noise and welcoming aroma wafting from the kitchen.

Sometimes the universe gave a *lagniappe*. Fully appreciating the little gift from the cosmos, he couldn't think of a better beginning to his day than sharing the kitchen with Laidi. Well, he *could*--but despite his feelings, he was nervous about crossing the workplace boundary. Maybe it was the hometown connection--as a fellow New Orleanian, she understood what it meant to be forced to create a new life in a strange land. Not that Georgia was completely alien; it just wasn't home.

And for Remy, Laidi Thibadeaux was.

He walked over to her and slipped a playful arm around her slim shoulders.

"Now what ya doin' here so early?"

Laidi threw him a halfhearted grin. She pulled her hands out of the enormous lump of bread dough, and brushed them off. A few tendrils of hair had come out of the loose clip she'd used to pull back her wavy, honey brown hair. Thanks to the flour, but unknown to her, Remy could see the streaks on her face where she'd wiped away tears. To save her embarrassment, he pretended not to notice.

Laidi leaned in to the half hug and weakly joked, "Arranging flours." Her smile dimmed as she looked back at the counter. "Comfort food. After yesterday, I need it." Her head tilted up to him. "Looks like you could use some, too." Her smile was faint. It was horrible enough to be this close to a murder. Worse though, was how this wasn't their first run-in with violent death--it was a reminder of the introduction. She turned to knead the dough again, but Remy pulled her back into the hug she needed. That they both needed.

Despite her size, Remy could feel the strength in her embrace. He shifted his weight and rested his cheek on her hair, while the scent of her filled his reality and tempted him to hold on a little longer. "You're a genius, you." He willed himself to let go. As he readied the French press, he said, "I'll make coffee." Reaching for the grounds, he noticed the large plate of fresh beignets. "*Chere*...?" He raised his eyebrow.

"Yeah, I've been here a while. Thought I'd might as well make the most of an early start."

Great minds, Remy thought. Great minds.

Laidi pulled him back into a hug. They held fast, oblivious to the set of inhuman eyes glaring at them from the shadows beyond the galley windows.

CHAPTER 11 - SHOUT OUT TO MARY P

Having finished the breakfast clean up, McAnrai filled the coffee tray with cream, sugar, and a carafe of Italian roast. He climbed the stairs to the living room.

Anya walked over from the dining room window, where she'd been watching the last of her thunderstorm. "How many murders are we talking about here?"

McAnrai sighed as he set down the tray. "That's what's hard to say. Columbus has classified fifteen deaths as murder this year."

"At the risk of sounding young and foolish--fifteen's a lot?"

"Not for somewhere like Chicago or New York, but here? Yeah, that's huge--especially since it's only August." He put his folders back on the coffee table and sat down while Anya poured them both more coffee.

Nestled in the deep cushions of the couch, Leanne asked him, "And you've been called to more than fifteen?"

He nodded. "In the past eight months, I've been called out to at least six deaths that were later deemed accidental or natural and so were not counted in the fifteen official murders."

Leanne mulled over his verb choice. "*Deemed*? If those were classified as murders, they'd up the murder rate here by what? Forty percent?"

McAnrai ran a hand through his hair. "Yeah."

Sitting on the floor, Anya's eyes ran over the coffee table, and the open file spread across it. "And you think some of them are murders."

"They're sure as hell unusual. Like no-official-cause-of-death unusual." He paused, trying to explain what was in his head--without sounding crazy. "They feel like murders but can't be. No evidence of anything criminal. But *something* makes me think they're connected.

"The problem is I can't *explain* why I think that, and," he let out a frustrated sigh, "if that weren't batshit enough, I'll be damned if Brad Casey isn't connected to these 'random' deaths as well," he mimed quote marks with his fingers. "And I don't have a goddamn thing to show the Cap. Nothing reasonable, anyway."

Leanne asked McAnrai, "You said there was something bothering you about some of the official murders? Something extra?"

"Yeah, and it's driving me crazy."

Leanne could recognize, practically smell, McAnrai's Talent. His instincts were deadly, and his mind automatically processed information missed by most. "Brad," Leanne said. "There's something about Brad that's worse."

McAnrai nodded. "Despite the deviations, and even though I have no evidence, I'm sure it's the same guy who did them all. It's just--" he broke off, frustrated.

Leanne nodded. "There was something about Brad's body that caught my eye--about his energy as I released it," she said slowly, still gathering her thoughts. "Something about it disturbed the hell out of me, and not because there was a body on the porch."

McAnrai leafed through the papers and photos he brought from the office. "I've tried comparing the pictures from each of the scenes, but...nothing in that." He dropped the pictures in exasperation and slumped into the cushions.

Anya shook her head. "No matter how good digital cameras are, it's tricky to photograph energy." The sisters exchanged a look.

"Fingerprints," McAnrai bolted upright as the word burst from him. "Or more like, finger-scents. Energy-scents."

"What?" Both women looked at him.

His brow furrowed as he tried to be more specific. "Something about the deaths felt the same, almost like how I know when you've just left a room." He glanced at Leanne. "I can smell you. The crimes had the same smell."

"I smell like crime. Fantastic."

Grinning, McAnrai squeezed her thigh. "No, babe. Well, not that kinda crime, anyway." He frowned at the tabletop. "I don't know how to explain it--it's a smell, but not. Like a smell you can touch, or almost see. Fuck, I don't know." He leaned back against the bookshelves' walkway, elbow on the back cushion, scratching the back of his head.

"The same smell, but a deviation in MO." Anya twirled the spoon in her cup of tea without touching it.

"And it feels like it's important, like I'm missing something huge. That's what makes it so frustrating. " McAnrai stood up and used a poker to jab at the empty fireplace, anxious to do something, anything. "I wish I could show you what I was talking about."

Leanne's brow wrinkled as she thought about what he said. A fingerprint you could smell. McAnrai's receptive Talents. She caught

Anya's eye, who lifted a brow ever so slightly. Leanne bit her lip and looked at McAnrai. Bringing her glance back to Anya, she nodded.

Anya caught McAnrai's eye. With a tentative smile, patted the sofa, inviting him to sit down again. "So, there's this thing that I can do."

"Ok…"

"Like Leanne, of course, I would never, ever--"

"Abuse your powers. Yeah. Of course not." He shot a bemused look at Leanne.

She nodded, "Anya can go into your memories with you, and you can show her what it was you saw at those unprovable murder scenes. She can see anything you choose to show her. She's hemming and hawing because she knows that if she chooses, she can see *whatever* she pleases, whether you offer it or not."

McAnrai's expression went blank as he processed the information.

"I would respect your privacy, of course," Anya hastened to add. "You would just consciously recall the scene, and that's what I'd see. I wouldn't go looking for anything. I'd stay still and you'd bring me what you've got."

"So," he gestured to Anya, then Leanne, "she reads information--thoughts--the way you read emotion."

Leanne nodded. "Yes. She controls it though--better than I do with emotions. We have to, otherwise shit gets really uncomfortable, really fast. If emotions are clothes, I still can't help but see everyone's," she paused to mime apostrophes, "'underwear'. However, it now takes a touch of effort to see them naked, or further." She paused, and looked at her sister, who was still looking nervous.

In an even, but cautious voice, Anya said, "It's up to you, of course."

"Do you think you could take me with you?" Leanne asked. "That might make it less nerve-wracking for both of you." She smirked as

McAnrai gave her a comical hairy eyeball. "Please," she added, "I can read you like a book anyway, and you know it."

McAnrai barked a short laugh.

Anya's head bobbed back and forth as she considered the suggestion. "I don't think it would be hard at all. We'd need to go upstairs though. Doing it like this will be like astral projection--we'll need to protect ourselves." She glanced at the man who had switched so quickly from a friend-of-a-friend, professional acquaintance to her sister's lover. "This is just one option. Instead, I could teach Leanne to do it herself, and in a few days--"

"Oh fuck it," McAnrai smiled. "I've always wondered what the Vulcan mind meld was like. Let's go check it out."

"Right now?" Anya asked.

"Why not? I trust you, and people are dying. Good enough for me. Besides, I want to see if I'm crazy for connecting these deaths or if Thuggy McBastard has something secret up his sleeve."

Leanne and Anya both looked at him. At once, they both asked, "Thuggy...McBastard?"

McAnrai was steady. "I don't know his name yet, and I'm sure as *fuck* not calling him anything cool."

***

There were four levels to the Gentry's Victorian. While the ground floor had the restaurant, bar/both kitchens, and the cellar served a few purposes (a couple more secret than others), the second floor acted as the rest of their private residence, while the top...

As he emerged from the spiral staircase, McAnrai took in his surroundings, and considering what he knew of the sisters, it was what he expected.

The open concept layout of the fourth floor was airy, and empty of furnishings beyond the folded gymnastic mats and meditation pillows. The walls were lined with their mundane, magickal, and medicinal supplies--candles, oils, incenses, and censers on the east wall, an extensive first aid/magickal apothecary station on the west. The northern wall had cabinets filled with their collection of rocks, crystals, stones and dried herbs, and its drawers contained a good amount of probably-useful-someday knickknacks. The southern wall showcased an enviable assortment of weaponry, ranging from traditional martial arts to modern firearms.

So it was almost what he expected. The weapon wall was a surprise. Though, considering the sawed-off shotgun that introduced him to Leanne... He looked to her, his eyes inquisitive.

Leanne followed his gaze and laughed, "What can I say? Being raised by an Irish wild-woman and an American Airborne Ranger makes for an interesting field of interests."

McAnrai nodded his head. "Fair enough."

There were no windows of the ordinary variety on this level. The hardwood walls provided an unbroken shield against any would-be prying eyes tempted to peep from the nearby buildings. The windows lining the perimeter of the ceiling provided natural light.

Like the rest of the house, the workroom had polished cabreuva floors--except for the circular area used for meditation purposes. Gesturing to it, Anya said, "When the renovations were underway, we allotted this area of the workroom to be maintained as a permanently safe, sacred space."

Leanne added, "We call it the Circle."

McAnrai nodded, thankful he understood enough of magick life to appreciate the significance behind the workmanship. Ten feet in diameter, floored with rowan wood, and outlined with a one inch band of elder, the Circle was sealed from the energies around it. This spherical area of protected space was created for raising energy, which could be used for anything from ritual work and spell casting, to out of body journeying, to mediation work...and now crime fighting.

The three of them sat down, knee-to knee in a tight circle. Anya grasped their hands in her own. "Mac will set up the conceit of what this will look like--just sit back, close your eyes, and think of whatever you want us to see. I'll pop in and draw Leanne with me."

"Like how they jumped into Bert's sidewalk drawings in *Mary Poppins?*" McAnrai raised his brows.

Anya raised her eyebrows as she considered. "Kinda. Our bodies will stay here, but our consciousnesses will pip over for a visit."

Leanne laughed, "Mary Poppins had to have been a witch--one with a ton of Talent."

Bringing them back to the point, Anya said, "Now think about yesterday."

In his mind's eye, McAnrai watched as the sisters meshed easily, water into water, and then flowed into him.

McAnrai took a deep breath.

Here we go.

CHAPTER 12 – THE PALACE PRESENTS

Each of their physical sights disappeared as their psychic sights opened to the inside of McAnrai's mind. McAnrai, Leanne, and Anya stood in a room that gave every vibe of being a luxurious library, except instead of books, there were doors--thousands of them. Doors to rooms, houses, cars, airplanes...ornate entries to businesses, rotted wood and peeling boards leading to crack dens...sliding glass panes of grocery stores, revolving entries to airports...battleship gray metal doors so common to military buildings. They varied in size, in proportions from mouse-sized to eighteen-wheeler loading bays.

Looking around, Anya nodded with approval. "Mac--I congratulate you on a well ordered brain."

Before he could respond, two of them jumped at a new, cheerful voice. "Well hello there!"

Just to the side, wearing a badge with the blunt label "LIBRARI-AN", stood a young man. Willowy in build, his light brown hair was thick and well groomed. His sideburns were long enough to mesh with his short, neat beard, and his eyes were hidden behind tinted, Old Hollywood-style soap star sunglasses.

Leanne slung her head around to McAnrai, her eyes wrinkled with mirth. She asked "Wow, you really enjoy those honey badger videos."

He met her gaze. "Apparently." Man, this had been a fucking weird thirty-six hours.

And counting.

In the unmistakably fabulous intonations of an equally fabulous narrator, the young man made a brisk approach and said, "How do you do? I'm the Librarian--but you can call me Libs--and I'll be showing you around today. I know you all, of course." He shot an extra glance and playful wink at Leanne.

Least startled of the three, Anya said, "Thank you, Libs. We'd like to see Mac's memory of Brad Casey's crime scene."

Nothing happened. Confused, Anya asked, "Mac?"

Still silence. Anya turned, and saw McAnrai and Leanne--inches apart, their hands wrapped around each other's forearms, and staring intently at one another. Anya blinked as McAnrai and Leanne went in and out of focus, visually sharpening back to themselves...

...but in different clothes...older clothes... At first Anya recognized each era's attire, but then the changings moved in and out of focus so rapidly, the shapes and styles of their clothes became mere flickers of movement around the edges of the blurred colors of the garments themselves.

Lifetimes they'd spent together. Dozens, no *hundreds* of lifetimes flashed before Anya's psychic vision as she saw for herself--why and how Leanne and McAnrai had known, so effortlessly clicked.

"Hey, break it up, you guys." The Librarian clapped his hands, breaking through the mesmerizing visual. "There's all kinds of nasty shit to deal with over here."

Anya shook her head a few times and looked from McAnrai and Leanne, still gaze-locked, then back. "Um, Libs?"

He let out an exasperated sigh and explained, "You're behind his defenses, Miss Thing. And you brought *her*. You can't be *that* surprised."

He reached above his head, just as an old fashioned bellpull handle dangled into his fist. "Now let's get these two back on track." Looking at Anya, he grinned and said, "Handy, isn't it? How he loves slapstick humor." The Librarian gave a great yank...

SPLOOSH.

...and several gallons of water splashed on the intimate moment.

Sputtering, soaked, and shocked into the present, McAnrai and Leanne turned surprised faces to Anya. Mac sputtered, "What the hell was that for?"

Before she could respond, the guardian of McAnrai's subconscious interjected, "Oh don't be such a crybaby. You'll thank me later. Move on."

Shaking his head, McAnrai said, "I guess it's pointless to argue with myself."

Leanne blinked several times, pushed her soaked hair from her face. "I feel like I've missed something."

Anya frowned. She glanced at the Librarian, who waved his hands in a "let's get a move on" way.

Anya let out a breath that could have been a short laugh. "All right, Mac. Call the memories down. Create doors for us here to step through."

McAnrai considered for a moment. "Seems easy enough." He glanced at Leanne, who smiled her encouragement. An applewood door appeared in front of them. Anya reached for the handle, but the Librarian intervened.

"Oh, honey. I would *not* open that door if I were you. You do *not* wanna see what's going down behind it. All *sorts* of shit to make even the best of us fucking *blanche*." Slipping his arm around her shoulders, he tried to redirect her, "Now, if I *may* make a suggestion, there's *this* bland, ugly door sealing off a drab, colorless corridor. It's ugly as *shit*, but that stubborn boy won't let me do a fucking thing about it. It's right over here, and *believe me* when I tell you, there's lots to see."

Anya sighed impatiently. She understood the Librarian's role was to help keep a daily diet of senseless violence from incapacitating Mac. She appreciated it and had dealt with far less congenial 'Librarians'. But as he said, they had shit to do. When she moved from under his arm, he flipped his hands, palms forward as he shook his head, his expression oozing of 'Don't say I didn't warn you.'

She opened the applewood door, and stepped through before skittering back out and slamming it shut. She turned her back to it, sputtering. "For the love of God, McAnrai! I can't *bleach* my brain. That image is going to stay with me *forever*!" Anya stepped away from the door, blushing a bright red. "*Forever!*"

"HA. I *tried* to warn you. Ever since *she* came along," the Librarian jerked his thumb at Leanne, "his ideas have gotten nastier and *nastier*. Why, just this morning, he wanted to--"

"That's enough out of you." McAnrai had his authority face on, belied somewhat by his blush.

The young man stood up very straight, and with a sassy hand on his hip, smirked, "Well fine then."

Curious, Leanne stepped forward and peeked in. "Oh, sweet man. Is this what you have on your mind right now?"

McAnrai leaned back, and with an expression both curious and cautious. Uselessly, he deflected. "Maybe." Different, additional knobs started appearing on the door, each decorated differently. One covered in lace, another with satin, one with black leather...

"HOLY CHRIST. Could we please get this show back on the PG road?" Anya was rubbing her temples in a vain attempt to clear her thoughts. *Especially* of what lay behind Door XXX.

Leanne couldn't help herself. "Well, technically, since we're investigating murders, we do need to brave the waters of R ratings."

Anya didn't find it as funny as her sister did. *R*-rated her classy, Irish *ass.* Rolling her eyes, and shuddering from her shoulders to her fingertips, she turned away.

With a sweep of her open hands, she gestured to the space in front of her. "Okay, Mac. How about a door right here. And concentrate on *Brad*, if it's at all possible. And *you* go first this time."

McAnrai was still having some trouble re-focusing. Maybe bringing Leanne along wasn't the best idea--it didn't help that she seemed more intrigued than shocked by what she saw behind the applewood door. Even worse, she tried to make it easier for him to move on by mouthing the reassurance, "Tonight."

In his physical form, McAnrai shook his head like a dog expelling water from its ears. In the mind palace, Leanne and Anya jumped as chains, locks, deadbolts, Bugs Bunny planks of cartoon-style wood and a nail gun attacked the door, sealing it shut. Leanne stifled a laugh while Anya shook her head.

Finally able to focus, McAnrai closed his eyes. The library emptied of all doors but one. It looked like the inside of McAnrai's work vehicle. They watched as the Librarian opened it from the other side.

With a theatrical flourish, he swept his arm to invite them through. "Here you go!"

They stepped onto the sidewalk in front of the Gentry's Table, and into what should have been McAnrai's memory of the crime scene. Instead of a lawn crowded with emergency personnel, both lawn and porch were empty.

"So here we are, in beautiful Columbus, Georgia. Home of the inventors of Coca-Cola." Libs added, *sotto voce*, "You're not gonna convince *me* it's from Atlanta. Bitch, *please*." Returning to his official, tour guide voice, he continued, "Ahhh...the hot Georgia sun...the humidity is nine thousand percent, but you don't give a shit. You're just here for the sunburn and heat exhaustion. Fuck air conditioning. You just wanna find a place to kick back and enjoy some ultraviolet radiation. So here you are. Come see the gardens, aren't they *gorgeous*? Beautiful shade and the *drinks--*"

McAnrai frowned in concentration as the would-be tour guide tried to usher them around the house to the *al fresco* bar. He must be more nervous than he thought, since his subconscious was literally trying to deflect their attention from the memory.

Again, weird thirty-six hours.

Again, and counting.

McAnrai eyed Libs, who mimed washing his hands. "Fine. Don't mind me. And don't say I didn't warn you." He waved his arm, and the landscape transformed to the crime scene. "You guys do whatever the hell you want. I'll be waiting the *fuck* over there." Libs gestured behind them. "Away from this nasty-ass business." When they glanced over their shoulders, they heard his muttering as his voice faded away, "That poor kid, how could anyone do that to a *kid*? Fucking bastard. I mean, what the fuck?!?"

They looked back, but he had disappeared, voice and all.

Then, as though none of that had happened, McAnrai took Anya's hand and concentrated. The car door disappeared, replaced by the "ugly as shit" door the Librarian originally recommended. In stark contrast to the polished woods and intricate metallic filigree of all the doors they'd seen thus far, it was painted battleship gray. Aged, dingy, the paint chipped and peeling in places. At eye level, a black plastic placard with white letters was mounted.

It read: DEATHS.

McAnrai took a deep breath, stepped forward and opened it. They followed him into the long corridor lined with dozens of doors, each marked with alpha-numeric labels, spray painted in stencil font. Upon seeing them, all the same battleship gray as the initial set of double doors, McAnrai felt the sisters recoil. So much death. From the corner of his eye, he saw Leanne give Anya an admonishing look.

Not that it mattered. McAnrai knew the contents of his memories well enough to anticipate their reactions. He had understood what he'd agreed to, even if they hadn't known the enormity of what they had asked. He gave a matter-of-fact nod.

Humbled, they nodded in return. The three of them stood together, facing the doors.

CHAPTER 13 - THE MIND-ALONG

McAnrai opened the door directly in front of them. Sunlight poured through. They stepped out onto the front lawn of their house. Brad's body sat propped against the pillar. Cops walked around.

Anya asked "Mac, can you get rid of everyone but Brad?"

McAnrai furrowed his brow and the memory was suddenly deserted, the landscape still. It was like standing in a photograph.

"All right. Let's see what we have here."

A creeping energy lingered over Brad's body. While McAnrai had shown up after Leanne had freed the boy's spirit, the defeated psychic ick still remained. Its hostility glowed like dying embers as it coated, oozed over the body.

"That's not how I remember it," McAnrai said, concerned that his recall was impaired.

"No, Mac. It's not what you saw, but that's what you *Saw*. You're more attuned to the esoteric than the average bear, so while you couldn't see it with your eyes, you could see it with your Eye." Anya touched the center of his forehead, his Third Eye, to help make the point.

Looking closer, they could see the substance marking Brad's throat, replacing the hand-shaped bruises, but it was thickest on his track marks and the bottoms of his feet. The sulky glimmer was dirty, like polluted water. Anya started when Leanne touched her arm, gestured up. The air above Brad's body had a sparkling quality, like golden glitter, flowing and swirling overhead. The higher they looked, the shimmering mingled with, then changed into, a wispy, spiraling cloud of silvery mist.

McAnrai's voice held a note of wonder. He asked, "That from you guys?"

Leanne nodded, her eyes a blend of wonder and relief, "I suppose so. I guess we managed to help Brad after all."

Anya said, "I've seen enough. Let's take a look at the others."

"Hold on." McAnrai gestured to a coal-black line drawn around the body. It was fine, so fine as to be easily missed. Without touching it, he traced it for Leanne and Anya to see. The sisters exchanged a glance--he was tracing the outline of where the hound from Faery had also focused. "What the hell?"

Leanne crouched low, head tilted to the side. Upon closer inspection, the coal-black line had a liquid glimmer to it, not unlike the polluted muck on the body. "I think this is a reverse blindfold." She looked up to McAnrai, whose expression had relaxed as comprehension dawned. "We all wondered how he could've gone so long without being seen."

"Then how *did* you see him ?" McAnrai asked Leanne. "Did the spell wear off?"

"I don't think it had anything to do with time." She frowned. "I think it had to do with me."

"You did something?"

"No." This time, it was Anya who answered. "Leanne must've been the key that unlocked the invisibility illusion." She added, "The killer meant for Leanne to be the one to find him."

At that, the ground began to rumble and everything slid in and out of focus--they looked at McAnrai, whose eyes were squeezed shut, fierce concentration in every corner of his face. After a few seconds, the ground stilled, obeying his command for calm. Opening his eyes, he said, "It's okay." His black eyes met their inquisitive browns and greens. In a voice that brooked no questioning, he said, "It's nothing. Moving on."

The sisters waited while McAnrai gathered himself, frowning as power flowed from him. As he shifted the reality around them, their eyebrows rose in tandem. Manipulating memories was difficult. Harder still when moving them in and out of chronological order. Yet he was able to do so. Leanne's mouth twisted in an impressed half smile.

A new door appeared, and McAnrai opened it. They stepped through, and onto a green field. Before them lay the fifteen bodies officially labeled as murder. Two of the bodies, one knife wound and one gunshot, were lined with the fine, black line of the murderer's invisibility spell, though lacking the magickal residue found on Brad. McAnrai nodded at the two outlined bodies. "I knew those two were related."

Suddenly, seven more doors appeared behind the official murders, each with an alpha-numeric label matching those in McAnrai's original Death Corridor. McAnrai, Leanne, and Anya exchanged glances. *What the...?*

Leanne looked at them both and asked, "I guess it's my turn?" She braced herself before opening the first door. Then the second and third. She shut the doors and turned to McAnrai. "They're deaths, but they don't look like murders."

Anya nodded. "These are the ones with the 'little something extra' you couldn't put your finger on." She walked to the closest door and turned the knob.

They found themselves in the middle of a rooftop garden. The sun was blazing overhead, beating waves of heat onto the body sprawled before them. The victim was young, maybe seventeen or eighteen, lying in the flower bed. She was wearing a loose, cotton sundress and her long, blonde tresses were dotted with fresh flowers, some tied with ribbon, others the fallen blossoms from the surrounding plants.

McAnrai cleared his throat. "Late June. No cause of death." His voice softened, "She was a little over six weeks pregnant."

Leanne took a closer look at the girl's abdomen. The faintest glimmer of energy remained in McAnrai's memory, fading as the baby's life departed.

McAnrai rubbed his face vigorously--Sweet Jesus. As necessary as this was, he wasn't ready for the rawness of it. He squatted down, attention riveted. "Look familiar?" He pointed to her neck, almost obscured by the girl's hair and bruised flower petals. On the smooth tan skin, there was a thick sludge of muddy glimmer.

"The print." Leanne had crouched next to him, trying to see from his angle. They both looked up at Anya.

Anya's mouth was set in a grim line. "But no black outline."

Leanne caught an epiphany breath and said, "Because it didn't matter when these bodies were found, or by whom."

"Right. Outline means hiding and splotches of gray slime mean magick as (or helping the) murder weapon." The tightness in McAnrai's voice drew their attention. "Next." They felt themselves moving backwards, almost sucked out of the scene, through the door, and watched it shut in their faces as the next one slid into place.

This body was a man in his thirties. He was sitting on his sun porch, a glass of iced tea spilled across the table in front of him.

"This one should've been easier. Wedge of lemon--rind and all--lodged in his throat means he choked, right?" He shook his head, "Nope. Oxygen levels were fine." He looked at the body from this new, metaphysical vantage point. "I can make a guess now." Sure enough, the man's throat had a thick slather of the same luminescent muck found on Brad and the summer girl. McAnrai looked up. "Aren't lemons used for purification?"

They nodded. Leanne spoke. "And healing. But if that's why this guy was trying to ingest it, that means he has knowledge. He's a practitioner." When she examined him more closely, her hand flew to her mouth. Turning to McAnrai, she asked, "When did he die?"

"Evening of May first. Why?" He turned and startled at the alarm on Leanne's face. "Why?"

But she had already walked to the next door. "We need to see the others."

The next three doors opened to the next three bodies. All dead without apparent cause, all covered in various places with the same toxic mire. They witnessed the retroactive rotation of the seasons as they progressed, Easter, late winter, just before Christmas...

Halloween.

At the last door, McAnrai's stomach knotted with dread. He took a deep breath as he read the dated label. He turned back and held up his hand as a warning. "This one is a child. Let me take out the others before you enter." He did, but not before Leanne and Anya heard the despairing wail of a mother. The silence that followed was as eerie as it was heartbreaking.

The boy's body lay on the apron of a pool. Leanne looked up to the balcony. He had fallen a solid two stories. She knelt next to him. "I remember this," Leanne said. "He's the mayor's nephew, isn't it?" McAnrai nodded. The strange energy they'd seen on Brad was there. Unlike the others, whose throats were tainted, the child's was clean. Instead, there was staining on the back of his shirt, almost like large handprints. They looked closer.

Gods. Not *like*. They *were* handprints. "Someone pushed him."

Anya struggled to calm her emotions. She needed to learn everything she could about this case, this boy. In the meditation room, her nails dug into the palms of her hands as she fought to hold in her revulsion, her outrage. "Someone he knew."

The sickening realization sank in. Leanne felt woozy, but she pushed it back. Had to. She saw Anya do the same. A wave of concern washed over Leanne as she felt her attention turn to McAnrai, as if drawn by an emotional form of gravity.

They needed to wrap this up, and soon.

The sisters exchanged a look. McAnrai was right. These deaths were connected, all committed by the same monster. They were now familiar with the killer's energy. It was ingrained in them, scored into their magickal awareness.

Leanne stood, hands as fists at her sides. Uncertain, she asked Anya. "Does something feel wrong to you? Something wrong with the bodies?"

McAnrai, on edge, interjected, "You mean besides the obvious?"

Leanne didn't answer but Anya said, "Yes. Something big."

They turned to McAnrai, the last confirmation. Leanne started to speak, but stopped.

The vision around them started to move in and out of focus. McAnrai started to shake as his control over the palace began to crumble.

In and out of focus...

And then to black.

CHAPTER 14 – THERE'S TOO MUCH TO SEE HERE; PLEASE DISPERSE

"**M**ac!"

"McAnrai!"

Anya and Leanne's voice sounded in the darkness. McAnrai heard his own voice rumble from inside, growing louder...and louder...

McAnrai shouted, the words inarticulate, but the command clear.

The darkness blinked out. The death corridor reappeared.

Leanne and Anya looked at each other, at the corridor, and then at McAnrai. His eyes squeezed shut, hands clenching and unclenching at his sides. He took controlled breaths. He was almost calm.

And then.

The ground rumbled, the walls shook.

And all of the doors opened at once. Through them came the sounds of machine gunfire, artillery explosions, the quick rapid fire reports of a pistol cracked the air. Following them, the screams of men, women and children, drowned in the roar of fire.

The stench of blood, of urine and feces leaked from the rooms, poured from McAnrai's carefully guarded memories. His trembling worsened as he sank to the ground. Drawing his legs up, McAnrai dropped his head between his knees to control his breathing. Tried to suck air through lungs that burned with smoke and fear and helplessness. "Oh God...gods..." he said, over and over again.

Leanne knelt in front of him, wrapped her arms around him. "Shut the doors, *a mhuirnín*. Just shut the doors."

"I can't." His voice was hoarse. "There's too many."

"You can. I'll show you." She lifted his head with a finger then moved to sit between his legs and face those open, reeking doors with him. "Wrap your arms around me. Just like that. Now watch." She reached back and cupped his neck, bringing his forehead, his third eye, into full contact with the back of her head. "Watch me do it. See what I do."

Anya watched in amazement as Leanne shut a door. She shouldn't be able to do that. These were Mac's doors, not her sister's. But one door at a time, they began shutting. Leanne stroked the arms around her waist, her touch gentle and reassuring.

The largest, heaviest door slammed, startling Anya. That must have been Mac. That door had a domino effect--soon, the extensive passageway was filled with the sound of metal doors slamming shut, bolts being drawn. The sisters could see flashes of the Librarian--checking each door as it shut, reinforcing each lock.

Leanne looked up, gave her sister a reassuring nod. She had this. While she had needed help to enter a mind other than Anya's, Leanne was capable of bringing herself and McAnrai back, and for that both sisters were grateful. It was intimate enough to enter someone's mind, and for that Anya had been invited knowingly. Neither of them expected the maelstrom of emotion that would be released--though they should have. For a man as good as McAnrai to be successful in a job littered with violence and spattered with blood, his best means of survival was to lock away the witnessed evils--sealed and guarded by irreverent humor. Helping him now belonged to the woman whom he had already welcomed to his contents and corners. Anya discreetly withdrew, from both McAnrai's mind palace and the workroom.

***

In McAnrai's mind, Leanne turned between her man's legs and knelt in front of him. His shivering had lessened and his breathing was even, though still wrought with emotion. He rested his head just above her breasts as she held him, stroked his hair.

The experience of having two people tromping around in his head, plus examining a series of murdered human beings, *plus* a flooding of older, fouler experiences, and all without the protection of his usual mental safety measures, left McAnrai stripped raw. Leanne knew any reassurance she could offer would push him into a true catharsis, and she neither could, nor should, choose that for him. She looked at his large, strong frame curled around his own heartbreak...

What he needed was an exit--and a distraction would do nicely.

Leanne heard a sharp whistle and looked up to see the Librarian. He threw--something. She reached up and easily made the catch. Leanne looked at the tool, then to the Librarian, and mouthed "Thanks" to the Librarian, to which he yelled, *"Don't just sit there, use the damn things"*.

"McAnrai." At the sound of her voice, and a strange, metallic jingling, he looked up. She was holding a crowbar with a key attached to the end.

"There are miles to go before we can use this tonight." Wink.

McAnrai blinked. The applewood door returned, and its virile clamoring replaced the death havoc.

In the third floor of the Victorian home, McAnrai and Leanne opened their eyes.

"Sweet Mother Mary and seventeen priests." McAnrai slumped into Leanne's lap, his breathing ragged. His arms wrapped around her waist, while she smoothed his hair with soft strokes. He wasn't tired, but he did feel punch-drunk dizzy. It was several minutes before the room stopped spinning and his vision cleared. When it did, he pulled himself to sitting. "You don't have to look so worried." He kissed her cheek and wiped her eyes.

Leanne wiped the tears from his eyes. "I'm so sorry. I had no idea it would be so--"

"Leanne, it's not like *I* didn't know what was there. And we got the information we needed--and now I know I'm not crazy for thinking they're connected." He stood up, reached for her hands and pulled her to standing.

"How are you now?"

"Now that we're back in the real world? I feel...amazing, actually. Lighter." He threw his arm around her shoulders as they walked back to the steps. "Let's move. Like you said, there's miles to go before we postpone sleep."

CHAPTER 15 – 'CAUSE WE ARE LIVING IN A MORRIGAN WORLD

Leanne and McAnrai descended the stairs to the sounds of a lively debate. Anya and Harley were in the living room, energetic discussion in full swing. When the other two walked in, they became silent. Anya looked up from the notes she was taking when she heard them come around the corner. Too tactful to ask out loud, her gaze was inquisitive.

"I'm fine. Better than fine." McAnrai had a spring in his step and a buoyancy about him that gave credence to his words. Leanne eyed the two Italian hoagies waiting for them on the table in front of her.

"Mr. Morgan's final interview. They're amazing." Anya pushed a plate on McAnrai and took another bite of her own meal. It was delicious, pure Northeast Philly, and she felt her own solidity reestablishing itself. After any astral or meditative work, especially an experience as intense as this morning's, grounding was necessary. This made food, and meat and salt in particular, more medicinal than optional. She looked at McAnrai. No doubt he felt lighter--even without a full cathartic experience, an indecent amount of noxious energy had been released.

Anya said, "Ok, so when I tried to look at the autopsy photos, there's a strange blurriness. In Mac's memory, the victims were covered with that bastard's energetic grime. Something important there."

Harley stepped away from his empty plate and looked over Anya's shoulder, "I'd say that's a good bit of glamour work." His large, green eyes darted to Anya, "You're going to have to examine that young man in person."

Anya closed and opened her eyes. As much as she loved Shelby, she hated visiting her best friend's workplace. She tilted her head in tentative resignation.

While her sister puzzled over the feet, Leanne read and reread the blood report. She couldn't stop herself from focusing on all of the grime Shelby found both in and on Brad. "Okay. Now while the drug isn't exactly a shocker, Shelby does note her surprise that Thuggy managed to kill Brad at all." She looked at the others. "Says here there's enough heroin in his system to kill him twice over." Her eyes softened as she reread the section. Gods, how did McAnrai do this all the time? Reconsidering, she supposed the experience upstairs answered that.

McAnrai reached over to Leanne, using his open hand to ask for the sheet she was already handing him. "And here--not *just* blood." He read from the paper in his hand, "This is some creepy-ass finger paint."

Anya's expression froze. A very nasty idea occurred to her. From the expression on Leanne's face, Anya could see they were thinking the same thing. "Harley's right. We need to see the second set of bodies in person. The not-murder-murders, as well as Brad. Especially Brad."

McAnrai flinched."Why especially? Didn't the field trip through my head cover enough?"

Anya fiddled with the papers in front of her. Without looking up, she answered, "Yes--and no. The muck on his feet was from the Faery Realm." She stopped, leaned back into the deep cushion as she let go of the sheets. Almost to herself, she continued her out-loud reasoning. "The "prints" on the bodies--that was all magickal residue. Which means, wherever Thuggy employed magick, he left those traces. But while he used magick at each site, not all of it was used to kill. At least half of the time, he was using it to hide things."

Harley added, "The recognizable murders."

"Right. He killed them the old fashioned way. But needed to--wait--", Anya paused, "why bother to hide them at all, if he meant for them to be found?"

McAnrai muttered as he concentrated on the photos. "Alibis."

As if she hadn't heard the exchange, Leanne continued, "The Faery plants also show up in his bloodstream analysis." She looked at Anya's notes, "It's a weird cocktail to inject," she compared the two lists. "Lots of heroin, of course, chicory and, good gods, hyoscyamine--" she broke off and looked at Anya, "derived from *mandragora officinalis*."

Anya stared at her sister for a moment. McAnrai waited with a look of expectation.

"In English?"

"Mandragora, mandrakes. A narcotic root, native to Europe," Anya answered.

"The screaming plants from *Harry Potter*?" Usually, the first thing a person learns when getting introduced to magick, was that it's a lot *less* like Hogwarts, and a lot *more* like Home Ec. A good eighty percent of it is just cooking, cleaning, dressing, decorating--stuff everyone does. That other twenty percent though...McAnrai had seen some pretty outrageous things in his life--to say nothing of the freakfest he just experienced in his own damn head--but this was...new.

"Well, Rowling took some poetic license with them, but yeah," Anya continued. "While the roots don't actually scream, they were pressed for juice, which was mixed with wine and boiled down--"

"Sounds delicious. What the hell--"

Leanne broke in, "These days, if you can even find one, you would use it to make a poppet." In response to his look, "It's the precursor to the idea of voodoo dolls--the roots themselves can look a tiny bit like a human body. Thousands of years ago, that wine concoction was one of the first narcotics considered reliable enough to use for anesthetic purposes. Dosing was tricky, though. Good for surgery, and maybe you'd wake up when it was done. Or not."

"What would this guy want with mandrakes, then? I doubt the killer was trying to lessen his suffering." McAnrai could've bitten off his own tongue for the look his last comment drew from Leanne.

Leanne went quiet, so Anya answered. "I don't know. It says there wasn't any in his stomach. Shelby proposes the mandrake traces were mixed with the heroin." She looked again at the Molotov cocktail manifest.

"And why drop the body on our doorstep?" Leanne muttered. "What did it accomplish?"

McAnrai's expression darkened as he deliberated over his words. "He was sending a message. Making it personal."

Anya's expression hardened when she met McAnrai's gaze, "He meant to make us afraid."

"Make. Us. Afraid?" Leanne's voice was so quiet, they felt, rather than heard, her question. Like so many quick tempered people, the bangs and booms of her tantrums were like Georgia's afternoon thunderstorms--loud, alarming to the uninitiated, but brief. They acted like pressure valves, releasing anger and aggression before it had a chance to build up. So was the usual flavor of Leanne's temperament. This quiet, calm, ice-cold fury was new.

To McAnrai, anyway. Anya had seen it once--and someone almost died from it being unleashed.

Harley's tail started to swish, a habit of his when he worked on puzzles. Recognizing his sign of progress, Leanne asked, "Harley, what do you think?"

He turned to Leanne, "First, I would suggest calling upon Remy and Laidi." In response to their questioning expressions, he added, "You said it yourself. VoodooHoodoo. Not all of it, but enough to imply a familiarity with the subject. Show our New Orleanian ex-patriots the list of Mortal world substances found on him, and the picture of his back."

Harley stood and stretched. "Leanne, you need to understand the significance of these deaths being linked, and--most importantly--*how* you know it." He looked at each in turn. "The same energy--the same magickal fingerprint." He tipped his head to McAnrai, then looked hard at Leanne and walked to her. "You think there is something special about it. Something unusual. There isn't. It's just a magical... fingerprint. What you aren't allowing for is that you, darling girl, *recognize* it." They were almost nose to nose.

Leanne blinked, then stared at him. She could feel the truth in his words, but still. Her life so far had been eventful, but happy. Wouldn't she remember something so vile?

"Still no?" He sighed as he sat on his haunches. "Yesterday, I told you why, in the years you've known me, my excursions into Faery have always been in your company. That, in addition to my life debt, I'd also been assigned as your protector. My Lady had taken a deep interest in your care, education, and protection"

Anya's face snapped in Leanne's direction. What? Leanne had a secret benefactor?

The Cait-Sith leapt from the table to the sill. Pacing, he continued, "What I *didn't* tell you was why I defied my orders and my obligation to you. What warranted my returning to Faery on my own." Harley's pacing increased in speed as his speech continued. Anya and McAnrai had to look away. Leanne was accustomed to it. "I recognized the energy, too." He looked up at her, "The person who's been committing these murders is the creator of the trap from which you freed me. His stench was strong enough, I could smell it from the second floor."

***

They sat for a full minute, processing that information.

Breaking the silence, Anya asked, "Um, first, I'd like to know more about this special patroness of Leanne's." McAnrai nodded in agreement, eyes wide and eyebrows raised.

Leanne bit her lip. "Uh, I didn't get a chance to tell you. Um, well, you know I've always felt an affinity for the Celtic pantheon..." As she tilted her head, her shoulders gave a half shrug.

"Yeah, we both do..." Anya leaned forward. "And?"

"And you know how they always say that the Celtic gods and goddesses call their own?"

Anya's expression was clear. *Spit it out.*

"Well, turns out they weren't kidding." At the look on Anya's face, Leanne hurried to the point. "I didn't decide to work with the Celts, they, er, *She* decided She wanted me to work for Her. For the Morrigan."

"*The Morrigan!?*" Anya's mouth gaped. Her mouth never gaped.

Leanne took a small moment to laugh. "I, uh, yeah. The Morrigan."

McAnrai was quiet, his expression contemplative. Anya explained, "She's a goddess. THE goddess, if you will."

"Uh yeah. My parents are Irish, too." With a touch of humor, he added, "And just *wait* til you two meet my grandmother." He smiled. "Though I admit, her stories always seemed like fairy tales." Harley snorted. Without missing a beat, McAnrai said, "*Gesundheit.*"

The man looked at the sisters. "But this is important...how?"

Leanne's expression became stony as she started making connections. "So we're up against the same guy I pissed off all those years ago, who's since moved from capturing and torturing faeries to using magick for serial killing. But no," her brow creased against the illogic, "that doesn't explain the switch from attempts to kill faeries, to whatever this is."

McAnrai shrugged, "Unless he's worried about getting caught? Magick's a little hard to prove."

Something in what McAnrai said registered as a nasty gut-punch for Leanne. Her eyes widened as her lip twisted. She set both hands on the table, took a breath. Without a word, she left the room. They watched as she stalked to the dining room. Out of sight, they heard the tinkling of glass, liquid being poured...

"The key is Brad. What's the clue there?" Anya stood, started pacing. "Brad was the only body who had evidence of both kinds of magick, because, because--"

Sharp words shot from the dining room. "He wasn't supposed to look like a murder either." Leanne set the bottle of whiskey on the table with a touch more force than she intended. "His tox report, the hex-painting on his back. His death was the *finale*." When they didn't respond, she took the moment to pour a second shot. "Wanna bet he was supposed to die on August first? Then he'd be like the other seven. Killed on a sabbat."

"Sabbat?" McAnrai was the first to speak. "Shit, shit, shit." He shuffled through the papers. "How did I not see that?" Paper flip, paper flip, paper flip. "Yep, yeah, and fucking yes. Both solstices, both equinoxes, equini? Halloween, Imbolc, Beltane and," he slammed the file on the table. "And Brad would have been Lughnasadh."

Anya's voice was soft, but icy. "A murder on each of our major holidays."

"Shall we assume, then, that our dastardly villain had something important planned for the day Brad was here?" Harley's voice was even, but his eyes had started to glow.

"It's the only thing that makes sense." Leanne fought against a flood of self recrimination. "My protection spell kept him off the murderer's radar until the day was over, until it was too late for his death to be *useful*." She spat out the word, then took a third shot as her voice rose to match her emotion. "What I did for Brad didn't protect him at all. It protected *us*." She turned and threw the tumbler into the hearth, enjoying the sound of the shattering glass. "And instead of a quick, painless death, I got him killed in a violent rage by an asshole who then decided to use his body as a goddamn calling card."

CHAPTER 16 – DUTIES AND DEBTS

A golden Irish Wolfhound trotted down Main Street, to her waiting master. Invisible to mortal eyes, she slipped through the front doors of My Boulánge.

Though hailing from a breed known for affable scruffiness, the Cu-Sith carried herself with an elegance worthy of her office. Her fluid, silky coat glimmered, reflecting the honey tinted light of her Court and the soft electric "candlelight" from the chandeliers hanging in the French bakery. As she walked deeper into the seating area, a fine mist rose, swirling in a gentle cyclone of glittery gold. When it cleared, the wolfhound had transformed into a woman. Neither young nor old, her hair, still the silky gold of her coat, framed her face as a ruffled bob, and her figure was the fit, sturdy figure of a competitive athlete. Only her eyes remained unchanged, dark, with a feral glint.

She padded through the tables, and sat in front of a tall, cheerful man with blonde, pleasantly tousled hair. He sat in one of the tailored, oxblood leather chairs arranged along the exposed brick wall. His clothes were a symphony of rich browns, the hues of warm sand and freshly sown earth. He appeared as a well-to-do businessman, blending in seamlessly to his surroundings, but for the battle spear leaning against the wall, and the sword sheathed at his hip.

She spread her arms and turned, as if to check her transformation skills against inspection. Her King nodded in approval, then asked, "Hello Sally. What did you find out?"

As he listened to Sally's report, his naturally sunny countenance darkened with concern--and anger.

Then resolution.

The iridescence of his glamour started at his wrist and his spear reduced to the length of an elegant walking stick. His sword shrank in his hand, smaller and smaller, until it fit in his palm.

"Well, I've always been a fan of human proverbs." Tucking the "pen" in his interior jacket pocket, he added, "Consider yourself a regular at the Brugh. Human, or invisible --as you choose."

With a derisive snort, the Cu-Sith faded into invisibility.

With a wink to the thin air, he said, "On that note, I do believe some cagey heroics are in order."

***

Leanne toweled her hair and checked her reflection; her dress wasn't too revealing, though it did highlight her curves. She hung up towel and let her hair fall in damp cascades; it would dry on its own. It was August in Georgia, after all.

As she finished preparing for the evening, Harley walked into her bedroom. He leapt up onto the bed and stretched in the afternoon sunlight. Answering his look, Leanne said, "McAnrai went home to change clothes and get some rest."

Harley nodded. "So on to business, then. My darling girl. You know I'm right." He rolled over and looked at her with amused affection.

It always made her smile when he called her that. Something about his accent sounded so old Hollywood, his 'dahling guhl.'

She replied, "Harley, I'm not saying you're wrong. I'm saying that I don't have the time to do anything about it today."

"Ah, but *that's* not a problem."

She stopped, slowly turned, and met his steady gaze. "What did you do?" Her look was curious and more than a little nervous.

"Oh, how do the kids these days say it? Let's just say I know a guy." Leanne was definitely apprehensive now. She could only guess about the kinds of 'guys' Harley would know. And what he would consider 'appropriate measures' when it came to protecting her and Anya. Harley added with amusement, "He owes me a Favor."

She swore she saw that cat grin.

***

Leanne's steps to the Table's dining room quickened at the sound of raised voices escalating to the knocks and bumps of furniture performing an impromptu dance recital. When she reached the main dining room, Leanne stopped short at the tableau before her.

A ruckus, an actual *ruckus* between two surly, obscenity spewing punks being escorted off the premises, none too gently, by a...a...

A *giant* of a man. At least six foot seven, he would make two hundred and fifty pounds look skinny. And he wasn't skinny. Nor overweight. Just muscle. Leanne stopped short. As he returned from the front door, he removed his hat and aviator glasses to reveal a clean shaven head and a calm but forbidding countenance.

The human tank smoothed his clothing as he returned to Leanne. With a faint smile, he offered her his open hand and said, "Warren Drake. I believe we have a colleague in common. He said you all were looking for help." His bass voice was formal, polite, and soft enough that his voice didn't carry.

However, Leanne wagered that, were he to raise his voice, the walls would, as the saying goes, come tumblin' down. Literally.

She took his hand. It was strong, warm, and enveloped her hand and wrist. While his touch was light, Leanne could feel a tingling sensation swirling around his hand and up her arm. Huh. It wasn't a surprise that he was involved in magick, whether as a human practitioner or someone from Faery. After all, if your recommendation comes from a Cait-Sith, odds are, you're in the game. Leanne was only taken aback at *how much* energy was coming from him--and she could feel a hidden reservoir waiting to be released. It was more than anyone she'd ever met, and that was saying something.

Mistaking her stare as a critique of his attire, he added, "I did not mean to presume employment. I just thought it would be best to be prepared." His voice was melodic, almost hypnotic. It reminded Leanne of...something. Her eyes swept his enormous frame. He was dressed in navy blue slacks and a white oxford shirt, the summer casual wear for the Gentry Table's staff. The sleeves were rolled halfway to his elbow, exposing his deep, golden tan. Leanne was sure that was as far the sleeves *could* go. His forearms were massive.

Lost for words, and still taking in that she was barely tall enough to reach his shoulders, Leanne shook her head, "Uh, well, oh, no, welcome aboard, I'm very pleased to meet you." Regaining her composure, she added, "Let me show you around. And introduce you to

Anya--you two should meet." She gave him a reassuring smile, and he replied with an understanding nod. "I think she's in the Brugh."

There were two connecting entrances between the Brugh and the Table. Leanne led Warren through the wider, taller one. Even so, his head narrowly missed the silver and gold filigree crowning the boundary. It was only a few minutes after opening, so the indoor side of the Brugh was still empty. Passing through the double doors to the *al fresco* area--Warren had to duck this time--they found Anya at the bar, talking animatedly with their new roundsman.

Leanne had wondered at her sister's impulsive decision to hire Troy. Not that she disapproved, quite the contrary. But going on pure instinct? Not Anya's style. Of course, looking at him, Leanne couldn't help but agree. Gorgeous energy, kind heart, and even Remy admitted he had more than enough talent to hold his own here. He *felt* older than his years, but to look at him, she'd say, 26, 27? Just what Anya needed--he would do her no end of good. And the way he was looking at her younger sister, she'd say he wouldn't mind a bit. Leanne cleared her throat.

Anya gave a little jump, and turned. Was she blushing? They were *definitely* going to have a little chat later. "Hey, Anya, I'd like to introduce you to--"

Before Leanne could finish the introduction, Anya blurted out, "Holy shit, that's a--"

"New hire." Leanne tilted her head to give her sister a meaningful stare. *Shut up.* The indoor area of the Brugh seemed empty, but ya never knew...

Leanne continued. "Anya. This is Warren Drake. He's here on recommendation from our colleague, *Harley*."

At the mention of Harley, Anya snapped her jaw shut. "Oh, I see. Well." She put on her best professional smile and stepped forward to take his hand. She started slightly when he took her hand, no doubt due to the same surge Leanne felt flow from him.

Leanne stole a glance over her sister's shoulder. The new roundsman turned as Remy's voice rang from the kitchen, and with a polite nod to Warren, the next-to-newest hire disappeared back to his duties.

CHAPTER 17 - LIGHTNING CRASHES, AN OLD FIGHTER DIES...

Anya walked through the chaos of the dinner rush. Remy and Leanne had things well in hand, she noted, as she made her way to the drive where Samson Ramsey's truck was parked. "Troy," she called over her shoulder, "come help Samson carry in the supplies."

The humid atmosphere was close, pressing in on her. The cloudy sky didn't look threatening, but Anya felt uneasy.

"Excuse me." Troy stepped past Anya, down the porch steps.

Samson turned his attention from the back of the property to the young man waiting for the first crate of produce. The farmer gave both of them a cheerful nod. "Afternoon. Here you go. First of five." He handed the box to Troy, who disappeared into the kitchen.

Anya walked to Samson. "It was so nice of you to bring everything yourself. I didn't mind driving out."

"Oh, I can't have you doin' that." After a quick smile and a subtle sweep of Anya's face and form, he shook his head a bit and turned back to the garden. "Have y'all done something different with your gardens? I mean, it seems different. Like it goes back further."

Anya's eyes widened as they followed his gaze. The Brugh's garden was lush and deliberately crowded, with the small bridge into the private--and supposedly *hidden*--garden.

To most, the view included a tall gardenia hedge, with a blanket of edelweiss and heliotrope at its base. In the corner where the hedge met the house, there stood a mock arbor arch laced with pink poppies.

To the Gentrys, the arbor was quite real, arching over a dainty stonework bridge, which itself led over the gurgling stream, the boundary of the garden they shared with the public, and the private one only known to their closest loved ones, mortal and fae alike. It also acted as a magickal privacy fence, a subtle invisibility veil preserving the secrecy of their garden from the casual observer.

With a forced laugh, she said, "Oh, no. That's always been there. Most folks just don't notice it." With a touch playfulness and an effort at distraction, she smiled beguilingly, "Not everyone is as tall as you."

Samson grinned at her remark, but his gaze never left the bridge he'd never noticed, onward to the trees beyond. He rubbed his chin and jaw with his hand, he asked, "And are those apple trees you got back there? They're beauties." Before she could answer, his expression changed as he processed a new piece of information. He turned to Anya and asked, "What kind are they, anyway, to be blooming this late?"

Taken aback by the implications of his being able to see the garden at all, let alone identify what was in it, Anya ignored the tiny pinprick of worry and pretended to think. "Lemme see. They were a gift--but it's been so long." Like he's going to believe she can't identify an apple tree. Scrambling, she turned to his truck. "These asparagus look wonderful." Anya tested the nearest crate.

At the buckling and scraping, Samson turned around and laughed, "Oh no you don't, Miss Anya. Not in that dress. Here." He hoisted the crate past her, and carried it to the porch. Handing it off to Troy, Samson ducked his head under the faery lights as he walked down the steps and back to the truck bed.

"No, really, I can—", Anya's protest stopped abruptly. The air hummed around her with the panicked murmurs of several sylphs. Something was very, very wrong. She looked back over her shoulder.

Samson stood a few steps down from her, eyes wide with uncertainty. "Um, Anya, you're, uh, you're glowing."

No time for the implied question--with a sharp shake of her head, she silenced him, addressed the faeries hovering around her. "Tell me more."

The sylphs' song-like voices were soft but hurried. "Lots of blood," the brightest one said. "Lots of pain."

"Not good, not good at all," said another. "She came through the trees. We found her by the pond."

Samson stood back a moment while Anya, for all intents and purposes, talked to some fireflies. Impatiently, he tried again, "What the hell is going--"

Ignoring Samson, Anya turned toward the pond and quickly asked, "Is she going to make it?" The sylphs glanced at each other before lifting shoulders and shaking their heads. Their incandescent wings sparkled in the sunset. Anya pushed past Samson and took off at a run.

She heard the crate of vegetables hit the porch floor as both Samson and Troy followed behind her.

In just moments, Anya saw her. A big, blue pit bull lay on her side under the blooming apple trees. She was surrounded by--

Dozens of gentle faery hands attempted to sooth the huge dog. Easily a hundred pounds, the skin of her quivering body rippled in pain and muscle spasms. Samson dropped to his knees beside Anya and whispered, "Are those *fairies*?"

"Yes, now please hush." Anya extended her hand. She had no fear of being bitten. Gentleness was written all over the enormous bull terrier--in her scars and in her soul.

"You're safe now, baby," Anya murmured, stroking her wide head, carefully avoiding what was left of her torn ear. "You're safe." The dog's tail thumped once, and hot tears welled in Anya's eyes.

She heard Samson talking again, but couldn't make out the words. Troy stooped beside her. "What can I do?"

"Get Leanne. She'll know what we'll need." Troy practically flew from her side.

"She's fading," the more talkative sylph said, stroking the dog's muzzle with a tiny gentle hand.

Heedless of her white linen dress, Anya stretched out in the grass beside the dog, her hand resting on the bloodied cheek while she gazed into the dog's gentle eyes. "Tell me, love. Tell me everything."

Much like she had with McAnrai, she allowed herself to sink inside the dog's mind. The hurky jerky images were disorienting at first, black and white and panicked. And pained. Anya gasped and reached involuntarily for her own ribs. She drew a deep breath and focused--then saw the dog's journey in reverse--the Faery Garden, the manicured lawns of the neighbors, the traffic of Veterans Parkway, an abandoned warehouse on 9th Street.

Inside, the warehouse was crowded with people, white, black, brown, the tattered, the well-dressed. The screaming of the crowd was split by the growls and sharp, staccato barks of scared and excited dogs. The air was thick with the filthy odor of sweat and blood and fear and money. A huge chunk of roof was missing. Paint peeled from the graffiti splashed walls.

There was no sweetness here, no gentleness. Hate mixed with blood lust, driving out any shred of integrity the people might have possessed. The very air was diseased.

Dogs on thick leather leashes strained and cowered in turn. Now Anya was in the center of the ring and time was moving forward fast. She felt the teeth of another dog tear into her host's hide. Her back leg was all but useless from an earlier fight. Desperation choked the big blue, and she knew it was kill or be killed. She bared her teeth and lunged for the mutt, throwing her full weight forward. Her teeth found their mark on the other's throat. She saw fear, relief...and then blankness in her opponent's face. A sonic boom crashed through the air, knocking the breath from the dog, and from Anya. The crowd erupted in a furious, perverted joy.

She saw a light-skinned man collecting wagers. He wore a uniform, his name embroidered over the breast. Benny. He stuffed the blood money in his pocket and came for the winning dog. Anya was wracked with pain again as he snatched the dog up and carried her over his shoulder toward a kennel in the corner.

Other dogs with listless eyes stared out from behind the bars. Some bared their teeth while others threw themselves at their cages, snarling, their lower jaws covered in spittle. Benny dumped the dog on the ground and reached for the lock. Near them, a door opened, and two more men with cowering dogs entered. Anya's host caught the scent of grass--something other than desperation awoke in her. She struggled to her feet, and with a burst of unexpected energy, she fled.

Caught off guard, Benny fell hard as the big dog cannoned past him and into the night. As she burst from the building, a flock of crows took flight, their mad, urgent cawing echoing in her ears. Hope pushed the dog forward. A path seemed to form in front of her, a faint tracing of delicate light, as if her own hope had sunk into the ground, illuminating a path for her to follow. Something glowed ahead of her. A clear, clean light, peeked through the wall of leaves opening for her, welcomed her in. It looked like safety. She felt lighter, almost carried by invisible wings, as she raced through the arch of vegetation. A small pond, a waterfall. An open field of green. The scene faded to peace, then nothing.

Anya sat up, gagging. It was unnatural. It was more than a dog fight, what this girl had been through. It was a sacrifice. Blood sacrifice. They were using the dogs for blood magic, collecting the energy it produced. Tears poured down Anya's face as she stroked the dog. The pit bull thumped her tail one more time, and then was gone. Petals from the blossoming apple branches dropped gently to her body, lightly kissing her injuries and disappearing as they landed.

The faeries blinked out, leaving Samson and Anya alone.

Samson helped her to her feet. He looked angry and astonished. "Are you okay?" He paused, then asked, "What the hell just happened? How can I help?"

Anya brushed the grass and dirt from her skirt. "It was a dogfight. She doesn't need help now."

Samson closed his eyes as his jaw tightened. His head dropped and he said, "I just don't understand how people could do that."

Troy ran up to them, held out the first aid kit from the kitchen. "Leanne's on her way."

Anya shook her head. "You're going to need a shovel, darling. Ask Leanne where we can put her. She deserves a nice spot." She turned from the young man's stricken expression and glanced to Samson. "I'm going to call the police. Maybe you could help Troy?"

"Of course." He followed Troy to the tool shed.

Anya turned away and headed back toward the house. Fury raged inside her. It had been a long time, a very long time, since she'd allowed herself to be overcome by emotion. But *this* anger, she decided, this barely contained desire to destroy was legitimate. Dropping her phone, she lifted the skirt of her dress in both hands and broke into a run.

The sky rapidly darkened as clouds flooded behind her step. The smell of ozone and rain blossomed in her wake; thunder growled as it rolled from the boiling clouds. The low rumble increased with her speed, rumbling behind her, accompanying, rather than chasing her. It grew to a thunderous bellow...followed by another, and another. Electricity crackled the air.. The street blurred in front of her as her feet carried her along the path the dog had fled. Fat raindrops hit the asphalt and steamed.

Screw calling the police. Screw the system. Screw Benny and every fucking person in that warehouse on 9th Street. If they were looking for a violent spectacle, Anya was happy to provide one.

CHAPTER 18 - ANYA BRINGS THE SMACK

Anya stood in front of the warehouse. It was utterly silent.

Silent? How could they have dispersed so quickly? No more than ten minutes, tops, had passed since the sylphs alerted her to the dog. She lowered her shields carefully, waiting to be bombarded by people's thoughts. Nothing. She wasn't even picking up on any residual emotional information that *all* buildings retained. Even brand-new construction would hold impressions from those who'd built it. There was *nothing*. Energetically, it was like the place didn't exist. Yet here it was.

It made no sense. Places *couldn't* be blank.

That was worthy of a pause.

Her rage cooled to a volcanic bubbling as she considered her options. Go home and be pissed--wait for the cops to act--maybe--or investigate the strangeness now. Her thoughts flashed to a vision of their private garden, nestled behind the Brugh's. She saw Leanne's alarmed expression as she looked from Anya's phone to the road. She saw Troy digging a hole. Next to him, Samson gently set the body down. As it touched the fresh earth under the apple tree, the vision faded, then disappeared.

Yeah.

Pushing her wet hair out of her face, Anya strode toward the front door of the abandoned building. The door gave with very little effort.

She stepped inside and was immediately engulfed in a miasma of corrupt humanity. She scrambled her shields into place, but not before experiencing a slap of the room's vitriol. The most awful things people could think or do or imagine, the most horrible tortures they could inflict and enjoy--this building was swamped in them. But none of that had been evident from the outside. Not even a wisp.

Fuck.

This was not good. This was *very* not good. Magickally speaking, this was a *minefield* of bad. It would take one hell of a practitioner to hide what she had just felt. She felt an achiness behind her eyes, a sure sign that a huge, long-term spell was in effect.

She was in over her head.

Anya debated a moment before deciding to go home. They would have realized by now she hadn't called the police, and Leanne at the very least would have called McAnrai.

She turned back to the door on the heel of her ruined ballet flat when she heard it. A pathetic mewling. The barest, most pitiable whimper an animal could make. She moved instinctively toward it, stepping around an old engine block, upended rusty chairs, and a box of old, greasy rags. In the corner was a puppy. It cringed when it saw her coming and tried to burrow under the lifeless bodies of its litter mates.

"Jesus, Mary, and Joseph." Anya dropped to her knees and projected all of the sympathy and kindness she could. The puppy stopped and turned towards her, its head lifting just a little. She patted her knees and the lanky thing scampered toward her, tail wagging hopefully. Anya scooped it--her--up. "You're going to be all right, my little love. I promise you." Setting the puppy gently back on the ground, she said, "Now, stay here another moment, while I take care of some business." She murmured a spell and a golden dome appeared briefly around the puppy before fading. It would take one serious motherfucker to break through it. Of course, that's exactly what she was dealing with, but she was gambling on a lack of interest in a single, skinny, left-for-dead puppy.

A sound caught Anya's ear while an interior door caught her eye--she went toward it. Cautious, she pushed it open a fraction of an inch. Blinding light...and the din, good gods, the uproarious, frenetic noise almost had her slamming the door shut again. What kind of magick could hide this much energy? This was more than just a glamour, much more than a parlour room spell. This was a gargantuan casting put in motion by a hard hitting sorcerer.

Anya slipped a mild veil over herself--no need to leave more evidence of her presence than necessary. The throng had not noticed her entry, and that was all to the good. As she walked, she could feel magick pulsing and being repulsed though none of it was directed at her. So where was it going? Against whom or toward what was it being directed?

Deftly, she slid through the crowd until she was on the inside of the ring. The cement floor was slick with blood as two exhausted dogs warily circled each other. The larger of the two was a gorgeous hound of some kind with a short brindled coat. The other was coal black and just as large. But there was a strangeness about them, like every other discovery thus far. Their shapes seemed to shift very subtly, almost like a blink. One moment one would be the size of a Great Dane, and the next, something closer to a...a bull? And when that shift happened, each of them rippled with a faint green shimmering. What the hell?

A dull glimmer of light from the brindle's neck caught her eye. Was he wearing a bent pipe as a collar? Unlike the other fight dogs which had been wearing leather collars or choke chains, both of these animals had what appeared to be thick metal...

Oh fuck. Oh fuckety fuck. These weren't dogs. These weren't *mortal* dogs at all. These were Cu-Sith. Faery dogs...But unlike the sunlit wolfhound who investigated the crime scene, these two were harbingers of death--Guides to the Underworld. Somehow, some way, the sorcerer protecting this place had managed to capture not one, but two *beansidhe,* or banshees. The collars were infused with iron, then.

They snapped at one another but neither seemed willing to move in for the kill. Anya watched as Benny stepped forward. He had a whip in his hand and cracked its threat as a perverse conductor leading the crowd's blood lust chorus. When neither dog lunged, he moved closer. This time the end of the whip caught the brindle and flayed open his hindquarter. He opened his mouth and bayed. The building shook to its foundation, and he bayed again. Benny moved forward and raised the whip again.

Anya acted without thinking. She stepped into the circle and threw her hands high into the air.

"*Lord of light and lord of power, let me use this thunder shower. Send me lightning, send the rain. Bring justice to they who bring this pain.*" Anya had to raise her voice over the third bay of the brindle. "*Nothing more than they deserve, your power here is what I serve. By the power of one times three, as I will so mote it be.*"

Glass blew out the windows, and the room went black but for a piece of sky visible through the hole in the roof. Screaming changed from blood lust to terror, and a cacophony of thunder brought down more ceiling. Blinding strobes of lightning struck all around. Fearless, Anya ran through it, reaching the black Cu-Sith first. He bared his teeth, but fleetingly.

She touched the collar gingerly. It was covered in a nasty powder--but the lock was easy enough to unlatch. The moment it fell from his neck, the Cu-Sith leapt away from her and vanished from sight. Anya moved to the brindle. He was lying on his side, spent. His blood smeared the cement floor. He didn't acknowledge her as she worked to remove the collar. Easing his head into her lap, she murmured encouragement. Leanne would be here soon, she knew. She would know what to do. Or at least Harley would. She hoped.

It took Anya a moment to notice the storm had abated and the building was utterly silent. The mob had not dispersed. They were lying or sitting on the floor, some holding their heads between their hands, others dazed and rocking. One person was still standing. Benny. Unlike the spectators, he was not in frightened awe of the lightning storm they just endured. On the contrary, *his* face was twisted with malice. His gaze swept the room, the floor, looking for the source of destruction...and then locked on Anya. He took a step toward her, the hand holding his whip swirling as he prepared to strike. He took another step, raised his arm...

One last bolt of lightning crashed through the remnants of the dilapidated roof. By trick of light, or fancy of imagination, Anya could see the faint outline of a man in the fiery bolt before her.

Despite her proximity, she was neither incinerated, nor blinded by the lightning, nor even singed by its heat. The stench of burnt something *did* fill her nostrils, and she fought the urge to gag.

"Anya!" Leanne's desperate voice filled the air.

She heard Samson boom, "Anya!"

"Over here." In moments, she saw Leanne crossing the debris filled room.

Leanne rushed to her sister. "What the *fuck* was that?" She looked down, and her breath caught. "Oh sweet, Mother Morrigan." Her voice choked--her shields were up and they were strong, but all of this? Holy Christ.

"We need Harley. This Cu-Sith is badly injured, and I don't know what to do for him." Leanne nodded at her sister, but before either of them had a chance to say more--

"Mortal medicine is a good place to start," the low rumble of a male voice surprised them all. While it was carried by an accent reminiscent of the British Isles, the specificity was hard to place. More than anything, it sounded rusty, exhausted. "I'm Ripley."

Anya and Leanne exhaled in relief, while Samson blinked with no small amount of surprise.

The sound of sirens filled the air. Leanne looked a bit sheepish. "It's entirely possible and or likely McAnrai may or may not have called in the cavalry. At my request."

CHAPTER 19 – FIRST AID FOR FAERIES

Armed officers ran through multiple entrances. "Police! Everyone stay where you are." None of the crowd seemed inclined to move.

McAnrai strode over to Leanne, Anya, and Samson. "Everyone ok?"

Ripley lifted his head and tried to get to his feet. Samson rushed forward to help steady the enormous dog, while Leanne knelt by him. McAnrai pulled Anya to her feet.

He gestured to her blood-soaked dress. "Is any of that yours?" She shook her head.

McAnrai turned and called over his shoulder, "I have a witness over here." He nodded to an officer supervising four other officers rounding up the crowd. She trotted over.

"I'm Officer Sanchez. Can you tell me what happened?"

The tremble in Anya's voice was genuine, even if her words were less so. "I'm afraid I'm not sure, Officer. I was walking to the Circle K to get a Thirstbuster, and I heard the most horrible sound. I, well, I know it was stupid, but I stuck my head in to see what was going on, and I saw all of this." Anya didn't have to fake the tears that leaked down her cheeks. "Then this storm just--just blew in--" which *was* a literal truth. "I think he was the ringleader over there." She used her chin to point in the direction of the still-smoking form of what used to be Benny.

"All right, ma'am. It's all over now." Sanchez gave her a thoughtful look, eyed the dress, the pearls, the ruined silk shoes. "You were walking to the Circle K dressed like that? From where? Weren't you concerned?"

McAnrai stepped forward. "This is Anya Gentry, Milla. She owns The Gentry's Table with her sister Leanne," he nodded to Leanne. "They could walk down Veteran's at midnight and not be worried."

Sanchez nodded in recognition. "I've heard about the work y'all've done--there've been articles in the paper. Financing the soup kitchen and domestic violence shelter. "

McAnrai nodded. "And all sorts of other adventures." He turned to Anya, "But right now?" He gestured to the room.

When the talk turned to the confiscation of the surviving dogs, Anya's expression froze as her eyes darted between Leanne and McAnrai. Mortal authorities unknowingly boarding an injured *beansidhe* would lead to some...complications...

Anya swayed on her feet as exhaustion hit her. Officer Sanchez lent a supportive arm and Anya took the cop's hand. Directing her attention toward Ripley, she said, "He's no danger. I saw the fight, and he never attacked the other dog. He is harmless. He is small." From the corner of her eye, she saw McAnrai lay a subtle hand on Samson's arm. The latter's face was knit with confusion, but he said nothing. Anya continued, "He's no danger to anyone. He is harmless. Small. We can take him with us."

Officer Sanchez's eyes rested on the enormous canine. "He *does* look rather small, doesn't he? And with that kind of damage, I doubt he did any of the attacking." Sanchez wavered. "He doesn't look like he'd pose much of a threat." She nodded to one of the younger officers, and said, "I'll have someone give you a ride home."

Anya bent down to Ripley and placed her hand on his head. She asked, "Can you walk?"

His head dropped a bit. "I'd love to say I could, but I wouldn't get very far."

Anya nodded and gestured to Samson. "Would you mind?" Ripley shook his head as best he could.

"I'll carry him," Samson said, leaning down. With the skill and strength of a man used to handling newborn calves and foals, he lifted the Cu-Sith.

"I'll meet you in just a minute. There's one more thing I have to do." Anya slipped away from the group and headed back to the building entry The shielded puppy practically wagged herself in half as Anya dissolved the bubble and scooped her up. "Hush now, love. You are my little secret." She touched lightly between the puppy's eyes, and they closed. With a touch of camouflaging glamour, Anya cradled the little stowaway and joined the others by the waiting police cruisers.

Leanne and McAnrai were quiet, and Anya could guess the reason--Ripley and Samson were getting situated in the back seat of the cruiser, but the door was still open. Anya stepped to the other two and the three exchanged a glance. When they heard the click of Samson's closing door, Anya said, "I'm going to ride with them--but you two," she faltered, hoping she was wrong, "did you notice--?"

They did. With a look of grim understanding, Anya joined Samson and Ripley as Leanne and McAnrai got into his car.

The warehouse, and everything in it, reeked from the residual magickal energy of the same monster whose handiwork they'd examined that morning.

***

Back at the Table, Anya led Samson and an unconscious Ripley around the porch, bringing them into the restaurant's kitchen through the emergency exit opening into the Faery Garden. The staff had cleared a path to what they'd nicknamed the Batcave--a narrow, dimly lit hallway connecting the Table's kitchen to the sisters' private one. With a look of instruction from Anya, Troy guided Samson through the kitchen. His dark eyes never left the limp canine, his fury reined behind a tight reserve.

The Batcave's door opened--Harley had been waiting for them on the other side. They followed him through the austere passage to the warm, welcoming glow ahead. Entering the pool of cozy light, Harley leapt onto the counter, to Leanne, who put her arm around him.

The kitchen island had been cleared, a cheap, plastic picnic tablecloth covering it. With McAnrai's help, Samson settled the large *beansidhe* on it. Both men backed away, and Leanne and Harley set to work. Samson looked down at Anya, placed his hand on her shoulder.

"Here." McAnrai had poured them each a whiskey neat. Anya shook her head at first, but he was adamant. "Your color is gone. Take a goddamn shot." But Anya remained focused on Ripley's care.

Samson took the glass from McAnrai and handed it to the woman at his side. "Here you go." Missing the hand-off, Anya absently took the glass from Samson, threw it back in one swallow and joined Leanne and Harley. The two men exchanged a look--McAnrai gave him an acknowledging nod. It was going to be a long night, but he couldn't help a tiny smile. It was always good to have an ally.

Taking this as a good of an opportunity as any, Samson turned to McAnrai and spoke in an undertone. "A talking dog. Fairies. Witches. A thunderstorm that would've scared Noah. Jesus Christ. Would someone please tell me what the hell is going on?"

Glancing first at Leanne, then Anya, who gave resigned half-shrugs. He turned to Samson, refilled the younger man's glass and said, "Well, brother, I've got good news, and I've got weird news, and either way, you're gonna want some more of this."

CHAPTER 20 - THE MORNING AFTER

Anya emerged from her second shower in ten hours. The first one had occurred shortly after she learned Ripley was in the clear. Or as 'in the clear' as a half-mutilated faery dog could be. Leanne promising to sit with him had also helped Anya drag herself from the Cu-Sith, even if only for the duration of ablutions.

When she'd returned to him, Ripley's eyes were closed, but now in a comfortable sleep. The blood had been cleaned up and McAnrai had assembled a makeshift recovery bed of blankets covered with a new vinyl cloth in the corner that was usually their breakfast nook

Arriving just in time to see Leanne and Harley moving him from the island to his bed, she looked at the nook's bench and smiled at her sister's efforts. Blankets and a pillow for her--good call, Leanne.

However, and despite the unexpected comfort of their breakfast furniture, Anya had slept sporadically. Instead, she had watched Ripley, his chest rising and falling. She had listened to his heartbeat--steady as his breathing.

Thank God, the gods, and the Goddess Herself. It would take some time--and a lot of care--but the magnificent Cu-Sith would recover.

As for now, the sun was up, the birds were singing, and she looked like shit. At least that's what Leanne said, though not in so many words. It was the best way to convince her to move upstairs--complimenting her comfort with letting everyone see her in pajamas and without make-up.

Anya fastened the buttons of her pale green sundress, pulled her hair back in a clip. Her face was on, and she walked into the living room with a bit more spring in her step.

With a little sleep, she was now able to think more critically about the events of the previous evening. It tickled her that the fight ring's Biblical destruction didn't interest her as much as Samson's matter-of-fact reaction to McAnrai's bite-sized tutorial on life, Gentry style. To be fair, it probably went so well because the guy'd already witnessed some hardcore special effects. By the time McAnrai had a chance to talk to him, *any* explanation was soothing. With any luck, the visit she and McAnrai were about to have with Shelby would go half as well.

***

Making her way down the steps, Anya savored the smell of freshly brewed coffee and friendly chatter. When her second foot hit the kitchen floor, a cup of hot, creamy Irish tea had been placed in her hand. "Mornin' *chere*. Where y'at?" Remy looked even less rested than she felt, but he wore tired well.

"Good morning, love. And thank you for this." She took a sip and followed her friend back to the island. Leanne and Laidi were already there, sipping coffees and discussing the notes McAnrai "forgot" to bring with him when he left for work. From the expressions on both Laidi and Remy's faces, she could at least tell they weren't confused by what they saw. Disturbed as hell, but not confused.

Um, yay?

"I tell you what, T-ya, dat dog's sumtin' tough and Harley," he sipped at his coffee, "he's some kinda doctor." He jutted his chin in the direction of the Garden. In response to her questioning look, he added, "He asked to go outside." Another sip of coffee for the night owl--Remy was not in the habit of being awake so early. "Ladybirds will tell us if he needs help."

Anya smiled with relief and at the playful nickname Remy had for the sylphs. Breathing easier, she reached for a folder, and asked, "What do you two make of it all?"

Laidi was no more a morning person than Remy. She rubbed her face vigorously and yawned. File down and coffee mug up, she sighed. "Whoever he is, he's one sick bastard. Sick and smart." She rubbed her eyes again and turned to Remy--who tagged in.

"Short version? Dis *fauyk* got at least a rudimentary understandin' of voodoohoodoo, and he's makin' like a shitty movie--" Remy paused at their questioning looks, then elaborated with sarcastically expressive hand gestures and facial emphasis, "Evil voodoo. Bad hoodoo. Scary *bokor* put *da conjure* on ya!" He took a drag of coffee and grumbled, "Like dere ain't enough stereotyped shit said about home."

Laidi patted his hand with almost comic sympathy, "Save your fight, hun. I'm sure we'll get our chance to discuss it with him." Her hand rested on his arm for a few extra beats. He stepped closer, resumed reading.

Switching to a more sober gear, Laidi continued, "Let's take a look at this laundry list of crap they found on this guy." She shoved the paper in question across the island,

"Waaaaait a minute," Leanne raised her eyes from the blood analysis and grabbed Remy's arm. "What do you use chicory for?"

"Coffee." He looked at her, "*Mais non*. Dat's not what you meant." He thought for a moment. "Invisibility. *Mais non*." He shook his head. "You could see him, you. How? Dat's *le tracas.*"

That *was* the problem. Leanne frowned. "What if he wasn't supposed to be invisible to *me*?"

Anya broke in, "Who else would he be hiding from?"

Leanne's expression cleared to something between triumph and oh shit. "What would a *witch* use chicory for?"

Grim understanding settled between them, and Laidi spoke. "Not who, *what*. Chicory is used for invisibility and *lock breaking*. That's how Brad got into the Garden Lounge without any of our knowing." She shook her head with an impressed air. Looking at Leanne, she said, "Girl, it's amazing you noticed him at all." It wasn't clear if Laidi was impressed by Leanne's senses, or the strength of the spell, or both.

"And here," Remy's expression hardened again to disgust. He passed the paper to Anya--Laidi waggled her shoulders with repulsion as it hovered in front of her, "Dis mess on his back. Blood, mandrake, asafoetida, Solomon's seal? Camphor? Dey're for power. For puttin' someone *under* your power, to be exact."

In response to the sisters' expectant expressions, Laidi explained. "This asshole had Brad under his will. Controlled him. No telling what he was making him do."

They all took a moment to willfully *not* imagine the implications of that statement.

Anya asked, "And sent him to us? Why?"

With a shrug, Remy said, "I dunno, me."

Laidi asked, "Maybe that was *Brad's* choice? Folks *do* know about us. Maybe he was instinctively looking for help."

"Not that it did him much good." Leanne clenched her jaw.

Remy and Laidi exchanged a look. It was Laidi who spoke, her voice tender. "No, hun. This boy here was *marked*. He didn't stand a chance." She pulled out the photo of Brad's hair. There was a black shoelace tied into it, behind his left ear, slightly into his hairline. "This here? It's black because it's burnt, and I'll bet Shelby found it soaked in oils from datura, yew, and grains of paradise. Confusion oil."

At that, Leanne turned a startled expression to Remy. He nodded. "Y'yeah, Leanne," he answered her with a sidelong look, "same one." Leanne nodded. It was a long time ago, and a story for another day, but that particular adventure's taste of Confusion left both of them with tidy blank spaces where the memories of an hour should've been. She grimaced.

Anya nodded confirmation without looking up from her reading. "Laidi's right. It soaked into the back of his neck and the hair that touched it as well."

Laidi continued, her delicate, dark brows furrowed in concentration as she stared at the papers and pictures in front of her. "Scrambling his brain, and the mentals of anyone he came near."

"Say that again?" Leanne cocked her head to the side.

Remy jumped in. "It means, *chere*, you got brain-whacked from bein' near him." He pointed to the shoelace. "Anyone would be affected by dis *gris-gris*." His expression, so hard from the horrors he was reading, softened a bit when he looked at her. "No way your mind was clear when you were wit' him. Pretty impressive you were functional at all." His warm smile was reassuring, as was Laidi's enthusiastic nod of agreement. Leanne welcomed the salve, smiled back.

Seizing the opportunity, Laidi said, "These designs, though. Why canine blood?"

Anya's hands shook with rage as comprehension grew. "Blood ink is crazy powerful--if charged with an entire dog ring's violence? That's the point of the dog-fighting. Raise energy, each fight pouring more energy into the 'champion' dog..."

Laidi grimaced. "So each victory charged her. To make her the ideal offering. To make her blood the base and power-source for the spell painted on Brad's back. Sweet Jesus."

In her own effort to bring her emotions under control, Leanne focused on the puzzle. She looked up, perplexed. Fighting to keep her voice steady, she asked, "All this to control a kid? That can't be the whole story. One person?" She slid off her stool and stood. Walking to the sink, she rinsed her mug and set it down. "Besides, with Brad already dead, these new dog fights, Ripley's--they were obviously meant for something else. I mean--" She stopped, leaned back, her expression darkening further as the pieces fell into place. "How much you wanna bet that this 'champion' has been fighting for a year?"

"In line with the sabbat murders?" Anya fought the urge to grind her teeth.

"Yes. And whatever it was, it didn't work, so he had to get a ton of energy quick--"

Remy's mouth set in a grim line. "To make up for a year of killin'--"

"Hence a Cu-Sith."

Laidi interjected, "Okay, nevermind **how** this guy managed to catch not one, but two *beansidhe*, ummmm, **WHY**?" Elbows on the table, she rested her fingers against her temples. "Lughnasadh is over. What's the point, now?"

Dropping her hands to her side, Leanne asked what they were all thinking, "What in the hell was supposed to happen that night?"

CHAPTER 21 - THE BABY DOWN THE HALL

After Anya left to meet McAnrai, Remy and Laidi exchanged a glance. It was a twisted temptation to spend more time discussing the grisly contents of the folder in front of them, but with a rehearsal dinner that night, priorities had to shift. Laidi pursed her lips, then said, "I'll go ahead and put these upstairs." Remy nodded, raised his mug in mock salute. Too tired for any attempt at subtlety, he openly admired her slim, tan legs as she climbed to the second story.

They both startled as a crashing metallic cacophony--and what might have been the shriek of a pissed off mountain lion--exploded from the loft style space overlooking the kitchen. Reaching the top first, Laidi froze at the entrance to the Gentrys' living room, just as Remy's large form barreled into her from behind.

Splashes and slides of water decorated the hardwood floor connecting the Gentrys' dining room on their left to the living room on their right. A tipped metal bowl rolled from a smattering of little brown, green and tan pellets, several small blankets, and an entire sports' section of newspaper (in varying states of soil and crumple). Darting quick zigzags through it all was a scrawny ball of silky, buttercream and caramel colored fur. Little snarls of delight squeaked and popped from the ball as it attacked fearsome newspapers and slid across the living room floor on the homemade slip and slide. It ricocheted off of the hearth, rough and tumbling its way to doors of the closet and, bouncing off it, stopped just in front of Laidi's feet.

"Awww! You poor little baby!" She squatted down, reached for the cloud of tousled fur. The puppy perked sharp, triangular ears in the direction of Laidi's voice, and scampered into her hands while wagging its tail with such vigor, the back legs repeatedly slipped underneath. Laidi scooped up the wiggly bundle. "Oh, you darling thing!" Cradling the puppy, she stood.

At the sound of a pointed throat clearing, both Laidi's and Remy's eyes followed the trail of puppy wreckage to the living room. What they saw petrified their expressions in every sense of the word.

"What da hell--what hap--" Remy's speech faltered as he took in the rest of the scenery. And when he saw Harley, he blurted, "Ho-ly shi--*UNGH*," he grunted at Laidi's elbow in his gut.

Harley, in all his dignity, was sitting on the living room floor. His eyes were at half mast, his expression deadpan. "It woke up."

Cautiously, so, so cautiously, Laidi spoke. "Good morning, Harley."

The haughty posture of the Cait-Sith was a grim blend of supercilious offense and despairing resignation to his plight. He was covered, from the tips of his velvety ears to the very end of his luxuriously plumed tail--with toilet paper. Sheets, shreds, a few wads at his feet. While some loose banners of it were flowing in the air around him, others were soggy, and melting into his (usually) impeccably groomed fur. His form looked less like a debonair lieutenant of a Goddess, and more like a caricature of an almost-drowned alley cat. He was perfectly still, other than one flashing swat of his paw sending the tipped water bowl from his personal space. The two humans flinched at the loud clang the bowl made against the surface of the hearth.

"Good morning? *Good* morning?" It took everything Laidi and Remy had to maintain straight faces at Harley's tightly reined voice. "Young woman, I have lived through wars, mortal and immortal. I have seen kings and queens rise and fall with their empires. I've been imprisoned by both merciful and sadistic wardens." He took a deep breath. "But I have never, in *all* of my days, been subjected to the ignominious indignities that I have suffered in the last twelve hours."

The puppy made her way up the front of Laidi's shirt and placed her paws on the woman's collarbone, grinning broadly. With a stern look, Laidi asked, "Have you been naughty for Harley?"

Ears flat against her head, the puppy's long face drooped. Her almond shaped eyes squeezed shut, and she buried her head in Laidi's blouse, whimpered pathetically. Remy's expression softened a little, and Laidi melted.

Harley was unmoved.

"Perhaps," he paused as he attempted to stand, snarling at the gooey toilet paper matted between his toes, "since you so obviously have an affinity for each other, you'd like to spend more time with the darling little waif." Remy and Laidi looked at each other, then at the puppy. The 'darling little waif' peeked one bright blue eye past the blouse collar. With a delighted, infatuated sigh, Laidi buried her face in the puppy's clean fur.

With a persuasive air, Harley hastily added, "*Yes*, Laidi, she's *adorable*. You look so *well* together." Harley had started walking around, extricating himself from the toilet paper plaster, taking unnaturally high and uncharacteristically clumsy steps as he attempted to free his paws from the sticky, pasty mess. Between hisses, and under his breath, he muttered, "You simply *must* save me from this insufferable situation." High step, high step, slip, *snarl*.

Running her hand down the light caramel streaks in the creamy white fur, she said, "Well, of course I will. You can come live by my house, darlin'. Yes you can. *Yes you can*." Nuzzle, nuzzle, nuzzle.

Harley's voice rang, loud and clear. "***Agreed***." At least within Faery, that was a legal passing of obligation. He disappeared without another word; a cloud of water droplets and bits of soaked toilet paper left a Harley-shaped cloud in his absence. The floaty mess that had moments before covered the Cait-Sith dropped to the floor with unceremonious *splats*.

Laidi dropped to the floor, unfettered joy in her words. "Oh Remy, isn't she sweet? And her fur, just like caramel, cream and sugar!" Yip, nip, lick...

Though he loved the sound of her laughter, Remy frowned. It didn't take much detective work to figure out where the little furball came from. Despite its youth and underfed state, if this girl was bred for fighting, he could only imagine her eventual size.

Remy asked, "Any idea of her breed?" He hoped he didn't know.

"Oh who *cares*? C'mere, Sugar. My little Cream and Sugar is so, so sweet." Laidi was crawling on the floor with, with--oh Christ, she'd already named it. "It's just me in that big apartment. I've got plenty of room." Her face lit up, if possible, even more. "And I bet they'd let me bring her by here, let her play in the gardens while I'm at work, so she won't be lonely."

"*C'est bien, mais nous faissons quois après*? Laidi, you may want to consider how big dis girl's gonna get." He sat down on the floor with them, petting Sugar, stroking her long, narrow snout. After a few thoughtful minutes, he said, "*Chere,* I don't t'ink she's a dog, me."

"Now what do you mean, not a dog? Don't listen to the mean man. He's just playing. Yes he is." The puppy was on its back, her too-long legs waggling in the air, her large paws swatting playfully at Laidi's hands.

"C'mon." Once on his own feet, Remy offered Laidi his hands, helped her stand. "Let's go downstairs and talk to Leanne." Laidi sighed, stood up, brushed off her shorts. Sugar scrambled to her own feet, tail wagging doubtfully, head tilted in query.

They started walking toward the stairwell. "So if not a dog, you must think she's a--" As soon as it was clear they were leaving, Sugar threw her head back and squeaked out a long, pitiful howl.

Remy's head dropped. He sighed with resignation as Laidi raced back to the pup, gathered it up in her arms.

"She's a wolf, *ma mie.* Dat *petit chienne* is a *wolf.*"

CHAPTER 22 - BEING DR. SEWARD

The ride to Muscogee County Morgue was spent in a companionable, if loud, silence. Both McAnrai and Anya were lost in their respective reflections with regard to the previous days.

McAnrai looked over at Anya. He'd always liked her--which was a damn good thing, considering how much their relationship had changed in the past...was it just three days? *Christ.* In three days, she had gone from someone he casually knew as Shelby's friend, and from the small town vibe of the summer concert series to.... Hell, now...she's riding shotgun on a ride-along, nevermind the goddamn *mind*-along from yesterday morning. And that's not even touching Leanne...

Well, there was some touching Leanne.

McAnrai's motives in asking Anya to join him were two-fold. Officially, the consult would be her knowledge of rare plant life. The second reason?

If he was right, this case might end up being easier to solve than they expected, but damn near impossible to prove or explain...or prosecute. Getting the Chief Medical Examiner to understand the magick angle of the whole situation was the first step.

As certain as he was about his guesses, and his conviction was only cemented by last night's events, there was no doubt today was going to be one enormous wake-up call for the coroner. The bombshell would get a better reception coming from her best friend.

***

It was well into Shelby's workday by the time Anya and McAnrai walked through her propped office door. As they passed the hidden sentinel, Anya suppressed a smile at Mac's shudder. This wasn't the time to tell him about Anya's role in Shelby's acquisition of that magnificent specimen. Or how it was actually--Anya shook her head. Really, today wasn't the day for anything pertaining to Beulah.

"Hey y'all! Be there soon as I can." Shelby hit a button on her desk phone, and went back to her conversation. Anya turned to find McAnrai had already made his way back into the waiting area and was talking to Garrett.

The assistant coroner was chipper today and beamed at the both of them. "I know you're here to see the body from Wednesday morning, but Shelby told me you also needed to see," he glanced down at his clipboard, shook his head. "Well, of the other ones you requested, only two of them are still here."

McAnrai grimaced. "I'm not surprised. It was a long shot to hope they all hadn't been claimed. I assume one of them is the girl from late June?"

"Right you are. She and the fellow from May. He willed his remains for science, so that was easy. As for the girl, few teenagers make wills, and her body was never claimed, so--". He broke off eloquently. "Neither had family, and the circumstances were so odd, we were allowed to keep them for study. Haven't had the chance to look at them for a while, though." He sighed as they walked.

He stepped with brisk precision through the aisles and rows of drawers. Gods, Anya thought, even with Shelby's decorating touch, this was a dreary place to work. No sunlight either. She shivered.

In an effort to comfort her, Garrett said, "It's not so bad. Most of the people here? This is where they come when the suffering is over. We get them ready for their loved ones--and help take down the bastards who brought them to us. Remembering that makes it better."

Like hell it did. Anya looked around the room of drawers, grateful for Garrett's sake he couldn't perceive what she could. There was a spiritual fetor flowing through the building--Anya reasoned it was comprised by the remnants of souls who, like Brad, had only partially moved on when they died. She shook her head. Focus on Brad.

Garrett slid open the drawer containing the young man. Out of consideration for Anya, and knowing what they were here to see, Garrett left Brad's face covered, and simply pulled back the covering over his feet.

Anya stifled a gasp. Thanks to what she learned on the mind-along they took in Mac's head, Thuggy's print was now visible without the help of McAnrai's subconscious. The plant life embedded in the soles of his feet? She knew exactly what the three plants were, but explaining it...?

"Hey y'all, sorry that took so long." Dr. Shelby Mitchell's steps were the same cheerful, quick tempo of Garrett's. "Hun, I got this--and you got a hell-stack waiting for you."

With a curt bow and a smile, Garrett was off.

It only took Shelby a quick glance at Anya's face to make the good guess. "You know what this all is, don't you?"

Taking a slow, deep breath, Anya said, "Shel, we need to talk." Her eyes darted around the room, wincing from the pressure of the darkening cloud. Pain and confusion swirled in wisps from most of the drawers, joining the undulating vapor above them. "But not here." She closed her eyes--she wasn't going to last much longer.

McAnrai jumped in, "How about we look real quick at the other two, then go out for Korean?" Anya brightened at the promise of not only getting the hell out of there, but then going to her favorite place in town--after the Table, of course.

Brad was sealed back up, and the second drawer was found.

"This is the man--Jason Blair," Shelby checked the clipboard, "came to us on May second, but killed on the first." She pulled the drawer open, and all three of them blinked in surprise.

The drawer may not have been empty, but it sure as hell didn't hold a body.

"What. The. Hell. Is. This?" Shelby stared at the drawer's bizarre contents.

"Shel, can we play a hunch first, and check the other body?" Anya looked at the unavenged souls swirling above...coming closer and closer to awareness. Once they realized she could understand them? There wasn't much time. "I *don't* know, not for certain, but I think...please?"

The weird, greenish tint to Anya's face froze Shelby's objection. The coroner stomped three columns down. Unlocked, pulled it open the drawer.

At which point, three things happened.

The coroner muttered a curse at another drawer filled with sparkling powder.

The telepath collapsed at the sudden rush of souls clamoring around her, begging for help.

The detective said, "Oh yeah, we're done here," as he caught Anya's body, mid faint.

***

Anya was busy inhaling the dinner sized portion of Golden Chopsticks' crowning achievement, *garbi*. Korean barbecued beef ribs, with their rich, sweet glaze, put any and all others to shame. Heresy for a Southerner, but as Anya's only south was by way of Ireland, she felt no remorse. With each bite of carnivorous heaven, she felt more solid, more herself.

Shelby poked at the *jap chae* noodles on her plate. "So let me get this straight. The plants on the girl's feet were, were--"

"Sominarius, Mervaalo--"

The coroner cut her off with a deceptively quiet voice. "I don't care what their *names* are at the moment. Explain how they're from *a-noth-er realm*?" Shelby was still regrouping. She knew about the sisters being witches, and a few of the friendlier pixie types had allowed her to catch occasional peeks. But there was a big, damn difference between believing in faeries and understanding the existence of the Faery Realm. Between knowing your friends perform spells and understanding those spells include the *occasional shopping trip to a parallel dimension of existence.*

Oh, and now she had missing bodies. And had just watched her best friend collapse for no apparent reason.

In an attempt at reassurance, Anya said, "I know it sounds insane. But I've always said magick is just another way to label the stuff science hasn't explained yet."

Shelby's mouth was open, as if trying to form words, but to no result. With an exasperated exhale, she sat back and said, "My God, I feel like Dr. Seward." Rolling her eyes at their blank faces, she commented, "No one reads the classics anymore."

Anya gave a short, weak laugh as she caught the reference. "Fortunately, I don't think our situation is quite as bad as that, though yes, I am making Van Helsing's point."

"Okay," McAnrai started, "I've caught up that we're talking about *Dracula*, but I'm still not following. He added, "And I *did* read it--just ten years ago."

Anya explained, "Okay, so you know in the story, Van Helsing is the first to figure out what Dracula is, and has to explain these so-called 'supernatural' elements to scientifically minded Dr. Seward." She gestured to Shelby, who gave a quick, if sarcastic, smile. "The latter is understandably resistant to the idea of a guy who can turn into a dog, bat, mist..." She took a sip of her Coke.

McAnrai's tone was deadpan. "I blanked on the name, not the plot. What's your point?"

"That scene illustrates Shelby's dilemma."

Comprehension dawned on McAnrai's face. "*'It is the fault of our science that it wants to explain all; and if it explain not, then it says there is nothing to explain.'*"

Responding to their surprised glances, McAnrai smirked, "Told you I read it. Wrote a paper on it, too." They continued to stare, so he muttered, "God, forget one character's name and the literary police show up." He dipped a fried *mandu* dumpling in the *cho ganjang* and popped it into his mouth.

The literary banter lifted Shelby's spirits a little, even if only enough to enjoy her *bul kogi*. "From what you two told me of this--I can't believe I'm saying this--magickal fingerprint, you said you could recognize it?"

"Yes." McAnrai frowned as he swallowed a bit of grilled steak. "Which gives us a whole new way of double checking our suspect pool. However--"

Shelby cut him off, "All of the evidence you have is useless in court."

Mouth full, McAnrai gestured his morose assent with a forkful of rice. "Useless anywhere this side of reality, actually."

They ate in silence for a few minutes. Shelby took a long sip of Coke, and turned to Anya, "So, all those times when you were talking about leaving offerings for the faeries, you weren't...weren't kidding?"

Anya grinned. "Nope."

Shelby shook her head. "I swear. Might as well change my name to Seward".

CHAPTER 23 - GUESS WHO'S COMING TO THE REHEARSAL DINNER

Considering the eventful week, the kitchen staff had resigned themselves to the prep and execution of the rehearsal dinner being an ugly monster. However, despite a week of both metaphoric and literal triage, everything proceeded with effortless fluidity. Moods were sober, but equitable. People were unrushed, but efficient. All arrivals--food, drink, dishes or linens--all on time, and in perfect order. Even the staff found themselves arriving on time (whether or not they'd been running late) and leaving just as their shifts ended--nothing left undone, but no overworking or rushing to make it so. It wasn't as though the Gentry's Table and Magick Brugh were usually disorganized places to work, but this was smooth, even for them. Eerily so, had any stopped to notice.

Finally, someone did.

Forrest was putting the finishing touches on the base to his champagne punch when Warren's large form sat down at the bar. He poured out and handed Warren a glass of iced tea, and asked, "Is it me, or has it been a little too calm?" In response to Warren's raised eyebrows, the barkeep exhaled a self-effacing laugh. "I mean to say, after all that's happened, folks should be frazzled. Biting each others' heads off. Ain't been none of that."

"Perhaps it's the lack of business?" Warren took another sip of tea and asked, "Do you often go this many days in a row without anyone in the Garden Lounge?" The bartender raised his eyebrows in inquiry. Warren elaborated, "I heard the members of the kitchen discussing it--the lack."

Forrest nodded, his eyes focused on the hand wiping down the counter. "The Lounge only ever has a few in it at a time, but I don't remember ever having a day without anyone." He lifted his head and frowned as he considered that point. "And definitely not three days. Huh. That *is* weird." He wiped his hands on his jeans, and said, "Be right back," before disappearing into the wine cellar.

Warren leaned back in the tall bar chair, his expression grim, but satisfied. He stood up when a blond man in a tan linen suit walked through the Brugh's porch entrance.

As the he approached, Anya's voice floated in from inside. "Oh, thank you. Just bring that tray in here. Yes." She smoothed the front of her dress as she walked in from the dining room. Troy followed, carrying an enormous platter of tiny bowls. "Right on this table. Thank you."

Anya arranged the bowls of candy coated almonds at intervals on each table, and then the bar, deliberately setting the last dish in front of the newcomer.

"Good evening sir. Welcome to the Gentry's Table and Magick Brugh." Smiling warmly, she extended her hand.

With a sunshine grin of his own, the man continued the handshake for an extra beat and said, "I'm delighted to make your acquaintance." He held her gaze and said, "You must be Anya Gentry."

Anya was taken off guard, less by the familiarity of the man's demeanor than by her comfort with it. Recovering, she threw back, "Indeed I am, though I'm afraid you have me at a disadvantage, Mr.--?"

"Forgive me. The name's Lou N. McCury." He extended his smile to the other three.

Warren slightly bowed his head, and murmured. "Good evening, sir." The man nodded back.

Troy poured a glass of champagne for Mr. McCury.

Her hand forgotten, Anya's gaze was thoughtful as her eyes examined the man holding it. "Do I know you from somewhere else? Not here--I'd remember that. But," she paused, lost for words.

McCury said, "Well, perhaps you've read my column? I have some connections with *Vanity Fair*." A flood of images rushed through Anya's mind, columns about celebrities, scandals, and crimes of the glamorous variety.

Of course. "Well, Mr. McCury--"

His bright blue eyes crinkled at the corners as he cut her off, "Lou, please. Call me Lou."

"Lou." She looked over his shoulder as the rest of the guests started filing into the main lobby. "It was a pleasure to meet you. I hope you enjoy yourself tonight. Please let me know if I can get you anything." She moved to walk away, but he held fast to her fingertips.

"Actually," he said, "I know you're about to be very busy now, but I'd love to talk to you about the excitement this week. Maybe a drink later tonight?"

Torn between her duty as the Table's proprietress, and the charming man asking her--on a date?--Anya shook her head. "I'm so sorry, but this event is going to run well after hours and I--"

"Oh, I'm so sorry, how thoughtless of me. Perhaps tomorrow morning?"

Between his insistence, and her fluster, she found herself replying, "Well, okay, then. That'd be lovely. Say, nine o'clock?"

"It's a date." Lou released her hand, and Anya felt his gaze watching her departure as she moved to greet the new influx of guests.

Lou turned to the bar, and accepted a glass of bubbly. He raised his flute to Troy and Warren. "Gentlemen, here's to what is clearly going to an interesting evening. As I trust you both know your duties," he grinned as they nodded. "I'll leave you to them."

***

In the galley, Leanne found herself with strangely little to do. Ordinarily, her job was far more administrative than she preferred, but that's what happened when your head and sous chefs were top notch. With the adjusted menu and added pressure of a formal occasion riddled with politicians and celebrities, she had expected to be run ragged. But Remy had everything well in hand, and what little he didn't directly supervise fell under the uncanny perfection of Troy's work. The pear and Gorgonzola salads were assembled, the tureens of spicy cucumber soup ready to ladle. She savored the rich aroma of the layered potato Napoleons as they finished baking, and after one last turning of the steak tips in their garlic-maple marinade, she turned to Remy. "I'm going to check on Ripley. You good to go?"

"Y'yeah. Take your time, *chere*."

Slipping through the Batcave, Leanne entered the soothing cool and cheerful noise of the smaller kitchen. Ripley was still on his bed, but in a different position. His eyes were open, and he was watching the source of the noise, the scrappy, cream-colored puppy Anya had saved and Laidi adopted.

"Good evening, Ripley." She squatted down to pet Sugar. "How's everything here? This one's not too much trouble?" Leanne smiled to herself as she thought of how Harley had spent the previous evening. No doubt he was making himself scarce on principle--she was going to need more than cream and a baguette to make up for *that* experience. In contrast to the cantankerous misery that had been etched into every ounce of Harley's being, the pit bull's expression was serene. To Leanne's pleased surprise, she could also tell his heart was also hurting a little less.

Ripley raised his massive, square head and his mouth opened in a smile. "I'm feeling better all the time, miss. And she," his expression softened even more as he looked down at Sugar snuggling herself into the crook of his front leg, "has lifted my spirits considerably." Sugar had brought a little blanket with her, and was tucking it in and around herself and Ripley's leg. She walked three circles over it, and curled into a tiny ball.

"Oh yes? She's darling, for sure, but," Leanne looked around the kitchen--the scattered toys, shredded rolls of paper towels, spilled food and splashed water-- "are you sure she's not too much of a strain?"

"I am most sure, but thank you." He nestled his head next to the sleeping puppy. "Would it be possible for her to stay with me while I recover?"

"Absolutely. Laidi needs time to prepare her place, anyway." Leanne paused before asking delicately, "You knew Sugar before today, didn't you?"

Ripley's voice was still weak, but it carried to the length of the kitchen. "While my compatriot and I weren't the first of our kind to be imprisoned there," he let out a long breath, "the blood on the body left for you to find is mortal canine. Blood from a beautiful, red--," he faltered, looking for the right word, "I believe humans would say, 'hybrid' named Waya."

Leanne's voice was soft with compassion. "Like Remy and Laidi said. The pattern on his back had meaning, purpose."

"Yes. Therefore the 'paint'," his furious disgust dripped off the word, "had to be special. Enchanted." His voice caught, and he breathed again. "Waya was the sacrifice." He looked at Sugar, and the love flowed from him, enveloping her in what looked like a soft, pink blanket. A happy sigh escaped from Sugar, and Ripley closed his eyes. "I didn't know any of her offspring had survived." His breaths were deep, but they shuddered with emotion.

"And Sugar's mother, Waya, was your friend?" Leanne's voice was tender, as was the soft touch of her hand on the back of his neck. She stroked his short, smooth coat.

"Waya wasn't my friend, she was *mine*. Which was why I went to free her." he tilted his head in Sugar's direction, "Which makes this one mine as well."

Leanne's eyes widened. The story was horrible, but it explained how Thuggy had survived the proximity of two Cu-Siths long enough to capture them.

CHAPTER 24 – SMOOTH OPERATORS

It might have seemed strange that the handsome reporter spent the evening almost entirely alone, but Lou McCury had a knack for being unseen when he wished.

There were at least a dozen Hollywood names in attendance, each with a glamorous date and a desire to be seen. The Who's Who of Columbus were also present, and could have given him ample angles and ideas for whatever article he planned on writing. Still, Lou neither initiated any interaction, nor was approached by any of the publicity-hungry guests. Intentional inconspicuousness had its advantages--he was there to watch.

He took an appreciative sip of champagne punch. The sweet kiss of early autumn honeycombs mingled with notes of lavender and vanilla. He glanced at the bartending brewmaster--the young man had a flair for his work. Setting the flute down on the bar, Lou's eyes ran the length of the *al fresco* porch.

The soft faery lights mingled with the glow from the lamps and candles. His gaze lingered on the young celebrities moving in and out of his line of sight, his view flickering back and forth from the fresh, innocent faces they once possessed and the deliberate attempts at art they'd become. Plastic surgery, he gave a brief, dismissive exhale. Helpful for some, but usually only erased the imperfections of beauty, replacing them with attractive interchangeability.

Beauty. He sighed. So few understood it, let alone valued it.

At that moment, he was drawn from his reverie by the piercing gaze of a woman. She wasn't a day under sixty, but possessed a vibrancy absent in the bodies and personalities of the youthful, glittering guests. He recognized her, of course--Dahlia Hilton, black sheep-turned matriarch of Columbus' first family.

Lou raised his flute in greeting--the smile she flashed in return was dazzling. In rebellion against her body's well preserved, but aged form, the charisma of that Cheshire cat expression held no less bravado today than it ever did. His own manner became pensive as he effortlessly visualized that smile as it had been when she was sixteen. It wasn't difficult to understand how it had moved mountains.

Aware of his recognition, Dahlia Hilton lifted her chin, the corner of her mouth turning up. She winked, and returned her attention to the young Hollywood couple. Lou's amused glance lingered an extra moment--the young man was completely entranced with the grand dame, while his nubile companion fought for attention.

Beauty. While few understood it, Dahlia Hilton embodied it.

Within moments, she made her way to him.

"My dear friend, it's been ages!"

"Dahlia." Lou took her hand, placed a genteel kiss on her fingertips. "You look as lovely as ever I've seen you."

She laughed. "I'd say 'liar', but I know you too well. C'mon. Clearly you've become addled in your old age." She looked up at him, her petite frame almost childlike by his not-even-six feet. "You don't come out to play very often, do you?"

"Only when invitation or duty calls." At his comment, a slight frown creased across her forehead. They stopped at the bar, and he handed her a flute of champagne. She accepted her drink, took a sip as she looked away.

With a quiet voice, she asked, "So who invited you?"

"No one." He took a long sip as she slowly turned back to him.

Her rich, brown eyes hadn't faded with age. They were now wide, and he watched as her face smoothed to an understanding she'd always resisted. It was but a moment, but it was all he needed.

Dahlia threw back the rest of her champagne, and with a playful elegance accepted only in delightfully classy old girls, she set the flute on the bar and announced, "Bartender, I believe I'll have another--but something with a little more kick," she pushed the flute toward him with a graceful, if dramatic, flourish, "so break out the goods."

Forrest made a movement for the ice, but Dahlia stopped him, "No, son, I take it neat."

"That's true enough," Lou's words were quiet.

Her head snapped around, her face losing none of its drama, but all of its play. Checking herself, she smirked. "That's a terrible pun."

"But an excellent point. Have you considered calling on him?"

"I can't." Dahlia leaned against the seat of the bar stool.

Lou shrugged his shoulders and accepted a refill. She accepted his offered arm, and they walked down the steps, onto the smooth stones of the Brugh garden's path-work. The party had all but migrated inside, with a few stragglers mingling at the bar's outdoor counter. Lou and Dahlia walked together toward the gardenia hedge. The woman leaned close to the blooms, inhaling deeply, while the man crouched lower, plucked a spray of purple flowers.

His eyes darted from the proud woman to their surroundings. Lou's attention swept the expanse of the enchanted garden and the length of the terrace. In less than a minute, they were alone. His words were kind, but firm. "Dahlia. You can and you should." He handed her the blossoms.

Her laugh was as soft as it was charged. "Heliotrope." She sunk her face into the petals, the delicate scent of cherry pie caressing her cheeks. With tears threatening the edges of her words, she amended, "I mean I don't want to." She turned away from the flat disbelief of the man's expression. The moonlight shone gently on Dahlia's face, melting away the years. Lines of reluctant awareness and rude awakenings fell from her. In that moment, she was an innocent girl with her whole life ahead of her.

"Dahlia," his voice was soft, but authoritative, "turn to me."

As she did, the years, the cares, the illness all flooded back to her, draining her vitality. In sharp contrast to the woman who had owned the evening only minutes before, she looked every inch of her sixty years. Wearily, she said, "I'm dying."

"Yes."

"He can't see me like this."

"Do you think he's unfamiliar with death?"

Blinking back tears, she whispered, "Leave me alone."

"That's not in anybody's best interest. Least of all yours." She didn't flinch at his hand on hers. He gave it a gentle squeeze. "Dahlia. You know what has happened. What's *going* to happen if we don't intervene."

She slowly pulled her hand from under his. They both turned at the subtle shift in the conversational noise floating from inside the Table.

"The wedding party is making their exit." Her voice was flat.

"Here." he swept his hand across her brow, and as it passed, her equilibrium was restored.

Dahlia smiled ruefully. "Thank you, kind sir." She swallowed her whiskey in one gulp and handed him the glass, "I have a wedding to attend."

Lou's thoughtful gaze followed Dahlia as she rejoined the party, resuming her role as beloved matriarch. He whispered, "Enjoy your party, sweet lady."

CHAPTER 25 - OUT OF THE FRYING LOUNGE, INTO THE GARDEN

Lou walked from the Brugh's porch to the Table's dining room proper. The last of the dishes had been removed, and most of the younger generation had departed from the formality of the Gentry's Table to wherever the after-parties took them. He exchanged a friendly nod with the guitarist as the latter packed his instrument. Strolling from the Brugh to the scattering of dignitaries and parental units in the dining room, his eyes focused on a tall man walking toward the back restrooms. Lou's concentration was so intense, he was barreled into by a young woman. Her hair was pulled into a low ponytail, and the white cotton of her culinary uniform was streaked with stains corresponding to the meal he'd just enjoyed.

"Oh, I'm so sorry, sir. I should've looked where I was going, I--"

He cut her off. "Not a worry, miss, it is I who should apologize. You must be one of the chefs? May I offer my compliments on a delicious meal?" He gave her a formal bow, punctuated with a winning smile. He noticed her blush slightly at the compliment, and a little more when he reached for her hand, kissing the top of it.

As his lips brushed the top of her hand, she peeked back up at him.

"Thank you sir. Please excuse me," Her eyes twitched toward the spinning door leading to the kitchen, "I need to see to my duties."

Lou released her hand, bowing his head as they parted.

***

Laidi stepped toward the Table's galley, but paused at the last second. She watched the departing crowd. The Hilton clan was leaving. Anya escorted them herself, everyone from Dame Dahlia herself, her creepy-ass son, Payne Hilton, all the way down to the almost-newly-weds. Laidi turned away from the entrance to the kitchen, toward the restrooms.

When she emerged from the restroom, her mind was troubled. She'd felt a little jumpy, ever since the reporter kissed her hand. It wasn't the usual flutter from flirtation--more the uneasiness of missing something important. Moving her head from the dining room to her left, and Anya and Leanne's private entrance to her right. She shook her head, took a step toward the kitchen, but then spun a u-turn. Her eyes widened with surprise as she froze at the sight of the Lounge's mural--it had transformed to the gate...

The ordinarily welcoming entrance was gloomy, its climbing vines brittle, and border flowers wilted. The gate itself was tarnished, and hanging open, creaking in a breeze only it felt.

Mesmerized, Laidi stepped inside, oblivious to the potential hazards waiting in the dark room. Her feet found themselves winding through the tables, chairs and plants, neither bumping nor tripping, despite her attention's outside focus. She registered the mild odor of decay, the smell of flowers overripe, petals browned, the sound of leaves being chewed by ravenous insects. Her eyes had found a mark--the silhouette of a large man furtively maneuvering through the garden beyond the glass. Heedless of the danger, she trotted in pace with the dark figure, all the way to the end of the room.

When he stopped at the trees, Laidi froze in place. The stranger crouched under the oak, ash, and thorn trees just beyond the glass, pulled something out of his pocket. It was the size of his fist--discernible by its slight, sickly glow. He set the large, dull object on the ground, brushed a few leaves, a bit of dirt over it, and stood up. With no regard to his surroundings, or the possibility of being seen, the man brushed his hands off, and broke into a light trot toward the front of the house.

Laidi exhaled--only then realizing she'd been holding her breath. Though her fear abated somewhat with the trespasser's egress, she was far from calm. She shook her head to clarity and ran her eyes over her surroundings--this time noticing the strangeness around her. Glancing toward the edge of the garden to make sure she was alone, she walked briskly to the light-switch...

And stopped, paralyzed by what she saw.

Under the last seat of the room, the floor was glowing. It shimmered with the same unwholesome seeping as the object outside--tendrils of glowing slime oozed in streams from an inky dark center, like grayish beams radiating from a blackened sun. Rising to her nostrils was a fragrance, one permeating its way through the fresh decay of the room, piercing her senses, triggering a memory...

"Oh no. Oh no, *no*." Laidi stumbled back a step, knocking into a chair. She turned and all but ran from the Garden Lounge. Once back in the regular hallway, she stopped, her hand resting on the wall as she fought the waves of nausea rising from her stomach. She looked toward the dining room--only a few people left. With a stride she hoped didn't look too much like a panicked run, Laidi made a beeline for the kitchen. This needed a second opinion, and it was everything she could do not to shout his name.

"Remy?" Busting through the spinning door, Laidi looked frantically around the room. Busboys, wait staff--where the hell was Remy?

"*Remy?*" Her voice was a little louder than she intended, but the volume was good for carrying. "*REMY?*" Louder still, the edge of panic attracting the attention of the other guys. She felt a hand rest on her shoulder--initially relieved, she spun around to see Troy. Barely hiding her disappointment, she said, "Um, I'm sorry. Didn't mean to shout. Have you seen Remy?"

"Is something wrong, Laidi Thibadeaux?" His face was creased with concern, his dark eyes boring into hers.

Ignoring his question, she repeated, "Remy. Have you seen Remy?"

"Right here, *chere*." With a look to Troy, he added, "No need to be so formal, chief." Remy bared his teeth in a grin and said, "An' I got dis."

Troy removed his hand, stepped back, but didn't turn away.

Raising a dissatisfied eyebrow, Remy turned, and froze at Laidi's face. Discarding Troy from his mind, he gently grasped both of Laidi's shoulders. "What's wrong, woman?"

Instead of answering, she shook her head. Her small, shaking hand reached up and grabbed his. She walked to the door, pulling him along. "You gotta come with me now." Without a word, he followed.

Dining room now empty, Laidi broke into a run, with Remy's long legs keeping easy time. They came to the Garden Lounge and found the Room was still open, its ornate gate still swinging back and forth. Creaking, no less.

"What in all hell?" Remy looked down at Laidi, whose eyes were large and anxious. He took the first two steps down into the room, turned to her. He noted the clenched muscle of her jaw as she braced herself to join him. He held out his hand, as if to help her navigate tricky ground. She took it, held it tightly. And jutted her chin to the end of the room.

Remy's eyes followed her direction, and joined hers in frozen surprise. "Go get Anya or Leanne. Go on." He stepped into the room.

"Like hell. Y'ain't going in alone."

"Seriously, girl? Go."

There were times when she found his low level chauvinism charming. This was not one of those occasions. "The hell with *that*. I need to show you what I saw." She pulled at his hand, and stepped around him, leading him into the room.

"What *you* saw? You were *alone* in here? *T'es fou toi?*"

Frowning at his attitude, but finding comfort in familiar banter and joined forces, Laidi walked him through the Lounge.

Remy flicked the light switch as they delved deeper into the room. The rest of the soft lights came on, illuminating the Room's grotesque transformation. "*Mere de Dieu.*" Jaw open, he looked around. The leaves were all drooping, the petals of each bloom browned at the edges. The fruits of the grapevines were rotting off of their stems, rancid juices dripping on the tablecloths. When they came to the anti-sun on the protection floor, Remy squatted for a better look. He took a deep breath, blinked in recognition.

Laidi nodded. "You smell it too, right? That's--"

"War-water. Oh *fuck*." Remy stood, turning as he yelled, "*ANYA*!"

Only to find Anya standing inches behind him. Reeling back from the power he'd poured into his call, Anya held her hands in front of him. "I'm here, Remy, I saw you walk in--what the--" Her eyes found the dark patch with the sick rays.

And a familiar glimmer.

Yelling as *she* turned, Anya called, "*LEANNE*!"

Who had also followed closely enough to be less than a foot from her called name.

"Okay, I could feel you guys all the way up in our kitchen, and when the lights flicked on under us, I wondered," Leanne's eyes fell upon the gloopy mess of malice on the floor, "what the ever-loving FUCK is that?" Leanne's eyes flickered back and forth between copper, hazel and...landing last on Laidi's clear grays, she pounced. "What happened?"

Laidi's expression flicked in annoyance, and Leanne apologized. "I'm sorry. I could just tell--" she broke off.

Laidi opened her mouth to speak, but Anya interjected, "Let's move this a little bit away from where we're standing? I'm not sure it's too healthy for us to be this close." Her eyes swept the extent of the wall, to its ivy creepers and climbing flowers--weakened and sickly.

"Yeah, you right, T-ya." Remy placed a gentle hand on Laidi's shoulder and another on Leanne's, pushing, er, guiding them to sit farther, at least to the happiness and health section. As the three of them walked away from her, Anya's eyes began to glow with a golden, metallic sheen. She reached her hands in front of her, speaking to herself. A golden orb enclosed the evil magick and the rotted floor surrounding it. When it snapped shut, the plants outside the orb, indeed, the Room itself, seemed to relax, to exhale with relief.

"I'd almost recommend leaving the Lounge, but I'm not sure it'll be able to let us back in."

Leanne nodded to her sister. "Agreed."

All four of them sat in the cheerfully painted wicker furniture. Laidi relayed everything she witnessed, while the other three sat in a stunned, alarmed silence.

"Once he was gone, I could move again, and I smelled it. I recognized it, and I knew it was from home, but I couldn't place it at first, just that it was bad, real bad--" Her voice started to shake. Remy slipped his arm around her shoulder, and she leaned to him. "It smelled like home, but everything bad about home, y'know? And all I could think of was home, so I ran, I ran to--", her voice cut off.

Remy cut in. "It's called War-water. As in, when you wanna declare 'war' on someone, you go by someone's house, toss it at da front door."

"So that's what that smell is?" While Leanne's scent palate was specialized to culinary endeavors, both she and Anya had noticed the strange addition to the room which had been organized according to her own magickal bouquet design. "Musky, but floral, and vinegar? I can also smell," Leanne grimaced, "is that rust?"

Laidi nodded, her eyes grim.

Remy added. "I've never made it, *non*, but I'm sure it'd be easy enough to figure out the recipe." His mouth was set in a grim line.

Anya had listened as Laidi gave her rundown. Though she was just as concerned about the room and the War-water, her mind had skipped to the next issue.

"We've gotta find whatever it is he put out there." Without waiting for the others, she marched deeper into the room, stopping just short of the spell she had cast.

"Wait a moment." They spun around to see Harley perched on the table next to the infected site and the glowing orb containing it. "It isn't advisable to do anything alone at the moment." He leapt in a graceful arc over the containment spell, and landed on the floor beside their feet. "Shall we?"

Anya concentrated, then put her hand on the glass pane aligned to the path between the money and protection plots in the Garden. At her touch, the glass rippled like water, evaporated into a silvery mist, opening to the Garden.

CHAPTER 26 - NO, IT'S PRONOUNCED "LA-BAHR-A-TORY"

L aidi pointed as they walked, "Right over there. Under those trees." Her directions weren't needed--they could all see the dim glow from...

"What the hell?" Anya reached her hand forward, but thought better of it. The enormous oak tree quivered, and a long, straightish branch dropped into her open hand. She looked up and into the intricate weaving of branches. "Thank you, love." Using the stick, she adjusted the dirt and leaves that had been used to hastily cover the creepy deposit.

Stripped of the shallow camouflage, a swollen mandrake root lay exposed. Its skin was stretched thin over the surface, and the root throbbed with a pale glow; its pulsing threatened an imminent burst. Aggressive tendrils of glimmering slime wandered toward them...

CRACK.

Anya, Laidi, and Remy jumped as Leanne's fingers flicked open, and an opaque sphere snapped violently into place. Smaller, tighter than Anya's, Leanne's orb swirled like liquid silver, its severe appearance cutting off the edges of the tendrils. They fell to the ground, squirming and flopping...toward Leanne. Harley's back arched, fur raised. He hissed at the scraps.

The ground shook, and tiny screams found their ways to the ears of the three humans watching. Harley's instinct for suave equilibrium was rarely shaken, and when it happened, it was worth witnessing. Leanne's hyperfocus never wavered, and Anya hardly reacted. Remy smiled with approval as Harley disposed of the little nasties

But for Laidi, who'd never seen Harley react with anything but stoic solidarity, this was a first.

"Um, uh, wow." She shot a half-grin at the Cait-Sith. "You're pretty badass, Harley."

Harley nodded in acknowledgement of the compliment.

Leanne's voice sounded in Anya's head. "It's poisonous, and it's strong. If we leave it out here, or touch it without protection of some sort...it's designed to permeate."

To Leanne, Anya responded, "Once downstairs, I'll be fine." Out loud, she said, "This way. Let's go in through the basement doors."

Anya could feel a wave of gratitude flow like a soft breeze through the limbs of the three trees whose side-by-side presence marked the boundary between the Room's garden and the Gentrys' private one.

As the humans approached, the sprawling hawthorn bush politely withdrew its branches, allowing them briar-free passage.

Looking away as they passed the fresh mound of Sadie's grave, Anya led them to the basement's hitherto hidden entrance. With a wave of her hands, she dropped the veil concealing the clean, smooth stonework of descending stairs.

"Well, learn sumtin' new every day, yeah?" Remy stood to the side, watching Anya and Laidi disappear into the blackness below.

He looked at Leanne and his expression changed from wonder to concern. It'd been a long time since he'd seen her eyes turn to silver, since he'd seen her do any physics-bending magick. Crazy cool to witness, but he didn't like the way her hands were shaking.

"Lemme help wit' dat, *chere*." Remy knew better than to touch the silver sphere, but he could assist in other ways. He wrapped his left arm lightly around her back, and cupped her elbows in his hands. As they walked down the steps together, he could feel the ribbons of his own energy manifest, slipping down her arms and around the sphere, supporting her spell that way.

They entered the sweet, cool dark of the cellar, and walked past the wine racks, across to the blank space of wall separating the beer and liquor storage. Anya placed her palms on the empty paneling, and for the third time that night, Remy and Laidi saw a previously unknown door appear.

To the left, a laundry room; to the right, a strangely angled corner of wall.

Laidi placed her hand on her hip and said, "Lemme guess. Another hidden door to a secret room?"

Anya grinned. As serious as the situation was, she enjoyed getting to share some of the cooler secrets of the house. What's the point of being an artist if no one ever saw the painting? "Better than that, love. A door to a secret *lab*."

***

By the time they had the protective sphere hovering over the surface of a stainless steel table, both Remy and Leanne were shaking. Whatever the hell this thing was, containing it was something beyond anything either of them had ever tried. Careful not to drop it, they steadied it over the metal surface as Anya touched the large, orange rocks on the corners of the table. When her fingers left the fourth, a gentle burst of energy surged from the edges of the table as four translucent screens of light shot up. They joined at the brightly banded, orange, cream, and red disc on the ceiling, giving the appearance of a shimmery mosquito net tucked around the "bed" of the table.

When the shield snapped in place, it severed the energetic cords connecting the poppet to Leanne and Remy, and the mandrake landed on the surface with an anti-climatic *plop*. Relieved of the burden, Leanne slumped back against the sinks, and Remy stumbled slightly. Without the glimmer of Leanne and Remy's combined shield work, the room sank into almost complete darkness. The only light came from the table's protection spell, and from several small, red lights floating in the inky darkness surrounding them.

Remy laughed and said, "Damn, I'm outta practice." He looked up at the shield anchor on the ceiling, and gesturing to the disc he asked, "Carnelian, yeah?"

Anya nodded. "Yes. Contains the nasty, and the way I finagled it, you can reach your hands in," as she suited action to word, the energetic field enveloped her hands and lower arms in a sheer, skin fit, "and work with what's there without getting hurt."

She withdrew her hands. Walking to the center of the room she addressed the darkness. "Could we have more light, please?" At once, the tiny, levitating embers seemed to spring to life, growing from small, wriggling slivers of reddish-orange to full-blown flares of glowing, golden flames. Visibility increased, and revealed several pairs of old-fashioned sconces mounted throughout the walls of the room, each pair flanking a long, narrow tapestry.

Laidi and Remy watched as the light gradually revealed the room. The stainless steel table before them and to their right, several drawers and a few narrow shelves. The latter was filled with beakers, bowls and various other vessels. The sink Leanne was using for support stood to their left, and just past it, a bonafide decontamination shower.

"*Cho*--you weren't kidding 'bout it bein' a laboratory." Remy's eyes widened in appreciation.

"Of sorts." Laidi eyes matched his as the far end of the chamber became clearer.

The shower marked the end of the room's resemblance to a scientific facility. Beyond it, Anya crouched at the end of what resembled a kitchen island. It was made of stone, and topped with a slab of beautiful Connemara marble. The counter top was clear but for a golden pentagram inlaid on one end, and an a deep, crescent-shaped cut in the marble at the other, hugging the cheerful hearth below. The hearth itself was built into the island, with an enormous cast iron cauldron suspended over the kindling.

Anya arranged two small logs and a dozen ghost peppers under it. The fire salamanders accepted the offering and erupted into cheerful flames. Anya turned again to the vessel cabinet, started rummaging through the drawers underneath. She pulled out several surgical tools, placed them in a wide, ornately carved, crystal basin and set it down on the counter next to the sinks.

Employing her best old-Hollywood horror flick emphasis, Leanne quipped, "Actually, we pronounce it 'la-BAHR-a-tory."

With a sidelong glance, Remy said, "Course you do, *chere. Mais bien sur.*"

Laidi looked around with approval. "Y'know, I'm not as surprised as I could be."

Remy let out an amused breath in agreement as they took in their surroundings.

Wiping the thin sheet of sweat from her brow, Leanne asked, "If you're good for now?" Laidi nodded, so she looked to Remy and said, "C'mon. We should leave them to it."

Remy nodded and added, "Good luck."

Leanne and Remy disappeared through the door as Laidi and Anya set to work.

CHAPTER 27 - SWING AND A MIST; SWING AND A DRINK

"Okay. Let's do this." They brought the tools to the metal table and considered the sight before them.

It had been years since Anya had seen a fresh mandrake--their scarcity and expense was one of the reasons most people switched to homemade dolls.

"So let's not forget voodoohoodoo." She spoke under her breath.

"My *nanan* used to talk about mandrakes, and how she used them as a girl, but I've never worked with one." Laidi held the poppet steady with a long set of silver kitchen tongs while Anya poked at it. There was a short incision between the mandrake's 'legs'. "Looks like the tips are cut off. You ever seen that before?"

Anya grimaced. "No...but it's probably metaphoric."

As the mandrake's long relationship with magick was closely linked to its roots' resemblance to the human form, complete with upward reaching arms in the stems, and two separate extensions of root to give the appearance of legs, the inference was unpleasantly clear. Laidi grimaced. "He cut off its feet."

"Something's wedged in that cut--but recently. The slit is new."

Laidi nodded. "Must be what I saw him do."

Anya frowned in concentration as the scalpel she was using to extend the opening bounced back from the mandrake. After several attempts, it finally slipped from her hand..

Leaning back with surprise, she asked, "Harley? Did you see that?"

Harley had perched himself on top of the decontamination unit. He tilted his head to the side as his eyes narrowed. "I did. That is sealed magickally. Therefore, that is how you must open it."

"*Scrobarnach-gaile?*"

"That would be my first suggestion. Do you have what you need?"

Anya considered for a moment, then nodded. "Yes, I'm settled. You're off then?"

The Cait-Sith's countenance wrinkled in disgust. "Considering what I think you're going to find? Oh, I do think it would be wise." Harley disappeared with a pop.

"Well, that's encouraging." Laidi turned to Anya, "Wait. Scrob--what?"

"*Scrobarnach-gaile.*" Anya answered. "Literal translation: scrub-steam. We're going to have to pull out the stops for this."

After several seconds of deep thought, Anya grabbed the crystal bowl and walked to the sinks, gestured to the cabinets across from the stonework hearth. "What we'll need are behind those."

"Since it's your spell, shouldn't you be the one--I mean, I could draw the water."

"This bowl is unsurpassed in its ability to absorb and channel energy for a purpose, but it's a little particular about who can touch it. It was originally made by my I-don't-know-how-many-greats grandmother, and passed down to me." She switched on the faucet, allowed the water to fill slowly. "Even Leanne's barely allowed to handle it, and usually just to pass it to me. If she tries any more than that, it gets twitchy--and our great-grandmother will kill me if I let anything happen to it." She twitched her head in the direction of the first tapestry, its subject a tall, beautiful woman with dark red hair.

"You're great-grandmother is still alive?"

"Not a bit. But don't think that'll stop her."

Laidi opened the sliding wooden doors, and paused at the array of bottled herbs and resins, dried roots and barks. Correctly interpreting her hesitation, Anya added. "Don't worry, the really dangerous stuff is down that way." She waved her hand toward the back wall.

Laidi's eyes widened as she read labels. "Belladonna and datura don't count as 'dangerous'?" she turned, eyebrows at her hairline. "Do I even *want* to know what's over there? I know you're not stupid."

Anya frowned. "Um, let's just say I hope we don't need them. There." She turned off the water, brushed her hands against her skirt. "We're going to need some bamboo chips and hydrangea roots on the fire, some vetiver in the pot itself along with some toadflax, and a little wintergreen--" Anya continued to list supplies while she carried the full basin to the heating cauldron.

Laidi added the ingredients to the lit wood. Fragrant smoke tendrils rose from under the cauldron, caressing its curves, and climbing past the rim to form a large, empty sphere of smoke. The vapor from the sizzling herbs coiled up, blending with the smoke in a web of perpetual movement. Once the web was complete, Anya poured the water slowly, a thin but steady stream spiraling from the center, filling the empty, protected space.

Anya set the empty bowl down, "Okay. Let me get behind you." She reached past Laidi's head and grabbed a bottle with a sealed wax coating. Addressing the bottle, she said, "Open." The intricate designs carved into the wax dissolved as the seal melted to the base of the bottle.

Anya splashed the ends of the tongs and the inside of the bowl with the brown liquor. She swirled it to lightly coat the inner wall. Returning the bottle to its shelf, she whispered, "Close."

Watching the wax reaffix itself to the bottle's opening, Laidi wrinkled her nose, "Smells like whiskey. What so special about it?"

"A little bit of American folk magick here--toadstools soaked in whiskey are great for countering hexes. The seal is because I don't want anyone to drink the stuff soaking the fly agaric." Anya carried the bowl over to the mandrake, lifted the root with the tongs, and gently set it in the bowl lined with the hallucinogen-laced whiskey.

Anya added, "Ideally, it'll loosen the hole so we can get whatever is in there out. Also, it'll draw out whatever's been soaked in."

"So it's just taking what's been combined, and separating them back to their original forms?"

"Yes and no. I mean I hope so." Anya bit her lip, hoping, praying she was wrong. "At the moment, the bowl is holding its energy, and I'll add my own shield while it's in the air. Once over the pot, the smoke should keep it safely contained."

"Should? Great. Just great."

"Yeah, I know. But it's what we've got." Anya nodded her head, though it was unclear if the reassurance in her voice was for Laidi, or herself.

Laidi rolled her shoulders, prepping herself. With a tilt of her head, she smiled. "Good times."

But before she could move, Anya stopped her, "Remember, hold the mandrake over--but not in--the cauldron. It's the steam we need."

"Okay." She reached forward again. Again, Anya stopped her.

"And make sure you grip it tight, at least until the spell can take over."

"Got it. Now cut it out. You're making me even more nervous." She took a deep breath. Laidi closed her eyes momentarily, centering, grounding herself. She allowed the enchanted smoke to circle her, absorbing its protective qualities. When she was ready, she opened her eyes, and grabbed the tongs. "Well, here goes."

Anya held the bowl at the edge of the marble counter, inches from the enchanted steam. Laidi reached toward the mandrake, but felt a resistance to her approach--as she got near, the tongs kept sliding to the left and right, as though she were trying to make two magnets touch at the wrong ends. Finally, she pressed through the invisible barrier and clamped down on the root. Laidi lifted it from the bowl and toward the smoke-steam infusion. There was another pause of resistance, but the spell took over, and sucked the poppet out of the tongs. The mandrake floated in the center of the swirling smoke-steam.

With a half smile, Laidi said, "Okay, that was kinda cool." Anya nodded, and they both watched.

The gorged root writhed in slow rotation. It pulsed, shriveled, expanded, and finally deflated in defeat. Reluctantly, resentfully, a red-brown fluid seeped from its crevices. It attempted to dissipate, but the magnetism of Anya's bowl was stronger. Once fully gathered, she picked up another dish to collect the second liquid, this one clear and pungent. Then another. And another. As the poppet dehydrated, the slit cracked open, releasing...

A black, glossy crystal detached from the root and hovered momentarily over the boiling water. Suddenly, both it and the ruined poppet dropped. Anya caught the root with a small dish she had waiting for it, but the crystal splashed into the water. Before either woman could react, the room started shaking, and a shrill noise rose from the vibrations, rocking the room in agonized shrieks. Without thinking, Laidi shoved the tongs into the boiling water and pulled out the round, black disc. Once out of the water, the noise stopped, the room stilled, and the women looked at each other--what the *hell* was that?

"May I?" Anya took the tongs and stared at the rock, "Onyx, I bet." As though speaking to it, she said, "Let's see what your story is." She walked to the other end of the marble counter, far from the heat of the hearth, to the gold pentagram inlaid there. She set it down in the middle of the protective symbol and focused while Laidi gathered all the other components and set to the challenge of identification.

They stood there, back to back, for the better part of an hour, Anya with the now-silent rock and Laidi with the mandrake and its evictees. The latter stared at the powders, herbs, the bowl of liquid and the small tray dotted with tiny dabs of essential oils. Only a few more to ID, then she'd be done for the night. She hoped.

Anya was feeling the strain of actually having to fight for access to something. Every time her mind pressed into it, she kept getting little flashes of the week's events, images from the mind-along they did with McAnrai, from the atrocities of the fight ring. But nothing from the onyx itself.

Turning away, she rubbed her eyes and laughed--she was *definitely* a little punchy. She couldn't help it. It tickled her, the visual image of what the scene would look like to someone walking in--she'd designed the room for practical purposes, but only now did the comedy of the room's set up suddenly hit her.

The lab could be split down the middle. At one end, Laidi worked at the modern, stainless steel dining table; her white chef's uniform almost looked like a lab coat.

In contrast, Anya's side of the room could have easily be confused for the set of an old horror movie, and her fitted, dark indigo tunic and a long, maxi skirt only accentuated the witchy vibe.

It was an honest-to-Goddess Jeffersonian/Hogwarts mashup.

Anya returned her attention to the crystal, the mystery of its contents. Her focus was so keen, she didn't hear Laidi speaking to her. After the third attempt, she got poked.

"Hey, you."

Anya jumped slightly, and turned. "Sorry. Got something?"

"Got plenty, and a real big problem on top. You ready?" Receiving assent, she squinted at the liquid, "This here is just mineral oil now. And these little spots are bergamot, black pepper and patchouli." She continued across the table, labeling the strange assortment of schmutz. "But no telling what kind of *gris-gris* is charging it all, still."

"I wouldn't worry about that. The steam from the cauldron neutralized the caster's intent." She grinned at Laidi's doubtful expression, "A concoction of my own, there. If it can take down a pissed off golem, it can clear a damn root." She glanced at the pitch black rock on the counter. "Okay." She straightened her back and said, "This is definitely onyx, and--"

"Actually, I wasn't done." Too tired to be apologetic, Laidi rubbed her hands over her face.

"Oh. Sorry."

"I can't be certain, since I don't know what was said, or what order the ingredients were used in, but this mess," she flicked her hand over the array, "It's either Essence of Bend Over or War Oil."

From the back of her mind, Anya could feel an alarm rising softly. "Or both of them?"

Laidi nodded grimly. "Yeah." She took a deep breath and pointed to the last pool of liquid. Anya grimaced as she waited for the confirmation of her guess. "Blood. Probably from the same poor animal used to paint the boy's back."

The words hung in the air for a full minute. Laidi was exhausted and simply ready for home. Anya was no less drained, but the pieces were finally starting to fit, and the barbarity of the finished puzzle gave her a shot of sour adrenaline. Horror crept across her face, while disgust twisted her stomach...

The fight to free Brad's spirit from the spell attached to her body. Witches murdered on sabbats. Something wrong about what they found--*didn't find*--on the bodies in McAnrai's mind palace. An entire dog fighting ring worth of violence being charged into one blood sacrifice. And now this, this abomination left on their property. At the foot of their...

Appalled, she slowly turned back to the piece of onyx.

Her voice was barely a whisper as she stared, wide eyed, at the innocent looking rock. "Sweet Mother Morrigan and the Blessed Virgin." Her hand covered her mouth as tears came to her eyes. "Laidi, this is so much worse. Oh gods," she ran to the back wall, to her hidden stores of magickal contraband. Her voice cracked as she said, "Go--go get Leanne. Remy if he's there."

Laidi shook her head in confusion, asked "I don't understand, what are you seeing--"

But Anya's panic silenced her protest. Without another word, Laidi took off for the stairs.

***

While Anya and Laidi deconstructed what they dropped on the large, stainless steel table, Remy and Leanne sat on the Brugh's porch swing, stiff whiskeys in hand. For a solid half hour, they sipped in silence. Out of nowhere, Remy started laughing. And laughing. He had to hand his glass to Leanne as he leaned forward, gasping for air.

"What is it? What's so funny?" Leanne's face crinkled with the pleasant expectation of someone about to hear a joke.

"*Mais non,*" Remy continued to laugh, tears running down his eyes. He gasped, "*Pomee,* me!"

"Yeah, I can see that. When you catch your breath--"

"A washroom!" Of all the things he could've said, that she did not expect.

"The laundry? What's wrong with it?"

"It's so, so...*normal*!" And he was gone again, laughing his way to the floor. He sat with his back against the outer wall, took deep, calming breaths. "*Mais non, non.* Just...I don't know what I expected to find behind magick-secret-door number t'ree, but just a plain ole' *washroom...*" He broke off in giggles. "Oh, me." He wiped his eyes, rubbed his face. "Ah *chere,* you and T-ya? Never a bore here, *mais non*!"

Leanne laughed and handed him his drink. Sliding to his end of the swing, she moved her back to the armrest and her feet onto the cushions.They sat for a while in a comfortable silence, sipping their whiskeys.

"*Merci.*" He was still shaking his head, but his face had cleared to a somber note. "What we brought in--" He paused, searching for the word.

"The mandrake."

"Mandrake. It was makin' da same damage outside as in da Lounge."

"Yep. Which means it was moved."

"Which means whoever planted it--"

"Had snuck into the Garden Room to fetch it."

"Which, since dat room's been closed since--" He caught himself. "Since Tuesday, means he was a guest here tonight."

"That's what I think, too."

Remy tilted his head up, looked at Leanne. "Where dat mess was. Dat boy must've dropped it, yeah?"

Leanne nodded.

"Suppose he meant to?"

Leanne considered her answer before continuing. They were outside, but other than a hint of Harley, she could feel they were alone. She looked at Remy for an extra beat before answering. Well, hell. If you can't trust your best friend, then who? "Sort of. I think he was compelled to drop it here. To plant it."

"On orders from--" He grimaced as he reached their shared conclusion.

With a humorous waggle of her head, Leanne quipped, "McAnrai calls him 'Thuggy McBastard'."

That earned a snort into the newly emptied glass. Remy collected himself, stood. "*Un de plus?*"

Before she could agree to another drink, both heads turned as Laidi emerged from the stairwell connecting the basement to the rear of the bar. "Y'all need to come back down. Now."

*****

It was well after midnight when McAnrai returned to the Table. As the front door locked behind him, he was hit by a cacophony of scent. Fingerprint scent, to be exact. Leanne's, Anya's, an unfamiliar one that reminded him of...Remy?, and another...that last one was also familiar...*oh fuck*...

He drew his sidearm, flicked on the flashlight attachment, and took measured steps into the lobby. Looking around the decorative walls flanking the hostess station, his eyes scanned the empty dining room. He hit the power switch. Bright, warm light flooded his surroundings. Following his nose, he moved through the arrangement of tables, chairs. The reek of that murdering bastard got stronger as neared... Oh Christ, near the residence's door. He passed the Garden Lounge's open gate, and the stench faded. He backed up, looked in. Low lights on, but an empty Lounge.

"The situation is secured, young man." McAnrai's head jerked in the direction of Harley's voice.

"Shit!" Relaxing his elbows, McAnrai brought the gun's barrel against his solar plexus, pointed down, to position sul. "Harley. What the hell?"

"She's upstairs. It's been a busy night."

"Busy, huh? What happ--" But after opening the residence door for McAnrai, Harley had disappeared. McAnrai growled as he holstered his weapon. "Fucking faeries." As much as he appreciated the reassurance, Harley's deliberate lack of elaboration was annoying as hell.

The debonair voice sounded throughout the room. "I heard that."

***

McAnrai hurried through their kitchen and took the steps to the living room two at a time. Once upstairs, he found Leanne asleep on the couch, surrounded by books, notebooks, and papers. He sat next to her, stroked her cheek. He jumped when she jolted awake.

"Holy shit. What time is it? How long've I been out?" Her hands scrambled through her books and papers.

"Hey, there, hey," He caught her hands.

Registering his face, his presence, Leanne relaxed, threw her arms around his neck. "You're back."

McAnrai squeezed her close, enjoying how she melted to him.

"Yes. I'm here, glad to be here, and fucking confused." He pulled her onto his lap. With a concerned smile, he said, "So start talking."

As Leanne listed out the adventures of the evening, McAnrai's features darkened. The rotting Garden Lounge, the blackened rot on the floor, Harley frying the wormy tendrils...what Anya and Laidi discovered when they deconstructed the poppet...

"Ow. Sweet man, I love your strong, strong hands, but ow."

Startled out of his reverie, McAnrai pulled his hands from her leg and waist. "I'm sorry." He rubbed where his fingers had been. "So the killer was one of the guests here tonight--"

"We think so."

"And he buried a plant and a rock in the Garden?"

"A soaked mandrake with a large piece of onyx inside it. Yes."

"And that's important because...it's a spell?"

"Oh, it's way more than that. I had to contain the energy before it was safe to carry the thing, and I still needed help. What?" Leanne paused as McAnrai's face relaxed in comprehension.

"And Remy helped you with that?"

"Yeah, he did. Once downstairs, Anya had to--" she stopped and looked at him, "--how did you know he was the one to help me?"

"Well, Leanne, don't take this the wrong way, but you absolutely stink of him."

"What? He doesn't stink." She lifted her right arm to her nose, inhaled. "I don't even smell his cologne."

"I didn't say his cologne. I said 'of him'." He smirked. "We'll take care of that later."

She grinned through her blush as she swatted him. "Brute."

McAnrai smirked, then kissed her cheek. "Go on, tell me the rest."

Leanne's voice got very quiet with the weight of Anya and Laidi's findings. "The piece of onyx isn't just a rock anymore. It's a battery, fueled by the souls of the people he murdered. Their bodies are dead, but their souls are trapped. Trapped in the onyx."

At that, McAnrai became very still, digesting the implications of her words. Finally, he said, "Now, based on what we learned at the morgue--the bodies weren't collected by the police, like we thought." McAnrai's brows furrowed in concentration. "So their souls did leave their bodies, not that we have any idea as to where those bodies are...."

Comprehension, horrified comprehension, dawned across his face. "And the onyx is contained by the mandrake, which was soaked in, among other stuff, the blood potion he used to control Brad."

Leanne nodded. "Their souls are being used as fuel, and the potion is controlling them."

"And what you're doing here," he gestured to the mess of books and papers surrounding them, "is what?"

"I'm trying to figure out what it's all for--and what to do about it. That asshole wasn't just salting our garden. Mother fucker positioned a magickal nuclear bomb at the base of our portal into the Faery Realm."

CHAPTER 28 - A MEETING OF THE MINDS

The predawn air hinted the promise of a beautiful day, hot and clear. The humidity was relatively low, and a cool breeze floated off the Chattahoochee. The night was still holding on--a midnight blue satin sheet, the millions of dazzling pinpricks fading with the morning light. The sun started to rise, and flares of pink and orange kissed the undersides of the clouds. The masses of deep pewter hung high above the horizon, forming a border between the vibrant hues reflected on the water and the silky, violet-sapphire blanket sliding into the west.

Two men walked in a pensive silence down Columbus' RiverWalk, the twenty-two mile paved walkway showcasing the beauty of the historic district against the lazy, flowing border between Georgia and Alabama. It was suited for walking or biking, and the mild weather had enticed a scattering of people to enjoy the early morning peace.

They seemed an unlikely pair, matched only in their accomplishment of careless elegance. As they walked, Lou got consistent admiring glances--his dark brown slacks fit him well, and the excellent cut of his golden shirt showcased his tanned, muscular build to magnificent effect. His appearance, finished with an easy smile, wavy blonde hair, and devil-may-care blue eyes, made a pleasing impression.

The other man wasn't any smaller, but one could mistake him for so. His age was also debatable--his apparent youth or maturity depended on the light, and on the perspective of the beholder. His dark hair was short and neat; his suit tailored in blending shades of grey and dark blue. In contrast to the welcome radiating from Lou, this man walked in subtlety, moving through shadows of his own design. So he drew fewer looks, though the ones able to find him were mesmerized by the gravitational pull of his livid-violet eyes, and the hypnotic effect of his smile.

As the lamps lining the brick trail turned off, they strolled in companionable silence. Eventually, Lou asked, "How's the wife?"

After a pause, the other man spoke. "Now why ask me that, I wonder?" His voice was soft and smooth. He took a deep breath, looked to the sky and said, "She's concerned, naturally. And there were words over it, of course, but when you've been married as long as we..."

Lou flashed a winning smile. "That's true enough." Sobering, he added, "Trouble is coming. It's nearing a level of destructive--"

An impatient gesture, an interruption, "Trouble is always coming, and thus already here. *War* is coming."

That drew a sharp look from the ordinarily cheerful eyes. "The treaties have stood a long time, my friend. And progress has been made toward equilibrium."

The other responded with a snort of derision. "*Progress*. Is that what you call it?" He pushed back the front flaps of his jacket and sunk his hands in his pants' pockets. "Letting our kind join their ranks, only to have them slaughtered? And for whom? Unbelievers? Unless we're speaking of tragic irony, that's *not* progress worth noting."

A small, yappy dog shot by them, chasing a smaller, quicker animal. The sun hid behind low-lying clouds, delaying daylight, but the sky was ripening to a bright, azure blue.

Avoiding a direction that would lead to unproductive finger-pointing, Lou switched tactics. "I saw an old friend of yours last night."

"I heard you went to the Gentry's Table. How are the girls?"

"You know that's not who I meant. And I doubt Anya and Leanne'd appreciate being referred to as 'girls'. But to answer? They're lovely. In figure, face, and manner." His eyes creased with a hint of anger, "And they're upset. It was not a wise thing for your boy to do, targeting them the way he has."

"My boy?" Thin black eyebrows arched. "He came to me for help, for guidance. To turn him away at that time would have been negligent. Or so I was told." In a quieter voice, he added, "You're not the only one with duties, responsibilities."

Seizing his opportunity, Lou said, "Dahlia looks as beautiful as ever."

Dark eyes flashed with a fierce, if fleeting, smile. "Of course she does." His expression flushed with satisfaction.

Lou continued. "Worried, though. She sees the darkness."

"She always had a gift for that." The shadows of the morning floated, caressed the ground around him. "It's been a long time since she's called on me." His soft voice held a faint note of regret. "Do you know I almost told her?"

"About her health?" Lou had *not* known that. He darted a quick glance before asking, "Why didn't you?"

His expression was almost wistful as he said, "I'd convinced myself she wasn't ready to know."

"And now?"

The walls snapped into place. "Now it doesn't matter."

The pain in his old friend's voice was evident, and Lou empathized too well with its cause. Not without compassion, he maneuvered away from the wound and pressed his original point. "As I was saying, Dahlia's worried. Deep down, she's known what he was, and is. Your influence can be of great use toward a peaceful resolution to the matter at hand."

This drew a second snort. "You know as well as I do--the Courts have made it quite clear that they will not approve my solution."

As he turned his face to the sunrise, Lou asked, "What if I told you I'm not asking on behalf of the Courts?" He smiled at the other's suspicious expression. "You may think your little pet is harmless beyond your use for him, but last night? Had I not intervened, his spell would have worked."

"Nonsense. Without my assistance, he would need his own blood to power that effort. He's far too fond of his own skin."

Recalling the events of the past twelve hours, Lou sighed and said, "What of Dahlia's vulnerability?"

The dark eyebrows arched, "If you are implying that I would endanger her, I *am* going to get angry. I have made my wishes clear. He would not dare break his *geas*." The shadows at his feet deepened as the color of his eyes swirled from their natural violet to empty blackness.

Lou held his ground, his own energy heating the surface below. Tiny spirals of steam rose from the crackling bricks as he snapped back, his voice urgent, impatient, "Do you understand so little of humanity to believe that a mere Old World taboo will be enough to curb his selfish hunger? He has killed. Over and over, often for nothing more than his own gruesome entertainment. Despite your reputation, we both know you have never embraced wantonness. You've tolerated his antics for the sake of his mother. Protected him from consequences for the sake of his mother. But no more, my friend. Now--"

Crackling bricks snapped into silent contortions as thin sheets of ice rapidly covered them. Darkness leaned into the light, their faces less than an inch apart. The chill of wintry breath crystallized the Georgian humidity, and tiny spears of ice dropped from the air between them, stabbing daggers into the brutalized walkway.

Ignoring the menacing glare, Lou continued, "And now, *now* he is meddling with Fabric. Oh yes," his voice rose at his adversary's slight start of surprise, "Yes, we *know*. Were we supposed to be impressed, when he left indiscriminate violence and started using his hobby with intent?"

At that moment, they heard an anxious cry. A girl, maybe sixteen or seventeen, was running toward them, her face contorted with urgent worry. They collected their tempers and turned their full attention to her. Subtle shadows obscured one man, as sunlight drew attention to the other.

"I'm so sorry, but my dog's gone. Have you seen her?" She was pretty, alarmingly so, with raven black hair and large eyes. Her face was flushed, evident even through the chocolate brown of her skin. "I'm sure she ran this way. I don't even know what she was chasing--she never runs away."

As though listening to the air around her rather than the words she spoke, the men exchanged a dark look. In the distance, several small clouds of smoke puffed and disappeared.

Lou reassured her. "Animals have quite the talent for finding their ways home. You'll find her there."

Her face creased in consternation. "I don't know, she's awful small." The girl's voice became filled with frustrated, frightened tears. "I don't think I could leave--"

Stepping into her field of vision and startling the girl into silence, a shadowy voice intervened. "Young miss, I assure you she's safe now. Go home. Right now."

He placed his hand on her arm, while his ageless eyes maintained a steady gaze with her young, frightened ones. As the connection held, relaxation flowed from her scalp to her feet. She swayed, lost in the inky blackness of his concentration. With a chaste caress of her cheek, he repeated, "Go home, *a stóirín*. Now."

The young beauty nodded. "I'll do that. Thank you, Mr...., Mr....?"

With the merest hint of a smile, he said, "You may call me Nate."

"Thank you, Nate." Another smile, and she left.

They watched her leave, her steps quickening as she passed a man sitting on a long, iron bench. Their attention shifted to the person whose presence made her hurry. They resumed walking, and after a few steps, were close enough to see him well. Muscular, mid-twenties, his pleasing, well-groomed appearance a slim disguise for his penchants.

With sickening focus, the man rose from the bench, his eyes tracking the girl as she headed home. He followed her--his predatory intentions naked to the ancient eyes watching him.

Lou's voice was even, direct. "I wouldn't if I were you."

The young man jumped, turned to them with a face both defensive and accusing. "Wouldn't what? Fuck off, man, I'm just going home." His clothes were far cleaner than his language, and the light tan of his complexion flushed with guilty anger. He took a few more steps.

"Now don't tell me you live that way." A peculiar light entered Lou's eyes--while no light at all reflected in those of his unnoticed friend.

"Look, man, I warned you to fuck off." He stepped closer, "But if you don't know how to do that, then I'm gonna--"

But whatever the rapist was going to do became lost in the splash of his body hitting the surface of the river, in the gurgle of its strong current. He didn't resurface.

With raised eyebrows, Lou asked, "I *would* say that was a bit of overkill, but--"

Nate returned his hands to his pockets as the two men resumed walking. "But it's just the right amount of kill." His stoic countenance almost hid the flickers of righteous anger behind his eyes. He continued, "His intentions toward that beautiful, untouched girl were unacceptable. To say nothing of habitual."

Having found a convenient outlet for their aggression, an air of camaraderie returned. Nate's satisfied expression was matched by a faint, grim upward twist to Lou's lips. The latter observed, "Our Lady always says you have a genuine understanding of violence."

A rare, but pleased, smile spread across Nate's mouth. "She does? It's a gift, that. A woman who truly understands." He took a deep, invigorating breath. "Breakfast?"

"Just coffee. I have a date."

"Of course you do." Nate smirked.

"Different kind of date. I need to ensure Fergus has the information he needs--without getting any inconvenient ideas in his head."

Nate nodded with contemplative amusement. "Young Fergus. I do like him."

"Yes, I thought he was your type."

The old friends continued to walk, each lost in his own plans for the coming days.

CHAPTER 29 - LAIDI ARE YOU OKAY?

It was well after midnight when Laidi and Anya finished in cleaning the lab. Ever the gentleman, Remy had waited, saying, "'Specially now, walkin' home alone is pretty foolish."

As Laidi and Remy walked home, she spent the entire trip fantasizing about her bed, just crawling in and passing out. So it was the strangest thing, when they opened the front door, walked in--the way she froze, didn't want to go upstairs to her place.

She could see Remy felt it too, but instead of saying anything, he said, "C'mon, *bebe*. It's not dat late, *non*. Not for us, anyways." He shot a second look from her to the steps, guessing her reluctance. "You wanna come in?"

Trying to remember how tired she was, Laidi looked up the stairs. But no. No way. She didn't want to be alone, and for some reason, she sure as hell didn't want to go upstairs. She turned to Remy. He felt so much...safer? Why would she feel safer at his place? "Yeah, sure."

She followed him in, and sat on the large sofa as Remy walked to the kitchen.

"Here you." He handed her a bottled water and walked to his media console. "Hey, I got me some--" he paused, "no, better for surprise. Get comfy, I got some home for us." After some fiddling with cases and remotes, an old rerun of Justin Wilson's cooking show started playing. "Now how's dat for--oh, *chere.*"

All at once, the enormity of the evening, the whole damn week, hit her. What should have been salve instead acted as the trigger for catharsis. Remy rushed over to the couch, put his arms around Laidi as she cried into his chest. "Naw, woman, you keep it up, you gonna make me cry, too." He patted her hair.

Her voice was muffled against his chest, but the words were clear, "You should. It'd do you good." They both laughed a little then, and when she straightened back up, when Remy wiped the tears from her cheeks, Laidi made a point of wiping the wet off of his face as well.

They held that moment--unsure of what to do next. She had known for a while that he'd wanted her--and it had taken her long enough to figure it out. Remy had always been attentive, but until recently, Laidi had never been sure if it was the hometown connection--a feeling of responsibility to look after her, or a real interest in something more. If she was going to be honest, the same could be said for her feelings. How much was genuine romantic interest, and how much was homesickness?

Sometimes, all it takes is a look. That long moment of held eye contact--it hit like a flood and washed away all confusion. It felt good to leave doubt behind, and a thrill like no other to watch his expression change when he saw her realize it. Remy let out a long, shuddering sigh, cupped her face in his hand.

But when he moved in to kiss her, she froze, pulled back. Surprised, he tilted his head and kept looking at her. Laidi pulled back, started to apologize--she felt awful, like she'd been teasing him. She ached for him, but... While she didn't know what held her back, it--whatever it was--stopped her cold.

She pushed away, but he didn't move--at all--his arm held her fast to him. "It's okay." Laidi's eyes widened as he leaned in again, but she needn't worried. Remy kissed her on her forehead, brushed her cheek with his thumb. "It's okay--*je comprends, ma mie.*"

She blinked a couple times--he wasn't mad. Maybe he did understand. She smiled and laid her head on his chest. Remy slouched into the sofa, getting comfortable, and she nestled in beside him, wrapping her arms around his waist. They fell asleep to the sound of old man Wilson's extrapolating on bayou cooking, his voice loud enough to keep them oblivious to the noises from the apartment above.

***

The sun was high when Laidi's eyes opened to beams of morning sunlight. She blinked, turned her head to the music from the bootleg DVD's menu screen. When she turned back to Remy, his eyes were open. They smiled as they became aware of their positions. Over the course of sleep, they had slid down and were now lying together on the couch. Her leg draped over his lap, leaving her almost completely on top of him. Laidi's eyes traveled up to his face, and she stared at him, weighing the pros and cons of her next move. Her heart was racing, her vague fear from earlier forgotten.

Thankful they hadn't been asleep long enough for morning breath, she moved to him. Their faces inched closer...

Other than moving his hands to rest on the small of her back, Remy remained very still, not daring to act as she made her way up to him. She could tell from his expression that what happened next was up to her--that he understood her caution, her need to make the call. Before she could overthink it, she leaned into him, covered his mouth with hers. His arms tightened around her, and she smiled through their kisses as she felt his hands travel, the care he took not to let them stray too far.

She kissed him again, and again, afraid of what would happen if she stopped, or pulled away. The intensity of the embrace rolled them to the side, and Laidi slid herself under him, wrapped her legs around his waist. Remy's eyes opened with surprise, and he paused, met her gaze. His hand slid down her slim side, and his eyes asked the question as he gently pressed their hips together.

At the pressure, Laidi's head tilted back as her legs tightened around him--a gasp of pleasure slipped from her like a song note. The sensation and sound brought a fierce grin to Remy's face, and this time he allowed himself to kiss her fully, passionately.

Though one leg still pressed hard at his side, she'd extended the other to rest a foot on the floor. Laidi caressed his face, his neck, played with his hair. Pausing between kisses, she suggested, "Upstairs. We should go--" but her words were lost in his soft groan and hard kiss. Remy's hands shook violently, held her tighter. It took all her willpower, but she managed to say again, this time with her hand pushing against his chest, "Hun, protection? Mine's upstairs."

"*Oh, remercier de le bon Dieu!*" Remy pulled himself off of her, his hands trailing on her skin, his fingers catching on bits of her clothes as she stood. Once the connection broke, he fell back on the cushion and caught his breath.

Laidi laughed as he remained seated. "Well, are you comin'?"

With a laugh of his own and a wicked smile, Remy bounced off the couch and over its back, landing on the floor just inside the door to the hall. He opened it, bowed and swept his arm outward, "*Apres vous.*"

They kissed and stumbled over each other several times on their way up the small flight, leaning on the railing and laughing. At her door, Laidi searched her pockets, finding nothing, until Remy's hand slipped up her front, keys from her front pocket pinched between his thumb and index finger. "Lookin' for dese?"

She fumbled with the keys, her concentration fighting against Remy's mouth on her neck. "Now you stop that," she breathed. As the lock gave, she turned and wrapped her arms around his neck.

"Not a chance, *chere.*" He lifted her up, and she kicked back against the door, swinging it wide. As Laidi kept her apartment spotless, and he was there enough to know the lay of the land, they could afford closed eyes on their way to her bedroom. Oblivious to everything but each other, they made their way through the once immaculate apartment, past emptied bookshelves and de-cushioned furniture. It wasn't until Remy put her down so she could leave for the bathroom, until he reached to pull back the covers, felt the rumples and feathers where a neatly made bed should be...

"Whaa?"

"What's wrong?"

Laidi pulled back the light-cancelling curtains. Bright sunshine glared on the ruins of her bed. The cover was on the floor. The pillows were ripped open, feathers everywhere. The sheets were shredded, the cuts sinking deep into the mattress, innards exposed.

They looked at the bed, then each other. Laidi's gaze slipped past him, to the violent disarray of her kitchen. "No, no, no!" She took three quick steps in that direction, set on discovering how extensive the destruction was. "Remy, leggo of me!" She struggled in his arms, but his grip was true.

"Wait, girl. Just *wait*." At the last word, he exerted an extra bit of force, pinned her to his chest, "First gotta make sure we're alone." He closed his eyes and concentrated. The anger would come, and soon, but right now, it was challenging enough to redirect his fear and the insane amount of frustrated tension, channel that energy to his Talent. He reached out, gave his ribbons free reign to explore every inch of the apartment. Satisfied at their solitude, and exponentially *un*satisfied with every other facet of his life, he opened his eyes and released Laidi.

"Sorry. I had to be sure, me."

"Yeah, I got that." Her pull away was sharp, and he flinched at it. Remy reached for his t-shirt, stretched it back over his head as he watched her leave for the kitchen. He swept the room, looking for any clue of what the hell happened here. Besides an attempt on her life, that is--he ground his teeth, fighting to control his rage. The bed was beyond repair, but the rest of her room was--just messy. Pictures knocked over, but not broken, jewelry box also askew, but whole.

"You can come outta there. Our plans for today just changed."

He flinched again and retorted, "Yeah, I got dat." He joined her in the living room. "Your pictures are fine. And your stuff. And da toilet. Just da bed is wrecked." He tried to keep the edge out of his voice, but hell. "It's what I was doin', me."

Laidi tried to smile. "Sorry I snapped."

Remy nodded, "I know." He rubbed his hands forcibly over his face. "Look, why don't you get cleaned up, ready. I'll call the police."

Laidi rolled her eyes. "Really? First of all, my place. If a call's gonna be made, I'll do it. Second," she looked around the living room, gestured to the closed, locked windows, "unless we're calling the Ministry of Magic, not much point, is there? This ain't a break-in. We're better off talking to Leanne and Anya."

Conceding her point, Remy added, "And Harley."

CHAPTER 30 – ...ARE YOU OKAY, LADY?

S leep had come to Anya but granted no rest. Her mind kept flashing to the poppet, to the fumes of poisonous magick radiating from it. She dreamt of her beloved garden, could hear the whimpers and moans from its injured population mingling with muffled screams from the onyx. Noise came in waves, and the first crescendo of sound woke her enough to look around her room.

Enough to register the black outline of a man sitting at her desk, watching her sleep.

Alarmed, she switched on her light, blinked through sleep dusted eyes--but she was alone. Calming herself, she rested her head upon her pillow. As before, she fell asleep...and immediately dreamt of painful echoes and mournful screams, seasoned with unintelligible whispers, angry and aggressive.

Once again, they rose in a violent wave, the crash of it waking her.

Once again, the silhouette of a tall man stood in her room. Now he was outlined against the window, his body at an angle to watch both her and the outside.

She turned on the lamp--but still alone.

Anya considered getting up, reading a book, but fatigue overwhelmed her, and her lids closed, almost of their own volition. Her night was a manic cycle of sleep, nightmare, startle wake, glimpses of a man in her empty room. Sighing, she resigned herself to a night of insane dreams--better to embrace it and learn, than to fight what her mind was trying to tell her. Once she solved the riddle, her brain would allow her peace.

Sleep washed over her, but this time, the hateful whispers had form. There were creatures at her windows, pecking at the glass, scratching it with their long claws. Occasionally, one would make its way past her wards, through closed windows. Once inside, the malice of its hissing echoed off the walls of her room. Anya marveled at her own detachment from fear--the nightmares should've been terrifying, but each time a flying intruder swooped in for an attack, a quick flash of light sliced through the air, through the predator, turning its flying form into a puff of smoke.

With each flash, she caught a glimpse of the sentinel in her room. Tall, fit, with curls of dark hair peeking out from under a helmet hugging his head, its fit smooth enough to be otherwise invisible. The flickering light from his blade reflected off of the silver chain-mail clinging to his broad chest, tapering at his waist.

She smiled at the humor coming from her subconscious mind. Here she was, up against a supernatural fiasco, and her brain decided to entertain her with an evening of Troy Morgan running around her bedroom, defending her like a knight from a fairy tale. When this hit her, her dreaming self almost laughed. If her mind wanted to sooth her tattered edges, couldn't she dream of him doing something else in her bedroom? Namely, in her bed?

As it often happens in dreams, when the thought hit her, it became known to Troy as well. He turned to her, smiled.

The effect of that smile almost woke her straight from her sleep. She fought the excitement--waited, hoped for him to talk.

Troy sheathed his sword and bowed. "M'lady, there is nothing I would enjoy more at this moment than to lie with you, and I am honored at your invitation. However," in a flash, the blade was drawn, spun, sliced another would-be attacker, sending it into the ether, "now is not the time. My orders are to protect you, and I must not fail at that mission."

Anya leaned back onto her pillows, disappointed in her subconscious' choice. At least it was letting her stay in her dream state, allowing her to watch the handsome knight fight a series of battles.

When dawn broke, Anya's radio alarm switched on, destroying her last vestiges of sleep by cracking her up with the lyrics: *"He's gotta be strong, and he's gotta be fast and he's gotta be fresh from the fight..."* Amused, she roused herself, her movements ragged, as though she'd not slept. Turning the music down, she considered blowing off her morning, taking it slow...but when she looked at the clock, her memory clicked. That reporter from Vanity Fair was due to arrive in fifteen minutes, and being a devout believer in Murphy's Law, she had the feeling he'd be early.

After her rushed shower, a quick glance at the clock told her she would have to bypass her usual hair and makeup routine. No one, but no one, ever saw her undone, but dammit, there was just no time. Wet hair and fresh face it was. Instead of her usual meet and greet clothes, she yanked on some pale green yoga pants and a simple t-shirt.

Anya looked at the clock. Two minutes. Leaving shoes behind, she hurried past the closed door of Leanne's bedroom, down into their private kitchen. She hated running late. She was never late. Gods, she was tired. Without pausing, she snapped her fingers to start the kettle and all but ran out into the restaurant proper.

She paused to compose herself before entering the Brugh. A quick touch to her hair reminded her it was still wet. She grimaced, but what could she do? Lou McCury was walking up the *al fresco* porch--when he saw Anya, he smiled warmly. She forgot about her hair and un-locked the door for him, greeting him with genuine gladness.

Lou apologized, "Hope you don't mind the impertinence. I fear I'm a minute or two betimes." He lifted a small paper bag from My Boulánge, "I brought pastries by way of apology."

Anya laughed and accepted his offered arm. As they walked back to the sisters' private entrance, she replied, "Not at all. I apologize for how I look this morning. I didn't sleep very well last night and overslept as a result."

"I'm sorry to hear that. I hope it will comfort you to know that you look every bit as beautiful this morning as you did last night." Though his tone was light, Anya felt sincerity in his words. As they chatted, Anya felt better. Warm pastries, lots of sugar and rich cream for the Irish breakfast tea had Anya and Lou conversing like old friends. As planned, they spoke of the wedding, the glittering guest list, the Hilton family itself. Less planned was the segue into discussions of a more personal nature.

Lou proved to be an excellent listener. His sympathetic air, the warmth of his manner, freed Anya's voice. The reserve she felt around almost everyone, even Shelby, had disappeared, utterly replaced by carefree familiarity. He disarmed her, but she felt no self-consciousness about what she was sharing. It felt to Anya as though she had waited her entire life to find someone with whom it felt so safe.

It was almost ten o'clock when they looked up from their tea and her confidences to the sound of steps descending from the living room. Leanne and McAnrai were making their plans for the day, and by the sounds of it, God bless him, Mac was going to spend it helping them clean up the mess in the Lounge, and the garden beyond..

"Sweet man, I know, but you do need that day off." Leanne's back was to the kitchen as she made her way down the steps, talking up to McAnrai as she used the rail as a guide.

"And you don't? Look, you crazy ass woman, don't worry about it. I love gardening, so don't--" McAnrai's words cut off as his eyes rested on the strange man in the kitchen.

At the sudden quiet, Leanne followed his gaze. Her eyes bypassed the man, instead focusing on her sister's appearance. Barefoot, feet up on the bench as she lounged down the full extent of it, wearing little more than pajamas and a smile.

Leanne's mouth opened to speak, but she shut it. Instead, both she and McAnrai continued into the kitchen. She turned on the coffee pot as he sat down.

"Well, good morning, you two!" Anya's voice was bright and welcoming, with no trace of her harried night. She started the introductions, "This is Lou. He was here last night, covering the dinner."

"Covering?" McAnrai's expression snapped shut.

Lou's eyes twinkled as his face creased cheerfully. "Ah yes, the famous Detective McAnrai. So glad to meet you at long last--I've heard such wonderful things." The men shook hands, and Leanne returned with the coffee.

She took a long sip of her coffee and slipped an interested glance over the man across from her. "Covering the wedding?"

He nodded. "Mostly the fal-lals surrounding it."

Anya added, "And he's known Dahlia Hilton for ages." With a mischievous glint, she said, "He's got some *stories*."

Leanne and McAnrai exchanged a quick glance. The man couldn't be much over forty--it seemed unlikely he'd be in the confidences of the grande dame. After another sip of rich, creamy coffee, McAnrai asked, "Oh? How do you know her?"

Before Lou could respond, McAnrai's phone rang. He grimaced at the name, and looked to Leanne as he answered, "Work." Grabbing his coffee as he rose, took a few paces, his attention never far from the breakfast table and its strange tableau.

Answering Leanne's gaze, Lou smiled. "Well, the Hiltons have a long history with the higher ranking members of those in my company." He took the last sip from his mug. "This was an opportunity for me to meet the whole family."

The comfort of his presence was contagious. Even Leanne felt relaxed, despite the grisly discoveries of the night before. She laughed, "With the turnout we had last night, you met the family and then some."

Lou nodded, "As you say."

From the corner, McAnrai's voice rose, "Sir, with Harris and Yeun on duty today--" as he listened to the captain's rebuttal, McAnrai's grimace became a scowl. "Yes sir. I'll be there ASAP." He shoved his phone back into the pocket of his cargo shorts, and let out a long, angry sigh. He started gathering his work gear, badge, wallet, gun from the counter.

Leanne's voice was sympathetic. "That bad?" She leaned to the island and pulled out a travel mug.

"Don't even ask." He accepted the mug with a smile and an apologetic kiss. "Sorry, babe. I'll be back as soon as I can." He disappeared through the door to the dining room.

Turning to Anya, Lou clasped her hand and said, "Well, my dear, I can't tell you the last time I've had such an enjoyable meeting. I hate to end it, but I have some unavoidable engagements today."

"Oh, that is a shame." Anya rose to join him. "Here, I'll walk you out." They walked out, arm in arm, and Leanne followed, fascinated by this interesting development.

CHAPTER 31 - IT'S NOT ALL GLAMOUR-- OH WAIT, IT IS

Columbus Police Department headquarters wasn't far from the Gentry's Table, and McAnrai was there in less than five minutes. Headquarters stood out among its surroundings on 10th--all glass and modern sleek amid the city's mill history of crumbling painted brick and railroad tracks.

Once inside, open blinds and glass walls gave McAnrai a clear view of the offices on his floor. Captain Roberson was at his desk, listening to the man sitting across from him. McAnrai recognized the mayor's brother, Payne Hilton.

Payne. Pain. Pain in his ass.

McAnrai had hoped to avoid having to interact with this particular member of Columbus royalty--at least until he could nail his ass for a plethora of shady financial dealings--but nope.

Roberson saw McAnrai, signaled him to wait.

Ten minutes and a clean desk later, McAnrai was still waiting, and growing more uncomfortable by the second. Something was wrong. Visually, there wasn't anything amiss--however, for the first time since joining the force, sitting in the precinct was making him damned uneasy.

He leaned back in his chair, called over to the desk by the window. "Hey, Yeun?"

Barbra Yeun spun around in her chair. "Oh, hey Mac." Her brow furrowed, "I didn't know you were in today?"

He rolled his eyes, "I didn't either. You know who's been in to see the Cap today?"

She looked over her shoulder at the glassed-in office. "That I know of? Only Payne Hilton."

"No one else?"

"Well, there's the guy who's waiting over there." She pointed her chin at the bench near the floor's entrance. It was empty, other than--McAnrai's eyebrows shot upward when he saw the relaxed form of the reporter who'd just breakfasted with Anya. "Hasn't been here long. Got here just before you."

McAnrai cleared his expression. He got here first? "Do you know what he wants?" Yeun shrugged. "Says he has an appointment."

"I see. Thanks." As McAnrai's gaze rested on Lou, the latter gave a matter of fact smile and a friendly wave. McAnrai nodded absently, his mind still trying to unravel the source of his own discontent.

Turning, he watched as Roberson shook hands with Hilton. The captain made a second gesture for McAnrai to wait, turned back to his desk, while the tall, grim form of the mayor's brother stalked to the exit. McAnrai stood, nodded as Hilton walked by.

Their eyes met for a moment, but in that moment, several epiphanies crystallized in McAnrai's mind.

The energetic miasma in the precinct was coming from Payne Hilton. He had Talent, and lots of it. Second, the man was exerting a good amount of energy to hide it. That wasn't surprising since, outside of New Orleans, very few people living in the Bible Belt outwardly practiced witchcraft--but it sure as hell shocked McAnrai that he could see it anyway. Which was nothing compared to its appearance--Hilton's Talent glimmered gray. And it reeked--of hate, of malice, of death. Of *specific* deaths.

McAnrai stood, frozen, not trusting himself to move, to react.

Then Payne Hilton was gone, leaving nothing but the odor of his own magickal machinations behind. McAnrai turned to follow, but Lou blocked him. The reporter's face was also wrinkled with distaste. "You're right. Some people have no business applying scent."

McAnrai's attention followed Hilton's departure, "What?"

"Your expression. You can smell him as well as I can."

The detective turned an interested face to Lou. The stench of the older man's Talent was so overwhelming to McAnrai's senses, he had no perception of any other smells in the room. And Lou could smell it? Well, maybe sickly sweet, metallic-y musky-turned-musty could be mistaken for horrible cologne worn by someone whose body chemistry clashed with it.

Lou's possible Talent was worth checking, but it could wait. Forcing a calm he didn't feel, McAnrai clipped back, "Yeah. Okay." He shifted his feet to step around the reporter. "If you don't mind, I've got to catch up with him."

Lou positioned his body to subtly block McAnrai's exit. Ignoring McAnrai's frustration, he added, "I can't place it, either. Never smelled it before last night."

"What?" McAnrai made another attempt to step around, watched the man from the corner of his eye. Feigning indifference, he asked, "Last night?"

"At the rehearsal dinner. I could smell it there but hadn't placed it to Mr. Hilton."

"Huh. Well, good talking to you." As interesting as this little discovery was, there wasn't much McAnrai could do with that information--yet.

He moved toward the exit, but before he could leave, Lou rested a firm hand on McAnrai's shoulder and whispered, "Easy there, good man. Can't do anything about him right now."

McAnrai looked at him. "You know something."

Lou looked over his shoulder, to the door behind him, his eyes tracking the path Hilton had taken. "And what I know will keep."

McAnrai's brain was working quicker by the moment. The guy could smell Hilton just as McAnrai could--which meant he did have some Talent. And the expression on his face? It didn't take a genius to interpret it--whatever information the reporter had, it was disturbing, and probably important. "What do you know about this?"

One of the rotating, desk mounted fans made its way back to blowing in their direction. As the air ruffled its way around Lou, the last wisps of Hilton's stench dissipated. Both men inhaled as the odor was replaced by the clean sweetness of new mown hay.

"Let's just say if it could wait this long, fifteen more minutes won't hurt. At any rate," the reporter jutted his chin in the direction of the Police Captain's office. "You're being summoned."

"Wait here. I'll be right back." McAnrai turned, took a deep, calming breath, and walked toward his boss' office.

Under an amused breath, Lou said, "'Wait here'. Adorable." He allowed McAnrai a few steps lead, then followed.

***

"You want me--to be *security* at the Hilton wedding?" For the love of God. Considering how he knew he'd react if put in close quarters with Hilton, McAnrai balked. For everyone's sake. "Sir--"

"Mac, before you get all fired up, you need to understand. This isn't my doing. Yes, we already have several plainclothes in attendance, but I had to pull most of the uniforms--after traffic control, they were only there for the potential tree rats, anyway."

McAnrai started to speak, but the captain stalled him with an open hand. "These past few days have been a clusterfuck of petty crime, and I need the manpower out on the street. Now, being tactful, while trying to convince that stuck-up sumbitch the safety of the city's a priority over his goddamn party?--ain't isn't as easy as it sounds. So when he said he'd settle for your presence, I took the win. Sorry, son."

"His request?". McAnrai contemplated Hilton's potential motive for this as he continued. "If he's so worried, I should be--"

"Specifically you. He's heard great things, so on and so on. And as far as days off go, you think I wanted to come in on a friggin' Saturday morning, just to be chewed out by that high-and-mighty asshole? *No.* I did not." Captain Roberson leaned back in his seat. "So go put on a penguin suit and think about the double overtime."

"Sir--" McAnrai's voice stopped at his boss' deadpan stare. "Aw, shit."

"Excuse me, if I may--?" Both officers jumped at the intrusion. McAnrai clenched his jaw as the captain ran an appraising look up and down...

"Lou McCury, and good morning to you." Lou's intrusion didn't charm the captain any more than it did McAnrai, but the senior officer had a far better public relations face. He rose and extended his hand.

"And you are," Roberson frowned. "Press, I suppose?"

"Yes, *Vanity Fair*." He extended his hand in greeting, shook with Roberson.

Roberson resumed his seat, and leaned back to cover his discomposure with his cheerful PR facade. "Ah, yes. How can I help you? Covering the wedding, I assume?"

"I'm certainly here for the wedding, but I'm far more interested in the several deaths committed with magick, and an abducted *beansidhe*."

McAnrai's jaw dropped at the plain speaking. He looked to his Captain and was doubly astonished, as the devout Baptist listened and nodded as if McCury had just said the most normal of things. Closing his mouth, McAnrai's eyes flickered between the two men. They were just talk, talk, talking away about magick and faeries, like it ain't no thing. His mouth opened again, forming silent words as they got back to "ban-cheese", as Roberson pronounced the term for the Angel of Death Cu-Sith now recuperating in Leanne's kitchen.

No words. McAnrai tried, but he had no words. He was snapped out of his reverie by Roberson saying, "Well, I'm sure Mac here would be delighted to offer you any help he can. How long will you need him?"

"Just as long as it takes to visit each crime scene." The reporter paused for an innocent smile, "It was set up for me to accompany him this morning to the sites of these alleged natural deaths. My editor was very impressed with his willingness to do that on his day off."

"Oh, yes, yes, yes. I see that right here." The captain nodded at the blank paper before him.

What. The. Fuck. The more McAnrai listened, the less he liked. His brain scrambled for sense. Obviously not a reporter, and guessing by the degree of magickal oomph required to glamour-slap the Cap into a state of amiable fugue, probably not human, either...

Before McAnrai could gather his thoughts, his captain was shaking hands with whomever--*whatever*--the fuck this guy was. Then the plan they had just agreed upon found their way into his brain...

"Oh, no, I don't think that's a very good idea, sir, I mean, I should--"

But Lou was unflappable. He piped in, "Follow up on new leads, cooperate with the press, make a family feel better. Good press for the Columbus PD is good for everyone. Seriously, Captain Roberson, look at his face. Just perfect for a magazine cover."

Ignoring McAnrai's apoplectic expression, Roberson grinned and said, "Well now, that's not a half bad idea."

***

Their brisk walk to McAnrai's vehicle, and the following drive, were spent in a combined silence of cheerful complacency and irritated suspicion. Arriving at the first murder scene, a secluded corner of Heritage Park, McAnrai put the car into park.

Doors closed, air conditioner running and no one else to listen, the detective took that moment to corner the slippery bastard. On the pretense of unbuckling his seat belt, McAnrai drew his Glock 9mm and pointed it at his passenger.

"Talk."

Lou opened his mouth to speak, but before he could, McAnrai broke in.

"You know what? I'll start. First, who the hell are you?" McAnrai paused as Lou, anticipating his next question, reached for his wallet. "And you can save that phony-ass press badge. I'm not buying it. Which means you and I are about to have a little talk about who you *really* are."

"Second, where do you get off glamour smacking my boss?" Again, Lou tried to speak. Again, McAnrai cut him off, his anger eclipsing the need for caution. "Not yet, brother. Third," Lou leaned back into his seat, resigned to the tirade. "What the hell do you know about Hilton? Besides the obvious, I mean." He took a breath and continued, "You weren't surprised by my reaction to the fucker, and I mean to know why. And--" he stopped, overwhelm swirling his brain to a less than focused state.

Pouncing on the pause, Lou volunteered, "If you're counting the implied question of my 'phony-ass badge' separately, the word you're looking for is 'fifth'."

McAnrai continued through clenched teeth. "*Fifth*, I want you to ask yourself why you think I agreed to take a liar with an unusual interest in magickal murders to a secluded pocket of Columbus on my fucking day off. And, for good measure," he leaned forward, "*sixth*, you're going to explain why I shouldn't fucking disembowel a guy like that *right now* for worming his way into the Gentrys' home, and getting Anya by herself under false pretenses."

The amusement vanished from Lou's gaze. "While I acknowledge your desire for a particular order," he winced as McAnrai shoved the gun further into his ribs, "Perhaps shortest answers first?" Interpreting a lack of spattered blood and guts as a tentative concession, he continued.

"I didn't lie about my name. Though," he grunted at the second jab, "I concede that I am neither from Vanity Fair, nor any other press. Shall I postpone that explanation until I've given the rest of the preliminary answers?"

McAnrai's eyes narrowed. But he didn't pull the trigger.

Lou sighed. "I'm here about the murder of Brad Casey, a teenager who's crime scene shows evidence of magick, but, as I said to your captain, also connects him to seven other murders mistakenly written off as natural deaths."

At this, McAnrai's eyes relaxed to their normal shape. He leaned back, taking the gun with him. But he didn't put it away. Growling, McAnrai said, "Go on."

"I apologize for the gaffe with your captain, but you may notice you're now out with me instead of watching a bunch of entitled people run around shrieking about caterers and flowers."

McAnrai moved to speak, but Lou raised a placating hand. "I know, I know. But you're not going to the wedding, either. If I may address your other questions before explaining how I know that?"

The detective responded with a steady glare.

"With regard to the Gentrys, I have a certain degree of responsibility in that quarter to ensure their safety. The killer has taken an interest in *them*, which means *I* have taken an interest in *him*."

"That just tells me you're obsessed with Leanne and Anya. Not a point in your favor, bud."

Lou continued as if McAnrai hadn't spoken. Smoothing invisible wrinkles from his shirt, he said, "Assuming your fifth and sixth questions were rhetorical--as to why you shouldn't, what was the phrase, 'fucking disembowel' me? As you may have guessed, I have several objections to that, not the least of them being the ruining of my favorite shirt, to say nothing of the damage it would to do the interior of your car."

Without waiting for a response, Lou continued in a matter-of-fact tone. "I don't know if your current state of mind will permit you to take anything on faith right now, but within the next few days, I will prove to be an excellent, even welcomed, ally in the impossible fight you have ahead of you."

Restored to his calm, but still wary, McAnrai asked, "Impossible?"

"Well, seemingly impossible. With my help, success is imminently probable."

"Oh really. Well, you've had your chance to give the short answers. I won't be going to the wedding because...?"

"Because you're needed elsewhere. The threat against Leanne and Anya--"

"Okay stop." McAnrai spoke through clenched teeth, "Once *again*, what the hell do Leanne and Anya have to do with this? Or you?"

"Detective McAnrai, Payne Hilton wasn't wearing any cologne."

"Yeah, so?" McAnrai didn't notice his slip until Lou pounced on it.

"So speaking of lies, now *you're* caught in one." Lou waited for the point to land. "You reacted to his Talent."

At this, McAnrai's eyebrows shot up. Lou nodded. "Yes, I know what Talent is. And not only could you notice his, you *recognized* it. His own magickal signature. And you know damn well what that recognition means."

The air calmed as the balance of power shifted to equilibrium. McAnrai stared, his expression teetering between incredulity and be-lief. The gun was still in his hand, but it rested in his lap as he di-gested the statement--and its implications. His mind replayed every crime scene he'd viewed or revisited over the last three days. Print on Brad. On the not-natural deaths. On the body snatcher glitter. The vomitous spewing of Hilton's Talent over the dog fighting ring. The reek in the Garden Room.

In his own precinct.

Nodding his head as the detective reached the unavoidable conclusion, Lou's voice was quiet, but absolute in its authority. "It means you're right--Payne Hilton is the murdering bastard behind this whole damned mess."

CHAPTER 32-
HEY, IT WORKED ON NORIEGA

Leanne zipped up the duffel bag on the kitchen counter and looked up when Anya walked in. Her sister had changed into more practical attire--jeans, t-shirt, work boots. With a wide, wicked grin, she said, "So, a good night, huh?."

"What?"

"Well, you've got the new roundsman under your thumb, and now an intimate little breakfast date with the sexy, charming reporter..."

"Wait, what?" Anya's smile was a little distracted, more pensive than defensive. "That's not it at all."

"Uh-huh. Here." Leanne placed a shiny piece of obsidian in Anya's hand. "Finished." Anya nodded and placed the crystal on the table, next to a new mandrake she'd prepared before finally going to bed.

Pulling out her sharpened athame, she dragged the silver blade in the same place they'd discovered the incision on the original poppet, and slid the obsidian inside. "There. Looks the same to me."

"And what about him?" Leanne asked, "Think it'll pass a closer inspection?"

"Sure do. That's most of what *my* mandrake's spell is for--I put extra emphasis on that--the illusion that it's his." Anya set the new poppet on the table. "Now, all we have to do is figure out how to help him steal it back without letting on."

Leanne nodded, "We'll deal with that later." She handed Anya a large Army duffel bag. "In the meantime, I packed us a survival kit."

Peeking inside, Anya raised an eyebrow. "Are we really going to need all of this?"

Leaving their kitchen, they approached the mural of a sad, hanging gate crowned with rotted vegetation. "I hope not." They stepped down into their once-beautiful Garden Lounge. The sickly sweet odor of rotting vegetation hung as a cloud of dank despair. Anya pulled the gloves over her hands and tossed the second pair to Leanne.

Leanne caught her pair and set them on the table next to the pile of CDs. She plugged in the first portable CD player as Anya set up the second. "I just wish we had something a little more old-school than these." Electronics were always iffy around magick, and they knew from experience that anything but the barest of devices could become frazzled within seconds of use in the vicinity of strong magick. "Tapes. Vinyl would be best."

"A crank turntable would be best." Leanne ran a compassionate hand over the drooping grapevine. "Let's start with something gentle. They've been through so much already."

Anya's eyes were sad as they swept the room. She nodded. "Yeah. I'm starting with Joe Wise." She held the discs in front of her.

Tilting her head to the side, Leanne popped a disc into her own player and said, "I've got Enya at the ready."

They pressed the play buttons. The two strains of music filled through the room. They should have clashed--but instead blended with remarkable balance. While the cheerful Catholic hymns brought with them the solid, almost tangible voice of humanity, the music from the Irish singer was as close as the sisters had ever found, mortal world-side, to the hauntingly beautiful melodies from Faery.

Joe Wise's warm baritone rose like a warm breeze from the other player. It blew through the room with the loving reassurance of a protective father. Anya's hands seemed to move of their own accord, following where the acoustic hymns chose to explore.

Enya's music flowed as water through the room. Like a mother tenderly washing the cuts and scrapes of her child, Leanne used her hands to direct the healing baths. She guided the ethereal melody through the room, allowing it to flow over the plants, down the walls.

Tears formed in the sisters' eyes as the cries of relief from the various plant life echoed through the room.

But the sounds of relief soon turned to shrieks of alarmed pain--the plants all began to swell, throb. Leanne and Anya slammed their hands over their ears, eyes squeezed shut. Fumbling to the players, they switched off the music. At the silence, the cries subsided, but the throbbing persisted.

"What the hell?" Anya looked to her sister.

The plants squirmed, continued to swell. Tiny bumps rose through the stretched surfaces, growing claws scratching to escape.

Anya grimaced in recognition.

"Oh shit." Leanne's eyes widened. She popped the Enya disc, re-placed it.

"*Olchanfae.*" Anya growled the word, suppressing the twist in her stomach as her memories replayed the last time she had encountered the small, but lethal, predators. "Why did it have to be *olchanfae*?"

Without looking, Leanne tossed a second CD to Anya.

Catching it, Anya read the label. "Boondock Saints? *Nice.*"

"Make it LOUD." Leanne's eyes darted through the room as the bulging plants sprouted emerging claws.

Their eyes met, and they exchanged a nod.

"NOW." The sisters stood back to back, weapons at the ready.

And then several things happened at once.

The music started, but instead of ringing through the air as normal sound, the melodies sunk into the Lounge itself. The blythe voices of Irish fiddles sprung from the walls, dancing in strange cooperation with the low, menacing bass guitar warning its way from the floor. As the latter came to crescendo, the songs met. Cleansing flames erupted around the periphery of the room as Mötley Crüe's '97 remix of Shout at the Devil exploded in time with the cheerful thunder of Blood of Cu Chulainn's bodhran drums.

At the music's crashing arrival, the invading enchantment responded by slamming the elegant French windows of the Lounge's outer walls shut. The glass panels suddenly riddled with spiderweb fractures, each cut bleeding the inky black substance they'd seen outlining each of the murdered bodies. The gate to the Table's dining room slammed shut and disappeared. They were trapped inside, sealed from the eyes and ears of anyone who may be near enough to help.

The bulging roots, leaves, and stems from the suffering vegetation all exploded, spewing at least two dozen purplish-black, foot-tall creatures with shiny ebony beaks and leathery wings. They flew overhead in a swarm, forming a circling net.

Standing back to back, Anya growled, "Let's do this."

As the first *olchanfae* made a diving attack, Leanne's bo staff swept through the air, sweeping several *olchanfae* in its wake. They crushed together, collapsing to the floor. Leanne stepped forward, drove the end of her staff through the pile, skewering them. They disintegrated into a pillar of rising smoke and powder, choking her as she felt claws pierce through her jeans, drawing blood. With a swat and a strike, the third attacker was gone in a cloud of smoke.

The air was thick with the poisonous dust of *olchanfae* remains, making it hard to breathe. Making it hard to *see*. Leanne could barely make out the bright blades of Anya's matching knives as they sliced through the air, dismembering and impaling as her sister ducked, swerved, spun and struck.

"Can you see how many?" Leanne shouted as best she could, but her voice choked and dry, came out as little more than a croak. She concentrated, focused on her sister while fighting off the creature clawing at her back. With her mind, she called to Anya, "How many more?"

Anya's voice sounded immediately, "Can't tell!"

Leanne felt a sharp pain engulf her left leg. When she looked down, her eyes widened in surprise. This *olchanfae* was three times the size of the others--almost waist high on her. A *mór-olchanfae*--big, evil faery. She reached down, grabbed the attacker by its neck. As she pulled, pain coursed through her body, shocking her into immobility. The faery had bitten down, its shark-like teeth sinking deep into the flesh of her upper leg. Leanne stumbled, fell back and into the table with their supplies, tipping it over. She cracked the back of her head on the floor, landing among the contents of her bag.

The pain from her leg was receding--which couldn't be a good sign. She struggled to sit and punched at the black, scaly head latched onto her thigh. The force of her fist caused it to pull back, almost tearing out a mouthful of flesh with it. She screamed, slapped her hand against the ground near her. Her hand finally landed on something useful--her own athame, its bright blade sharpened to a razor point.

Turning back to the *mór-olchanfae*, Leanne slammed the hammer side of her fist on the back of its head, shoving its mouth closer to her, causing the jaws to open wider, the teeth to withdraw. Once dislodged, she grabbed it by the throat, choking it as she flung it at the flames of music. She sent her ritual knife sailing after it, impaling the imp to the fiery wall. It exploded on contact.

While the sound of its scream was drowned out by the cacophonous melodies, the impact of its death rippled through the room like depth charge.

At that moment, the remaining *olchanfae* froze. Anya stepped forward, stabbing through the two faeries before her, floating in absolute stillness, mid-charge. They crumbled into the powdery smoke, their remains swirling through the air as the flurry of retreating faeries raced for the cracked windows. Hitting them en masse, the windows shattered, a messy exit for the horde.

With their departure, the Lounge relaxed, and the gate reappeared, reopened. Harley charged through, eyes glowing with rage. The bronze flecks in his fur flashed like chain mail in the dappled sunlight.

"You're hurt!" Anya scrambled to Leanne's prone, bleeding form. The left leg of her jeans was shredded and bloody.

After ensuring they were alone, Harley reached Leanne, looked at her leg. "Anya, leave this to me."

Nodding, Anya leaned away, watched as Harley held his front paws over the mangled flesh bleeding through the tatters of what was left of Leanne's jeans. Translucent indigo light shimmered into the wound, and the ooze turned from the crimson of Leanne's blood, to the brownish, mustardy yellow of the *mór-olchanfae's* venom.

Once freed from the influence of the numbing paralytic, Leanne could move--and feel. "Fucking *OW*." It came out, perhaps, a little louder than she intended.

"No need to shout, little one. I hear very well indeed. Now stop squirming." Harley's glamour faded from watery blue to gleaming white. The white energy field shrunk to the shape of a long, thin thread. It wove itself through Leanne's wound, stitching it shut. "I apologize for the lack of anesthetic, but you well know--"

"Yeah, heals faster without, got it. *FUCK*." Leanne mumbled a series of cathartic expletives through gritted teeth. Turning to her sister, she growled, "You wouldn't mind getting the fucking whiskey, would you? GAH!" Leanne threw her head back as the knitting finished, and knotted itself off with one last tug.

Ignoring the tirade, Anya looked at Harley. "You good with her?"

Disregarding Leanne's glare, Harley agreed, "Yes, I can handle our little princess for the moment. Get the bottle."

"Princess? Fucking really?"

"Enough sweet talk from you, darling girl. You need to rest. But before we ensure that," Harley's eyes swept the room, missing nothing. "You killed the male, but where's his mate? They always travel in pairs."

"The poppet." Leanne gritted her teeth as she pressed against the wound. Harley leapt to the overturned piece of woodwork. "Is it gone?"

Craning his neck, Harley checked the table and the floor around it. "Looks like."

"That's where she went."

Anya returned with the bottle. "Yeah, now we just have to worry about the fall out."

At that moment, three heads turned at the sound of uneven footsteps. A woman, dark brown hair, light brown eyes, medium build. Expensively dressed, in a beaten-and-bloody-chic sort of way. The bruises on her face and neck marred her young beauty.

"I'm, um, I'm here. But I'm not sure, I don't know--" she swayed on her feet. Anya rushed to help, and caught Ursula Hilton just before the youngest of the Hilton siblings collapsed, unconscious.

CHAPTER 33 - THE EMPTY DEN

M cAnrai leaned back in his chair. He spent a full ten seconds evaluating the man in the passenger seat through half-closed eyes.

"That's quite a statement."

"It is indeed. As I was trying to tell you, the threat against his family is very real. In fact, his own sister, Ursula, was violently assaulted and left for dead not ten hours ago."

"He attacked his own sister?" As a man who erred on the side of old fashioned chivalry, McAnrai was ready--had *been* ready--to tear out Hilton's throat. Now he wanted to rip the bastard limb from limb. He clenched his jaw, concentrated on the part of him that was all cop. Put that guy in charge. "That breaks pattern, for one thing."

"Are you sure about that?"

"In fairness? No." Unsatisfied, but letting it go for the moment, McAnrai asked, "What evidence do you have to prove that he's the killer?"

"That would be useful in a Mortal court? None." Lou paused, then added, "I can't even prove Ursula Hilton is dead."

"Then...?" McAnrai's look dripped with impatience. At the other's silence, he pinched the bridge of his nose.

After several tense moments, Lou suggested, "Perhaps a reference would help?"

"I already know you're connected here, so that doesn't--" He stopped talking as Lou wrote a phone number on the back of one of McAnrai's cards.

Reaching for it, McAnrai said, "I don't know what you think this is going to do for you, but--" when he read the number, he stopped abruptly. "I know this number."

"Of course you do."

McAnrai slammed the hand holding the card against his thigh. "How do *you* fucking know it?"

"Just make the call."

Thunder in his expression, McAnrai flicked the card into his cup holder and hit the speed dial on his phone. The voice on the other end was a kaleidoscope of laughter and charm. As always, she answered in Irish.

"Well, good morning, Fergus! How are you, my darling boy?"

Shaking his head, McAnrai considered his company, and decided to answer in kind. His Irish was rusty, but still fluent. "I'm well, Nana. I know this is a little sudden, but, I've had a bit of a surprise."

"Life's never dull for you, is it? What's going on?"

Shooting a look at the passenger seat, he said, "Well, you're not going to believe this, but you've been given to me as a reference."

"That *is* new." Her voice dripped with intrigue. "Okay, who's the poor bastard who needed to rope in a delicate old girl?"

"Calls himself Lou McCury. Though I have to say, I--"

Her voice snapped from play to business. "Trust him."

"Excuse me? What did you say?"

"You heard me. Trust him."

He could not believe the words coming out of his cell. "Nana, I'm going to need more than that. How do you know--"

"Fergus," He flinched at the second use of his given name, but clenched his jaw and listened, "I can't talk right now. Your Aunt Sarah and I are heading out for an early dinner."

"But, Nana, how do you--"

"Love you darling. And do what I say. Talk soon?" *Click*. The line went dead.

McAnrai turned to Lou, but before he could speak, Lou cut him off. "How about this? Give me this morning, and see where it takes us. If, by lunchtime, we're not on the same page, we'll re-address the situation?"

Unsure if he was relieved or alarmed that someone else had come to the same problematic conclusion about the murders, McAnrai contemplated the offer. Lou wasn't armed, and though he had been nothing but a series of discomforts, the detective was intrigued.

Sensing a temporary victory, Lou piped, "C'mon." He opened the car door, stepped into the hot humidity of the deserted park. "You can always shoot me later."

Grinning at the thought, McAnrai climbed out of the car.

***

The morning was quick work. At each of the visited crime scenes, the man McAnrai's grandmother vouched for went through the same, strange ritual. Heedless of McAnrai's suggested points of interest, he walked the perimeter of each scene, as though he knew where the original stretches of police tape had hung. McAnrai's initial suggestions were politely ignored, so he watched as the not-reporter walked ahead, placed his open right hand consistently on the tree or potted plant closest to where each body had been found. Each time, white mist swirled, floated over the man's open left palm, coalescing into a small white rock, which was then slipped into his front pocket. Then, without word, they were off to the next site.

McAnrai had seen enough magick in his life not to be freaked out, but there was something uncomfortable about watching this stranger effortlessly perform such a powerful spell.

Repeatedly, no less.

Happy to be spared the answering of awkward questions, the silence gave McAnrai time to ruminate.

In terms of magick, the guy was clearly a heavy hitter. That explained a few things--how he slipped past the station's reception desk, and, just maybe, gave a slight edge of believability to his claim to have a reasonable interest in Leanne and Anya's safety. Looking back, it was true neither sister had treated Lou as a stranger. As the man had disappeared while McAnrai had been gathering his things, there hadn't been a chance for them to be formally introduced.

A magickal lifestyle could also be how the guy knew Gracie O'Flanigan. McAnrai frowned. It did *not* explain her quick endorsement of the fellow. Nor her unwillingness to discuss it--early dinner with Aunt Sarah? Since his aunt was making daily Facebook posts chronicling her trip to South Africa, that was a lie unbecoming of his Nana's acumen--therefore her way of telling him to shut up.

They arrived at the last address. The one he'd been dreading--the home of Oliver Montgomery, the Samhain victim, Payne Hilton's nephew. It was now the home of single mother, Ursula Hilton. When McAnrai's knuckles hit the front door, the light impact sent it swinging inward. Clenching his jaw, he paused, then drew his gun.

"You won't need that. There isn't anyone in here but ourselves." McAnrai twitched at the voice coming from the formal living room, just right of the foyer. "Not anymore, anyway." Lou emerged from the soft lighting and pastel shades of a room that belonged in a museum exhibit designed to illustrate upscale Southern life.

"Seriously? Where, how--?" The detective's nerves were on edge, and he was finished with surprises. Exasperated, he asked, "You were right behind me. How did you--?"

Though not a direct answer, Lou continued, "There is still plenty to see." He tilted his head through the open hall leading to the kitchen. McAnrai took light steps in the indicated direction.

They stepped through the kitchen arch. The last time McAnrai'd been in this room, it had been cheerfully messy. Lived in, with evidence of cooking, baking, eating. With toys on the floor, and muddy sneakers propped against the door to the garage. It had been messy, but joyful and welcoming. And echoing with the heartbreaking sound of a young mother's anguish.

Today, it was sterile. Extravagant renovations had left it open and airy, with natural light pouring in from tall, slender French windows leading to the patio, to the emptied pool. The room didn't smell of food, or show evidence of there being any in the house. As devoid of life as the non-living room, the barren kitchen told the men everything to know about how Ursula Hilton had channeled her grief. Replacing the hand painted canisters were wine racks, and a display of Waterford glasses. Tumblers stood at the edge, acting as an introduction to the contents of the elegant, glass paneled cabinets, where behind gleaming wood and sparkling glass stood a grand assortment of bottles. Some half empty. Several with unopened replacements behind their nearly consumed counterparts.

The showcasing of Ursula's descent into alcoholism only held their attention for the seconds it took to recognize it. For all of the kitchen's well-ordered sterility, the trail of smashed knickknacks spilling from the living room spoke of violence. McAnrai nodded as Lou pointed to the drops of blood from where someone's head had clipped the wall separating the rooms. They followed the narrative of broken glass and spilled wine into what used to be the family room.

The den was still decorated in warm browns and tans. The tattered fabric of the couch cushions peeked from under blankets with large, cartoon race cars printed across them. From their arrangement, and the clumped up pillow with the pillowcase to match, it was clear they were standing in what had become Ursula's bedroom. It was cozy, well worn, its walls pathetically covered with the charming, smiling face of a little boy she hadn't seen in person in over a year. Pain threatened the barriers of McAnrai's heart--he had long since desensitized himself to the immediate aftermaths of tragedy, but he seldom revisited a home that had time to form scar tissue. They were standing in the den of a momma bear, robbed of her cub.

And it was trashed.

Each of Oliver's faces smiled at them from strange angles, their frames tilted in response to the struggle they had witnessed. Several of the boy's portraits, including a framed finger-painting of mother and son, littered the floor around the TV.

"Sweet Mother of God." McAnrai's voice was barely audible, his face desperately blank.

"Over here." Lou's voice was gentle, but commanding. He led the detective to the small area between the back of the couch and the sliding doors. The impact cracks radiated outward from a small, bloody hand-print--Ursula had tried to steady herself before falling back onto the floor.

After the events of the week, McAnrai was hardly surprised to find a human-shaped pile of sparkling white, glittering powder. Nor that he could see, without telepathic assistance, the powder was liberally mottled in murky, gray slime. He chanced a quick glance at Lou, who looked neither confused nor shocked. Just sad.

Lou ran his a through his tousled blonde hair, and squatted down next to the used-to-be-a-body. Before McAnrai could stop him, he pinched a tiny bit of unpolluted faery dust. "This is how I know about the murder, and how it can't be proven." Without touching Hilton's print, he gestured to it and added, "And how I know it's Payne Hilton."

"You can see that?" McAnrai considered a moment before shaking his head and asking, "Wait a minute. You know what's going on. What that crap is. But these bodies that, that--?" McAnrai's head started spinning with revelations, summations and questions arising from both.

"Bodies don't matter at the moment. Not from the Mortal Realm's forensic point of view." Lou stood, delicately brushing the dust from his hands. As the sparkling flecks returned to the large pile of shimmering powder, every last speck of the faery dust and Hilton grime disappeared, leaving empty floor space. "But to answer your questions. Yes, I can see the evidence of Hilton's Talent. Yes, I know roughly what's going on. And yes, I know what this substance is." He extended his hand, gesturing to the front door. "Let's talk."

CHAPTER 34 - CAN WE TALK?

As they left the living room, McAnrai pulled out his phone and reported the situation. "...home invasion, physical assault, possible kidnapping." At the last one, Lou nodded his head back and forth, as if mulling over the believability of the spin. McAnrai ignored him and gave dispatch the address.

Ending the communiqué, he turned to Lou, "They're on their way." He closed the front door behind them before they walked through the porch and onto the the sun-drenched lawn. "Now, about that responsibility of yours?"

"Master Payne has been killing for a long time. It's only been this last year, though, that he's been using magick as his weapon, targeting practitioners, witches." Lou sighed. "As long as he kept to mortal methods, Hilton was bound to be caught. You're an extremely able fellow." His simile had less smirk than the words implied. "But now?" Lou nodded to McAnrai's holstered gun, "Your means of stopping him are practically useless."

"Are you seriously saying 'your weapon, you will not need it'? Thanks, Yoda."

Lou blinked at the reference, then answered the question literally. "Not at all. You need all the weapons you can get. I'm saying that your usual mortal resources will be inadequate to this fight. Which is where I come in."

Well, it's about damn time. McAnrai waited for the explanation.

"You've been watching me all morning, no doubt wondering at my actions?"

McAnrai nodded.

"By choosing to target magickal practitioners, and by killing them on holy days, Hilton was both clever and stupid." The sun beat down on them as they walked down the steps and to McAnrai's car. "Clever, because it would get him, how do they say, 'more bang for his buck'?" At the second nod from McAnrai, Lou continued, "But stupid, since he went after people who not only had powerful friends, but attacked them on days when they'd be surrounded by those allies."

"And now, you've lost me."

Lou placed his hand on the pocket full of white rocks. "No doubt you're curious?" He took a long breath before continuing. "These are the physical remains of the faeries who've spent their, *báisteach*, their lifebloods, in exchange for stock bodies."

Stock bodies? McAnrai's mind flew to his childhood, to the stories his Nana told him about the times before faeries and humans were estranged from one another. Stories of grand love affairs and inter-marriages. Of alliances and gifts--and of sacrifices.

As comprehension spread across McAnrai's face, Lou gave a short nod of approval. "Not that I ever doubted your grandmother, but it is good to see that her efforts toward your education were not wasted."

In answer to the look *that* drew from McAnrai, he grinned and said, "I'm a little older than I look."

Oh Christ. McAnrai's first instinct was right. Lou's not a practitioner. He's a *faery*. Shaking his head, McAnrai made a choice. They could discuss *that* later. Right now, stock bodies. "Ooookay. So what we saw in there," he pointed to the house, "is the same as the stuff as in the drawers at the morgue?"

"Yes."

"So the bodies collected originally, weren't bodies at all?"

"Nope. Just glamour and dust. When the deaths of those humans became imminent, their friends," he held his hand gently against the full pocket, "gave their lives in exchange for stock bodies to replace the person getting killed."

Wait, what? "So Hilton *didn't* kill any of those people?"

"He thinks he did. He attacked, the bodies went limp, they got collected by the authorities and so on. He thinks all of his victims are dead, but that's only true in the cases where he didn't use magick."

"But those he attacked with magick, they're alive?" Excitement started coursing through McAnrai's veins. "We can save them?"

Lou's response tempered McAnrai's hope. "Yes, their bodies are in Faery, and yes, they are alive. Technically. But they are unresponsive--comatose. There was a complication." Again, he gestured to his pocket, "This glamour was used here to save lives, and save those they did. But Hilton wasn't after lives."

McAnrai's thoughts flickered back to the previous evening, what Leanne had told him. "He was after their souls."

The fury rippling from Lou hit the detective with a force both invigorating and alarming. McAnrai noted the scent of Lou's wrath--searing hot metal with a sharp stab of ozone.

"The fae sacrifices were enough to keep their human friends from death, but not to keep their souls from Hilton's grasp." He tilted his head, "Not until Brad Casey. He was a practitioner, a witch, but an unhealthy one. He didn't work for good, and though his crimes were almost always against himself, by never following the Rede--"

McAnrai interjected. "'An' it Harm None, do as thou wilt'." What little of McAnrai's childhood was spent learning actual witchcraft, The Rede was the one thing he was expected to non-negotiably understand. While violence had its place, both for the emergencies of self defense and defense of others, when performing any other magick, harming none--not even oneself--was the most hard and fast rule of the entire lifestyle. A rule that, if broken, had dire repercussions.

"Just so. As he didn't follow that, natural consequences ensued. He had no friends, no allies, no help. Until--"

"Until Leanne."

"Right. The Lounge did its part in protecting the Gentrys. Brad as well, for that matter. It called, invited him in, thus distracting him from planting the poppet."

"He dropped it in the Lounge, instead of burying it in the garden." McAnrai nodded. "And the food she served him kept him hidden from Hilton. At first, anyway." Just like Leanne had said.

Lou corrected him. "Oh, it did more than that. It kept him safe from harm." In response to McAnrai's look, he added, "It kept him safe from the *greater* harm. If he'd internalized the entire spell by finishing the water as well? Stayed in the Lounge, eaten more, who knows?"

"The greater harm?"

"Hilton's pull, the power of his efforts, was strong enough to keep Brad's soul from moving on, but couldn't rob him of it. That is what

Leanne's spell did; she kept Brad's soul out of Hilton's grasp, thus it was still there so she and Anya could release it."

"But that body won't turn to faery dust?"

"Correct. Brad is dead. But for the intents of Hilton's plan, the timing was off, the poppet was out of place, and when Hilton tried to harness his soul, he was foiled by Leanne's spell. That, plus his recognition of Leanne's Talent on the boy?" He raised his hands, exposing his palms in a gesture of 'well, there you have it'. "Hence his rage."

McAnrai's mind flashed to the note Shelby had shown him, and bit back the fury. He took a deep breath, exhaled slowly. Forcing calm. he asked, "So if Ursula's stock-body-switch only happened last night, and that replacement has already turned to faery dust, why did the other bodies last long enough to be collected and transported to the morgue? Even long enough to have autopsies performed?"

Lou smiled at the question. "Level of expertise and intent. In the days when faeries and humans had a more comfortable relationship, it wasn't uncommon for humans to be taken into Faery. It was often done by the grace of a befriended nature guardian, a flower sprite or a sylph, but could also occur without the human's knowledge or lucid consent."

"Being faery-led." McAnrai's mind flickered over childhood stories of people stepping into faery rings, or disappearing near the enchanted mounds, never to be seen again.

"Exactly. Bringing humans to live in Faery is a long practice, and the process of doing so discreetly has been consistent, overall. The exchanges for Hilton's magickally committed murders? For the most part, those spells acted as they always did--body switch, facade maintained until human attention ceases."

"And all of them were willing to give their lives so their human friends can live in Faery? No offence, but that doesn't sound like typical faery MO."

"Because it has never happened until now. Under normal circumstances, performing this glamour would weaken its caster, but only temporarily. These faeries," he patted his pocket, "died because they weren't merely helping a human escape into another realm. Those gentle beings were playing a spiritual tug-of-war, competing in a challenge they didn't expect."

"And lost."

"Lost their lives, yes. But their sacrifices ensured us the chance both to bring those people back, and to thwart his larger plan."

"All of this still doesn't explain why Ursula's body, or her not-body, deteriorated faster."

Lou's expression was inscrutable. "Ursula's switch was done by one who has no use for secrecy."

"*Has* no use? I thought they all died."

Lou flashed a fierce smile. "To Ursula's savior, Hilton's Talent is no more than a collection of cheap parlor tricks."

Oh sweet Jesus. McAnrai's thoughts came to an abrupt halt. "So beyond Hilton, we're also up against a being who is not only powerful enough to survive against magick poisonous enough to kill faeries, but can bend an ancient glamour to its own preferences?"

Smiling, Lou corrected him. "No, you're *allied* with a being who is powerful enough to be completely unaffected by a human's best efforts, and can bend an ancient glamour to his own preferences." Lou lightly tapped McAnrai's shoulder with his fist, "You should take some comfort in that."

"Well, I don't." Another question popped from the back of his mind. "How did Hilton recognize Leanne's print?"

Raising one finger to punctuate the correction, Lou said, "While she had never been face to face with Hilton, in her childhood, Leanne interfered with something enormously important to him."

"When she freed Harley." Uncharacteristically, McAnrai found himself speaking openly with the man who, until a few moments ago, had been nothing more than a progression from annoyance, to potential threat, then intrigue. He was beginning to understand the effect of the faery's personality. Eliciting comfort in Anya, acceptance from Leanne, and absolute faith from his grandmother--and here *he* was, speaking freely--with someone he barely knew--about magick, about faeries. Shit--about his *job*, complete with details from his caseload.

Lou nodded with satisfaction. "Leanne dealt him a devastating blow that day."

"How so?"

"Harley was intended as a sacrifice. The torture and execution of such a powerful faery--oh yes," Lou paused at McAnrai's expression, "The Harlequin is far greater than you know. His execution would have produced an extraordinary amount of force. That assumption also fits with what we have here--" He let his head tilt back and forth, as though weighing information, calculating formulas. "The souls of eight humans, sacrificed on holy days? If the victims were powerful witches, that could come close enough to the impact from sacrificing a faery of Harley's stature."

"Sacrifice? But isn't that more for worship? And if so, who the hell was he worshiping?" Great. All he needed was to have his first pagan god meet-and-greet to be with the blood sacrifice-demanding type.

Accurately interpreting McAnrai's expression, Lou grinned. "I wouldn't worry about that. Payne Hilton has never known what it means to worship. The attempted sacrifice was intended for his own benefit."

"And that is?" McAnrai grimaced, "Killing animals and peo-ple--just for the sake of killing--doesn't help a person."

"I'll give you, there are other methods that are far more effective." Lou nodded. "But, if done properly, violence can be used to enormous ends." Lou added, "You, of all people, know that."

McAnrai's eyes dropped at the truth of those words.

Lou pulled out his pocket watch and held it for McAnrai to see. "Our morning together has elapsed, and I await your decree. Am I well enough in your good graces for us to continue our collaboration?"

The two looked up at the crunch of tires on gravel. As the cruisers pulled into the long, crescent driveway, it was McAnrai's turn to ig-nore a question, allowing his duties to save him from giving a quick response.

Once back in his car, McAnrai turned to Lou and spoke with prudent calculation. "Obviously, you know a thing or two, and have more information than should be running loose."

Leaning back as he started the ignition, McAnrai sighed, "And I guess it doesn't hurt to have as many friends as possible." And having a faery indebted to him could be a very good thing one day. He adjusted the volume on his radio, planning for the music to provide a cushion of space between them. "Easier than getting rid of you, I imagine." He pressed his preset station buttons, one after the other, only to find static--even on the satellite radio.

"You're too kind." With as much of a bow as his seat belt allowed, Lou added, "If I may?" At the random twist to the tuner dial, music erupted from the speakers.

Whoa, we're halfway the-ere...whoa-OH livin' on a prayer...

McAnrai rolled his eyes with an exasperated exhale. *Seriously?*

CHAPTER 35 – CURBING PAYNE

Twenty minutes later, the dark car pulled to the curb, two blocks from the majestic edifice of Columbus' First Baptist Church. Between the local politics, the Hollywood element, and the guests themselves, they weren't getting any closer. McAnrai clicked the doors unlocked, and Lou stepped onto the white-hot sidewalk.

McAnrai leaned over to look out the passenger window. "You sure you wanna be here? Doubtful this kind of congregation welcomes your type."

Lou beamed with approval. "Well done, detective." His grin spread to the crinkling of his eyes as he leaned down to speak through the open window. "Not to worry. People only dislike my kind when they recognize us. Which is seldom, these days. But I like how you think." He gave the sill of the door a brisk tap. "And don't worry about leaving. I can handle Hilton."

For the first time since meeting him, McAnrai felt a genuine flow of warmth toward Lou. With a nod of thanks, he put the car back into drive and said, "I supposed I'll be seeing you...?"

"When next I am needed. We Celts take care of our own."

For some reason, those words sent a chill down McAnrai's spine.

"And now I've answered your question regarding my interest in the Gentrys, and in you, for that matter." Mischief danced in Lou's eyes as he walked away, "Farewell for now, Master Fergus. See you soon."

Immediately cured of the brief warmth, McAnrai snapped his attention back to the passenger window, but Lou was gone. "Seriously?" He pulled into traffic, turning in the direction of the active crime scene at Ursula Hilton's home.

***

The ceremony had been brief, and pleasantly lacking in brimstone. Now at the reception, with formal pictures completed, Lou watched the guests mingle as they sipped sweet tea and nibbled delicacies. His gaze rested on Mayor Shetland, a woman clearly divided between her diplomatic duties as mayor and hostess, and cheerful behavior toward her daughter and new son-in-law, while the worry for her sister undermined her ability to do either believably.

His eyes traveled the expanse of glittering dresses and charcoal morning suits, and found Payne Hilton. With grim amusement, Lou made his way over.

"Not too pleased with your head count, I see."

Payne Hilton took a moment to collect himself before turning toward the unwelcome observer.

Lou continued. "Oh, I wouldn't be so hard on Detective McAnrai." His affable tone was belied by the chill in its delivery. "The lad's hard at work on your sister's behalf. Surely you don't object to his priorities?"

Hilton bristled. "I don't believe we've been formally introduced." His voice was saturated with the full command of his Talent.

The directive rolled off its target. To highlight the miss, Lou brushed imaginary dust off of his sleeve. "Oh, my name wouldn't impress you anyway. You couldn't possibly object to--"

Hilton rushed into speech. "I object to being ignored, to having an arrogant, glorified *thug* defy his orders by--"

"Get used to it." Lou's voice cut as an icy blade through Hilton's speech. "I was quite justified in sending him on his way."

Hilton's eyes flashed. "What do you mean by that?"

"Come now, Payne. We both know how," he paused, "*unorthodox* your ideas about familial relations are."

"What did you call me?"

"Your name, you insufferable ass." Lou took that moment to enjoy watching the blood rise in the taller man's face, deep crimson flushing through the salt and pepper beard.

Hilton's voice shook with fury as his words flew out in a harsh whisper. "How dare you speak to me in this way?" His voice lowered as he loomed over Lou, "I will--"

"*You* will enjoy these last happy hours of revelry with your family." Lou's voice was firm.

The frigidity of Lou's voice slapped Hilton to a surprised silence. He looked down his long, straight nose and asked, "Last?"

"For most people, loss of a family member is a source of sorrow. Right now, your sister there," Lou's scotch tilted in the direction of Mayor Shetland, whose expression was a rotating motley of politic aplomb, worry, and fear, "is putting on a good face for her daughter. Who, in turn, is pretending as hard as she can to not worry about the whereabouts of her young aunt. While you are whining," a mean smile crept across Lou's face, "over someone proving to be the better man."

Hilton's checked rage oozed into his words. "I do not tolerate such insolence, not from you, or--"

"Oh Payne, do be quiet." Dahlia Hilton had made her approach subtly, and her arrival startled her son. She took Payne's arm, and turned to Lou. "Now don't pay any attention to him." Looking up at her son, she said, "Run along now. And behave yourself."

Hilton's face transformed to a horribly serene facade. "Certainly, Mother." He nodded to her. Ignoring Lou, he strode off.

Once he was out of sight, Dahlia let out a long, sad exhale. With a quick glimpse at Lou, she asked, "My daughter?"

"Is safe. For now."

"Thank you." Blinking back tears, she whispered, "He's never going to stop, is he?"

Lou's eyes were still on Dahlia's son. "No."

"I didn't want to believe it of him." Steeling herself to ask, Dahlia closed her eyes. "What are you going to do?"

Gentle pity washed over Lou's face. "A great deal of that depends on you, Dahlia. You know that."

***

The text alert on McAnrai's phone sounded, and he snatched it: Remy.

<Entre nous> Laidi's place has been ransacked. She's okay. I think it's the Other Crowd. I'm sticking with her until further notice.

Holy shit. McAnrai considered calling--but clearly Remy couldn't talk.

WTF? Get out of there. Go to Leanne and Anya. Tell them everything. I'll be there ASAP.

McAnrai shook his head--one supernatural-friendly cop in the whole fucking town. Muttering to himself, he wove through the traffic. "Shit, I need to figure out how to recruit some guys into this clusterfuck. I need some goddamn backup."

The coincidental comedy beat of Remy's text reply elicited a short laugh from McAnrai.

Ya fuckin' think?

He'd driven barely a block when his phone rang. What now? But this time it was Leanne.

"Hey babe."

Bypassing any kind of greeting, her voice was terse. "You want to get over here."

"Right now? I'm headed for a crime scene. Related to the mess we're in."

"Crime scene?"

"Ursula Hilton has gone missing, and the official report is that she's less missing and more murdered."

"Well, *a ghrá*, then you definitely want to stop by." There was a pause as McAnrai heard a mixture of other voices speaking in the background, one calm, the other... "'Cause Ursula is here right now, and she might be a little swirly in the head, but she's pretty spry for a dead woman." The noise from Leanne's end rose to a crashing cacophony and she hastily added, "Um, I gotta go. See you soon?" Leanne ended the call, but not before the sound of breaking glass and hysterical sobbing blasted through the connection.

McAnrai stared at the blank screen on his phone for a full second before he dropped it into the passenger seat. Flashing his blue lights to make an abrupt u-turn, a grim laugh escaped him--he was leaving the forensic unit to figure out what they could, while he left to interview the would-be victim.

CHAPTER 36 - BLOOD WILL TELL

When McAnrai arrived at the Table, Harley met him on the front porch. The Cait-Sith tilted his head toward the gardens and said, "This way."

When they entered the sunlight of the Gentrys' private garden, McAnrai could hear the blend of country-meets-reggae beach music coming from the back of the house.

"Jimmy Buffett?"

Harley's voice as his form disappeared. "A quick injection of positive energy. Master Buffett makes some of the most cheerful choices available in the modern era."

When he turned to face the building, McAnrai stopped short--stunned by the view. The vast wall of glass was riddled with shattered, jagged edges, the Lounge's garden doors almost indiscernible. Shocked, his eyes explored the garden itself. What was left of it, anyway.

McAnrai's hand covered his mouth as he took in the surroundings. The ground immediately surrounding the Garden Lounge was cleared of any vegetation, leaving mounds of overturned soil behind. He looked at the latticework wrapped around the side walls and roof of the glassed in room--also stripped clean.

An expanse of bare, loose dirt stopped just short of Anya's prized pear trees. Under those trees, but beyond the reach of their shade, was Anya's reclining form.

Turning at the footsteps behind him, McAnrai's eyes widened in alarm as Leanne limped over to him. Eying the blood soaked jeans around the bandage, he fought to keep from growling as he asked, "What happened?"

Leanne kissed him on the shoulder, but instead of answering, turned to Anya and said, "Sleeping like a baby."

Anya nodded once, rested back in her lawnchair. Leanne turned her attention back to McAnrai.

"I guess I should start with the failed clean up attempt."

"How about you start with the leg?" McAnrai's voice was soft.

Waving aside his offered arm, Leanne smiled softly and said, "Later. It's fine."

McAnrai was unswayed. "That's a lot of blood."

"And Harley took care of it. C'mon." Leanne made her slow way past McAnrai, and gestured for him to follow her to one of the openings in the glass wall.

When they entered the Garden Lounge, McAnrai caught his breath. The beautiful room had also been stripped to its bones. The furniture was gone, pitifully replaced by the long cushion from the bench of their breakfast nook. Lying on it was the sleeping form of a woman, not so tiny as her mother, but not so tall as her sister, the mayor. Ursula Hilton's long, dark hair was messy, but arranged as well as possible over her shoulders. Her expression was peaceful, but the bruises on her neck and across the right side of her face bloomed in grisly shades of blue and purple. She and the mattress were enclosed in the golden shimmer of Anya's protection spell.

McAnrai moved to approach her, but Leanne held his arm. "She's not going to wake--not soon, anyway."

McAnrai ran both hands up and down the front of his face. "Do you mean to tell me, on top of everything *else*, *now* we've got a stolen page from the freakin' *Grimms*, and we're dealing with Sleeping-fuck-ing-Beauty?"

Leanne smiled. "Not so bad as that, thank the Goddess." They strolled over the steps leading to the garden, and sat in the sun. "Anya gave her something to help her sleep. The woman was hysterical."

She extended her arms to show him her own scratch marks. "And all we did was offer to call the police, or her family. Take her home."

McAnrai nodded his head. "Well, that would do it." He relayed the story of *his* morning.

Disgust washed over Leanne. She leaned forward, put her head between her knees. "Sweet Jesus. I feel like I'm going to be sick."

McAnrai cleared his throat. "So, besides the top secret nature of your mauling, how was your day?" He pointedly looked at the length of the Garden Lounge. "Looks like you've been cleaning house."

Leanne took a long breath. "That bomb I told you about?"

Cautiously, he said, "The one you said was neutralized? Yes."

"Well, we contained it, yes. But we couldn't undo the damage it caused before Laidi found it."

"In the Lounge, you mean? That's why you shut it down?"

"I wish it were that simple." Leanne's voice was calm, but her own anger and fear seeped into it as she explained. "It wasn't only a bomb, or a battery." She looked around the skeleton that used to be their

Garden Lounge. "Last night, when we first got in here and looked around, it was like a swarm of locusts had made a pit stop--but only staying long enough to do damage."

"Yeah, I saw the room before I came up."

"This morning we realized they weren't insects, so the sustained damage wasn't the regular kind."

"Then what did all of this?"

"Now we're getting to my leg." She recounted the disastrous effect of the first music, the ensuing battle, Ursula's arrival--but her voice choked when she started to describe the aftermath. "Well, we threw out the furniture, and had to rip out the plants." Her voice caught, but she continued. "It's like the plants were begging us to do it. To end them. So we..." She wiped her eyes, sat up a little straighter. "We did. It was awful."

He slipped his arm around her shoulder and kissed her forehead. "Go on, babe."

"They were sick. Poisoned. It *poisoned* them all."

"The rock poisoned the plants?"

Leanne shook her head, but it was Anya who answered. "The spell cast on the poppet. The onyx was just the power source." Her lip twisted in disgust as she added, "Our plants were being used as hosts."

"Hosts?" McAnrai hoped he didn't know what she meant by that.

Leanne continued, "Initially--take a look around--it was a poison pill. *And* it was some sort of twisted homing beacon, calling every nasty fucker in the vicinity to visit. And *then* it was to act as a bomb."

"Excuse me. Homing beacon?"

Gesturing with a sweep of her arm, Leanne said, "*Olchanfae.*"

Oh holy shit. *Olchanfae.* Irish for Evil Faeries. McAnrai remembered how his uncle had loved to terrorize him with bedtime stories about those things. And now, Hilton had taken the liberty of inviting a bunch of goddamn hate mongering faeries into the heart of downtown Columbus. No wonder petty crime had taken off this week.

"How many?"

"This morning? Only a couple dozen."

"Only." He pointed in Anya's direction. "And the sunbathing?"

"The fight, and then putting Ursula to sleep, took a lot out of us, and especially Anya. So we're recharging--sun is the quickest way." She wiped her face with the hem of her shirt as her thoughts traveled back to the most dysfunctional family since the Goebbels.

"He tried to kill his own *sister*?"

"He *actually* killed her son."

"And you can't prove a goddamn thing."

With a long, slow exhale, McAnrai sighed as he listened to the lyrics floating around him. "We'll burn that bridge when we come to it."

McAnrai and Leanne turned at the noise of footsteps approaching from around the side. Leanne rose, limped over to Laidi and Anya. Remy sat next to McAnrai, and handed him a beer.

They exchanged a look of commiseration, and clicked glasses. "So here's to a shitty morning?"

Remy let out a short, sharp exhale in agreement, took another draw from the bottle as he looked around the gutted room. "Ah man, you got *no* idea." Remy tilted his bottle up, gulped down a good third of the bottle in that first swallow. "Don't know how you do it, Mac. I wanna' fuckin' kill someone, me."

"Honestly, I spend a lot of time thinking the same thing."

Remy snorted. "Looks like dere was some trouble here too, yeah?"

McAnrai nodded as he drank. When Remy's eyes stopped at Leanne, he asked, "An' what about her leg?"

McAnrai told him.

Forcing calm, Remy asked, "How about Anya? How'd her night go?"

"She was talking about having weird dreams. Like all night battles type of dreams. Not sure, but--"

"But she wasn't dreamin', was she?"

"I don't think so--not after what you told me about Laidi's place." After a thought, McAnrai added, "Nothing like that happened in Leanne's room."

"Nor by my place. Which means dose two girls were targeted." Remy tilted his head as he frowned. "For dissectin' dat poppet?"

"That's where I'd lay my money."

"So dese fuckers not only knew Laidi and Anya worked on it, but also dat Leanne and I didn't." He worked his thumbnail against the paper on the beer bottle, tiny, ribbony shreds peeling off under the pressure. "*And* where dey live, which rooms, even."

"Looks like."

They spent a minute drinking their beers, processing the implications.

"So. An *olchanfae* spy, or spies, took notes, reported to a shot-caller."

McAnrai nodded in agreement. "Who sent a squad of hit-faeries." His voice was tight with controlled rage. "Timing wise, they must've hit Laidi's place first--if Anya's 'dreams' didn't start until later."

"Not if it was two groups, hittin' at once. Must've been waitin' for her when we got home. We felt it, Laidi and me." In a quieter voice, he added, "I guess dat's why she didn't want to go upstairs."

The detective shot a quick glance at ... *Oh...*

"Oh dude, that sucks." McAnrai knew sympathy would just sound like blown sunshine. Instead, he worked the bottom line. "That instinct saved her life. I'd call it a good thing she had somewhere safe to go, somewhere she was happy to be."

"Yeah, I guess." Remy's jaw muscle worked as he watched Laidi, Leanne, and Anya reach the same conclusions.

Remy became very still as he watched McAnrai from the corner of his eye. After a pause, he said, "So here's an interesting question."

"Yeah?"

"Is it still murder to kill faeries who look like people?"

A small, grim smile played at the corners of McAnrai's mouth. "Can't murder something not legally recognized as real."

"Good." Remy finished his beer and stood. "And what about dat *fauyk*, Hilton?"

"Unfortunately, he's human enough to matter."

Remy grimaced as he rose, walked toward the kitchen. He called over his shoulder, "One more?"

"Might as well bring a bucket."

Once Remy was out of earshot, McAnrai added, "Matter to the legal system, anyway."

CHAPTER 37 - HANGING BY A THREAD

As Remy's steps faded, the hairs on the back of McAnrai's neck suddenly stood on edge. He turned to face... the Portal.... then the noise started...the ethereal music that ordinarily heralded its opening was replaced by a mess of off key notes in minor chords. He jumped to his feet and asked no one in particular, "You expecting anyone?"

Anya answered, her eyes narrowed with suspicion. "No. I put the word out we'd be closed for a while."

Leanne grumbled, "This can't be good."

The noise from was not the usual combination of merrymaking and sociable chatter. Instead, they heard the muffled noises of clanging of swords crashing against battle cries. Laidi and Anya started toward the Portal, Leanne limping behind.

All eyes focused on the Portal. The metal veins marbling the stonework were vibrating, shivering. The ornate doors rattled, though not quite enough to loosen the hinges--yet.

"What fresh hell is this?" Leanne looked from McAnrai to Anya to Laidi, each of whom responded with an assortment of shrugs and head shakes, eyes focused on the open Portal. McAnrai started toward the noise, drawing his Glock.

Eyes widened as the vines framing the Portal rapidly dried, blackened, crackled, turned to dust. The drying rot spread outward as the double doors shook harder, then vomited smoke as they burst open .

Smoke billowed from small fires scattered across the wide, rolling fields of Faery. Swarming above flames and through clouds of smoke were hundreds of *olchanfae*.

McAnrai holstered his gun, grabbed one of the Portal doors, yelling, "We have to close it!"

At the sound of his voice, the noise from the battle ceased as the combatants in Faery became absolutely still. In exact synchronization, each being turned to the now-open Portal.

"Oh. Shit." Leanne pushed through the pain to help McAnrai with the door, but her leg screamed in protest.

The lines of *olchanfae* cheered at their successful breach, and charged toward the Portal. In response, a portion of the defending warriors scrambled to protect the now-open Portal to the Mortal Realm.

Laidi and Anya grunted as they threw their weight against the other door. Almost to closing... pushing... straining... almost there...

With a mighty crash, the doors once again swung outward, flinging all four of them onto the lawn as the huge *mór-olchanfae* burst through and into the open air of the Gentrys' private garden.

The *mór-olchanfae* threw its grotesque head back, roaring in triumph as it flew in a tight circle over the bodies on the ground. On the other side of the Portal, the battle raged on, with more and more *olchanfae* slipping past the *carafae* blocking access to the Portal.

The onslaught was met by several deep, sonorous barks. Leanne turned to see Ripley ambling toward them, Harley at his side. The Cait-Sith cut a swath through the *olchanfae* swarm, creating a space for *beansidhe* to lean back, open his mouth, and his voice boomed into the air.

The force from Ripley's howl knocked several of the airborne assailants back through the Portal, into Faery.

He took a deep breath and called again...

The second was weaker, and the remaining attackers thudded to the ground, disoriented, but only temporarily thwarted by Ripley's efforts. Harley's movements were hard to track, evident only by flashes of his brass armor.

The air was thick with *olchanfae* remains, but more kept pouring through.

Exhausted from the exertion, Ripley's third attempt was faint, and he collapsed as Anya reached him, letting out a soft howl as he did.

The howl was answered by a distant baying.

Then a second call...the baying closer...

Battle cries from Faery drew their attention back to the main skirmish.

Leanne's leg refused to move. She squeezed her eyes through the pain, and blinked as she looked up. Paralyzed by pain, she watched the *mór-olchanfae* swoop through the air. Closer and closer, with more joining it by the second. She saw it focus its gaze on her. Its mouth opened wide, exposing rows of needle sharp teeth.

"Shit!" McAnrai brought the barrel of his gun to sight, and shot into the air. His aim was excellent, but the faery was faster. The bullet ended the three *olchanfae* behind it, and he lost the *mór-olchanfae* in the haze of their smokey remains. That moment cost him, as the faery had swept around him, ramming him from behind. McAnrai rolled with the momentum, then bounced up to his feet, sights trained on the *mór-olchanfae* circling over Leanne.

The baying sounded again, closer...

Before he got a second shot off, an enormous, golden wolfhound leapt in between the open Portal and the dive bombing *olchanfae*. Her chest expanded as her mouth opened, and when she threw her head back, the sonic boom of her voice shook the ground, the Portal, the very air around them. At the noise, the *mór-olchanfae* exploded, nasty little bits of it falling in ashy flakes on the ground around them. The remaining *olchanfae* scattered as the golden hound leapt through the struggling Portal.

McAnrai threw his body over Leanne, shielding her from the fallout as best he could, instinctively trusting the motives of the heavy footsteps rushing toward them.

When he looked up, McAnrai saw Remy raise his arms, his power channeled into glowing, orange-red ribbons burst from his hands. The fiery energy swirled in the air, spiraling toward the Portal's crumbling filigree. As Remy stepped closer to the Portal, his ribbons fastened to the edges of the it. Then they entwined, insinuated themselves into the stonework, the Portal stilled, settled...the doors closed as he pressed his hands flat against the closed doors.

Shaking, Remy held fast...

Until the strain of maintaining the integrity of an interdimensional Portal proved more than one young mortal could handle. Remy's powerful frame dropped to the ground just as Laidi reached him. The remnants of his spellwork remained for a few seconds, but as he lost consciousness, the ribbons faded, along with the stability they provided.

The Portal trembled, threatened a second unraveling...

BANG

The Portal went nova, briefly blinding them all. When their vision blinked back to functional, they watched, amazed as the silver and gold strands of the threshold, rather than regaining their original form of elegant filigree, wove themselves into a tight rope. The rope sharpened itself at one end, its razor edge acting as a threaded needle, stabbing through the air around them, disappearing, reappearing, leaving sections of itself visible as it did so.

In a matter of seconds, their quaint doorway into Faery was now entirely golden--whether gilded or solid, they couldn't tell and didn't care. It was stable, but impenetrable. Confused, they all looked around for the source of the transformation.

Lou McCury walked to them, and with each step, the faint haze of a golden aura faded to nothing as the metallic sheen of his eyes returned to clear blue.

In answer to the eyes upon him, Lou shrugged and said, "Like I told the good detective, I have a knack for showing up when I'm needed."

Lou's eyes scanned the scenery. Anya ministering to an unconscious Ripley, and Harley unharmed from his corner of the fight. To Leanne and McAnrai, one still bleeding, the other just angry. He walked to Remy's prone form and squatted down. After a few moments, Laidi turned to Lou and asked, "He'll be all right, won't he?"

Lou's nod was untroubled. "Yes. He's in excellent physical health. The young man is powerful, but I'm guessing he does not often make this kind of magickal exertion?"

"None of us has, until recently." Leanne rubbed her temples as Lou crouched to her level and pressed his hands against the reopened gash on her leg. "This might be a restaurant with mystical benefits, but it's not like we're running some sort of magickal boot camp."

Lou looked at her and murmured, "Are you sure about that?"

Quickly turning to him, she asked, "What do you mean?"

"What if I told you," Lou's expression was serious, but his eyes twinkled, "you are?"

CHAPTER 38 – COMFORT FOODS AND UNCOMFORTABL[E] TRUTHS

Anya leaned back in her seat, sighing as she rattled the ice in her almost-empty whiskey tumbler. The day had been a series of minor catastrophes topped with a trainwreck, and the effect of skipping lunch in exchange for emotionally traumatizing garden-gutting, hysterical woman wrangling, and supernatural warfare had caught up with her.

She looked around the indoor side of the Brugh, taking a mental inventory. Lou had carried Remy to the upstairs couch while McAnrai settled Ripley into the kitchen. The *beansidhe* himself was in a deep slumber with Sugar cradled between his jaw and his front legs.

A few minutes after McAnrai joined them, Lou entered the room. Taking the bottle from the bar counter, he refilled each glass before sitting, answering the silence as he did. "Each will sleep until their strength returns."

Leanne was nestled in the loveseat with Mac, his arm around her shoulders and Harley asleep on her lap. Anya looked from her sister's rapidly healing leg to the *Vanity Fair* reporter whose hobbies apparently extended to interdimensional architectural alchemy and whose knack for magickal triage amped Harley's ministering. She cocked her head to the side and asked, "You're a...healer, then?"

"Among other things."

Uh huh.

Since the doors connecting the Brugh to the kitchen were propped open, Anya had a clear view of the activities therein. She watched as Laidi bustled around the Table's kitchen, reflecting on her friend's comparable day. Trashed apartment, seeing her friends banged up, and her home away from home wrecked harder--Laidi had a lot of stress to work out of her system. Refusing any help beyond letting Anya set the table, she had set straight to her favorite coping strategy--making a delicious, if eclectic, assortment of foods--"comfort fusion", she called it.

Some sauteed shrimp with garlicky butter and wilted arugula, baked macaroni and cheese, blackened steak with loaded mashed potatoes later, and everyone would be feeling better--or at least full.

***

Once their physical needs were met, curiosity regained control of the room. Each person had taken a turn serving their pieces of the information pie, and as McAnrai finished his part of the tale, the story naturally flowed into the role Lou had played thus far.

When Lou started speaking about tears in the Fabric of Existence, Laidi interjected. "Say that again? Tears? Fabric?"

At her question, Lou looked up from his grilled peach and praline bacon salad. Wiping his mouth, he clarified. "As you know, the Fabric separating our worlds acts like actual fabric, flexible, breathable to a degree, but one needs an actual opening to travel freely between the realms of Faery and Mortal. When the energy between the two worlds is balanced, Fabric is strong, and the only way to travel between the two Realms is through established portals."

"Like ours?" Leanne asked.

"Like yours." Lou agreed. "However, human disbelief acts like an abrasive chemical, burning holes in the border between our two realities. Look--" Lou picked up a napkin, and with a touch of his finger, burned two oval holes, one on each end.

"For millennia, these tears have all been in clusters, and relatively easy to identify and address." Lou leaned back and said. "But the carnage from the Industrial Revolution was nothing compared to the devastation the Technology Wave caused. The new order religion of Science has had a mortally corrosive effect on the Fabric between Mortal and Faery realms--it has worn so thin, tears are happening on their own. When the Lady commissioned *this* portal--"

"Commissioned?"

"Yes. There are several Fabric tears in west Georgia, two in Columbus itself, and two just a bit north. Of those, one is still hidden from the mortals near it, but another is on the Hilton family property and was discovered some years ago by Dahlia's Hilton's son.

"Trespassing between Mortal and Faery is bad enough--but when Payne Hilton started hunting faeries, that is when the Lady got involved, calling Leanne to her first quest." He tipped his hand to the brow of his imaginary hat as he added to Leanne, "And congratulations on a job well done."

Anya asked, "By freeing Harley and inadvertently sealing the opening behind his cage, she actually sealed a tear?"

"Yes. Thus temporarily stopping Hilton's interference with the Faery Realm--though also introducing him to Leanne's magick-print. To protect Her powerful, but newest, and thus least experienced, protegee, the Lady assigned her lieutenant as Leanne's teacher and guardian."

Anya nodded, then asked, "You said there were four tears?"

"There were two here." Lou swept his hand in the direction of their newly gilded-shut Portal.

Leaning forward, Leanne said, "Which is why the land and building were in such bad condition when we purchased it."

"Yes. The Lady facilitated your settling here," Lou added, "and the complexities of the purchase itself were smoothed over by Her decree."

"I'm sorry, what?" Anya's head.

"When it came time to create this Portal, you were granted far more help than you realize."

Leanne looked at Anya, who nodded as lots of little mysteries cleared up at once. Buying several properties at once, destroying and then rebuilding a house like theirs--city politics alone, there should have been miles of red tape. Add in the complete lack of problems with contractors, construction crews, hell, even the federal laws affecting some of the foreign plants they imported. It should have been a nightmare.

McAnrai pointed to the holes in the napkin. "So what happened to the tears on this property?"

Lou addressed the answer to Leanne and Anya. "When you worked together to create your Portal, the Morrigan Herself folded the two holes over each other." He folded the napkin as a business letter, a hole in the top third, a hole in the bottom third, and a healthy sheet between the two openings, "With Her help, you two sliced a clean rip through the middle panel." He placed his finger through the opening, ran it down the center, slicing as it went, "Then, you used that divinely cut Fabric to 'sew' a proper seam around the edges." The two, clean slices rolled over the sides of the layered holes, and threads of light sewed them into a seam. "And there you have it. Brand new, extremely stable, Portal into Faery."

"Wait," McAnrai asked, "I don't get it. What's so bad about the random tears? Wouldn't it help with belief, what people would see if they go wandering in and out of Faery?"

"When it's the occasional small tear, that *is* how they mend themselves. Through them, relatively harmless faeries move freely, cause a little havoc, make believers of the local human community. Much like how a human's fever is unpleasant, but is the body healing itself. However," Lou took a sip of whiskey, "Fabric is aptly named, it *literally* acts like fabric. An official, *well-sewn* Portal is fine--use it all you want. But a *tear* large enough to accommodate a *human*? When a human enters through a tear, rather than an actual portal, that person is plucking and pulling at already frayed Fabric."

Leanne's brow furrowed as she asked, "What you said earlier, about our running a boot camp?"

Since Leanne alone heard Lou's earlier comment, everyone else turned in mild surprise. Lou smiled, and answered, "From Faery's perspective, the time has come to choose between leaving Earth to the destruction humanity is nursing into ironic health, or finding a way back into full participation and cohabitation of Earth's natural world."

"I'm sorry--what?" Leanne shook her head. "Look, it's been a day. I need this in Captain Dummy talk."

Lou thought for a moment, then said, "Faeries draw their power from the Faery Realm. They tend to Nature, and thus the health of the Mortal Realm. Human belief fuels the Faery Realm. Human disbelief weakens it. The Faery Realm, and all in it, are fighting for their survival. The survival of the Earth as we know it--both Mortal and Faery sides--depends on humans believing in faeries. So steps are being taken."

"By faeries choosing to be born as humans."

"For many, yes." Lou continued, "Many as writers and entertainers--using the arts. In this way, we've been able to revitalize the Old Ways, bring new life to the Old Stories."

Nodding her head with an expression of 'aaaaahhhhh', Laidi said, "Just like in Peter Pan, the more folks believe in faeries, the stronger they get."

"And the Earth is correspondingly healed."

Anya asked, "So in addition to faeries who simply look like humans, there are people walking around that actually *are* sylphs, or gnomes?"

"Or leprechauns, or mermaids--" Lou nodded.

"Or *olchanfae*." McAnrai said.

Lou's mouth tightened. "Those, too."

"Umm," Leanne tapped her fingers on the table. "Back to the boot camp thing?"

"For many of these beings, maintaining and functioning in a human body is a new experience. They come to places like the Brugh to practice. See if they can pass for human--most can't on their first try."

"Well, that explains a lot." Laidi chuckled. "So many people recklessly partying, sex, drugs, rock and roll--with no thought to the consequences."

Leanne nodded, "Millennia of living for pleasure, not having to worry about mundane responsibilities--even down to taking care of a physical body."

"So they come here to try out their 'human act'--a place to safely interact with mortals. If they screw up, no harm done." Laidi smiled at the discovery. "Not a bad plan."

"Just so." Lou smiled.

McAnrai shifted in his seat. "Okay. But what happens when someone tries to dislodge an official Portal?"

Lou looked at him with approval. "Yes, that's what young Hilton is trying to do."

"But why?"

"Despite his disparaging words, he has an excellent appreciation for your talents as a policeman. He realizes it's just a matter of time before you," he tilted his glass to salute McAnrai, "bring him to justice for his various sallies into financial wrongdoings. Oh, and murders--at least two of his victims were killed by mortal means."

"He's planning on running away to Faery, like other criminals escape to tropical islands?" McAnrai fought to control his voice. "All the months I've spent building the case against him--and the bastard is going to go free anyway?"

Anya muttered, "Talk about avoiding extradition agreements."

Moving on before McAnrai could react, she said, "But all he had to do was sneak onto our property once--he could just go through our Portal, and be done with it."

"If escape was his only desire, yes. However, he wants to maintain access to Mortal."

"Why?"

"Sadism." All heads turned to Leanne. "Every predator needs a hunting ground. He's powerful here, but he can't hunt in Faery."

Anya's eyes narrowed. "He wants a hideaway home in Faery *and* his own private access to mortal victims. So he's trying to blast our Portal to his property, like a goddamn cannon."

Lou rocked his head. "More like a lasso. He placed his--what did you call it?--homing beacon here, and has thus made two blessedly failed attempts to trigger the spell from a distant location."

"Trigger?"

Lou grimaced. "I think we can assume that this spell is designed to be ignited by murder."

Anya counted out on her thumb and index finger, "First Brad, then Ursula."

Frustrated almost beyond speech, McAnrai sputtered. "And what, we follow him around, hoping to catch him in the act of trying to murder someone else somewhere else?"

Sighing, Lou shook his head. "I don't think that will be necessary."

Leanne agreed. "He's coming to us--make sure it goes off without a hitch. The personal touch."

Anya agreed, "He's done taking chances." She then added, "But he thinks it will work like a lasso?"

"It will certainly be effective in dislodging your Portal, especially since *olchanfae* have been chewing at its borders--hence the incident this afternoon."

Leanne chanced an interruption, "Thank you for your help."

With a slight smile, Lou said, "And you can pay me back by continuing to protect it. But back to Anya's question. Hilton has no understanding of Fabric. He thinks stealing your Portal will be like moving a gate to a different part of fencing, but he'll actually be ripping an enormous hole here, and creating a sloppy--and unstable--wormhole between Mortal and Faery."

Anya's eyes moved to the ceiling, as she put her ideas in order. "Technically, any portal is a wormhole, right? And usually about the size of a door?"

"Yes."

"And this one will stretch the distance between our properties."

Anya groaned. "So, even in his best case scenario, he'll rip a gaping hole in the Fabric of Reality, one with *miles* of frayed ends and loose strings."

McAnrai rubbed the back of his neck in agitation. "That would destroy Columbus, entirely."

"Columbus would be the *beginning*." Leanne shook her head.

Anya took a deep breath before saying, "An apocalypse."

Lou gave a short nod. "Hopefully, the damage will be limited to this planet."

It was McAnrai who asked what they all wondered. "So what do we do?"

"If stopped at the right moment," Lou said, "we will prevent a catastrophic event, and permanently secure Columbus' Fabric weaknesses."

"Awesome." McAnrai's voice was pure deadpan. "And if we don't?"

"Boom."

"Oh, even better. Chances of success?"

"With each of us using our full strength, and with luck, there's definitely a chance of success."

Leanne looked at her healing, but still bandaged leg, at Anya's exhausted face, thought of Remy, recuperating from what was a comparatively minor tussle. Laidi was, as yet, unharmed, but her mastery leaned toward brainwork and magickal puzzle solving. Her five foot nothing frame wasn't much of an encouragement as far as brute force goes. Harley was an absolute badass, but they could be going up against an army of Harleys. That left McAnrai. Their eyes met, and she could almost hear his wheels doing the same math--and reaching the same conclusion. Yet Lou didn't look as worried as he should. She asked, "Is there any upside to this situation at all?"

"Having failed twice already, he'll want to ensure success for his third attempt. The success-oriented energy of Sunday, combined with the energy of a late fourth quarter moon? He'll wait til tomorrow, probably sunset, so he can harness all three powers for his spell."

"So what?"

"There is time to get a good night's sleep."

They all rose together, and McAnrai cleared his throat. "Best news I've heard in days. *If* you're right. But what if--" But when McAnrai turned to ask his question, he was speaking to open air. Lou had vanished. Rolling his eyes, he muttered to himself, "Fucking faeries."

CHAPTER 39 - DEFCON 2

"Hey, Mac!" Remy called to the tree canopy as he walked outside. "I got here some *cafe au lait* wit' your name on it." Remy jumped as a two by four fell, missing his head by mere inches. "Shit!"

"Oh--sorry, man." McAnrai flinched as the heavy piece of wood landed with a thump on the soft lawn below. The strong scent of chicory-laced roast wafted up to McAnrai, its appeal adding a bit of chagrin since he almost concussed the guy offering it.

"Uh, yeah" Gesturing with the large mugs of coffee, Remy set them on the grass, freeing his hands to steady the ladder. "*Ça viens?*"

"It's going." Hooking the hammer in the loop on his belt, McAnrai slipped his legs over the side of the wooden ledge he'd just secured in the canopy of the enormous tree. Grabbing the nearest and sturdiest branch, he descended slowly and, hanging from the lowest limb, he let go, dropping to the ground.

"Leanne said you'd be out here, makin' yourself a place to wait for Hilton." Remy handed over the steaming brew. "Dere you go."

"Yeah. I just finished." McAnrai took his first sip. "Damn. You know your coffee. This is great."

Remy stared at the platform for another second before turning to his friend. "T'anks." Raising his own cup in a slight toast, he drank as well. His eyes flickered from McAnrai to the platform and back. "You mind runnin' all dis by me again? All I know is dat sumbitch is comin' back at midnight to kill someone...and what, trigger an apocalypse?"

"That does sum it up" Rubbing the kink from his neck, McAnrai said, "He's got to come back with the poppet, and try to kill someone to complete the spell--"

"Which will blow dis Portal--?"

"To his property. Yeah. Only it won't--it'll rip a wormhole from south Columbus to Waverly Hall."

Remy let out a low whistle. "But he'll be usin' dat poppet Anya made--so it won't work?".

"Right. But we have to prepare for the worst." Jerking his head in the direction of the treetops, McAnrai added, "I'll be waiting for him--to stop the murder. Then Anya takes over, triggers her own spell, which--."

His words were cut off by the soft sounds of grinding metal and tinkling bells. The men turned to the Portal, pausing to watch its gradual transformation to its original appearance. It was soothing, almost hypnotic, to watch the solid gold fade as the movements of the silver filigree stretched and curled from beneath the warm glow.

Answering Remy's look, McAnrai added, "Lou said the glamour he used should hold until tonight. It'll look normal by the time the action starts."

Remy asked, "But it won't be normal, *non*?"

"No. Whatever it was that got left here last week, it's been weakening the Portal's hold ever since--or at least until it was removed. But the critters it attracted," McAnrai pointed to the disturbed ground around the Portal, "they've been chewing at what anchors it here."

Following his own train of thought, Remy asked, "Girls are goin' by Hilton's later?"

"*I* am going." The muscle in McAnrai's jaw clenched. At the other man's doubtful expression, he grumbled the addition, "With Leanne."

"Sounds more like her." Remy smiled. "But don't you need to be here?"

"Not if we do it soon. Lou said the next best time for Hilton to attack is midnight. Meanwhile, Anya's cooking something up for us to drop there." He looked at his watch. "We're leaving soon. His sister said he always goes to Sunday church. Time it just right--we arrive just after he leaves."

Remy nodded. "An' we trust her?"

McAnrai's voice was quiet. "He murdered her son."

Remy exhaled sharply. "*Mon dieu.*"

"It's a gamble, but we're hoping he's intent on keeping up his 'respectable' appearances til the last possible moment." Brushing the last of the tree debris from himself, McAnrai gathered the rest of his tools and the two men started for the house. "Drop the whatever the hell it is Anya gives us, haul ass back here. Then, tonight, when he tries to to trigger the spell--"

"By killin' someone here--"

"By trying to murder someone here." The correction was soft, but cold.

Remy another look over his shoulder, to where he knew the platform must be, all but invisible thanks to the leaves. "Dat's a long way to jump, bruh."

McAnrai continued as though Remy had not spoken. "Once that is settled, Anya will do her thing, which essentially sends the magick version of Minuteman to that asshole's base of operations. Game over." They stepped through the gutted Garden Lounge, toward the passage connecting the private kitchen to the Table's dining room.

Remy nodded again. They reached the door, but as McAnrai reached for the knob, both men turned at the strange mixture of sound coming from behind. The Portal had morphed again, one step closer to its normal, increasingly vulnerable, state.

***

"This," Anya held up a small, velvet bag, "Is a homing beacon. Once I redirect Hilton's spell, it's going to lay waste to the general vicinity of wherever this bag is. So you need to drop it in his space, and get the hell out of there."

"Won't that worsen the tears there?"

"The resulting waste should act like platelets--clotting at the opening, giving Nature a chance to heal itself."

Leanne nodded as she pocketed the grim talisman, but McAnrai looked at them pointedly. "'In his space' is... not as specific as it could be."

Leanne elaborated. "His magickal workspace. This bomb has to go off in the very foundation of his power."

"So we need to find his version of your upstairs?"

"Yes. All we have to do is drop it and go." Tightening the laces of her boots, Leanne said to Anya, "Don't worry. We'll figure it out."

McAnrai rolled his eyes and mumbled, "What could *possibly* go wrong?"

***

Anya stood on t the Brugh's porch, watched Mac's SUV turn at the corner and out of sight. Her mouth was set in a grim line. She raised her hands, and with a fluid motion, sealed the protective wards she, Leanne, and Harley put in place earlier that morning.

The Gentrys had always made protection a high priority, and had put a great deal of effort into the design, implementation, and maintenance of their home's security. Or so they thought, Anya mused. If nothing else, the events of the last week had shown them just how much they had to learn about protection. This ward was intended for emergency purposes only, its extreme measures untenable for normal living.

She let out a short, cynical laugh. Normal living. Whatever the hell that was.

What it wasn't? Casting a wide-net deflection spell to make the property, and everything in it, practically invisible to, and instinctively avoided by, innocent bystanders. Nor was it normal, living in a building whose outer walls were enchanted to incinerate anyone foolish or unlucky enough to touch it. They had gone to a state of battle readiness and heightened defenses akin to that last step before nuclear war--and while Anya was sickened by the situation, her pragmatism held true.

She sighed and turned from the newly activated wards, fingering the amulet hanging from the chain around her neck--or 'pass-ward', as she liked to call them. The small piece of rose quartz, identical to the ones worn by Leanne, McAnrai, and Harley, hummed with soft energy, and was the only means by which someone could cross through the defenses unharmed. Anya pulled the other four from her pocket as she walked inside to where Remy, Laidi, Troy, and Warren waited. They had all insisted on staying--refused to leave, actually--until, as Remy put it, "dis whole clusterfuck is cleaned up". She understood why her NOLA family had dug in their heels--and she knew from experience how well seasoned they were, even against magick-wielding attackers. Warren had a Faery debt to pay--and she had no doubt that his massive build was merely a hint of what he brought to a fight. But Troy. Battle dream aside, he had no experience in warfare, magickal or otherwise. Yet nothing she said could dissuade him from staying.

She handed out the first three pass-wards. As Warren carried Ursula to the relative safety of the private kitchen, Laidi and Remy busied themselves at the other end of the bar. Anya turned to Troy. She held the last amulet a touch longer, imbuing it with a little extra 'oomph' before handing it over. Just in case.

Smiling faintly as he examined the quartz, Troy asked, "So this keeps me safe from harm?"

Anya shook her head. "No. It grants you safe passage on and off of the property. That's it." She put a hand on his forearm. "I do wish you'd stay out of this--you have no stake in our mess."

"I am stronger than I look." He lifted the chain around his neck and fastened the clasp, the crystal laying against the center of his collarbone. "But I thank you for this." His smile was wide, warm, and made her feel even worse about his decision.

"Fine." Anya sighed as she turned in the direction of the Batcave. "Look, strong is great, but you're also unarmed. You should come with me upstairs, and--"

"Or I can just use this." Troy stepped beside her and held a black, knobby walking stick at his side.

Anya blinked. "Oh, that belonged to my great grandfather. It's only out for decoration, since..." Troy's expression cut her short. "You know how to use a *shillelagh*?"

He grinned. "Well, enough even, to appreciate the knob is weighted. Filled with lead?"

Anya nodded, thought for a second. It may be an innocent walking stick now, but all things considered, her great grandfather's *shillelagh* had seen some shit...

Slipping his hand through the leather strap, he spun it to grip. "Properly balanced, too."

And Troy knew how to use it.

"Okay then."

She didn't like it. But she didn't like anything about what was coming.

At least they could control the timing of the showdown. Nothing less than a deity could get through her wards without an invitation.

***

A dark man in a dark suit climbed the front steps of the Gentry's Table. He stood at their front door, examining it, and the walls around it, with an expression both curious and impressed. He placed his open palms against the ward. With no more reaction than a flinch, the high voltage defensive measures coursed harmlessly through him, escaping into the ether beyond.

When the last of the wards faded into nothing, he turned to face the street.

"Well?" Payne Hilton stood on the sidewalk, waiting, his hands clenching and unclenching at his sides.

Refusing to be rushed, Nate took slow, deliberate steps toward the impatient man.

Forgoing the pretense courtesy, Hilton stared hungrily at the rambling Victorian house, and raised his voice, "Did you strip it off? Is their protection gone?"

Raising an eyebrow at the rudeness, Nate waited an extra beat.

Heedless, Hilton persisted. "Well?"

The skin around Nate's eyes tightened at the repeated demands. He turned back to the Gentry's Table, and smiled to himself. As he walked away, he turned his head in Hilton's direction and said, "The way is open."

Payne Hilton climbed the steps of Leanne and Anya Gentry's livelihood and home, Bailey Traywick at his heels. When he paused at the entrance, his not-so-secret son hurried around him, opened the hand-carved door. They walked to the empty dining room, stopped at the hostess station. Hilton's eyes swept the room, and smirked at the helplessly visible creaking gate, swinging from the entrance of the Garden Lounge. He looked through the windows, to the decimated garden beyond.

He looked at Bailey, then pointed to the gate. "Go to the Portal. Wait for me there." At Bailey's hesitant glance toward the Lounge, Hilton said, "I can see you're nervous."

"Oh, no. It's not that. I just," he stammered to a halt.

"Bailey," Hilton rested his hand on the young man's shoulder. "It's natural to be afraid. But I'm telling you--there's nothing back there that will harm you." Hilton's eyes followed Bailey's gaze toward the Lounge, the busted gate offering a glimpse of the wreckage beyond. He looked back at Bailey, and suppressed an impatient sigh. "Bailey. I am your father. You are my blood. There's no future for me in Faery without you."

Bailey's face flushed with emotion. He patted the gun in his pocket, nodded and left.

Hilton rang the service bell sitting on the edge of the podium.

CHAPTER 40 - A LESSON PROVIDED

Remy's quick glance at the bottles Laidi had lined up on the bar turned into a double-take. "I like your idea, *chere*, but dat proof, it's too low. *Ils ne vont pas prendre feu.*"

Without looking from the line of bottles, Laidi let out a sharp laugh. "They'll burn if I fucking tell 'em to. And the sugar content makes the fire sticky."

Remy blinked at her language and picked up the closest nip. "Well, damn. Shit done got *real*." He grinned at her. "Dis some flashy *gris-gris*."

Anya returned to the Brugh and Remy opened his mouth to speak, but his eyes narrowed at her expression. "What is it, T-ya?"

The menace of Hilton's thoughts had hit Anya before the bell answered Remy's question. The delicate 'ding' echoed in a deafening silence.

First to recover, Anya turned to Troy--the best she could do was direct him away from where the fighting would be. "You have the vegetable Garden. And you two," she looked at Remy and Laidi and jutted her chin toward the Brugh's porch, and the garden beyond. "The Brugh's."

Laidi nodded, and slipped behind the bar. Remy hesitated, and eyed Anya, "Sure you don't want some back up, you?"

The corners of Anya's eyes creased at the offer. "There's no way he came alone, and we need to cover any access to the Portal. Besides," She nodded at Warren, who had just returned from securing the private kitchen. "I'm not alone." She rested her hands on the garden shears hanging from the front of her utility belt. "And it's time this asshole and I had a little chat."

Once she turned to walk out, Warren and Troy exchanged a look and a nod. Warren walked toward the Garden. Troy followed Anya.

***

Exuding a calm she did not feel, Anya walked into the dining room. Her eyes swept over Payne Hilton. The mayor's brother. Dog fighting ring owner. Murderer.

With her coldest, most professional, fuck-you smile, Anya said, "I know it will come at a great inconvenience, but we are closed for renovations."

Hilton made a show of taking in his surroundings. "Oh yes. Quite a lot of damage has been done here." His eyes spared a quick glance at Troy, who had stepped closer to Anya, barely a foot behind her.

Anya waved off the gloat. With a careless 'pfft', she said, "Oh don't you worry. Barely scratched the cosmetics, and we were due for a touch-up anyway."

Hilton's eyes flickered at the dismissal. Turning his attention back to Anya, and gesturing over his shoulder, he said, "But yes, that would be an inconvenience. I have a party of over three-hundred hungry mouths. And I," Hilton's gaze slid lazily over Anya's figure, resting at the neckline of her shirt, "was looking forward to the pleasure of your service. You--and your sister, of course--have quite the reputation for...hospitality."

The lines around Anya's eyes and mouth hardened. She tuned out the rest of her surroundings--trusting their care to Warren's vigilance. Nothing but Hilton, and the unmistakable intent of his words. Anya concentrated on her hands, letting her wrath flow into them. The channeling was so intense, she could feel the gentle jingle of her charm bracelet as the surge of power rushed to her hands, and into the garden shears her left hand rested upon. The force coalesced so quickly, she could practically hear the sounding of a sword being pulled from its sheath.

With an exaggerated "aw shucks" click of her tongue, Anya shook her head. "I'm afraid we have very strict, non-negotiable requirements for service here."

"Is that so?" Hilton made a show of looking for a sign. "There aren't any posted."

Anya waved her hand in mock apology. "I keep forgetting." She nodded to the wall behind Hilton. "Some need even the simplest of concepts spelled out for them." At the snap of her fingers, a chair slid behind Hilton, the sudden impact buckling his knees and dropping him into the seat. It spun to face the wall of the entrance foyer, to the Daily Specials board, whose words shuffled and resettled.

In a carrying voice, Anya read:

"Tie and Jacket Optional

Decency and Class Required

If One Is In Need of Either, A Lesson in Both Will Be Provided"

"Cute." Hilton smoothed imaginary creases from the front of his slacks as he rose to his feet. "Well, little girl, this has been fun," he let out a long, slow breath, his eyes twitched behind her, then back, invasively savoring her curves. "But I am sure you can do better than that."

"That's true enough." In a blur, Anya's hands dropped to her right side and swung behind her, as though winding up for a pitch. She torked her arms forward, unleashing a hurricane level current of rain soaked wind at Hilton's torso.

With an amused wave, Hilton redirected the gale to his left, twisting in the direction of the torrent. The brunt of it hit the double-doors to the outside, blasting them open. Hilton stuck his hand in the coursing attack, grabbed, and held.

The degree to which Anya had poured her Power into the attack, combined with Hilton's hijacking of it, held them frozen in an energetic tug-of-war. Though brief, the sharing of energy space gave her a closer understanding of his intention, the degree to which his twisted lust had distracted him from everything. Including the Portal.

Which was useful information. Repulsive, but useful...

Encouraged by her recoil, Hilton leered, "Looks like you need to learn a lesson, honey. How about you come closer, so I can teach you how to behave?"

Well, he did ask. Anya relaxed her resistance to his pull.

Mistaking her slow slide to him as weakening of resolve, Hilton's expression relaxed in lazy triumph. He said, "Now that's a good girl. Not that it matters, but you might even enjoy--*oof*--"

When he called her "girl" for the second time, Anya ceased all resistance to Hilton's thrall. Their bodies crashed together--though differently than he expected. As she allowed the power of his need to draw her body to his, Anya chambered her right arm, fist poised and ready. She drove her fist into his throat, then grabbed the collar of his shirt, steadying him as she slammed her knee into his groin. He gasped, doubled over, wheezing as she shoved him to the floor.

The thump of his impact acted as a firing shot, signaling the charge of his army.

***

Once the others left, Remy walked behind the bar, pressing past Lai-di. He stretched to his full height as he reached over the top shelf of bottles, to the staff hanging above. It was over six feet long, and hand-carved to look as though comprised of several thick vines bound together. He grabbed its center, pulled it off its wall mount, and hopped a seat onto the empty half of the bar. Laidi automatically ducked as he swung his long legs over the bar, the 'decoration' spinning overhead.

Remy's feet landed on the floor in time with the end of the staff. At the impact, red ribbons of power streamed from his hand, weaving and winding into the now glowing vines. They pulsed as the energy poured from his hand. He grinned at Laidi's admiring look.

"Not gonna lie, honey. You got panache." She climbed onto the step stool behind the bar, and grabbed a small leather purse--no bigger than a whiskey flask. She opened it, murmuring as she did. It opened wide, wide enough to accommodate a basketball. Looking at Remy, she asked, "A little help?"

"*Mais certainement.*" He touched his bo staff to the tip of the bar. A ribbon of pale pink light shot out, formed a lasso around the charged tiny bottles, then slid them into the purse. He smiled as elucidation dawned.

"I'd wondered why you bought a case of nips, when you already work at a bar."

With a touch of playful sarcasm, she shot back, "I wondered why you keep a heavily charged weapon, hanging it as art-deco for a bar."

"*Touche, chere.* Always battle-ready, me."

"So you get it." Grinning, Laidi quipped, "I call them, 'cinnabombs'.

Before Remy could react, both heads snapped toward the dining room--the sound of a chair sliding and Anya's slightly raised voice reading the scroll.

"Won't be long now." Laidi's voice was low--held a note that brought Remy's attention back to her.

"You got dat right. Look. If dis goes sideways, maybe we should--"

Without another word, Laidi grabbed Remy by his lapels, pulled him to her for a fast but fierce kiss. Remy wrapped his bo arm around her, careful not to clock her, as his left hand held her close. Hot, hard and intense, each of them pouring what they had to say into the embrace.

When their lips parted, an explosion of noise crashed into the Brugh. A swarm of *olchanfae* billowed in as a dark cloud, blackened smoke lined with cruel eyes and fanged mouths.

Anticipating Remy's reaction, Laidi harnessed the spin from his release, and dropped to a crouch as she threw her first fire-bomb shouting its command, "*Wrap!*". The enchanted nip hit its mark, and the fire-engulfed *olchanfae* screamed as it swerved in the air, igniting its fellows on its way to the floor. Back on her feet, cinnabomb in each hand--she tossed them into the air. They floated, waiting on her words. Pointing her aim, she cried, "*Bind!...Pin!...Engulf!...*" The enchanted nips suited their action to her words, then exploded.

In the movement of releasing Laidi, Remy spun the bo down and back. He thrust his left hand forward, palm out. Red ribbons flew from his open palm, each wrapping around the throat of a nearby attacker. Sizzling at contact, and constricting at the command of his closed fist, each throttled *olchanfae* exploded. He swung the staff across his front, and clasped it with his left as it swept the *olchanfae* before him.

Laidi and Remy fought as the swarm poured into their home away from home.

***

You're my blood.

The words echoed in Bailey's mind as he crossed the dining room, and into what was left of the Garden Lounge. The validation did what the attempt at reassurance did not--propelling him forward to a future at once exciting and terrifying. Faery. The Faery Realm. He was going to live there, with...

I'm your father.

So focused on his own reverie, Bailey didn't hear the sliding chair, nor the ensuing skirmish behind him. The weight of his steps squeezed creaks from the hardwood flooring as he strode through the bare bones of the scraped out room, and continued out to the garden beyond the glassless walls.

He looked around. The garden was empty, just as his father had said.

His father.

He'd waited his entire life for the man's recognition--but it wasn't until the words were spoken did Bailey realize he'd never expected to hear them.

"This is private property. You are trespassing. You must leave now."

Bailey spun his gun in the direction of the deep, rolling voice, squeezing the trigger as he did. He fired until the trigger pulls clicked on empty, but the bullets bounced harmlessly off the big man's chest. With sharp *tings*, each fell to the ground, flattened and spent. Bailey blinked.

Warren asked, "Is there anything else you'd like to try, or are you ready to converse?" The complete lack of irony in the bouncer's courtesy robbed the words of condescension.

Bailey felt a wave of relaxation wash over him. With childlike candor, he said, "I need to go to the Portal."

Warren's face broke into a sad, gentle smile. He rested his large hand on the same shoulder Hilton had held. "It is not safe for you here. Leave while you can."

The soothing energy from the bullet-proof behemoth washed all fear and tension from Bailey, leaving only weariness behind. He whispered, "I can't leave. I have to get to the Portal."

"I know, lad, I know." Warren slipped his arm around Bailey's slumped shoulders, turning him, guiding him to the front of the property. He continued speaking, his soothing words swirled around them, a stream flowing away from the Portal...

CHAPTER 41 - THE HOME FIRES ARE BURNING

A nya's attention snapped toward the Table's entrance as the doors blew open, and an eruption of *olchanfae* poured into the room. Grabbing her shears, she concentrated. Golden flecks of light flickered over the handles and blades, and with a sparkly little *pop*, her shears disconnected, elongated to a pair of gleaming scimitars. The sudden outstretching of her arms disemboweled the first two *olchanfae* to reach her. She sank to a watchful crouch--and rising, allowed her arms a helicopter interpretation of a *port de bras* as she resumed her full height via *pirouette*, slicing all the way.

Though the air became thick with the dusty debris of exploding *olchanfae* bodies, Anya caught glimpses of silvery light coming from ...Troy? The white oxford and navy slacks of his Table uniform were gone, replaced by a black and silver tartan kilt, shimmery chainmail. Small locks of black hair curled from beneath the helmet he had worn in her dream.

Oh.

In her not-a-dream.

Whatever reason he had for hiding his faery nature--was obsolete now. Troy's form came in and out of view, though Anya wasn't sure how much of that was *olchan-dust*, and how much was glamour. The arc of his broadsword cut a series of swaths in the onslaught. Feeling her gaze, he turned to Anya and yelled, "Behind you!" before disappearing again.

Anya spun around, decapitating one *olchanfae* and skewering another, then another, and another, in a razoring dance.

Hilton grasped the podium as he gave his own powers time to subdue his pain, regain the focus of his strength. Once upright, he used the cover of the *olchan-dust* to cross the room, closer and closer to the Lounge. As he passed by the open fireplace, he reached toward it, igniting the cold wood by sending surges of energy to each of the fire salamanders sleeping there--yanking their bodies as Christmas crackers, their combustible innards splattering across the decorative wood. Hilton laughed as the enormous flames erupted from their screams--he reached forward and clenched his fists, pulling the flames from the fireplace, caressing them into a weaponized shape, and directing the blitz at Anya's back.

Troy thrust his shield and himself into the onslaught, absorbing the brunt of the attack, and the pressure of the fire blasts knocked both Anya and Troy to the floor. In one fluid movement, Anya spun to sitting, and blasted Hilton with hurricane knot winds. The gale lifted him from the ground, blew him past the hallway to the Lounge, and knocked him not only against, but *through* the south wall of the building and into the vegetable garden.

At the pause, Troy appeared at Anya's feet. Clasping his offered hand, she stood. Looking him up and down, she opened her mouth to speak, but he cut her off. "Later, m'lady. Now, we pursue."

They climbed through the blown-out wall, following Hilton into the gardens, and to the Portal.

As they neared the front porch, Bailey's eyes flickered toward the Table's dining room windows, and the melee they framed.

He couldn't make out the form of his father--just the stream of fire bursting across the room...

Startled out of his compliance, he pulled away from Warren, and said, "I can't. I have to get to the Portal. My father needs me."

Warren's hand tightened, and he asked, "Aye lad, but for what?"

Before Bailey could respond, a smoky cloud of dust, shattered glass, and splintered wood erupted from the Victorian, catapulting one very pissed off man.

Hilton crashed into his son, sending them both sprawling into the watermelon patch. Bailey felt a surge of cold as an invisible blanket enveloped them as they scrambled on the ground.

"Come on." Payne Hilton had hardly landed before he was back on his feet, and dragging Bailey with him. "This way."

They ran in the direction of the Portal, with Anya, Troy, and Warren close behind.

***

The bare minutes of fighting made the Brugh's patio and garden an ashy mess of *olchan-dust*. Remy could barely see his hands as he attacked, though the glowing eyes of the swarming *olchanfae* were clear enough. He sent his ribbons to the left, over and over, catching, throttling, throwing the beasts into each other. On the right, his bo cut a swath through the throng, incinerating those it struck. As for him, he had a couple knicks and nips, a scrape or ten, and like Laidi, he was holding his own...

But the *olchanfae* numbers never thinned.

"*Burn! Engulf!*" Laidi's voice rang through the air as her cinnabombs executed their orders, and their targets. She had a gash on her leg, and a pattern of scrapes as sets of teeth had come close enough to mark, but not so much to sink in. She felt in her bag--she was running low, a dozen nips and one industrial sized bottle. Holding a cinnabomb in each hand, she sent them to her right and left, yelling, "*Commandeer!*" Upon impact, those two nips lit the first *olchanfae* they hit, but with such force as to have them collide with their fellows.

But more kept pouring into their Brugh.

"We need a new plan!" She tried to shout it, but her words came out as coughs. Practically blind, she moved toward the flashes and flames that did not come from her. "Remy!"

"Woman, where y'at?" Remy choked on his words. He felt rather than heard or saw her approach. Using that as his guide, he moved in her direction. Upon meeting, they stood back to back, covering each other.

"How many dem bombs you got left?" Kick, ribbon, squeeze, poof. "How long til you gotta go old school?"

"Just a couple." Laidi held the largest bottle in her hand. "And I never left it."

At the words, Remy shot a glance over his shoulder. Sure enough, she was fire-bending with one hand, rolling pin bludgeoning with the other, and damn, if she didn't just tork her body to the left, kicking the nearest *olchanfae* into the three next to it.

He was impressed as hell, but the seconds he spent watching her ass-kicking cost him. He shouted, grabbed at his face as a claw sliced down his cheek.

At Remy's shout, Laidi turned and yelled, "Duck!"

Remy dropped as Laidi tossed the economy sized cinnabomb into the thickest patch of *olchanfae*. "*Divide! Commandeer!*"

The bottle exploded, sending shards of fire-soaked glass in a radius extending outward from Remy and Laidi. Spread thin, tiny bits of flame attached to each *olchanfae*. Enough to hurt, but not instant death.

Enough to cause the *olchanfae* ranks to spin into a full-fledged panic. Each hit faery started screaming as small fires started on them, an attack gradual enough to replace quick deaths with panicked, aerial free for all. Within seconds, dozens of attacking *olchanfae* became double dozens of screaming balls of crazed, semi-sentient fire. The firestorm persisted despite all efforts to extinguish, escalating panic to full-on hysteria, flames spreading from faery to faery to faery...to...

The air was so thick with flaming bodies and floating dust, the only reason Remy and Laidi knew the house had also caught on fire was the three story glow from the eruption.

The two people froze in horror--stillness in a tempest of screams, flames, and smoke.

Remy's eyes were wide. "Oh *merde*."

"I've got an idea." Laidi took a few steps behind Remy. "Ready to share?" At his nod, she yelled, "Power up!" She ran to him, jumped, slammed the palms of both of her hands onto his back, pouring her own power into him.

Anticipating the energy boost, but expecting something like how he helped Leanne carry the poppet, Remy was ready for her plan, but was surprised as the impact of her power--and its delivery--knocked him forward, down onto his hands and knees. He felt the surge of his ribbons, propelled by their combined forces, but when the energy went into the ground...

Nothing.

Until dozens of ribbons shot simultaneously from the ground, grabbing every *olchanfae* in sight. Grabbed, squeezed, then more *olchan-dust* as damn near a hundred of those bastards exploded at once.

The air was now so thick, they couldn't speak at all--but if there was one thing a couple of top-notch chefs know, it's how to cooperatively put out a fire. Usually a little smaller than the side of a three-story house, but the principle was the same, right? Laidi's control of fire and Remy's telekinesis worked in perfect cooperation--gathering the dust from the surfaces, from the air, forming into a blanket large enough to...

They concentrated, and slammed their 'blanket' into the north side of the building. Its impact shook the structure to its core as it smothered the fire.

Laidi sank to her knees, moved up to Remy's side as he leaned back on his haunches. They watched as the dust smothered the flames, while the fire reduced the malignant residue to harmless oblivion.

Alone in the garden, Laidi and Remy looked at each other, and each let out a half-hearted laugh of disbelief.

And then the sound of Anya blowing Payne Hilton through the Table's south wall cut their celebration short. They looked at each other.

"Portal?"

"Portal."

CHAPTER 42 - "I BELIEVE IT'S CALLED A 'LAIR'"

Traffic on Manchester Expressway north wasn't too bad as most religious services were well underway, and once they passed Peachtree Mall and the Chevrolet dealership, there was nothing but open highway until the traffic light in Ellerslie. McAnrai leaned back in his seat, mulling over the plan.

"So we get there, find the mystical spot of badness, plant the rock, and run."

Leanne nodded. "Pretty much."

"And how, again, are we supposed to know where that place is?"

McAnrai startled as Harley appeared between them and answered, "Chances are excellent it will be very, very obvious. At least for eyes that can see."

"Vaguely direct. Of course." McAnrai applied a little more pressure to the gas pedal. "And hi there."

"Hello, young man."

Leanne suppressed a smile at the exchange.

Oak Mountain Estates was a few miles north of Waverly Hall proper, so they had plenty of time, but Leanne could tell McAnrai wanted this part over. She glanced at him. McAnrai's expression was almost inscrutable, but she knew warriors well enough to recognize the glint in his eyes. As a former sniper, he was accustomed to advancing past the regular lines of enemy boundaries. But to find a place to hide himself--and even then, still from a distance. Openly strolling into the danger zone was not his speed at all. And he *hated* having her here with him, driving straight into danger.

"I'm going to be okay, ya know." The corner of Leanne's mouth twitched to a half smile. "Promise."

"Hmmph." He cast her a sidelong look. "I guess it's my turn to say it's going to be okay."

Her voice was quiet, her question more of a statement, "You're going to kill him, aren't you?"

McAnrai couldn't bring himself to lie.

"Yes." He took a breath and added, "It's the right thing to do."

"Is that supposed to make me feel better?"

"Was anything going to? Be reasonable."

The miles ticked by, and eventually, they turned off of the highway, and through the entrance to Oak Mountain Estates. Several minutes and a few winding roads later, McAnrai nodded his head at the GPS. "Here we are." They looked at the long, straight driveway. Newly deposited gravel against the deep orange-red of the clay on each side, plus the bulge outward at each end, gave the illusion of a bloodied bone. It ended to the right of a cottage, whose distressed finish gave the illusion of age and wear. McAnrai turned the car toward the street, then put it in park. They each looked to the Cait-Sith.

"Harley?" Leanne turned and looked over her shoulder.

His answer was soft but certain. "No humans for acres, my girl."

"Let's do this."

They climbed out of McAnrai's SUV and stepped onto the fine gravel. McAnrai immediately started walking past the front porch of the house, but Leanne and Harley took a moment to take in the rest of the surroundings. The faux-vintage cottage had a picturesque garden--she had expected an exotic display, but no. Just the usual suspects, azaleas, roses, gardenias, four o'clocks. Instead of facing the garden, or the lawn, the house looked over the end of the driveway, down into the ravine mere feet beyond the edge of the gravel. Growing from the bottom of that gorge were enormous, dark trees. They formed a solid wall between the house and what otherwise would have been a spectacular vista. Weird choice for a view, but whatever.

McAnrai back turned to Leanne and Harley and grimaced. "And now for the breaking in and entering part." With a sigh, he turned toward the house, but Leanne stayed his arm.

"Look."

McAnrai turned around, his gaze following the trajectory of hers. While the entire house looked to be drizzled in Hilton's "signature", there was a distinct increase toward the far end of the porch. It spilled onto a paved walkway leading a quarter mile past the building, down the steep hill, and into a grove of what looked like cypress trees. They followed the steps, careful not to touch the slime. The closer they drew to the trees, the larger the pools of slime became, finally coalescing into a perverse stream, flowing downhill into the little patch of woods.

McAnrai snorted. "Oh, that might be it."

Turning to look at the policeman, Harley offered, "At least now you're only trespassing."

"Not much better," McAnrai grumbled. "Here we go. Follow the slimy brick road; follow the slimy brick road..."

A few steps into the darkened grove, a mournful wail sounded. Wrenching calls echoed through the darkness around them, trying to escape into the sunlight beyond.

"What the HELL was that?" Leanne's voice was brittle.

Instead of answering, Harley said, "You stay on your task." Before either person could object, he disappeared into the darkness.

Leanne and McAnrai stared into the woods. Up close, it became clear the trees were...different than they expected. Definitely not cypresses, nor birches, and probably not even from the Mortal Realm.

The branches entwined with one another, and the tops leaned inward, forming a thick canopy overhead. The trunks looked like thick locks of silver hair, their loose braids leaving gaps of inky black hollows where animals should be making nests. From their upper branches, trailing vines dangled, the dark green of their leaves barely discernible from the black stems.

They stepped carefully, as the roots had all but undone the outer curbs of the paving, leaving the center of the walkway smooth and well worn.

"I half expect to see pairs of eyes flashing from inside the hollows of these tree trunks." Despite her effort to keep the tone light, Leanne felt the heavy malice weighing on her, pulling at her ankles as she trudged further into the darkness.

"Yeah, you can practically hear them thinking."

"So how far down do you think this goes?"

"I think we'll know it when we see it."

They continued to walk, the mark of Hilton's magick now so co-pious as to cover the entire walk space. Leanne muttered, "At least it's not sticking to our feet. It could be worse--*whoa*," Leanne swayed on her feet, catching McAnrai's arm as they both reeled from the stench of slaughtered animals, followed by a wave of energy, a ripple in the air knocking them off balance. As suddenly as it came, it disappeared, returning them to mossy air and solid stance.

It was McAnrai's turn to say, "What the HELL was that?" He coughed the words out, fighting his nausea.

"I don't know, but it probably means we're getting closer."

"Fantastic." They walked on, but slower, bracing themselves for the repeated waves of disgusting smell and disorienting energy. The waves kept coming, a few steps of fresh air, wave. A few more steps, wave.

Finally, they arrived at a small clearing. Twenty feet in circumfer-ence, and empty but for three things: a thick hanging rope with a bar tied to the end, a basin of black water, an enormous pyre, its surfaces blackened with repeated use, and a large, square slab of rock, stained beyond recognition.

"Safe to say we found it." Leanne looked around, and up. She could see small creases of sky through the leaves of the canopy. "Even the sky looks darker from here."

"I don't want to touch a damned thing."

She grimaced in agreement as she looked around. "I bet that's a literal description of everything here."

Before he could respond, both Leanne and McAnrai turned at the sound of an unmistakably feline howl of pain.

"Harley?" Leanne stepped toward the noise.

McAnrai stopped her. "We finish here first." Anguished, Leanne looked in the direction of the cry, then back at the rock in her hand, then to the ground before the bloodstained altar. She dropped the crystal, and with a wave of her hand, drew some nearby leaves to cover it.

Her love for Harley, accentuated by her fear for his safety, gave Leanne the strength to free herself from the swoozey pull of the energy waves. Freed from their hold, she ran to his voice, as fast as she could.

CHAPTER 43 - ENTER THE GARDEN

R emy and Laidi skidded to a halt in front of the large oak tree, catching their breath as Anya and Troy arrived from the other side of the house, with Warren close behind. All but Warren were pumped on adrenaline and battle ready, if a little bloodied.

But No Hilton. No Bailey.

At the conspicuous lack of bad guys, Anya snarked, "Oh good. Hide and seek."

"Y'yeah," Remy agreed. "You know dat *couillon* didn't just give up, *non*." He looked to Laidi, who was bent at the waist and breathing heavily. "You all right, woman?"

"I'm fine." She lifted her head a bit, her hands lost in her thick hair, as though holding her skull. Her eyes darted across the ground between them and the others. "No...it's...Just my head. Spinning a little."

Following his own train of thought, Troy tipped his head to the side, then slowly closed and reopened his eyes. "Hilton is still here." He murmured, "Veiled."

Anya nodded in agreement, "I can sense him, too."

Laidi straightened to standing. Holding Remy's arm for support, one hand still gripped the back of her head. When she spoke, her words were mumbled.

Remy leaned to her, "What's dat, *chere*?"

"***EXPOSE***!" She flung her last cinnabomb nip at the empty air between them and the Portal. It found its mark, and exploded into flame.

"What the HELL, Lai--" Anya's alarmed cry was cut short when the flames exploded further, extended to envelope the upright forms of two men.

The flames ate at Hilton's veil until both men were visible. Hilton's teeth were bared in a vicious smile, while the younger man hung a couple inches off the ground, the last twitches of his death throes subsiding.

All but Troy flinched at the crunching noise as the final clenching of Hilton's grip crushed Bailey's throat, snapped his neck.

Anya gaped, horrified, when Bailey's empty form crumpled to the ground. As Hilton's casting grew, she held her breath, praying to the Lady and all Her gods for the plan to work. The Portal shuddered, the tremors extending into the ground around it in a horribly similar manner to the unraveling attempt from the day before. But before she had a chance to panic, the shaking stopped--everything stopped--the stillness was absolute, freezing out even the sounds of the traffic from the streets around them.

As if burning from the inside and soaking out, light emerged from the lines and creases of the Portal, growing brighter and brighter until they coalesced together, shining hotter and hotter...

And in one fluid motion, the light erupted as flames into the sky, the blinding light briefly forming a giant hound before soaring northwards. Anya let out her breath, turned back to face Hilton.

"Not so glamorous now, is he?" Remy shot a lopsided grin at Anya and said, "Looks like ya did it, *chere*."

She didn't return his smile. Her eyes were riveted on Hilton, watching as the seconds ticked closer and closer to his understanding. "Oh, I did it, all right." Anya resisted the urge to take a step back when she saw comprehension spread across Hilton's face. "Here we go."

It took Hilton several seconds to register the bait and switch of Anya's spell. But when he understood... His expression mutated from anticipation, to confusion, to tightly contained rage...

"Oh, you did *something*, Anya Gentry." Hilton's voice was deep and his words were slow. Malice throbbed from him as a stench. He smiled, stepped toward her, and asked, "What was it?" Hilton's voice held a command, freezing each human in place, enticing them to speak. Anya looked to Remy and Laidi--they too were struggling to remain silent...

"I--I--" Anya choked on her words, fighting the order to answer. She attempted to draw away, but her feet, her legs, refused to cooperate. As the power for Hilton's command grew, the three of them gradually aware of the gripping sensation tightening around their feet and lower legs. Paralyzed...

...until the hold of their beguilement was shattered by an inhuman roar.

"***Sorcerer***!" Warren's voice bellowed through the Table, the Brugh, the grounds. The noise echoed through the gardens, and inside of their heads, the cry of a mountain lion with the lacing of a cobra's hiss.

Even Hilton staggered; his hold wavered. Free to react, to move, Anya, Troy, Remy and Laidi all turned to gape at Warren. Transfixed, they all watched, mouths open--

Warren's skin had deepened from warm tan to metallic gold as illusory clothing rippled away, exposing a body growing both longer and taller. By the time his transformation was complete, the top of his head was even with the roof of the Lounge. His face elongated, and his jaw extended to a sleek, shimmering snout filled with rows and rows of needle sharp teeth. Enormous eyes of smokey quartz blinked in the dazzling light of the garden, their vertical pupils constricting to narrow strips. Leaning forward, Warren's arms landed on the ground as they transformed to match his legs--now even wider around, with razor edged talons protruding from the tips of his claws. With a final ripple of his serpentine back, a tail at least twenty feet long flicked outward, knocking the last of the *olchanfae* to the ground, and into dust, as it did.

"Is that, I mean," Laidi's mouth kept moving, but no words came out.

"Well damned if he ain't a--" but Remy's response was drowned out by a second roar from the *oir-drakan*, Golden Dragon. Even Hilton paused at the spectacle, his eyes widening at the challenge.

Now freed from Hilton's thrall, Remy swept his bo across his front, stepping into the attack.

He wasn't quick enough. Anya watched in horror as Hilton flicked his hand in Remy's direction and screamed silently as the big Cajun's body crashed through what was left of the Lounge's glass walls, slamming into the brickwork beyond. She heard the anguish in Laidi's battle cry as Remy's body slumped to the floor. She watched as Laidi charged Hilton, rage blinding her to the false step.

Hilton turned to Laidi, rolling his eyes. "Oh, shut UP." The back of Hilton's hand landed hard on the side of Laidi's head, sending her sailing through the air, following the same arc as Remy. Laidi's petite frame collapsed over Remy's long legs.

Black, inky smoke spiraled from the ground, twining and swirling around Hilton's legs, then slipped up to his arms, and gathered in his hands. Anya and Troy stood, mesmerized, as shades of gray and black smoke curled and furled around each other, faster, faster...

A third, earth shaking battle cry reverberated off the Table's walls, the Portal, the ground itself. As the sound died out, the dragon inhaled, practically sucking all the air from the vicinity. Warren arched his back, ribs pumping rhythmically as they glowed from inside, the contents of the fiery forge building in urgency.

Hilton threw his arms out to his sides, then bent his elbows, bringing his hands to his shoulders, palms out, as though to do a standing push up. His mouth formed words, but their sounds drowned out by the priming of the furnace brewing in the dragon.

Suddenly, Hilton thrust his arms forward, loosing thousands of envenomed arrows from his hands, racing toward Anya, Troy, and their motionless friends.

They sailed through the air as Warren's chest puffed, mouth opened wide, and unleashed a river of fire and smoke.

Anya gasped, first at the sudden lack of oxygen, then at her solid impact with the floor. She landed with an ignominious grunt, a heavy weight on top of her. From her low vantage point, she watched as Warren's jaws opened wider, releasing a second eruption of flame and vapor. Head spinning, she was vaguely aware of Troy, Laidi, and Remy's fallen forms, of the flames erupting overhead, crashing spectacularly with the poisoned spears. Her mind drifted to the magickal bomb she had sent to Hilton's lair...

Before losing consciousness, Anya's last thought was of Leanne, Harley, and McAnrai, and the feeble hope that she hadn't murdered them.

CHAPTER 44 - 9 SWORDS

The noise did not stop with Harley's cry. Once his voice faded, others called out. Leanne and McAnrai followed the cacophony up the hill, past the house and into a clearing. Along the back edge of the property, they saw several kennels.

The ground around the kennels was clear of life, the grass burned down to the ashes of its roots, bright orange clay singed and darkened to dirty rust. Leanne strode forward as McAnrai paused.

Shaking his head, he said, "Something's off." He barked out a laugh. "This fucking week, man. We're surrounded by evil slime, threatened by trees, wading through invisible water--but *now* I'm thrown because something feels 'off'." He looked around. The air around them hung heavy with menace, alive with the electrical charge of the coming thunderstorm. Even the sunlight reflecting from under the thunderclouds seemed to pulse with urgent warning.

The sunlight...from *under* the clouds. "What the hell?" He spoke louder, pushing his voice to Leanne's back, but her focus was unshakable. "We were in that grove for--what?--fifteen minutes, tops?"

He dug out his pocket watch, muttering, "What the hell time is it?" McAnrai blinked. "Oh shit. Leanne, Those waves of energy weren't protective barriers--they were tears in Fabric. We've been walking in and out of *Faery*."

Despite her lack of response, he kept talking. "Fifteen minutes to us, but depending on what section of Faery we walked in, we could have been gone anywhere from hours to weeks, to years over there. Are you even listening?" He jogged to catch up with Leanne, calling her name.

No, Leanne was not listening. Her eyes were hyper-focused as they searched the grounds for Harley. He wasn't in front of them, nor within the clearing at all. At the far edge, her eyes finally rested on a familiar form. "Oh sweet Mother Morrigan." She ran.

The copper flecks in Harley's coat flickered in the late afternoon light, accentuating the darkness of his fur. He was moving, attempting to stand. Leanne rushed to his side, dropped to her knees. While running, her mind had been so engrossed with concern, the rising noise ringing at the edges of her awareness. Once her knees hit the ground, the muffling disappeared, and she was hit all at once by the cries coming from all around her, loud, hysterical, and all but drowning out the noise of McAnrai's approach.

She did hear him say something strange. "Thank God. Only a couple hours."

Leanne heard his words, but she had eyes for Harley alone. He was alive, though injured. Leanne looked up, searching for the source of his wounds. By forcing attention outwards, the owners of the crying voices came sharply into view. She caught her breath.

The Cait-Sith had fallen before a circle of small buildings, a dozen kennels, each containing several cramped, but beautiful...

Both humans' mouths dropped open. Faeries. Incarcerated faeries. *Dozens* of them.

"I tried--" Harley's voice whispered in their minds, faded and weak. "Getting past the wards was...easy...but the border...hidden ...I couldn't..." He gestured with his front paw. Both Leanne and McAnrai grimaced at the condition of its pads--they were covered in what looked like severe chemical burns. Leanne gently moved his other front paw--it was also burned and bleeding, as were Harley's legs. Comprehension dawned as they followed the direction indicated, toward the ground before the nearest kennel. There was an actual line drawn in the clay, a band of gray-black powdered iron, two inches thick, and stretching entirely around the faery jails. As Harley had stepped nearer, the particles of iron fluttered up into the air, coating him in a thin mist of...

"Faery napalm. That asshole." McAnrai nodded, his mouth set in a grim line. "Makes sense, though. The single way to contain faeries by brute force. Okay." He stooped down, joined Leanne as they brushed the remaining traces of iron from Harley's thick fur, "We need to do this quick and get the hell out of here."

When they were done, Harley's breathing became less labored. Leanne stood and turned to the cages, but McAnrai dug his hands into the ground under Harley and said, "All right, brutha. You're not going to like this, but we've gotta get you home--"

"Don't think we're leaving them, do you?" Leanne gestured to the captives. Their eyes were wide, intelligent, scared. Many of them showed evidence of iron burns, and all had battle injuries in varying shades of gaping to scarred. "Iron doesn't slow us down." She brushed her hands on her pants, and kicked aside what was, to humans, just a line of iron dust. At that, both McAnrai and Harley made noises of protest.

"Leanne, look at Harley. Then take another look at them. And look at the sk-"

"Right. Get Harley to the car."

"*Look at the sky, woman.*"

"What?" Leanne looked up--and recognized the import of the lowering sun. She turned back to McAnrai and Harley, "How long were we in that grove?"

By the look of Harley's paws, legs and patches of coat, it looked as though he had walked through it, tried to shake it off, only to have it sprinkle all over. But...she looked at the poison powder border--it was disturbed, yes, but hardly displaced enough to cause the extent of damage, unless...

"Faery? Only minutes. But the grove? By the looks of Harley's injuries, I'd say a couple hours. If the spell goes off as planned--"

Leanne's voice was low with pain, "Then this place is gonna go boom any second now." Her movements quickened, hurried, but careful. "Leaving them is a death sentence."

McAnrai shook his head, addressed the back of her head as she scrambled, looking for a shovel, a rake, anything to make an opening in the iron thorough enough to create safe passage for the faeries, "No. *Freeing* them is a death sentence--for all of us. We don't have time. And look at them." She didn't turn. He raised his voice and shouted, "Goddammit, Leanne, look at them!"

At the shock wave of his voice, Leanne paused, looked again at the brimming cages. The prisoners all seemed to be benign Fae, but even the most kindly of faeries could be lethal when provoked. And long, cruel captivity had added an edge--friendly they may have been, once. Now? At best they were feral. Freeing them may save most of their lives--if they did it before the bomb went off--but releasing what looked to be over fifty terrified, wild creatures with lethal magickal powers? There was no telling how that would go, other than badly. Leanne's heart fell, and shame reddened her cheeks as she saw the prisoners read her expression.

McAnrai turned and started toward the car, a squirming Harley cradled in his arms. They were well down the driveway before realizing he was alone with the Faery officer. In his mind's eye, as clear as if it were happening in front of him, he could see Leanne casting, eyes silver, raising her energy...

"Oh fuck." He looked from the path to the kennels, toward the car. Harley sighed, struggled for speech.

"Leave me, go to--" Harley's voice trailed off.

Ten feet from his car, McAnrai gave up on delicacy and ran the last stretch of driveway. The rear of the SUV lifted open of its own accord, and the big man all but tossed the semi-conscious faery into the back. He turned and started to run back.

But then he saw Leanne running toward him, a throng of fear-maddened faeries in her wake. They overtook her, disappearing one by one. Without breaking stride, Leanne yelled, "Run! It's coming!"

Leanne continued to barrel toward him. Her eyes were solidly silver, and the sheen of them extended over her body, a faint metallic light covering her entirety. The wild, dangerous beauty of it immobilized him, but his senses returned when she dropped her weight. She crashed into him, sweeping his legs as if he were standing on home plate, and she was sliding in. They rolled, stopped in the ditch dip past the driveway. McAnrai pulled himself over Leanne's body, covering her as best he could. He closed his eyes, unaware that her silver shield was now enveloping them both.

In that instant, the sound of a sonic explosion shook him to his core, and the source of it swept over their flattened bodies, tearing at Leanne's energetic protection, scraping the shirt from McAnrai's back...and blasting the SUV several feet into the air. McAnrai and Leanne were hardly aware of the mundane and magickal shrapnel hailing down around them--their eyes followed the SUV as it arced through the air...

The vehicle landed, rolled, losing its passenger just before crashing down into the gully across from the property and erupting into violent flames.

"No. NO. NO!" Leanne scrambled to her feet, and took off down the hill, toward the wreckage of the burning car, following the path of fire and metal left in its wake. As she ran, the heavens above split open, spilling massive drops of rain onto the scorched land below. Heedless of rain or wind, ignoring the lightning and thunder, Leanne stumbled down the steep hill.

Toward Harley. Harley's body.

"Oh gods, no. No, no, no..." Her words cut off, choked through sobs as she reached the limp form of her closest, dearest friend. So much more than friend. She dropped to the ground, desperate to hold him, but afraid to touch--if there was even a chance he was still alive, one wrong movement could be fatal. She crouched on the ground next to him, searching for any sign of life at all.

Already weakened by the iron, Harley had been in no condition to defend himself from the effects of the crash. His coat was burned off in patches, exposing the gashes in his skin from the glass and metal torn from the SUV. Lying in a pool of his own blood, his eyes were closed, his mouth open.

Leanne held her hand over his head, slid it down over the rest of his body, inches from his skin. She closed her eyes, working to keep her breathing even, frantic to sense any life in the Cait-Sith.

Nothing.

She withdrew her hand, curled into fetal position as tears wracked through her.

CHAPTER 45 - TIME IN A THROTTLE

The heavy thuds of a man's approach drew Leanne's attention. So blinded by emotion, she didn't recognize the footsteps as McAnrai's. Raging grief propelled her over Harley's form, a vain attempt to protect him from further harm.

McAnrai froze at the sight, his heart wrenching from his chest. "Oh God help us." McAnrai whispered as he dropped to his knees. "Someone, help us."

As quickly as it started, the weather subsided, warm sunshine replacing the violent gales from seconds before.

"Well, I doubt I'm who you meant, but I am here." Lou's steps were brisk, his face serious, his eyes locked on the fallen Faery warrior. Just behind him, a parked Shelby Cobra stood, its canary yellow paint almost blinding in the bright sunlight.

"Where the hell did you come from?"

"You need help, and I'm here." Lou reached for Harley.

Leanne snarled as she instinctively dug her fingernails into the ground around Harley's body.

"*Leanansidhe Gentry, allow me to help.*" The power from his words washed over her, flooding her throat and chest with a quivering sensation. In spite of herself, Leanne relaxed her hands, and allowed Lou to touch Harley's blood soaked fur. She watched as his fingers lay on her beloved friend, only gradually aware of the changes in Lou's appearance. His fingertips shone with golden light--her eyes followed the shimmer up to his face. His eyes were solid gold, the same transformation she'd seen whenever Anya had performed intense magick. Unlike Anya, this alchemy spread beyond his eyes, to his hair and skin--the man was comprised of differing shades of sunlight, buttery tans for his clothes and skin, spun cornsilk for his hair.

Glowing liquid flowed like honey from his fingertips, and within seconds, Harley was completely ensconced. Unlike Anya's protection spells, which presented as fine, shimmery cords of swirling golden thread, the protective spell congealing over Harley looked like the actual metal itself.

Lou's words fell soft around them. "He is not yet gone, though no more is he healed."

Leanne's eyes skittered back and forth over Harley, her voice tight. "What did you--" her voice stopped short when she turned to Lou. His appearance was returning to normal--within seconds, he appeared once more as a dapper reporter. "What did you do?"

"I have given him time." His voice was tender. "It is not my place to save him, but I can do this. He is safe, but frozen. He will not heal, but he will not worsen either." He slipped his arms under Harley's form, and lifted him effortlessly. With a nod to his car, he said, "Make haste. You must get him to the Table, to the healer there."

McAnrai and Leanne were already on their feet, and walked with Lou. McAnrai climbed into the passenger seat--Leanne slipped in the backseat and reached for Harley. Lou set the Cait-Sith's head on her lap, the weight of it settling into the flesh of her thighs.

The engine came to life as Lou's hands rested on the steering wheel. With a faint smile, he said, "Hold on."

On the ride back to the Table, Leanne's heart and mind were playing a tug-of-war for attention. The weight of Harley's solid gold head had her legs almost numb and her heart close behind. But...even with the hours they lost in Faery, they should have made it home before the bomb went off at Hilton's lair.

As though reading her thoughts, McAnrai said, "Hilton's already been to the Table--set off the spell."

Lou nodded, but said nothing.

But who did he kill? Neither he nor Leanne could bring themselves to ask, holding off the tragedy they feared.

***

The Cobra pulled onto the Table's front lawn, and all the way up to the porch. Opening the doors, Lou lifted Harley from Leanne's lap. She scrambled out from under them, and after a pained look at Harley, ran inside. Through and past the caked debris of *olchan-dust*, the broken furniture strewn through the dining room, through the goddamn enormous hole in the side of the building, dread ever rising as she screamed her sister's name.

Garden--empty. Empty but for a dead body. Repulsion mixed with guilty relief as her steps slowed...definitely a man...and too blonde to be Remy...closer...closer...Bailey? Bailey Traywick?

She looked to the house and into the skeletal remains of the Garden Lounge. Ordinarily, finding a thirty foot long, ten foot tall, fire breathing dragon just chillin' in your home would be a point of interest. But Leanne barely registered Warren's true form before running to the four bodies prone on the ground next to him.

"Anya! Remy! Laidi?" Closer, she scrambled over furniture pieces and plants and chunks of scorched wall. She fell to her knees at her sister's head, taking her pulse. Steady. She looked to the next prone form, as if noticing him for the first time. To be fair, the Faery armor was new. She whispered, "Oh gods, Troy?" Her question held a mixture of wonder and dread--clearly a warrior from Faery, and by the Celtic design and somber coloring of his armor, from the Court of the Morrigan Herself. She touched his neck, searching for a pulse. Searching, searching. Eventually finding it--also steady, but so faint. Leanne groaned. If a soldier from the Battle Goddess Herself had fallen, what chance did her sister, or her friends, have?

McAnrai stifled a moan as his footsteps slowed. More acclimated to violence, to wreckage--but still sucker punched by the scene in front of him, recalling past experiences, scenes with other friends lying still.

The sound of the dragon's voice poured salve onto their tortured thoughts. "Be at peace, both of you. They are alive."

Both Leanne and McAnrai exhaled in relief as they saw the immediate proof of her sister stirring.

As Anya woke, Lou entered the Lounge, carrying Harley. He laid the gilded warrior between Warren's front legs.

After several moments, the dragon's eyes closed and his head sank. "Forgive me, my lord, but I cannot cure him."

Lou's expression creased with compassion. "I know, my son. But you can maintain, can you not?"

"Yes, my lord. But only for a while."

Oblivious to that exchange, Leanne, Anya, and McAnrai were attempting to revive Remy, Laidi, and Troy.

"Why won't they wake?" Anya's voice crept closer to panic. "I woke. Why won't they?"

"You weren't hit, Miss Anya." Warren's voice echoed through the room. "Your protector shielded you from all but the remnants of the spell."

"My protector?" Her eyes went to Troy. Even in battered unconsciousness, his features were more beautiful than before. Without his human mask, his faery nature glowed through his countenance.

"Troy Morgan was assigned to protect you, Anya Gentry." Lou placed a gentle hand on her shoulder. Answering her silent question, he added, "As per his standing orders, once Hilton's poppet was dropped in the Garden Lounge, Harley alerted our Lady of the situation."

Eyes wide, Anya turned to the Cait-Sith's golden form. "Harley hired a bodyguard?"

"*Harley* didn't. The First Lieutenant of the Morrigan commissioned a foot soldier from his Lady's Court."

"So those strange dreams--" Anya's words confirmed her earlier guess.

"Weren't dreams at all. That was your bodyguard, following his orders."

Anya mentally slapped her hand against her forehead. *Troy Morgan*. Foot soldier to the Morrigan. Of course.

McAnrai's voice was all business as he interjected, "When will they wake?"

Finding escape in logic, Leanne mused aloud. "Hilton must have cast a blanket curse--and Warren," she gestured to the dragon, whose head bowed in encouragement, "You filtered, weakened it."

"Not weakened. Slowed." Lou's voice was quiet but urgent. "They are dying. And they will die, unless--"

"Unless what?"

"Unless the spell is lifted."

"Unlikely to get him to agree to that." McAnrai muttered. "What else will work? There has to be a way."

Lou met McAnrai's gaze. After a few seconds, McAnrai gave a grim nod of understanding.

Lou turned to the prone friends. "Let's move them closer. No, my friend," he said as Warren started to speak. "Conserve your energy. We'll bring them to you." They moved the bodies to the dragon's side as Lou explained, "The more of them touching the more of him, the more in tune they will be with this healer's energy."

"This won't hurt him, though," Leanne looked to Lou, "Will it?"

"No. He is holding them to life by welcoming them into his own life force. Energetically, they are part of him now."

"So, alive unless he moves."

"Alive for now unless he moves." Lou looked at the three of them. "We need to plan. For Hilton's next try."

Anya's eyes widened as she followed the natural progression of his thoughts. She said, "We still have the onyx, and it's still filled with souls." She tilted her head to the side, "Assuming we figure out how to free them, he'll be done. Right?"

Lou shook his head. "Remember, he is a powerful sorcerer. He could still use his own blood."

"The amount he'd need, though," Leanne's countered, "Pretty sure he's not suicidal."

Lou opened his mouth to speak, but stopped himself. He pointed to the Portal. "Their bodies are in Faery. I'll hold the Portal open while you empty it. Hopefully they'll find their own ways home--if not, well," he shook his head as he strode to the Portal, "we'll figure something out."

"Again, we don't know how to empty it."

"I find, when the time is right, solutions make themselves known."

CHAPTER 46 - POKING THE BEAR

Ursula Hilton opened her eyes, blinking at the daisies floating all around her head. It had been a slow waking--she had no idea how long she'd been asleep, nor how long she'd been hovering between slumber and awareness.

She also didn't know where she was--other than hating it. The cheerful kitchen mocked her as she held as fast as she could to the memory of her dream. Nightmare though it had been, she could hear Oliver. Ollie. Her boy. He was alive in the dream. He was scared, but alive. She could hear him calling for her--she could save him. A desperate fantasy. And now, nothing.

She sat up, slightly dizzy. The room sank and swam around her, and in her disorientation, she could still hear him calling from her dream. "Mommy! Mommy!" Ursula choked back a sob. If she could hear his voice even when awake--she grabbed two handfuls of her long, dark hair. She was losing her mind.

"No, no, no," Ursula cried, slumping back against the lower cabinet. The attempt to speak hurt like hell. Her throat hurt. Not the usual burn from the alcohol, but a duller, deeper, wider burn. Her hand moved to her throat, and she winced at her own touch, and the return of her memory. Her pain. Pain.

Payne. That murdering bastard. Fury writhed in her chest as her memory returned in a flood. How did she get away from him? More importantly, how could she find him again? She welcomed the sensations that came with her violent fantasy--the pleasure of wrath temporarily numbing her pain.

"Mommy!" She heard it again. " Mommy! I'm right here! Can't you hear me?" Oliver's voice was louder this time. It carried through the tiny kitchen, bouncing off the surfaces, struggling against her ears, for access to her rational mind. "MOMMY! MOMMY! MOMMY!"

Louder and louder, insistent. "Ollie?" Ursula croaked out her son's name, and tears rolled down her face--her heart not allowing her to hope...

"In here, Mommy! I'm here!" Ollie's voice was louder, clearer. But coming from...

She looked around the room, for where the voice could be coming from. Scrambling to her feet, she grabbed the edge of the counter to steady herself. Her fingertips brushing the edge of a smooth, shiny black rock.

"MOMMMMMMYYYYYY!" Louder, louder than ever. He wasn't only in the room with her, he was shouting at her. Shouting at her from...a rock?

She grabbed the shiny piece of black. "Ollie?" Desperation pushed the words from her mouth. "Oliver! Can you hear me?"

For the first time in almost a year, Ursula Hilton heard her son's laughter. The pain of that joy almost brought her to collapse.

"Yes Mommy! I'm here! Help me!"

The noise of a door opening cut the conversation short. Snarling, she whipped around, ready to murder the cause of the interruption.

But she didn't know where she was. If whoever was walking toward her was dangerous... Ursula looked for something, anything that could be used as a weapon. Knives. She grabbed the largest from the wooden block on the counter. She turned at the hurried, approaching footsteps, knife in one hand, the rock with her son's voice in the other.

***

Considering the events of the day, Anya wasn't sure what she had expected to find in her kitchen, but a half-crazed, Columbus socialite clutching her bosom with one hand and swinging a butcher knife with the other wasn't it.

"Ms. Hilton. You're awake." Anya flinched at the expression on the woman's face. Ursula's most recent memory was probably of getting wrestled down after she and Leanne tried to take her to her family--maybe reminding her that Anya was the one who knocked her out wasn't the best choice.

"Get away from me!" Ursula clutched--oh hell--the *onyx* to her chest, brandishing the knife unsteadily.

"Ms. Hilton, I am here to help you." Anya tried to send calming energy to Ursula, but her powers were so diminished, she had none to give. She could still hear thoughts, though. And Ursula's mind was roaring, inarticulate with primal passion.

Slow and calm words, Anya. Slow and calm. "Ms. Hilton, I need that rock." Gently, Anya reached for the rock, then jumped back to avoid the stabbing blade.

"Stay away from me. From us. I will *kill* you if you try to take my baby away from me."

Okay, she'd figured out what was in the rock. Or rather, who.

The truth. As strange as it was, it was the only chance of reaching her right now. "Ms. Hilton, I know."

Ursula's face contorted in confusion, hope, and wariness. "You can hear him too?"

Okay, the truth might need a little tweaking. "Yes, Ms. Hilton, I can hear him, too. And the others--"

"I have to help him. He's trapped in there. He's scared--my baby is scared."

"Let me help you." Anya reached again for the onyx, but slower, and with an eye on the knife.

"We have to get him out." Ursula turned to the counter, and tried to slam the rock on the marble surface.

"NO!" Anya's voice still held a little command. Enough to stop the frantic mother from accidentally killing everyone in her hands.

"I have to save him."

"And I know how." Okay, so a lot of truth bending. To be fair, the only part Anya was sure of was that it would be disastrous to just break it to pieces.

"You can save my boy?"

"I can try."

Ursula's face contorted in pain. "No, you can't. He's dead. He can't be alive. I can't be hearing him." She rounded on Anya again, waving the knife. "He's gone. I can't be hearing him!"

"**MOMMY**!" This time, Ollie's voice was loud enough, both women could hear him.

Ursula gasped, and in her surprise, dropped the onyx. Seizing her chance, Anya caught it.

The second Anya's fingers clasped around the onyx, time froze. Anya watched the change in Ursula's eyes as the rock left her grasp. Wide, wild, feral. In that moment, Anya realized she was no longer talking to a grieving mother.

This was a momma bear.

And Anya had just taken her cub.

"Oh shit." Anya turned and ran. Ran faster than she knew she could fly, strangely thankful for the hole in the building's side as a bellowing roar shook the world.

***

As Lou opened the Portal, Leanne and McAnrai spun in defensive surprise at the spectacle of Anya running toward them with the primal form of Ursula Hilton charging after her. The setting sun played on the dappled shade, the shadows and beams playing tricks on the eyes. Ursula, in and out of the golden light and purple shadows, flickered between her pixie build and the looming force of a full grown grizzly bear chasing down its prey.

McAnrai muttered, "Oh hell."

Anya barrelled into them, Ursula snarling behind. The four of them collapsed, struggled to disentangle, but it was Ursula who found the onyx. Leanne, Anya, and McAnrai knew better than to fight her. She clamped it between her hands, and when her mouth opened in a bellow...

The ground shook. The Portal shook.

Lou held the Portal steady. The humans covered their ears.

Ursula roared at the rock--and the onyx trembled. Piercing through the thunder, screams of fear, screams for help, and one clear voice of a boy calling for his mother.

At the sound of Oliver's voice, she bellowed again. At the noise, the onyx cracked. Light poured from inside. A young woman flew out, her wispy form sailed through the open doors of the Portal. A man...his form shot like a bottle rocket into the Faery Realm.

Ursula howled.

A smaller outline. A boy. A young boy emerged--hovered. At his appearance, Ursula relaxed into a portrait of pure joy. She reached for her son, only to grab thin air as the lights composing his outline compressed and zoomed into Faery.

With an anguished cry, Ursula dropped the onyx and disappeared through the Portal, into the Faery Realm.

Anya and Leanne picked up the onyx--concentrating all their will to summon the other souls. Moved by pure instinct, McAnrai shut his hands over theirs, felt the rush of energy channelling from the ground, through his body, into his hands.

A fourth light emerged, flew into Faery. And a fifth.

Leanne and Anya and McAnrai shouted, together and separately, three voices as one...

As the sixth and seventh souls began their exit, there was a great crackling. Screams of horror, of pain. The onyx exploded, its shards scattering to the air, to the ground.

To the silence of Death.

The sensation of feeling those two last souls struggling to escape, struggling for life--to then be ruthlessly crushed into non-existence... Strangers or not, the anguish, the loss cut to each of their hearts. The three humans stared, horrified, as the last soul perished.

"They...they're...are they--" Leanne's shoulders slumped.

"Dead. Yes." Lou's voice was sad.

"What happened? Did we--" Anya could not bring herself to finish the question.

"No." Leanne answered with a certainty that surprised her. "We didn't kill them. It was something, else."

"That it was." Payne Hilton chuckled as he walked through the garden. "Silly girl. Didn't anyone tell you it's rude to play with someone else's toys?"

CHAPTER 47 - THERE'S BLOOD ON THE LAWN

"So sorry to interrupt." Payne Hilton's voice dripped with sarcasm, "Except that I'm not."

Hilton took slow, deliberate steps toward them, as though making a formal entrance to his own play. The same calico light that played with Ursula's appearance was very still--the shadows obscured everything behind him. Now close enough to speak softly, he nodded at the Portal. He said, "And after the destruction of my home, there went the last of any and all evidence against me."

"Evidence?" McAnrai's voice was grim.

Ignoring him, Hilton continued, "I have been working to right a wrong. A wrong done to me many years ago. The theft of my passage into Faery. This," he pointed at the sealed Portal, "is rightfully mine. That my hobbies gave me the means to reclaim it, all the better."

"Hobbies?" Leanne sneered. "Torturing and murdering animals, faeries, and humans are your hobbies? Dude. You need to get laid."

Hilton turned his full attention to Leanne. After a few seconds, he said, "Okay."

Leanne's eyebrows shot up, and McAnrai took a step forward, but before either of them could respond, a noise carried through the air. From nowhere, from everywhere, soft crying echoing through the garden, through their minds.

"The hell?" Like the others, Anya was looking in every direction, searching for the source of the crying.

Hilton continued, "I had resigned myself to leaving a mess behind when I gained my prize. But that little poppet switch? Neater. Teaches you a better lesson." He tilted his head back, smirking. "The first of many lessons I'll be teach--"

Lou's voice rang clear and true, cutting Hilton's monologue short. "Payne Hilton, I say to you now. Remember your debt to your master. The obedience you owe him."

Hilton turned, looked at Lou as though seeing him for the first time. After a moment, his face transformed with recognition. He scoffed. "Master? Me? I have no master." There was no mistaking the mockery in his voice when he added, "Oh Fair Haired *King* of the Autumn Court."

King? Three sets of eyes looked at Lou. Anya met his look, her silent question eloquent. Lou reminded them, "I've already told you my names."

Anya's mind raced to their introduction: "The name's Lou N. McCury." In a flash of discovery, she heard it again, now properly, "The names: Lugh and Mercury."

Lugh, Celtic god of the First Harvest. God of Lightning. Tender of the Golden Apples of Life. The Oath Binder...

Anya's memory flashed to the destruction of the dog fighting rin g...the man in the lightning...

Leanne's mind replayed Harley's gilding, the freezing of his wounds...

McAnrai heard the words echo in his head, "No, you're *allied* with a being who is powerful enough...can bend ancient glamour..."

Mercury Quicksilver, the Messenger, god of travel, communication, eloquence, trickery...and apparently the Autumn King's Roman counterpart.

Lugh smiled faintly at their collective epiphany, but his eyes never left Hilton, who was dragging the source of the echoing sobs...

Hilton jerked his arm forward, tossing a small woman into the pool of light before the portal. Dahlia Hilton's arthritic frame crumpling as she did. The disoriented woman didn't attempt to stand, instead crying in a heap on the garden lawn. Vibrating with outrage, McAnrai whispered, "Holy shit, that's his *mother*."

Leanne, Anya and McAnrai all gasped as Dahlia's magick poured from her, swirling in a thick, opalescent mist. Though physically weak, the air throbbed with the unused Talent Dahlia had held in reserve for so long.

Trembling with horrified realization, Leanne whispered, "Holy shit, she's powerful enough to set off the spell."

"Indeed she is. I always thought it a waste, her never using it. Handy now, though." Payne Hilton extended his hands toward his mother, his fingers curled as claws, clenching against the mist surrounding her. At his touch, Dahlia screamed, her physical and emotional agony melded together, lifted from her...

As life left Dahlia Hilton's body, the spell ignited. She resisted, her attempt at a protection spell lit up as a dome of encasing light. It was strong, but only slowed Hilton down, since his killing curse fed off of the dome instead of Dahlia. Frustrated, Hilton poured more energy into his attack, becoming oblivious to his surroundings.

The ground around the Portal started to disintegrate, its woven branches unraveling from the wispy threads of Fabric holding them in place. Thunder rumbled as clouds flooded from all directions, and swirled overhead, leaving just enough sky to show the waning moon.

The Portal was coming apart at its seams.

When the dry screams of the elderly woman crackled through the air, Anya turned to Lugh for help--but her stomach plummeted at the look of satisfaction on the face of the sacrificial god.

The sight of Hilton torturing, attempting to kill his own mother was too much for McAnrai. He charged forward, potential apocalypse be damned. His fist found its mark, and Hilton spun in the direction of the impact, landing jaw first on the ground.

At the break of his concentration, Dahlia screamed for help.

At her cry, sudden blackness swept across the sky, cloaking them from the waning sunlight. Within seconds, all became darkness but for the light from Dahlia's shield. From the reflected glow, Leanne could see the darkness had form, a fluid smoke gurgling around them.

Hilton pushed toward his mother, his hands opening and clawing shut as he attempted to throttle her through the barrier she had cast. The barb-wire light sphere cracked, and Dahlia screamed again.

Everyone froze as the shadowy blackness poured smoothly from the sky, and seeped through the cracks in Dahlia's magickal spell. Once inside, the smoke engulfed the woman, abruptly cutting off her screams. Shining in the now moonlight, her protective cage flaked and dissipated. Dahlia's words pierced the ravaging weather, and Leanne heard her beseeching the darkness, as though it had awareness of its own. "Take me, please take me from this."

The black presence coiled from liquid darkness to the form of a man. With neither face, nor feature beyond his human shape, he crouched to the prone woman, cradled her in his arms, kissed her. As the shadow-man's lips caressed her face, Dahlia Hilton aged in reverse, returning to the full bloom and beauty of her youth. Her eyes were dazed, unfocused. Returning the embrace with the vigor of young womanhood, both Dahlia's soul and her savior disappeared, leaving her broken body behind.

***

A ground-shaking roll of thunder tore Anya, Leanne, and McAnrai's attention from Dahlia's death. Frantic strobe-styled lightning exploded across the sky. Hail, rain...

The ground shook harder as the Portal continued to writhe. Thunder crashed around them, the sheer impact of the noise causing the larger pieces of hail to burst midair. Tiny spikes of ice stabbed at their skin and steaming hot rain scalded them.

Anya looked around--as the fight over the Portal shook the weather conditions from bad to worse, the dramatic exit of Dahlia and her lightless rescuer...

Ignited the spell.

There's loud, and scary loud, then super scary loud...and then there's the terrifying epiphany of absolute silence. The crisis tension of the Portal's detaching from both realities gave the illusion of immobility. Anya looked to the people around her--Leanne, Mac, Hilton--completely still. Even the winds and rain and hail--all still, frozen in the moment. The only movement of sight or sound came from herself, Lugh, and the Portal.

With unspoken cooperation, Anya and Lugh raced to the Portal. On instinct, Anya slapped her hands against the flat of the door. She felt them get sucked in, then spread to the full width of her open arms, pulling her flush against it, hugging the door as her arms disappeared into its glowing surface. Her surroundings abruptly changed, caught between Earth and Faery. The Portal was in front of her but behind her as well, moving from clear focus to blurred splitting, like the double vision effect of blow to the head. In an instant of complete overlapping, she could see clearly into each realm--her home to the right, the fields of the Autumn Court to her left.

When they split again, Anya found herself caught in what looked like a fiber-optic car wash, threads of Fabric flurrying wildly through the air. She tried to pull herself out, back to the garden, but a voice sounded in her head.

"No! Grab what you can and hold fast!" Lugh's voice reverberated, loud enough to fill her mind entirely, but soothing despite its volume. Anya's head moved back and forth, looking for him, but she was alone in the maelstrom.

Until she looked up.

Lugh was taller--much taller, and now able to reach around Anya, and grab the splitting Portals by their sides, uniting them. His hands glowed with the silver and gold lights of the metal filigree, flashing with the lightning bolts stabbing the earth around their feet.

"You're the anchor! Its link to the mortal world--hold on!"

Anya tightened her embrace, barely feeling the tight cuts of fiery cords of Fabric. Desperately, she concentrated on maintaining her grip without unleashing the force building up in her. Too much was at stake--the universe was literally falling apart, and if she lost control now...

"Control. Control. Maintain control." Anya's mantra pounded in her head, through her body. She imagined herself as stone, solid, strong and unmoving. She sank her weight into the earth below her, and gripped the fraying Fabric harder. She felt the joints in her hands burning with the effort, the skin across the front of her body straining between the Fabric squirming for freedom and the internal twisting of her own power as it struggled to unleash itself.

"Stop fighting it--embrace your power, woman!" Lugh's voice carried a command almost impossible to resist.

"But I can't--can't control it!" Her entire body started to shudder as the esoteric suction from the Portal played tug-of-war with the magick coursing through her.

"I am a *GOD*. I will help!"

A crack in the ground opened at their feet as the earth quaked on both sides of reality.

For the first time, Lugh's voice held a note of panic. "Anya, there is a time and a place for unbridled power. THIS IS BOTH!"

Time froze in Anya's mind as a moment of clear epiphany. The power inside her? Maybe she didn't know how to control it, maybe she couldn't, not yet anyway. But this was about more than overcoming personal doubts.

What was faith worth, or the point of spiritual devotion, if when the moment of crisis arrived, she couldn't trust her god?

If she couldn't trust Lugh, she had no business doing business. And if she didn't have the courage to woman-up and do what needed to be done, she had no right to the calling of Witch.

In a perfect moment of understanding, Anya surrendered herself to the power flowing from and through her. She felt it erupt from her solar plexus, radiating outward, joyful and fierce and primal. It flowed from her feet as her awareness embraced the mortal earth, dissolving any sense of personal being from the waist down. It rushed from her heart, her hands, as the upper half of her body became indistinguishable from the realm of Faery. The sudden rush of knowledge, empathetic understanding for all beings, both mortal and immortal, animal and plant, good and evil, flooded her mind, overwhelming her as a tidal wave of information and emotion.

There should have been pain. There should have been agony. But in the momentary sharing of Lugh's reality, Anya felt nothing but ultimate burden and infinite peace. She watched as the blurring, double-vision warble of reality bounced one last time, then overlapped into clarity.

Anya collapsed to the ground, drained but exhilarated. The Portal was stable. The Fabric mended. As her eyes lulled to the seduction of exhausted blackness, she smiled as the sky cleared and the wind stilled, wholesome reality once again asserting itself.

***

The reassertion of reality also set everything back in motion.

With the final negating of his spell, the ultimate undoing of his life-long plans, Hilton's eyes went livid with the malevolence of his intent.

Leanne braced herself as he raised his energy. *Bring it, bitch.* She dropped her own awareness into the ground, rooting herself into place as she called upon the Waters with her Talent. Her eyes closed slowly, then flashed open, their usual green replaced with swirling quicksilver.

Drowning was too good for him, but it was what she had. Leanne brought the Water up, swept her arms to the side and back like a double handed pitch from a baseball mound. Leanne unleashed the Waters, pouring everything she had into the execution before her.

The Waters hit him with crushing force. Hilton went down with a thud as the indignity of Leanne's overpowering attack held him fast to the ground, a savage current whirling over and around him. He struggled for several seconds, then went still. Leanne was dizzy from the effort, and she leaned forward, her hands on her knees, taking deep, recovery breaths. Though water was her metier, an attack of this enormity cost her.

The currents flowing over Hilton slowed, then ceased. Leanne and McAnrai exchanged a quick look of confusion as the Waters disappeared--instead of returning to the ground, to their source, they seemed to sink into the prone man. Attracted by the spectacle, new *olchanfae* swarmed over him, hundreds of them, as he twitched on the dry earth.

"Oh shit." Leanne straightened to her full height, praying she was wrong about what she saw.

Hilton's eyes snapped open. He sat up.

She was not wrong.

***

McAnrai watched the monster's eyes bore into Leanne. As Hilton rose to his feet, his expression became a showcase of sadistic anticipation. This is it, McAnrai thought to himself. The bastard was about to make his final attack. The man's intent drew from the *olchanfae* unfortunate enough to be nearby--their essences vaporized and absorbed into the sorcerer, fueling his immediate need for power.

Hilton raised his hand above his head, a whip materializing into his grasp as he coiled it, preparing to strike. The gleam of its bladed tip reflected in the dim light.

McAnrai wanted nothing more than to kill Hilton with his bare hands--but there wasn't time. He brought his Glock from his side, leveling its sight on Hilton's chest.

Hilton smiled, stepped quickly to his left, released his attack.

And impaled McAnrai.

McAnrai blinked, then stumbled slightly as his gun lowered. Blood dripped from the blade protruding from his back. Hilton pulled the whip to him, torking his body to the right, ensuring the blade casually sliced through McAnrai's chest as it did. The sickening sound of bones snapping, blood gurgling wrung at each of the onlookers. Still aware, if only for seconds more, McAnrai snarled as he brought his gun back to level, squeezed off one shot before collapsing to the ground...black eyes open, empty pools under a merciless sky.

CHAPTER 48 - AND I AM THE MORRIGAN'S GIRL

T he very air vibrated with a scream. Anya's eyes opened as a tide of anguish coursed through her, bringing her recovery nap to an abrupt end. Her eyes searched wildly for the source--for Leanne. Then for the reason her sister--

Oh Lady, oh gods. Waves of horrified nausea threatened her as tears blurred her vision, obscuring McAnrai's mangled form.. She looked back at Leanne.

Pain, grief. *Wrath*. Leanne's Valkyrie call came from all directions, shaking the trees, plants, the ground. The remaining *olchanfae* fell, either from their perches in the trees and plants, or from the air. They each hit the ground, their gloating forgotten as they clutched their ears. Their mouths formed in wide screams, noiseless against the cacophony of Leanne's anguish. Her cry continued, and Anya watched in heartbroken amazement, as each grisly faery exploded in a puff of black smoke. Within seconds, Hilton was alone against them.

As Leanne's voice subsided, the garden became silent.

Raising her left hand, Leanne beckoned the water from the small, crescent pond under the old willow tree--it came at her call, slamming into Hilton's back, engulfing him in tightly in a series of foaming currents. He struggled, stumbled, and almost fell. Spent from loss and exertion, Leanne dropped to her hands and knees.

But Hilton remained upright. Once again, he absorbed Leanne's casting into himself.

Anya watched helplessly, first at McAnrai's dead body, then at her sister's collapse. At first, she thought Leanne had passed out, but her sister remained on her hands and knees, neither falling completely to the ground, nor attempting to stand.

Hilton's mouth curled to a gloat as his steps circled around her, pausing again as he stood directly behind her. For one terrible moment, Anya watched the man's energy flicker in the direction of grabbing her sister's hips, his desire to add violation to her defeat.

It was only a flicker, but it was enough to move Anya past her own fatigue, galvanizing her into action. She scratched and scrambled to her feet, moved to attack--but Lugh grabbed her arm. She heard his voice in her mind, urgently stilling her. "This is not your fight."

Her own response came out in snarl, "Like hell it isn't. You know what he wants to do."

"We aren't the only ones who know."

Lugh gestured to Leanne. Though the silence continued, the ground shook around them, and threads of silver flowed from the ground to Leanne's arms and legs. They coiled up her limbs, weaving themselves into an undulating, metallic skin, replacing the pale pink of her natural color. The tendrils crept into her hair, lining the long, red curls. The silver threads flowed past her body, coiling over her back in the outline of an enormous serpent. As it gained in form, as the rage pulsed from Leanne's heart, more threads crept from the ground, from the air around them. These threads were black, shiny but supple, the tiny details reflecting the starlight as black, glossy feathers. They filled the silver-outlined snake, giving it form, muscle.

Without warning, it lunged, curled around Hilton, and flung him back to the ground where he had broken his *geas* by attacking his own mother. Where he'd killed McAnrai.

He landed with a grunt, and clambered to his feet.

Leanne rose slowly, the silver and black slid back into the ground at her feet, creating a small pool of energy below her. In a hoarse whisper, her voice traveled through the garden, a noise more felt than heard. "You have taken from me and drawn it into yourself."

"Little girl, I can take whatever I want." He swept his arm toward the Table, to the bodies he left there. "You're boyfriend in there, he tried to kill me. And couldn't."

Standing now, he laughed through his words, "And the *mighty* Cait-Sith," he sneered as he swung his arm at the Lounge again, "He's never waking up, you know. Not without the grace of a god, and as you can see," He gestured to his mother's lifeless form, "they are notoriously fickle. Not that it matters."

Leanne stood as a cast statue against his taunts. Her voice was calm and clear. "You have taken from me and drawn it into yourself."

Ignoring her, he went on, "All this time, I worried there was something special about *you*. Something in you that kept thwarting me. But it seems that the only skill you have is the ability to get men to serve you." His steps found their way to McAnrai's body, and he squatted down at the man's head. "And now you've lost your last protector." He straightened back up, brushed imaginary dust from his front.

With an air of mocking curiosity, he asked, "So what are you going to do now?"

Leanne stood perfectly still, only her eyes moved, tracking his pacing form. He walked to her, bending down so they were almost nose to nose. "What are you going to do, now that you've been stripped down to nothing more than a worthless piece of ass? Do you still think you can kill me? Or are you going to accept your proper place in this world? I could always use a concubine." He brushed Leanne's cheek with the back of his fingertips, dragged his hand down her front.

The ground rumbled again. The grass surrounding the black and silver pool withered, browned and crumbled into dust as the humidity in the air disappeared completely. The crows and ravens riled again, wheeling in circles, their raspy cries cutting the dry air like sharp scissors through tissue paper.

Hilton stepped back, smug smile in place.

Anya watched as the pool at her sister's feet disappeared, rushing up her legs and forming spheres of power around her hands. Leanne drew back and pitched her attack again. Again, the rushing currents flowed from the palms of her hands.

Again Hilton fought against the strangling currents. Again the absorption.

Her voice was still hoarse, but it was also still clear. Louder than before, Leanne declared, "You have taken from me and drawn it into yourself."

At this third utterance, Hilton did not laugh.

He was frozen in place. Anya could see his body jerk slightly, as if he were trying to move a mostly paralyzed body. Her eyes widened in time with his, as they both reached the same illuminating conclusion:

he hadn't deflected Leanne's spells--by absorbing her attacks, he'd allowed her magick into his body.

His attempt to weaken her by absorbing her power enabled her to influence his actions.

Leanne's hands, which had been palms out, flipped inward, her fingers curling as if each were beckoning a follower. Her voice raised to a thunderous pitch as she shouted, "I call upon Blood, as from Blood all force of will comes!"

Anya's heart froze in her chest. Oh shit. Working with Water was one thing, but working with *blood--*

Leanne's skin started to glow, a cool shimmer in the dark garden. The light became brighter, pouring from her and irradiating Hilton. His skin darkened, suffusing with shades of purple and blue. Leanne raised her hands slightly, her blank, metallic eyes devoid of emotion, and nothing but the tilt of her head to indicate her interest in the scene before her. In response to that gesture, Hilton raised his own hands, brought them near his throat.

Anya watched, horrified, as he jerked helplessly against Leanne's direction, fighting uselessly against the open, claw like hands that had strangled so many others. His eyes widened with terror as he grasped his own throat, and started squeezing. Oh no, oh no, oh sweet Lady, *no.* Anya broke herself free from Lugh's firm grip, and charged to her sister, shouting.

"Dammit, no!" Her voice was little against the cacophony rattling around her, but she had to try. "Leanne! LEANNE! NO!" Anya yelled, she screamed, she shouted until her voice gave out. Nothing. She reached out with her mind, but the usual, sardonic welcome was gone, in its place a wall of sheer energy, silvery gleams and threads of black formed a barrier. Anya pressed harder, but to no avail.

Hilton dropped to his knees. Tears streamed down Anya's face, and she turned to Lugh. "Stop her! You've got to stop her!" But Lugh was engaged in his own contest of wills. Flares of lightning flickered through, in and around a mass of pitch black smoke--the same blackness that had engulfed and taken Dahlia Hilton's soul. It was less a battle, more a dance, rhythmic and flowing. The ebb and flow of it hovered over McAnrai's body, slinky black breaths washing over him, then getting flicked away by flashes of light.

She turned back to her sister, her sister who had decided to twist her own Talent to murder. Anya frantically examined her options. Lugh was unavailable. Her Talent had been sealed out of Leanne's mind. Hilton was dying, and each tiny bit closer he came to death was reflected in the diminishing humanity in her sister's energy--if Leanne managed to kill him, she'd end up destroying herself, too. And McAnrai was dead--oh God and the gods, that's what pushed her over the edge. That last thought broke Anya's restraint, and damn near broke her heart. Her own mind flooded with the rapid-fire memories of what she knew of Leanne over the last two and half decades.

Suddenly, Anya stood firm, her calm restored as her heart emptied of all panic.

Her telepathy may not be of any use, but her love...

Anya harnessed that love, focusing it, letting it flow into her hands. She closed her eyes, reached forward, released her energy to the air between Leanne and her victim.

Almost instantly, the connection between Leanne and Hilton snapped. He fell back onto the ground, choking, gagging for air. Leanne stumbled back, her color returning to normal, her hair reddening from the white locks they'd become. She looked at her hands, wonder in her eyes, then looked at Anya. She swayed on her feet, and Anya ran to her, caught her.

The crackling of lightning blended almost seamlessly with the caw-ing of the ravens, the crows, and the whooshing wind of the billowing black smoke. The cloud of electric light and shadowy black eclipsed their view of McAnrai's body completely, and for that, Anya was grateful. The sisters watched as the avian dance continued, its steady movement hypnotic. Leanne looked at Anya, and asked, "What is--?"

"I thought it was a fight, but now--?"

Her words were cut off by crass, ugly laughter. "That? Oh, that's nothing more than fire and smoke, called by me." Hilton pulled him-self to his feet, his strength seeming to return as he did so.

Leanne and Anya ignored him, so mesmerizing was the marbled sphere of fluctuating energy. Anya felt herself pulled toward the whirling clouds, her feet stepping of their own accord as she moved to the small electrical storm.

"They wait there for my orders, obedient to my will."

But his voice barely reached Leanne's awareness as she let her mind become lost in the blissful oblivion before her. It was a curious sensation, this brief reprieve from suffering. McAnrai was dead, she could see him, right there. With him, still so close to him she could almost touch, went her warmth, her love, and even her interest in... She paused, the periphery of her awareness clouded somewhat by a nagging, whining voice. She'd lost interest in it, and in all humanity. In her own humanity... Little more than an afterthought, she noticed a numbed void where her Talent for empathy should have been...

Hilton's voice thundered through the night, "*Bitch, you'll look at me when I talk to you!*"

A rush of poisonous energy sped past Leanne's pensive form, wrapped itself around McAnrai's body, and snatched it away from the dancing lights and shadows, through the air, to the ground between Hilton, Leanne, and the apple trees.

At the profane treatment of McAnrai's body, the shadows and lights ceased, their offended outrage so palpable, Leanne could feel it in her bones, despite her deadened state.

Leanne's eyes followed McAnrai's slung form.

When he landed, her restraint snapped. Severed her intellect, her emotions, and her awareness from anything and everything but her wrath.

And Hilton's punishment.

CHAPTER 49 - THE UNINTENTIONAL VOW

Golden apples of the Sun,
ever loving, ever tending,
Whose tree shall bloom to hail those passed
to lands of summer never-ending
Golden apples of the Sun,
honey sweet, Life giving,
Wake the warrior from untimely slumber
charge to him the task of living...

Leanne's voice echoed through the land and the heavens, shaking the very ground and air.

"I call upon the Natural Worlds, that I may wield your power for the task before me!"

Sweeping her arms behind her, then in front, gestured to Hilton.

"Again, I call upon Blood - for it is through blood all senses exist." Faster than before, Hilton's blood rushed to the surface of his skin, reddening him with the illusion of shame he couldn't feel.

"Drop." With the lowering of her hand, he fell to his knees.

"Beg for forgiveness." Unable to resist the order, he opened his mouth to speak. Instead of words, blood poured from his mouth.

"Behold!" At the flick of her wrist, Hilton's head snapped up, his eyes writhing with hatred and fear.

With a satisfied smile, Leanne said, "*You* will look at *me* when I talk."

Her voice dripping with cruelty, she directed him, "Submit." The front of Hilton's pants drenched with reeking submission.

"Feel!" Leanne's hands gripped into tight fists as she squeezed with everything she had, twisting and pinching each and every nerve in his body. Through the squawks of the crows and the cries of the ravens, she thought she heard something else, a woman calling her... She felt her fingernails dig into her palms, enjoying her ability to be aware of Hilton's physical agony.

***

"Leanne, no!" Anya shouted as her sister again disappeared in a melding of black and silver energy. Despair ripped at her heart as she watched Leanne torture Hilton. Desperate, she appealed to Lugh. "Stop her! Stop this! Isn't that why you're here? To help us?"

Lugh's voice was carefully neutral. "I cannot defy my Lady's will. It is not my place to stop Leanne's evolution."

"Well, what the hell *can* you do? We have to do something!"

"Have faith."

Faith? Her god may have helped her for his own ends, but now, when she needed him...what good was faith?

***

"Listen!" Blood dripped from Hilton's ears as he writhed in suffering humiliation.

Leanne's arms stretched over her head.

"I call upon the Morrigan, Queen of the Living Waters, Divine Lover, Mistress of Blessed Death!"

Her call lifted to the skies as her power became infused with the soil below her feet. With open arms, she shouted, "Make me your Priestess, your weapon of Divine Justice! By the offering of my blood and the power it holds, I stand before you now, my honor willingly betrothed to the safety and sanctity of the worlds, both Mortal and Fae!" The entirety of Leanne's awareness was wrapped in the darkness flowing in, from and around her. Streaks of icy silver flashed around her eyes, up and down her person. She watched as Hilton suffered, her empathy well aware of his desire to die...he was now begging of his own accord...

She had no intention of granting him that mercy.

***

As the echoes of Leanne's vow faded, the black, inky clouds once again unfurled across the night sky, smothering the natural light. In the perfect absence of sight, the shadow boomed, "I accept your terms." As suddenly as the darkness had come, it disappeared, leaving them in a bath of clear, clean starlight.

Anya turned to Lugh. Without a word, he turned to the apple trees flanking McAnrai's body. Their non-seasonal blooms glowed, reflecting in the moonlight as teardrops of delicate honey. At once, each petal quivered, detached themselves from the trees, swirled in the air. Closer and closer to each other, drawing themselves together, coalescing as a golden apple. It hovered, then floated into the open palm of Lugh's hand. He knelt, cradling McAnrai's head. The apple liquified, then poured as rich, golden honey into the dead man's open mouth.

Lugh turned to Anya. She whispered, "What did you do?"

When the last drop disappeared, Lugh stood, smiled lovingly at Anya. His form disappeared, but his voice sounded through the garden.

"I fulfilled my role."

Leanne wallowed in the icy numbness of her attack. She didn't feel anything at all. Even the enjoyment of Hilton's suffering had left, leaving in its place a blank emptiness. As her interest in his torture faded, the energy around her shifted, from a black cloud with silver streaks, to gray and metallic, to a shimmering, silvery light now laced with the occasional flare of black. Her will to hurt dissipated with the rest of her heart's contents--into nothingness.

She released her hold over his blood, over him--allowed his body to crumple into a heap of bone and flesh. He was still alive, and cognizant, and even able to move. But he lay there, mostly still. And what triumph she may have felt was empty--everything was empty, but for the cold.

So this was death...She hadn't meant to kill herself, but by the Lady, she had to stop the bastard. If his defeat came at the price of her blood, so be it.

Her arms dropped and her eyes closed, tears welling up in her eyes.

She was barely aware of anything beyond her own emptiness--not Hilton's attempt at movement, not her sister's wide-eyed astonishment at the way Lugh vanished into thin air...leaving Anya all alone...

She had left Anya all alone...

The enormity of the moment hit her. Dying meant she was leaving Anya, and oh gods...she cried harder.

As tears fell down her cheeks, dripped across her shirt, the coldness gave way. Warm air ruffled around her, drying her tears as they continued to fall. In her mind's eye, she could see a cloud of magickal energy--like hers, but not. A white cloud with golden threads wrapped itself around her, interacting with her energy.

As the white and gold blended into Leanne's energy, the threads of her power coiled together--white threads coiled with black, creating a rope of deep, soothing neutral gray. The clouds of silver mixed with gold, giving a marbled beauty to the mist engulfing her. The heat against her front increased, as if the source of it were coming closer, the sunny beams of light growing as the cloud's bright center gave shape to the form of a man.

Leanne opened her eyes, and cried with relief. McAnrai was standing in front of her, his smile full of love and concern. He gathered her into his arms. "Shhh. It's not as bad as all that."

She laughed bitterly through her tears. She looked past the brilliance of air around them, past it to the dark of the moonlit garden. To Hilton's body, struggling to stand. "I just wish I'd taken him with me."

McAnrai kissed her forehead. "Take it from me, Leanne, you don't. You don't want that on your heart." They both looked up as the crows and ravens started fidgeting. "And you did plenty. Even gave him some time to wallow in his defeat."

From the corner of her eye, Leanne saw Hilton crawl to where McAnrai had originally fallen. Crawling in the direction of the Portal. Someone had reopened it, revealing the forbidding landscape of what looked like an Irish moor. "What's he doing?"

Guessing the goal, McAnrai asked, "May I have the honors? I owe him one."

"Well, if we weren't dead, I'd say hell yeah."

"Babe, the report of my death was somewhat exaggerated." McAnrai strode over to Hilton, who had managed to stand up, McAnrai's pistol in his hand.

As Hilton brought his arm up to shoot, McAnrai kicked him, square in the chest, sending him flailing through the Portal.

The silent swarm of ravens and crows exploded into a frenzy. They flew as one murderous conspiracy, through the Portal. Once in Faery, they attacked, dive bombing the man, screeching as they tore at his body, hunks of flesh and pieces of bone scattering over the land, each bit crumbling into dust as Hilton's blood drenched the ground.

Once all trace of him was gone, the birds flew in a tornado fashion, funneling themselves into the shape of a tall woman with ivory skin and dark, auburn hair. She was clothed from the deep plunge of her neckline to the ends of her wrists and ankles in a gown of raven black feathers. Looking at Leanne and McAnrai, she gave a small nod of acknowledgment, then vanished as the Portal shut.

CHAPTER 50 - HEADCOUNT

"Did we just see...was that--"

"The Morrigan?" Leanne took a long, tremulous breath, exhaling as she wiped the sweat and tears from her face. "I think so." She leaned into McAnrai's open arms, rolled her face into his chest. "I thought I'd lost you--just when I'd found you."

McAnrai held her tighter, his words muffled into her hair. "Woman, it'll take more than that for you to get rid of me."

They turned at the sound of a throat clearing. Anya's eyes were big, her usually serene face flushed. Without a word, she rushed forward, gathered them both in a tight hug. Through sobs, she choked out, "Don't you ever, EVER fucking scare me like that again. *Never*."

***

At Hilton's death, his spell lifted from the Garden Lounge, and all in it.

Remy's eyes blinked open. He was sitting up, propped against a surface at once warm and giving, but also cool and dry...like heated snakeskin. He looked around the room--putting his tangled thoughts in order. The last thing he remembered...was soaring backwards across the garden, going through some glass... And maybe something about a big...

There was a soft, humming vibration, and Remy startled when he realized he was rocking, ever so slightly, back and forth.

Something about a big dragon.

He looked down, sighed with relief as Laidi's eyes fluttered open.

"Don't be so quick in your movements, Remy. Nor you, Laidi Thibadeaux." First to regain consciousness, Troy was sitting across from them, bruised and bloody, but smiling. "The Dragon Watchman must not be disturbed."

Dragon Watchman?

As one movement, Remy and Laidi looked at each other, then slowly to the large, vibrating surface supporting their backs. Thousands of golden scales interlocked across the soft metallic skin of the enormous leg holding the chefs in place. Their eyes slid over the rest of Warren Drake's true form, finally resting on the golden cat cradled between the draconian bouncer's front legs.

Confusion gave way to alarm, and Troy nodded sadly. "Aye. My commander, the Lieutenant Harlequin, has fallen. Not," he hastened to calm them, "not in death--but he is very near. Though were it not for the healing gifts of the draco lord, he would have perished. And us with him."

"That big blast of fire and smoke?" Laidi asked and answered herself, "Of course. It intercepted Hilton's spell--made it less lethal."

Troy rocked his head back and forth. "Close enough. Keeping us from death was close work. Our adversary was formidable."

"Was? He's gone?" Remy shifted gently from Warren, and stood, faltering, as though just getting from bed. He offered his hand to Laidi. As she accepted and rose, his head snapped left and right, sweeping the room. "Wait. Leanne an' Anya. Mac.. Dey're not--" the words caught in his throat.

"Hilton is gone." Troy smiled more broadly. "And our friends are fine. Outside still. And now that you're both awake," he directed their gaze back to Harley, "the draco lord can focus all his art upon my commander."

"But he'll survive, won't he?" Laidi's eyes were wide with concern. Despite Remy's support, she also stumbled.

At the dip in her movement, Troy leapt to his feet. "There, Laidi Thibadeaux. Give yourself time." He guided her to his chair, and looked up to include Remy in his words, "Both of you. Waking from an enchantment of that kind takes time for a mortal body to recover."

Laidi gratefully accepted the help, but caught Troy's suppressed grimace. Looking over his frame, she saw places where his blood had seeped from under his armor. "Oh hon. You're bleeding. Here, let me--"

At her offer, Troy's expression flashed social horror. "Oh no, I could not accept such an act of kindness from--" His words trailed off as the blood drained from his face.

"The hell you can't. Remy, you go--" But Remy was already headed for the first-aid locker.

***

"Laidi Thibadeaux, I am certain I will be fine." Troy flinched as Laidi poured iodine on the open gash.

"Damn right you will. Now hush and sit still." She shook her head as she smiled. "This won't take but a minute, and if you leave it, infection's gonna' get in." Her brow was furrowed in concentration as she discarded the bloody linen napkin and picked a fresh bandage from the box. Just then, the box tumbled to the floor as a newly woken--and very active--Sugar grabbed the last bit of gauze and took off to showcase her streaming prize, yipping all the way.

"Oh, yes. Very nice, indeed." Ripley licked the top of Sugar's head, sending the little ball of fur rolling. Laidi smiled at the gentle indulgence Sugar got from *beansidhe*.

When Remy stepped forward to help, she shot him a stern look and said, "And you make sure we keep all those together. Don't want anyone getting his blood." Remy pursed his lips as he swept it smoothly into the bag he had prepped for the incinerator. So her tone was a little sharp. Remy deserved it. While helpful, Laidi found his motive for assisting her treating Troy's injuries a little questionable. Less like support, more like hovering.

Remy handed her the clean replacement. As he walked to the small incinerator, he grumbled, "Woman, I know how to dispose of blood."

She smiled at the shocked expression on Troy's face, and wondered if he would ever get used to their banter.

Without taking his eyes off Remy, a strange, almost formal, reserve entered Troy's expression. He said, "Laidi Thibadeaux, I am in your debt for this ministering, and for the care you are taking for the future safety of my person."

With an easy smile, Laidi said, "Oh please. I don't even know how many times you saved our butts in the last day alone. That's not even counting the stuff that probably happened when we weren't looking."

Troy considered the truth of her statement. Emboldened, he asked, "If it is true, that our debts are even--"

Laidi interrupted, "I'd say better than even, hun."

"Well, if it is so that you are in mine, may I ask a question?"

"Ask anything you like." Before he could speak, she leaned around his shoulder, looked him in the eye and added, "And I've told you you don't have to be so formal. Not with me, not with anyone else here." She moved behind him, refocusing on the open gash across his back. Not as bad as she expected, but then again, one never really knew what to expect from Faery physiology. So intent was her study, and so soft were his words, she only half heard his question. "Sorry, hun. Say that again?"

He swallowed and asked again. "Why is it that an individual of your standing need answer to Remy?"

"Don't be fooled, Cap. Dat girl answers to no one." Remy grinned as he handed her a new, tightly wrung, hot cloth.

Laidi tilted her head and her mouth curled around an amused grin. "Well, that's only at work. Though he's technically my boss, we're really friends--" She stopped short as she caught Remy's eloquent eye. Laidi eyes dropped as she felt the blood rise in her face, grateful Troy's back was to her.

"What I mean to say, is that we are peers."

Though an answer to Troy's question, she addressed it to Remy. She wasn't ready to make any kind of public announcement, and he was going to have to be okay with that. From the expression on his face, her blush satisfied what the words left empty. She turned her attention back to the faery soldier's injury.

However, and to the surprise of both Laidi and Remy, Troy blanched at her words. He turned to her and said, "Remy is also Peer of the Realm?" Heedless of the barely applied bandage on his lower back, or the frustrated profanity that slipped out of Laidi's mouth as his jump sent first aid equipment flying, he turned to Remy and bowed.

"Lord Hawkins, I offer my most humble apology for any offense I may have incurred by failing to address you as your position warrants."

Surprise turned to shock as Remy watched Troy bow so deeply, the cuts on his back resumed bleeding. Almost speechless (but not quite), he laughed, "Hey heyyyy. Better calm down dere, you." He gently grabbed Troy's shoulders, lifting as he did. "And stand up. Else you're gonna bleed all over."

Troy straightened to standing, and immediately swayed on his feet. Remy reached out and steadied him, while Laidi redirected. "No, you sit the hell *down*. Right damn now. And don't get up til I tell you."

"Yes, Laidi Thibadeaux." He eased back onto the stool, his expression mortified.

Troy's reaction to her words was so sudden, to say nothing of strange, it took Remy a few extra seconds to appreciate the wording. "Whoa, whoa now." He turned to Laidi, jerked his thumb at Troy. "He just call me '*Lord* Hawkins'?"

Enlightenment dawned on Laidi's face. Closing her eyes, she exhaled a breathless, "Oh!" Of course. Troy Morgan. *Troy Of Morrigan*. He had been so thoroughly undercover as a mortal, they were still processing that he was, in fact, *not human*. Not even a little. What's more, he was not only a faery, he was a *soldier* in service of the Morrigan--*in her role as Warrior Queen*--from Her Royal *Court*.

Faeries were hard core about etiquette anyway, but if he was a member of the Court of the Morrigan Herself...All this time, he'd been calling her *Lady* Thibadeaux...and Remy had been treating her as he always did, and oh gods, the way he'd been treating *Troy*...and now he thinks Remy is also nobility...but is about to find out neither of them are anything of the sort...

She looked at Remy--who had come to at least a similar conclusion, complete with the potential for political catastrophe if they offended the warrior fae in the process of setting him straight. Hell, the physical consequences alone--even injured, a soldier of the Morrigan Court was beyond deadly to a couple of mortals, magickal or not.

But it was funny...in a terrifying sort of way.

Shit, shit, shit...

Biting the inside of her cheek in an effort to keep a straight face--while Remy turned away and made himself a drink--she patted Troy on the shoulder. "Oh hun, no. No, no. Not Peers as in royalty. I meant peers like we're equals, Remy and me. And Laidi isn't my title. It is my *actual* name."

"I do not understand. Do mortals often name their children after offices?"

Laidi turned back to her work, biting her lip. Folks from the Faery Realm embraced the concept, 'he needed killin' as a legal defense, and with even more fervor than any southerner she knew--and her daddy was a Texan. She watched Remy's expression as he swallowed his bourbon, and could tell he was thinking the same thing. His daddy was a Lone Star native as well.

Having taken his moment--and a second sip--Remy intervened, "N'no, Cap, er, Troy. Her name is *Adelaide.*"

Laidi smiled at the confused warrior. Maybe a little formality will help. "Troy of Morrigan, please allow me to formally introduce myself. I am Adelaide Marie St. Jean-Baptiste Thibadaux." In reply to Troy's blank stare, she added, "Laidi is short for Adelaide. My name."

"I see." The faery nodded as he worked it out. "You are not members of any Court. But here, you answer to Leanne and Anya, and the other people do what you say." He looked back and forth between Remy and Laidi. "And you are equal to each other."

Jumping on the loophole lifeline, Laidi said, "Yes. We run this kitchen, which is owned by Leanne and Anya. So, not royalty in any sense of the word, but in human terms, peers, equals, with each other, and working for Leanne and Anya."

"So your position here is like mine in my Lady's Court." He nodded.

Perhaps too soon, Remy flashed him a big grin. "You might even say da t'ree of *us* are peers."

At Troy's raised eyebrows, Laidi interjected, "In the mortal sense of the word."

"Ah yes. I like that." Troy smiled at Laidi, more warmly than before, bringing a slight blush to her face.

"So, what now, Troy?" Remy's interruption was not as smooth as he would have liked, but fuck it. "I hate to lose a good roundsman, but, I mean, you prolly have some Court duties, *non*?"

Laidi rolled her eyes, and Troy's expression twinkled. Conceding, he said, "Yes. The Autumn King has given me my orders. I'm to leave as soon--"

"As soon as what?" Three heads and a dragon's eye turned at the question. Anya, Leanne, and McAnrai stepped from the garden, into the hollowed Lounge. After giving Remy and Laidi quick hugs, Leanne walked to Warren, crouching on the floor. At his nod, she cradled Harley's head in her lap. McAnrai gave the room a quick glance over, and walked through, into the Table's dining room.

Anya asked again, "Leaving as soon as what?"

At the ladies' entrance, Troy started to stand, but both Laidi and Remy stilled him to the seat. "M'lady, Anya," he looked at Anya. "You three," his gaze now included Leanne and McAnrai, "managed to save five of the captured souls. The task of accounting for them falls to me."

"So you're leaving?" Anya tried to keep the disappointment from her words.

He nodded, "As soon as I am able. By morning at the latest." At her expression, he asked, "Is that a problem?"

"No. Of course not. It's just--" Her words stammered to a stop.

Laidi to the rescue. "It's that we've all grown quite fond of you." She shot a warning look at Remy, ensuring his silence. "We'd hate for you to go."

"Will you ever be back this way?" Anya regrouped. "We'd love to see you."

Before he could answer, they all turned at the sound of tinkling glass and pouring liquid. McAnrai had returned, and brought with him tumblers and a bottle of the house whiskey. As he opened it, he said, "Yeah--I'm opening a tab."

Leanne smiled as she accepted her cup. "It's on the house, sweet man."

Remy and Laidi grabbed the other four.

But Troy's and Anya's eyes had never left each other.

In an effort to change the subject with some grace, Remy turned to Laidi and said, "But she does insist on misspellin' her name, dis one." He brought his glass to his lips, and before pouring the rest in his mouth, he caught Troy's eye and explained. "'Laidi' should end wit' an 'e', and she uses an 'i'."

"Oh yeah?" Laidi's glance was so quick, Remy didn't notice. Timing it to coincide with his mouthful of liquor, she retorted, "Well, giving a guy your name and number is well and good until you find out he thinks you wrote "laid" on the paper." Raising her eyes in innocent surprise, she smiled sweetly and asked, "You okay, there, Rem?"

Sputtering through his intermittent chokes, and eyes burning from the unintentional sanitizing of his sinuses, Remy took out his handkerchief and wiped his face. Suppressing his coughs as well as he could, he dumped the dregs of the exhaled bourbon and reached for another glass. "I'm good--I'm good. Just swallowed wrong, me."

"Uh-huh." Laidi grinned at him.

From the floor in front of Warren, Leanne asked, "So it's done, then? Everything is back to normal?" She sat at Harley's head, stroking his coat--or rather, his gold-encrusted fur. There were peeks of sable here and there as the Cait-Sith responded to the healer's ministering.

McAnrai laughed. "If drinking with a faery soldier while a thirty foot dragon doctor's taking up residence in a monster-gutted lounge belonging to my girlfriend-of-five-days, to care for a gold-encrusted faery cat, all while we recover from the aftermath of an interdimensional apocalyptic battle between two gods, the Goddess, and a sleazy serial killer...if that even has the chance of something one can call 'normal'? Sure!" He chuckled into his next sip.

And then there's that whole, 'coming back from the dead' thing, McAnrai thought to himself. Aloud, he said, "Yeah, I'd say we all had a helluva week."

CHAPTER 51 - AND YOU GET A HERO MOMENT!

A week had passed since the averted Armageddon, and the crowds at The Gentry's Table were winding down for the day. The damage sustained from the "freak lightning storm" and "tornado touchdown" had drawn the goodwill of Leanne and Anya's neighbors, many of whom had stopped by to help with the clean up. Though the Table still hadn't reopened formally, Remy, Laidi and Leanne had been busy cooking for the dozens of people who had shown up with rakes, hoes, mulch, and even some potted plants.

Anya let out a long, deep breath, "God, I'm tired." Just as she closed the door after the last neighbor, a hand shot in, preventing the latch. Surprised, she opened her mouth to say 'thanks but no thanks'--but the words froze on her lips as the light from the setting sun shone like a halo around Lugh's head.

"You called?"

Anya's surprise must have shown plainly, because Lugh's gave way to a short, knowing laugh. "I suppose you're still getting used to the nature of our relationship?"

"Maybe a little." She opened the door wider, and stepped back, "You are always welcome in our home."

"You are too kind." He stepped across the threshold.

She couldn't help but stare. Lugh seemed to have aged several years in that night in the garden. The gray at his temples was barely noticeable, and the lines on his face were only a touch deeper, but he was older, late forties, maybe fifties, rather than the early-mid thirties from mere days ago.

"Cheer up. I'm not a frail, old man, yet." He grinned. "In fact, I think we should raise a glass to that very fact."

Anya smiled. "Right this way, then."

***

"If this all revolves around the Morrigan, and Her plan, why wasn't she more involved?"

Lugh had spent the last half hour filling in the blanks for people seated around him. Looking from the sisters, to Remy and Laidi, then to McAnrai, he answered the detective's question.

"Besides ordering the creation of this Portal, declaring the property as Neutral Ground and granting it Protection of the Seasonal Courts?" Lugh's eyebrow rose. "It's the nature of the Many-Faced

Queen to rule from a distance. Hers is the duty of the larger perspective."

Leanne asked, "But what's Her interest in the Brugh, with us?"

Gesturing to both sisters, Lugh asked, "When the two of you have visited through your Portal, you've noticed the changes in scenery?"

They nodded.

"That wasn't the caprice of the Realm. While the Portal remains stationary in your garden, the location of the Faery side changes. On the four major Sabbats, our side changes to the next season's Court. As of August first, the protection of you and yours fell under the jurisdiction of Autumn."

Laidi asked, "Wait, autumn in August?"

Anya explained, "First harvest, thus the connection to Autumn."

"Just so." Lugh took another sip of his whiskey, "Brad entered the Garden Lounge on the eve of Lughnasadh Sabbat, and he entered it bearing an enormously malignant piece of magick-work. There isn't a word for it--the effect an attack of this magnitude has on its guardianship in Faery. The noise reaches past Fabric, and in this case, alerted the entirety of the Autumn Court."

McAnrai slapped his hand on the table. "And *that's* where you come in to all of this."

Lugh grinned. "Yes, one of my names is Lugh, King of the Autumn Court, husband and consort to the Morrigan in her face known as Áine."

Frowning, McAnrai asked, "And the shadow-phantom guy who has the power to start and stop an apocalypse?" To say nothing of the ability to decide whether a guy gets to live or stay dead...

"Isn't."

At the dissatisfied stares, Lugh elaborated. "Dahlia has long been my comrade's devotee. As a rebellious teenager, she was eager to throw herself into what are misnamed as 'evil arts', but are more accurately described as 'shadow arts'.

McAnrai nodded. "And like attracts like."

"As you say. When she explored Celtic history, her attention was drawn to a little known--and even less understood--god. The sheer degree of her Talent, combined with her tastes, inevitably attracted the attention of my Winter counterpart. When the beautiful girl called upon him, he was quite willing to introduce himself."

"As you can see," Lugh gestured down the front of his person, "we are perfectly capable of appearing as mortal, though we have no use for the arbitrary moral codes of human culture. Their relationship was intense, passionate, and anything but a secret."

"I hardly need say her family didn't approve of the affair, and took what steps they could to separate the two by sending her to boarding schools, both here and abroad."

Leanne snorted. "Not much help when your boyfriend is a god, though, right?"

Lugh's reply hinted at a private amusement. "No, it is not." In a pensive tone, he added, "I honestly believe he loves her."

Anya blurted out, "He loved her so much, he *killed her*?"

Lugh's voice was stern. "When she chose to be his, she deliberately, knowingly, put her trust in him. They are two sides of the same coin--god and devotee. She understood what that entailed. Granting her death *was* an act of love. One she knew was coming, asked for, and welcomed with open arms."

A very nasty thought crossed McAnrai's mind, "Hilton wasn't his son, was he?"

There was no mistaking the gratitude in the shake of Lugh's head. "No, thankfully. Dahlia's family married her off to an unpleasant, but wealthy Louisiana businessman who was willing to overlook the wildness of her youth. It soon became clear that their son had inherited the unfortunate combination of his mother's Talent...and his father's personality."

"So the Winter King took Hilton on as a protege?" Leanne's tone was skeptical.

"It would be more accurate to say he was willing to protect Dahlia's interests, and if doing so also forwarded his own agenda, more the better."

McAnrai asked, "Agenda?"

"While Faery, and its inhabitants, need humanity to *believe* in us, there is nothing that says you have to *like* us. There are many among us who see fear as an acceptable, even *preferred* form of belief."

Anya had been restless in her seat. "So people are just acceptable casualties?"

"Obviously not to all of us." Lugh's expression brooked no argument. Brightening a bit, he said, "This war is far from over, and your roles are far from finished." He paused for effect, then added, "But Life is supposed to be a grand story--an adventure with loss and gain, tragedy and victory. There's enjoyment to be had in the fight, children. And none of us should want to miss out on that."

Lugh set his hands on his thighs with a deep breath. "It's getting late, and alas, I have duties which have been neglected." He stood, finished his glass.

One by one, the women and McAnrai said their goodbyes and left.

Lugh and Remy were alone in the bar.

Silent until now, Remy had listened to the explanation exposition, his countenance darkening by the second. By the time Lugh had finished, the young man could sense the ribbons of his own energy sliding on his skin, as if he were a snake charmer, surrounded by entranced--and angry--serpents.

The young man approached the ancient deity.

"*Pardonnez moi.* I need to get one t'ing straight, me."

Lugh waited with a polite, if smug, expression.

"I get how you knew Hilton was da killer, and how he'd be in da garden. And I get how you knew what he was doin'." Remy paused, choosing his words with great deliberation. "But dere's one more t'ing."

"Yes?"

Keeping his voice carefully devoid of emotion, Remy continued, "After da rehearsal dinner, how did Laidi end up in da Garden Lounge at all?"

"I saw Hilton leaving through the emergency exit, and it was necessary--"

Remy cut him off. "Y'yeah, I know how we *benefited* from her goin' in. I'm askin' *how* she got herself in an empty room, watchin' a serial killer incriminate himself wit' nuttin' but a sheet of glass in between. Did she tell you she saw sumtin'?"

The ribbon-snakes quivered, coiled close to Remy's body.

Lugh's mouth broke into a wide, relaxed smile. "Oh, I see." He set a hand on the big man's shoulder. Remy looked pointedly at the Celtic god's hand.

"I gave her a little nudge, that's all."

Remy met Lugh's gaze. His eyes narrowed. "You sent her?"

Lugh waved a flippant hand and chuckled, "Oh that. Well, with my kind of powers, it's not like there was any real danger of her getting hu--"

***

CRASH.

The noise of a door slamming against its frame caused Laidi to drop the pitcher she was carrying. She ran toward the cacophony of breaking wood and running feet, arriving on the Brugh's porch just in time to watch the flying form of a well dressed man burst across it. Lugh hit the porch railing with a loud grunt, then somersaulted backward and down into the garden.

Into the rose bushes, to be precise.

In the tussle of cries, grunts and curses, Remy slowly stepped through the man-shaped hole in what used to be the screened French window connecting the inner and outer Brugh. He stood at the steps to the garden, arms crossed, watching his friends help the Celtic god extricate himself from the thorny briers.

Lugh raised his hands, "I'm all right. I'm all right." The others backed away from the figure seated on the lawn.

"Remy! What the hell did you do???" Laidi marched over to him, grabbed his arm and turned him to face her.

He moved easily at her pull, and looked at her with a satisfied smile that didn't reach his eyes. "Don't worry. With his kinda power, dere was never any real danger of his gettin' hurt."

Lugh's expression was blank. "I've killed better men for lesser indiscretions."

Remy slowly let his head turn in Lugh's direction. After a moment, he allowed his body to follow and meet the god's stare. "I'm certain you have."

"Does that not concern you?"

The young man slowly walked down the steps and squatted down. He said, "Sir, where I come from, we don't deliberately endanger our women." His hands shook with rage, but he clenched them against his knees to hide the motion. "*Et ma maman,* she raised me better dan to treat a woman like a piece on a damn chessboard." He stood again, stepped back. "You wanna kill me, dat's your business. But it won't make you right. And it won't make me wrong, *non*." He took another step back, and waited.

After a full minute of silence, Lugh inclined his head, conceding the point. "Well reasoned."

Remy gave a sharp nod in return, and stepped lightly onto the porch. He left without another word, grabbing his hat on the way.

Laidi looked from the scene on the lawn to the empty porch to her left. "Oh, *hell* no." She grabbed her purse and followed.

***

Once Remy and Laidi were out of sight, Lugh laughed. With a shake of his shoulders, the briers withdrew their tendrils, and the thorns fell from his clothes on their own power. The Celtic god bounced to his feet, brushed his impeccable suit from imaginary bits of flora. He pretended to not notice the stares as he climbed up the steps and approached the bar. With a smile and a gesture, the Autumn King requested a refill.

"Um?" It was Anya who asked.

"What? Oh, that? Meh." He checked his hair in the bar's mirror. Unnecessarily. It--like his clothes--kept no evidence of the tussle. "He'd earned a hero moment, and she's the type to react favorably to a grand act of chivalry." Addressing Anya, he asked, "She did see the whole thing, right?"

They all paused as the shouts of her 'favorable' reaction faded in the direction of the chefs' home.

"Oh, she saw you fly through the door, all right." Anya paused again--unsure if it was okay to laugh.

"Well, that's good. It'd be a shame to waste a perfectly good deck and throw for nothing."

Leanne had been noiselessly forming words with her mouth. Finding her voice, she asked, "You aren't mad?"

Lugh laughed again as Forrest poured him another large glass of Gentry's Own. "It is one of the less pleasant parts of my role, but if being a sacrificial god was easy, there'd be no impressing the ladies with my skill in it." He winked at Anya, raised his glass to the room, "*Sláinte.*"

At that, they all laughed, then Anya suddenly exclaimed, "Oh gods!"

Ignoring Lugh's facetious "Yes?", her hands flew to her cheeks as said, "I'm so sorry—between all of the events this week, we never celebrated Lughnasadh."

Lugh shook his head. "Don't be--you honored it better than you realize." In response to their confusion, he clarified. "War games. All of those activities, sporting events? They started as training exercises for war, and later, for replacing battles altogether." Finishing his drink, Lugh wiped his mouth and stood. "So feel proud of yourselves. You did my holiday more justice than it's had in ages."

"You're staying for dinner, at least?"

"Afraid not, my dear Anya." he touched her cheek. "However, I shall be free to visit when the season turns."

She smiled, "We would be delighted if you joined us for Mabon."

"Well, that's settled then." He grabbed his walking stick, and gave a light salute to the room before disappearing into the golden sunlight of the faery garden.

CHAPTER 52 - MABON

The Gentrys' Mabon dinner was well known. As the original, and literal, thanks-giving for the harvest, the sabbat of Mabon was to the Gentrys an opportunity to throw an enormous appreciation banquet celebrating their family of friends, both mortal and Fae.

The patio had several long tables set at accommodating heights, all laid out with delectables designed to please faery palates. Bowls of tender lettuce and ruby red pomegranate seeds alternated with bowls of freshly churned honey butter and lengths of warm baguettes. Hot, buttery paninis filled with garlicky fiddlehead ferns were devoured by the fare-welling fae, as were the tureens of butternut squash soup marbled with heavy cream.

Every year, the Gentrys and their extended mortal family hosted this grand do for their friends and allies from Faery--the dawn of the Autumn Equinox kicked off an even twelve hours of revelry. Music, dancing, feasting and laughter carried the spirit of camaraderie through the entirety of their unorthodox clan. At dusk, after saying their annual fare-thee-wells to the spring and summer elementals as they departed through the Portal, the mortals at the Table moved the party indoors--to their own holiday feast.

The music was festive, even if the haunting, minor chords hinted at the melancholy of the waning year. The late September air was still warm, but that was to be expected. In Georgia, the summer lasted far into what more temperate places called autumn. The Brugh was clear of any Columbus patrons--though attendance from the Other Crowd had the place bursting at the festive seams. Forrest was proudly sharing the first sips of his Harvest Brown lager with McAnrai and Warren. They sipped with appreciation as the barkeep disappeared into the kitchen.

McAnrai's eyes followed Harley as the Cait-Sith stepped into the gentle sun at the end of the porch and curled to sleep. Gesturing past the napping feline, to the garden hidden behind the hedges, to the happy yips and squawks coming from it, McAnrai sighed. "I still can't get over how quickly they've recovered." Ripley's huge form could be seen in flashes as his playful jumps cleared the top of the shrubbery, while Sugar's creamy coat peeked here and there through the undergrowth. McAnrai lifted his glass to Warren. "There were some miracles worked there, my friend."

Warren smiled in acknowledgment, and both looked up at Forrest's return, Remy on his heels. The latter said, "Now, I can understand you two, fine gentlemen feelin' you can't cook to my standards, but dis a family affair, and you can peel like five or four potatoes as well as anyone. *Allonsy*--dinner's gotta be ready for eight--dat's not much time." As if on cue, the thick, rich aroma of a classic turkey dinner melded with the spicy accents of Laidi's oyster and andouille stuffings floating from the indoors.

***

Since most of the attendees were of comparable human-ish form, the good number of wings--feathery, dragonfly, butterfly and otherwise--made the sudden presence of a well dressed, thoroughly human-looking man a surprise. At least, that's what Forrest assumed to be the cause of the gradual slowing of the music, and the steady decrease in party goers. The bartender watched the newcomer closely, while making a decent show of wiping down the spills and drips littering the length of his bar.

By the time the dark, quiet man reached him, the two were alone, and the young bartender had a pretty good idea as to this new fellow's identity.

"How can I help you, sir?"

The answering voice was deep, yet soft. He looked at the syllabub and smiled. "While I do love a good, old fashioned punch, I'd prefer a taste of the blackberry cordial, if you please."

"Coming up." Forrest paused as he placed a tumbler on the bar. "Rocks or neat?"

Crinkles of humor creased the corners of the patron's eyes, and he answered, "Oh, 'neat', by all means. *Neat.*"

Trusting his instincts, Forrest reached for the top shelf, uncorked a new bottle of Leanne's homemade cordial. The look of approval was a relief, though the bartender didn't breathe any easier. He poured a generous glass and returned to wiping the counter.

Nate leaned comfortably into the plush backing of the bar seat. He rolled the dark, sweet liquor in its glass, rocking the tumbler along the edges of its base. His violet eyes traveled the room and its garden, as someone taking the time to enjoy his surroundings, truly experience the atmosphere. "I've heard so many interesting things about this place. It's good to finally experience it for myself." Sighing, he took another long, savoring sip. "If I could bother you with a second request?"

Forrest raised his eyes. "Yes, Sir?"

Nate leaned forward conspiratorially. "I am sure the two young proprietresses are quite busy at the moment, but I do desire a word with them. Would you mind?"

Forrest nodded and left. While he was gone, a second man walked into the Brugh. Older, white haired and leaning on a cane, his wizened face creased in a smile as he gingerly lowered himself into the rocking chair just inside the front steps. Nate tilted his head to acknowledge the newcomer, his expression remaining sober as he waited for the sisters.

"Hey, Leanne? We have a bit of a situation." Looking up, Leanne pulled her hands out of the vast bowl of potato and onion stuffing. "There's a man here, wants to talk to you and Anya." Forrest was calm, but the wariness in his expression gave her pause. She wiped her hands down the front of her apron.

McAnrai reached around her, dipping a spoon to make a taste test. "Needs more black pepper." He added a few more shakes, grabbed the spoon, and took his turn stirring the thick dressing.

Addressing the bartender as she removed her apron, Leanne's brow furrowed. "Brugh should be closed to people, Forrest. I'm not sure--"

Forrest interrupted, "Didn't come in through the front." He tilted his head over his shoulder, "And the place emptied pretty fast."

Oh.

"I see." The words came out as a breath. She turned to face the door opening from the dining room. Anya walked through it, removing her own apron.

Brushing a loose lock of hair from her face, Anya asked, "What is it?"

Leanne bit her lip and shot a look toward the bar. "We have a visitor. Came in from the back--and cleared out the side."

The younger sister took a deep, bracing breath. "Okay, then."

Leanne grinned, "Well, at least now we'll get to see what he looks like."

Anya muttered, "You say that like it's a good thing."

As they left, McAnrai lifted the large bowl and moved to the counter near the opening to the bar.

***

Leanne and Anya walked through the galley's revolving door and the lifted counter of the bar. The events of the last month had left them with a good sense of caution and a whirlwind of flurried memories. The being they had first experienced as a terrifying, vengeful agency of holy justice was now presenting himself as a man, and a prepossessing one at that. His short dark hair was neatly combed, and his deep violet eyes were smooth satin. In stark contrast to the flying force of Nature they'd already met, this man was quietly intense, his lean frame almost wiry, and a few inches shy of six feet.

The sisters exchanged a glance--Leanne's half smile seemed to say 'Well, here we go', and Anya's teetered between professional decorum and healthy fear.

"Good afternoon." Anya stepped to him, and extended her hand. "I don't believe we've been formally introduced."

Nate set his drink on the counter and turned his chair to face them. He looked at her hand, politely reluctant. When she nervously withdrew it, his response was a small, but kind smile. "My dear, I'm not certain you'd enjoy my touching you." His voice tolled as the melodic bells of a Dublin cathedral. "But you're right, of course. You are Áine Gentry, and you," he turned to Leanne, "are Leanansidhe Gentry."

They nodded and Leanne asked, "And by what name would it please you to be known by us?"

His eyes twinkled with approval. "Such lovely manners." Lifting his chin, he stated, "I am He Who Leads the Valiant Warrior in Battle, He Who Leads the Legions of the Mighty Dead. I am Neit, God of Battle, of War, of the Passionate Fight." He finished his drink and said, "But that's a bit of a mouthful, isn't it? So we can leave it as Neit." He pronounced it 'net'. "Or 'Nate', as most mortals say."

He gestured to the steps leading to the garden patio. "Shall we sit together?"

Only slightly reassured by his courtesy, they followed him to a small table. Sitting around it, Leanne braved a question. "If I may make an inquiry?"

Neit nodded.

"We were most fond of Mrs. Hilton."

His face went blank. "That is not a question, child." His eyes flashed from violet to livid and back. "And her name is no longer bound by the title of 'Mrs.', nor by the branding of 'Hilton'." The intensity of his disdain for her marriage was matched by the pleasure he'd taken in negating it. "She is simply Dahlia."

Shielding herself and her sister as best she could from the god's reaction, Leanne pressed forward, "I stand corrected." She swallowed subtly, and asked, "Is Dahlia well?"

The corner of his mouth twitched with the barest hint of humor. "She is well." He added, "But I didn't come here to discuss the complications of married life."

Married life? In response to their confusion, he elaborated, "I am the Winter Consort to the Morrigan, husband to Her face known as

Nemain." The pause following his statement may or may not have been for dramatic effect...but it made one.

Leanne waited an extra beat before asking, "And to what do we owe the pleasure of this visit?"

Neit leaned back into his chair. "To be oblique is the nature of my world, and most of us delight in the exploitation of human misunderstanding. However, our circumstances are entirely too serious to allow for games--confusion can lead to unnecessary harm."

Wow. Both sisters' eyes widened at the plain talking.

He leaned forward. Though he addressed both of them, his gaze never left Leanne as he said, "We take care of our own. *Never* forget that."

The force accompanying the statement was palpable, and Anya suppressed a *gulp*. Looking at Leanne, she was surprised that her sister's reaction was a mere cocked eyebrow. Something just happened there...

Leanne said, "We are listening."

Neit tapped his fingers in a slow staccato on the table as he spoke, his tone pensive. "Humanity knows very little about me--not that I've taken too much of an interest in them either--and what they know focuses upon my relationship with Violence." The tone of his voice explicitly capitalized the word. "But I am equally invested in Justice and in the survival of the Faery Realm."

Leanne felt rather than saw Anya's quick, alarmed glance. Was this going where they thought it was?

"Payne may have wanted the Portal for the base satisfaction of his own hubris. But," the inflection of his voice became casually matter-of-fact, "but it was only useful to him if it were in excellent working condition--and if Faery was still there, and healthy. So, for a time, our goals overlapped."

"But those innocent people--?" Anya knew it wasn't the best idea, calling him out, but her moral outrage got the upper hand. "How was that useful?"

Neit answered, "His blatant use of magick, both in the fight ring and sabbat killings brought attention to our world. We need humanity to *acknowledge* our existence. Fear is a powerful form of belief, children."

The complete lack of emotion in the god's logical assessment was far more unsettling than if he had been frothing at the mouth and spewing a diatribe. While neither evil, nor a sadist, the utter rationality of his concept of justice, or *Justice*, made Anya's blood run cold.

The Celtic God of Battle's tone was dismissive as he spoke, "What he did in his spare time was not my concern. When he got into trouble with the *wife*?" Neit's eyes widened for emphasis and rolled in annoyance as he shrugged again. "He knew better than to attack one of Her protegees. I helped him as I could--but for my Dahlia. Never for him." At their expressions, he let out a breath of amusement and clarified, "Nemain and I have many loves, not the least of which is for each other." His mouth twisted to a smirk as he added, "You can trust me on this, ladies, life is far more interesting when love is diverse." His eyes swept Leanne's form up and down. Slowly.

Satisfied with the bright red blush his gaze drew from Leanne, he relented and said, "Not that anything I say or suggest should be taken as a slight against young Fergus. In fact," he leaned away from the table, shot an approving look in the direction of the kitchen, and the big man keeping an indirect eye from within, "I like his style." He sighed, "it was a wrench to let him go."

Though still flushed, Leanne met his stare steadily. When she spoke, her voice was soft, but her words were clear. "I thank you for that."

It was Neit's turn for raised eyebrows. "So eager are you, to place yourself in my debt? Be careful to whom you give your thanks, my dear."

Leanne shook her head. "Spoken or not, the debt is there. I would honor it either way."

A rare, broad smile spread slowly across his face. "The passionate loyalty of a good woman. I trust young Fergus appreciates what he has in you. But no. It served my purposes as much as yours, if not more, to restore Fergus to the mortal world." Neit took a deep breath and stared meaningfully at Leanne when he added, "I am certain that decision will ensure fruitful results."

Leanne tilted her head, and Anya's brow creased-- *fruitful*?

The God of the Passionate Fight continued. "Power is intrinsic to duality--we are, each of us, stronger when in a balanced partnership with an equal, but complementary force." His eyes held a tiny glint of mischief as he said, "Even the many-faced Goddess needs Her gods."

Tenderly clasping Leanne's hand, Neit said, "Leanansidhe, you have already made one promise to which your blood is bound, and," his glance flickered to and back from Anya's widened eyes, "neither of you, ever once, has broken your word."

He paused, allowing the import of his statement to ripen in their minds.

The sisters looked at each other. The God of Battle, War--more importantly, a god who rarely took any interest in (living) humans--had been keeping tabs on *them*?

Amused by the succession of emotions crossing their faces, when Neit spoke again, his voice dangled the words in the air as though offering a treat. "You may want to accept my offer of not accepting your thanks."

Struggling to keep her voice even, Leanne said, "I accept your offer of non-acceptance."

"Then our business here is settled." He finished his drink and stood. "I have no doubt the conditions of the truce will be honored to the letter, and that I will never have reason to regret the acceptance of your terms."

The Gentrys rose to join him, though they were both too shaken to speak.

As though he could read their thoughts, Neit smiled again, seduction and ravenous adventure swirling around him with the shadows spreading from his presence. He stroked Leanne's cheek with the back of his fingertips in a gesture of departure. Turning to Anya, he kissed his fingertips and said, "As their patron leaves, so yours arrives." Addressing both of them, he said, "Fare thee well, *mo daor cailíní.*"

He walked in the direction of the Portal, the shadows of evening playing around his footsteps as he faded from their view. Once gone, the golden light of a rich harvest afternoon bathed the garden in warm hues, and the cheerful noise of a rowdy party flooded their ears as the party-goers returned in a rush.

"So is it me, or are we in some trouble?"

Anya retorted, "*Ya think?*"

***

There were layers to that talk, Leanne was certain. Layers they missed--even if he claimed to be direct, Neit was still of Faery.

She shook her head. There were still some last touches to put on the holiday dinner, and Remy had been cooking since yesterday...

Tabling her new set of concerns, Leanne returned to the kitchen, leaving Anya to her thoughts.

The sound of footsteps on the Table's porch drew Anya's attention to the elderly gentleman approaching her. He was familiar, but his eyes had faded to watery blue. His wavy hair had turned from sunny gold to pure white, wispy and receded.

But the smile, the smile was the same.

"Lugh?" She caught her breath at the change in her god's appearance. He'd lost weight, and his shoulders stooped as he leaned on his cane--he looked as though he'd aged no less than thirty years in the weeks since she'd last seen him.

"Trust me, dear, I've looked worse. In fact, I will look worse shortly." He winked and offered his arm. Anya took it, and they strolled through the garden. The warm sunshine played the illusion of goldening his hair, but there was no questioning his health. Lugh was dying.

"Surely, Anya, you're not surprised?"

Anya tried to lighten her expression. "Of course not. But--does this happen...?"

"Every year? Certainly it does. And every Yule I'm born again. I won't look like myself as you know me until the late summer," he gave a shrug, "but they're all good looks."

"What do you mean, don't look the same?"

"You'll find out in good time. As for now," Lugh's eyes creased with affection. "Let's address those concerns of yours." At Anya's surprised blink, he specified, "My comrade does have a way of...making an impression." He patted her arm and let his gaze rest gently on her face. "Don't have any worries. You could have a worse taskmaster."

With a not-amused laugh, Anya retorted, "No offense to the God of War, but he scares the shit out of me."

"Oh, that wouldn't offend him." Lugh chuckled. "But the title of Oath Binder is mine."

Relief flooded through her. "Oh...right."

"Besides, weren't you listening to him?" His frustration was palpable. "We take care of our own."

He smiled at her. "Now to more pressing matters." As they walked to the dining room, he said, "I took the liberty of having my contribution to the celebration delivered ahead of time." Lugh nodded to the previously empty buffet, where a dozen bottles of wine now stood. "It's a brew of my own."

Anya's thanks were cut short by the scents and sounds of the approaching dinner. Literally approaching, as folks emerged from the galley, each carrying a covered dish. Leanne carried a large tray of potato and onion stuffing, and Laidi followed with her oyster dressing. Samson had a tray, and on it were the first round of vegetables--a tureen of decadently creamy spinach, a wide, crystal dish of fresh string beans, their bright green speckled with bits of crunchy bacon and flashes of dried cranberries.

The procession continued-- Shelby also carried a tray, hers held the baby romaine and arugula salad, shiny pomegranate seeds sparkling against the creamy hunks of goat cheese, along with the ambrosia and her homemade cranberry relish. McAnrai cradled the mashed potatoes in the crook of one arm, the sweet potatoes in the other, and the mixed scents of buttery earth and rich, brown-sugary cinnamon glaze wafted through the room. Drake's enormous form filled the archway connecting the Brugh with the dining room. He ducked slightly, and turned to set down the warm loaves of French bread and freshly beaten honey butter.

"Eh HEM," All heads turned to the archway connecting the dining room to the Brugh. Trusting no one else to carry it, Remy entered with slow deliberation, carefully balancing the enormous, stuffed turkey in front of him. Everyone exchanged amused glances--the man never passed an opportunity to turn a meal into a showmanship expression. Not that they could blame him--the bird was beautiful, marvelously golden, and the andouille stuffing burst from the opening like the contents of a generous cornucopia. He set the large platter on the table, stood back, and with a flourish, said, "Have your enjoys."

***

After the plates filled, emptied, refilled, then emptied again, the pleasant haze of 'turkey coma' filled the room, and the talking slowed. The pleasure of the meal mellowed to the quiet contemplation of what forces had been set into motion.

Into that quiet, crept a sense of dread.

Bracing herself to cheer the room, Leanne tapped her glass and stood.

"We made it through. Even if only through the beginning, or the beginning of the end...in any case, we've reached a good reason to raise our glasses." She suited her action to the words, and said, "Drink up, drink deep--we're gonna need it where we're going."

Remy leaned to Laidi and muttered, "Whaaa?"

Laidi said, "Looks like more went down than we know."

Remy's brow creased. "Yeah, but what?"

"By the looks on their faces, nothing good."

Everyone drank. Emboldened, Leanne added, "To Life! May we live it, love it, and not soon lose it. But, in the event we're about to lose it, may we lose it well, and may there be enough drink that we don't notice so much. And that it won't seem so terribly unpleasant, and possibly gruesome..."

Anya leaned to her sister and said, *sotto voce*, "I thought this was a toast to life?"

Leanne's mouth stretched to an 'oops' grimace as she sat, "Well, it started that way..."

There was a pregnant pause. Eventually, all eyes turned to Lugh. Smiling, he rose to his feet.

"I have always been a fan of some well-placed irony. In that vein," the Sacrificial God cleared his throat, and lifted his voice. "To Death." He grinned at the raised eyebrows and sarcastic laughs of thanks.

Undaunted, he continued. "To Death. It can be frightening, and yes, sometimes it hurts. But much more often, it is peaceful, welcomed, even. Over the years, I've had all of them. Many times each." He paused to let his point land.

"And here I stand, for in all my millennia, I've never not come back.

Learn from this--for I speak the two absolute Truths of Death.

It is inevitable.

But also...

It is temporary.

You don't cease to exist til the work is done--and children, it is never done. Thus, the sleep of Death is but a nap. The rest can last a year." He bowed slightly.

"Or can be measured in mere minutes." He tilted his glass to McAnrai.

"And sometimes, centuries." There was a pause, and a private acknowledgment of sadness flickered across his face.

"And yes, for humans, if the rest is long enough, you wake with only the buried memories of the history before. And yes, in that, there is loss. And the threat of that pain is very real.

But take this from one who never experiences the forgetting--it is a gift."

Again he paused, as poignancy fell soft upon the room.

"Yes. At some point, you will experience the agony of losing each other. But know this: You have, and will continue to, reunite. And that is a pleasure so real, it's enough to draw the envy of the gods." Lugh cleared his throat.

In a voice which held the echo of his lost vigor, he cried, "To the Enduring Battle, the Joyful Quest, the Reality Made for Pleasure. To Death. To Life. To the Loving Wheel that Turns Them Both."

He raised his eyes, his glass, and the spirit of the room.

"*Sláinte.*"

In one voice, the room answered, "*Sláinte.*

CAVEAT-ING LANGUAGE

A nd now, my language research adventures...

Concerning Irish:

It is exceeding difficult for someone in North America to learn Irish when most available resources are limited to vintage books (which I bought), what's found online (which I sought), and a purchased computer program (which for me was bought...I'm here all week, folks...).

This difficulty was compounded by the heartfelt disagreement in Ireland herself discussing the preserving of traditional Irish dialects vs. the standardized form officially taught in Irish schools (the latter being what the computer program teaches).

So I made a command decision.

My choice of Munster Irish is not an endorsement of one side, nor slamming of the other. I am of Irish descent, but I'm also an American. I am not entitled to any opinion at all on that debate.

Within the context of this story, it makes *narrative* sense for my characters to be fluent *specifically* in Munster Irish. The Gentry sisters are the latest generation of a cloistered, home schooled family from Cork. Said family had/has very little need to speak *An Caighdeán Oifigiúil* (The Official Standard).

Anyway. While I took liberties in making up words for fantasy terms, when it came to the characters' actual dialogue, I did my very best to find words/spellings that both made narrative sense, and had a ring of authenticity.

And I am all but certain I screwed up at least some.

Though yes, I am leaning hard into the excuse that their accents/word choices are flux as they do have an American father (who's active duty military), and like all military families, the Gentrys developed a multi-cultural hodgepodge lexicon specific to them.

Hey, they say write what you know. I am an Army brat and can speak for that aspect of military culture.

So for any glaring mistakes...

I am sorry...and I absolutely welcome being corrected. Please @ me with corrections/suggestions--and thank you, thank you, thank you in advance.

***

Concerning Cajun English/French:

Unlike Irish, Cajun English/French is a dialect as opposed to an official language, with variations throughout the parishes in Cajun country.

Without an official version, there genuinely wasn't any way for me to *officially* learn anything.

Also, while it is (and will remain) plot relevant for Remy to be Cajun, it wasn't my first choice to write his dialogue to reflect his accent—it felt disrespectful for obvious reasons.

Then two of my familiar-with-Cajun beta readers called me to task on it--to the tune of one of them refusing to discuss anything plot related until I, and I quote, "Fix(ed) Remy's speech--why the hell is he pronouncing the 'th'es in his words? Yeah, yeah, yeah. Plot's fine. Whatever. Fix that shit, or you're gonna have some pissed off Cajuns on your ass".

So his speech is presented phonetically.

I worked as best I could to educate myself, from playful books on Yat, to hours spent online perusing unofficial Cajun "dictionaries" and YouTube videos sent to me by NOLA friends...and the cross-referencing of the three by having said friends as beta readers.

I did my best to make Remy's speech, lexicon, syntax, and pronunciations realistic and respectful. Though, like with the Irish, I am confident I could do better here as well--and again, I beg forgiveness for mistakes, welcome any @ me corrections/suggestions, and—again—thank you, thank you, thank you in advance.

THE VERY SO THANK YOUS

This book took a crew, and it's time for some ginormous thank yous...

To Amanda, your idea for a book about a restaurant with enchanted food has come a long way from that night in Kansas. I hope I did it justice.

To Aiden and Liam, thank you for being the oxygen in my lungs, the blood in my veins...and for being patient with me when I get mushy. Thank you for allowing me to monologue my way out of plot holes, and for making me laugh.

Aiden, thank you for recognizing when I need a hug, plate of mozzarella sticks, or a margarita...and especially when I need all three.

Liam, thank you for reminding me of the outside world by way of days at the beach, and for always keeping me grounded when I get flighty.

You two inspire me, and I love you with everything I have.

To Jessica, my soul sister from another mister (and missus), Murph to my Connor, Bob to my Jay, and Terry to my Doolittle...thank you for being the only person who could assuage my fear about a certain character. She absolutely is our love child (were it scientifically possible for us to be in the baby-making business). I love the hell outta you.

To Douglas, thank you for supporting me during the years it took to get this all out. Thank you for your insight re: law enforcement, all things gun, and for helping me work out the blocking for fight scenes (Remy sends his compliments).

And most of all, thank you for understanding when I had to amend my promise to make McAnrai nothing like you, instead keeping his personality/private side different beyond recognition, while allowing him to remain the cop I need him to be. (I mean, let's be real—if all cops were like you, the world would be a better place.)

To Mark, thank you for getting fed up with my not having a cover artist, and lighting the fire under that step.

To Tara, thank you for feedback, for insights, for being a sounding board extraordinaire...and especially for making me laugh when writer's block hit.

Finally, thank you for pulling Steven into the No Res Book Party, and thus...

Steven, thank you for sharing your amazing talent.

To the both of you...*go raibh maith agat, ohana mia.*

To Jen, thank you for your extensive help on all things NOLA, Yat, and Cajun related--Remy and I owe you, *beaucoup.*

To Kristi, you Wonderfully Sick goddess of media and its appreciation. I never intended to share my little Mardi Gras story, let alone expect someone to insist upon reading it. In the years since, your reaction to that doodle-turn-backstory-canon saved this book **repeatedly**. *No Reservations* would **not** have survived its infancy without you. I cannot thank you enough for your unwavering support. I feel it still, even through the Veil.

Last, and definitely most...

Molly.

Without your brilliance as both Idea Bouncing Genius and Editor Extraordinaire--*No Reservations* literally would not exist. It had been decades since I'd done any writing beyond advocacy letters, and man, did it show. Your gift for balancing directness with humor-laced tact transformed this story from a (very) rough draft to an honest to God, the Goddess, and the gods book.

My darling, darling sister. In both our professional and private lives, you are the multicolored glitter glue holding the Universe together, and I love you more than you have ever, or will ever, realize.

Born in Philadelphia, Pennsylvania, E.V. Touchton spent her Army brat childhood as a neurodivergent GenXer with a penchant for daydreaming, learning about anything *other* than what her teachers assigned, and talking too much in class.

She eventually channeled her wayward talents into the written word, devouring books, English classes, and any available creative writing courses. Armed with an English/Education bachelor's from St. Joseph's University, she set out to lure others into a lifetime obsession with literature (ie., teach high school English).

However, Life had other plans, and decreed her young mother years to revolve around special needs advocacy. Not one to fight the Universe (much) she then spent two decades working with/on behalf of children who are undoubtedly magickal.

This series of extraordinary experiences, combined with her early 2000s hyperfocus interest (witchcraft, paganism, and their influence on modern culture) paved the way for her Queen era.

Ms. Touchton works from her home in foliage famous New England with her very own Cu-Siths. These charming canines protect her from the dangers of the mortal world, while she hangs out with her invisible friends, recording those adventures here, and in the installments to come.